MURDER ON
CAPE COD

MURDER ON CAPE COD

A Jane Adams Mystery

B.H. GATES

gatekeeper press

Columbus, Ohio

This book is a work of fiction. The names, characters and events in this book are the products of the author's imagination or are used fictitiously. Any similarity to real persons living or dead is coincidental and not intended by the author.

Murder on Cape Cod: A Jane Adams Mystery

Published by Gatekeeper Press
2167 Stringtown Rd, Suite 109
Columbus, OH 43123-2989
www.GatekeeperPress.com

ISBN (paperback): 9781642372663
eISBN: 9781619843462

Printed in the United States of America

Dedication

THIS BOOK IS dedicated to my husband Clark who has had total faith in me and got me through all the mishaps and mayhem of crashing computers and total frustration with technology when it is supposed to be so easy. It's not! And thanks for parting with his "famous" Caesar Salad dressing recipe that our entire family begs him to make quite frequently. To my parents who also shared my husband's faith in me and to my sons for inspiration, thank you. With special memories of Davis Plunkett, and my dearest friend, Julia Haslam, they both shared my love of reading and their spirits are in this book. I owe a huge debt of gratitude to my brother, Ted Hewitt, for his help with my book. I want to thank Beth for telling me to let the book go and to Rob at BookBullet.com for getting it out for you to read. Also, I give special thanks to my good friends, Mary and Tony, who goaded me on. Here it is! I hope everyone has fun in Herring Run!

Thank you for reading Murder on Cape Cod. I hope you enjoyed your time in Herring Run and with Jane and look forward to some of her new adventures that will be coming soon. The author looks forward to seeing your reviews and thoughts on Amazon and at Goodreads.

Contents

Prologue

ROUTE 3 SOUTH from Boston was bumper to bumper, backed up for miles from the Sagamore Bridge. The evening was hot and muggy with no breeze to move even the smallest leaf on this tree- divided highway. On the radio, the weatherman was predicting that the hot, uncomfortably humid weather on Cape Cod would break in the next few days.

With her well-manicured hand, Sara lifted her long, blond hair off her slim, damp neck as each car in front of her edged forward inch by inch. This after-work traffic was worse than last week's Fourth of July back up she thought with annoyance. She rued not having the car's air conditioner repaired as it hardly let out a puff of air. Letting her mind wander forward to her room at the Tara Inn in Hyannis, which she knew would be blissfully cool, maybe even cold from their usually blasting air conditioning system, helped her deal with her current discomfort. She'd call room service, order a gin and tonic with a wedge of lime, shrimp cocktail, a steak with a small salad and maybe even a hot fudge sundae topped with nuts and whipped cream. Yum, she thought at the thought of this delicious meal. Going on with her reverie, she decided that while she waited for the food to arrive she'd enjoy a refreshing shower to get the dust of the day off. After dinner she'd slide between the crisp, clean, white sheets in her new sheer, pink, shorty nightgown and watch a sweet, romantic movie on the hotel's in-house movie service while she waited, hopefully, for Sam to arrive. Sam and air conditioning for an extended weekend, ah, paradise.

Sara had been so pleased when Sam had asked her to take off from work on this Wednesday afternoon so they could have a four-day tryst instead of their usual hurried two days of the weekend when he'd fit her in at odd moments. His wife, Joanna, had wanted him to come down to the Cape early to catch the junior tennis matches that her sons from a previous marriage would be playing in at their club in Herring Run. That would be happening on Thursday so he thought he could get away and spend some time with Sara for a bit each evening and during the days under the guise of an errand, a morning sail or a round of golf. It would be heaven to spend four days on and off in the luxury of a hotel room with Sam. When he wasn't around she'd head out to do a little shopping in Hyannis at her favorite store, Islands, where maybe she'd treat herself to a skimpy, colorful island bikini or a new pair of sunglasses or she could just browse through Kennedy Studios to look at some artwork! Then she'd head down to the beach to get a little color.

Dinners with Sam would probably have to be in the room, if at all. They couldn't take the risk of being seen in public, running into someone who knew Sam and his wife on the Cape. Sara longed for the day when she and Sam could be together as a real couple, not just business associates out for lunch or a drink after work with others. For Sara, living with two other young women was getting old and she was ready to move out.

Private time together was never easy, public time nearly

impossible. Sam had hinted that he had some good news to tell her so maybe it wouldn't be long now before Sam told Joanna the truth about them and then she'd be Mrs . . . a honking horn brought her abruptly back into her hot, little, red Honda Civic with a sweltering reality as she realized she still had a ways to go but at least she could move up another couple of feet toward the Sagamore Bridge, Cape Cod and Sam.

Wednesday, July 7th

J ANE ADAMS WAS in a race with the clock again. After relaxing at the beach all afternoon, she tried to quickly blow dry her short blond hair so she could throw something together for dinner for her older son, Ian, before he had to rush off to work. He worked days as a lifeguard at their beach club until five and several nights a week at a surfer clothing shop in Hyannis called Islands, with an hour in between to shower, change, eat and get there. How he could manage such a schedule she didn't know. Maybe, she thought, she could nuke the remains of last night's dinner. They'd had chicken and vegetables done on the grill and had plenty left over and it would warm up nicely. Later she could make something cool for herself and Trey, her younger son who worked at the tennis club until six. Thank goodness, she mused, Trey had finally expanded his repertoire of food to include salads and vegetables. It made life so much easier now that he wasn't such a picky eater. She remembered, not too fondly, the days when all he would eat was macaroni and cheese that came from boxes, baked chicken breast and raw celery!

Multi-vitamins must have sustained him, she thought as she gave up trying to get her stick-straight hair into anything resembling something out of a fashion magazine in this sticky, humid weather. Turning off the hot air that spewed from the blow dryer, she threw it back in the drawer, took one last look in the mirror and sighed. Geoff, her husband was back home in Arizona so she'd probably spend a quiet evening alone with a book, so why was she torturing herself? Vanity, probably. What a waste!

With a sleeveless, pale green shift on, Jane emerged from her room somewhat coifed smelling faintly of Jo Malone's Vetyver, one of the few fragrances her sensitive nose could tolerate and that she loved. At the same time, Ian came bounding up the stairs wrapped in a towel, still dripping from his outdoor shower. At six foot one he was a handsome boy that Jane was quite proud of and for good reason! He worked hard all summer to help pay for his college expenses, he was well liked for his easy going personality and he had a truly compassionate heart. He seemed quite unaware of the fact that his comfortable good looks attracted many an admiring female eye. She noticed that his brown hair glistened from the water that still clung to it and when he caught sight of her his tanned face broke in a huge grin as he rushed past her on his way to his room.

"Hey, Mom! No time for dinner tonight," Ian yelled as he ran into his room. "I've got to stop back down at the beach to pick up my guitar before leaving for work. Matt and I are playing at the Fog Runner tonight. Why don't you and Mrs. Sanders stop by for a set? We go on at ten."

"Really? If I can stay awake until then I'd love to go. I'll call Marti and see if she wants to join me. But you've got to eat something. How about something quick or I could make you a sandwich that you could take with you?" Jane yelled up to her son while thinking that with the prospect of somewhere to go tonight, there was justice for the time she spent torturing herself under a blow dryer!

"Nothing for me, mom, thanks. I'll get something to eat at work. See you tonight at the Fog Runner. Love ya!" Ian said as he rushed back down the stairs, started to run by her but stopped just in time to give her a quick kiss on the cheek and then he ran out the door, his shirttail flying as he went. Jane was left with only the lingering scent of her freshly showered son. *Egyptian Cotton soap*, she thought, *heavenly. God, men are lucky. From shower to dressed in two minutes and they look great. Well, one down and two to go,* she thought as she entered the kitchen and poked her head into the refrigerator to see about dinner for herself and Trey, who happened to walk in at that moment, poking his head in with hers.

"Don't plan anything for me tonight, Mom. Nick and I are off to the Pizza Shack, meeting some friends. See you later."

And with a quick kiss from Trey and the slam of the screen door Jane decided that was the end of any dinner plans for the evening. Used to their chaotic summer schedule, Jane pulled her head out of the fridge and immediately switched gears, deciding it was time to rally the troops for a mom's night out. She picked up the phone and dialed her good friend, Marti's number thinking a glass of wine, being waited on, eating someone else's cooking and an adult conversation seemed like a wonderful idea for dinner, not to mention someplace that was air conditioned, as well! Marti agreed. So after tying her favorite navy and pale green summer scarf around her neck to add just a little panache, (for scarves, Jane thought, could make or break an outfit and were truly her one addictions. Though, Jane thought it might have something to do with the gathering of wrinkles on her neck, but no matter), Jane felt ready for a fun evening out. She gathered up her keys and purse and was out the door and on her way to pick up Marti, feeling free and happy.

After a delicious dinner of fried fish platters that included shrimp, scallops, scrod, stuffed quahogs, creamy coleslaw and an overabundance of fries, topped with a few onion rings at a local fish restaurant overlooking the colorful Hyannis harbor, Jane and Marti lingered over cappuccinos as they watched the ferries and pleasure boats coming in for the night. Both ladies knew how lucky they were to be able to spend their summers in Herring Run, a small village made up of mostly summer residents situated along beautiful Nantucket Sound on Cape Cod. The village had one way in and one way out and, in fact, was filled mostly with one-way streets that were really little lanes lined with trees and filled with speed bumps. It had started as a camp meeting ground back in the 1800s on lots where people pitched tents that now held their cottages. Some cottages faced the Green, which was the heart of the village, a few were situated on a bluff overlooking Nantucket Sound, others were down a road that meandered through the woods while still others were on a great pond that was filled with lily pads, fish and snapping turtles. The Herring Run Beach and Tennis club was only a five-minute walk away from both of their homes. Though there weren't any stores in Herring Run, it did boast a tiny post office, a tabernacle and an inn where people from the Boston area flocked each summer.

Marti and Jane had been close friends since they were little girls playing on the beach at Herring Run and as tennis partners on the club's courts as teenagers. They had both grown up in a small town in Connecticut summering with their families in this quaint little village but after college their paths had gone in different directions. In the winter, Marti lived in a small town outside of Boston with her husband Bob and two sons, Matt and Nick. Her husband worked as an attorney for a law firm in the Boston area and could come down every weekend. Jane now lived in Tucson, Arizona in the winter with her husband, Geoff, a doctor. While Jane was in the village all summer, Geoff only made it for a few weeks at the beginning of the summer and maybe one or two at the end. Every few years a bonus weekend got thrown in if Geoff had a conference on the East Coast. The two ladies had continued being best friends, renewing their friendship each summer on the tennis courts and under their beach umbrellas, sitting in the same spot of sand year after year. And now their sons and husbands had continued on their tradition, having bonded summer after summer. Jane and Marti tried to keep their forty-something bodies fit by walking some mornings, playing lots of tennis and only occasionally indulging in their some of their favorite fat-laden foods, like tonight's splurge of deep fried madness!

These days, they were watching each other's children have summer romances, go off to college and tonight to see Ian play and sing at a local hangout with Marti's son, Matt. The boys were less than a year apart in age and had had many wonderful summers together, swimming at the beach, wake boarding from a friend's boat and fishing in the pond. They had both played on the Herring Run tennis team, as did most of the kids in their small summer community. When they teamed up in doubles they were usually unbeatable. Now on their summer breaks from college, they were lifeguards at the Herring Run Beach and Tennis Club where they bunked together over the club's bathhouses. The ladies' younger sons, Trey and Nick, were both going to be seniors in high school and had been best friends since they were born just a week apart from one another. They worked at the tennis part of the club, helping with lessons, manning the phones and doing any gofer work the pro had for them. At times it seemed that they were joined at the hip for the months of July and August, so rarely was one without the other. These days the empty-nest-syndrome thoughts were starting to creep into the women's conversations as they fast forwarded their lives to a year from now when Trey and Nick would be off to college in the fall.

"What will you do with your time when you're not spending every spare moment on all your school committees?" Marti asked Jane as they waited for the waitress to bring their check. "I mean, will you get a 'real' job once Trey is in college or will you just join another tennis league?" Marti teased, who spent her winters teaching nursery school.

"I've decided to become a jet setter and divide my time between the Cote D'Azur in the winter and Herring Run in the summer," Jane replied with a laugh. "No, really, I've been taking a course in home staging over the winter and I've been working for a woman in Tucson staging houses on a part-time basis. I'm hoping to make it full time in the fall."

"Wow! That's news! So, when were you planning on telling me this?" Marti asked, a little surprised at not being in on Jane's career plans sooner.

"Actually, I haven't told anyone else here. I wanted to see how it went, you know, maybe start my own home staging business if all goes well and I think I can really run it and get enough customers to make it worthwhile. Meanwhile, let's keep this on the q.t. if you don't mind. I'd like to get my feet wet first before I tell everyone I have a new career."

"My lips are sealed," Marti promised. "Anyway, I don't even know what a home stager is, so how can I tell anyone about it?"

"Well, we get houses looking great so when they go on the market they are more likely to sell quickly. It's lots of fun and lots of work. The woman I've been working for has got a great eye for it, plus a great business sense. She's sorta taken me under her wing, which is nice. But she only uses me when she needs me so, like I said, I may want to start my own business if things look like the market could use another stager and I have a friend that is planning to go in with me. But, just keep this under your hat; I'm still a bit a novice at this and want to get my feet wet first."

"Speaking of jobs, I have a feeling that our 'friend', Joanna, will be needing one soon." Marti speculated. Marti's husband, Bob, saw Joanna's husband, Sam, lunching at one of the many Italian restaurants located in the North End of Boston with a very sexy, young blond and it seemed that lunch was not all they were having. "He said it reminded him of the lunches Joanna and Sam had had while Sam was still married to Julia: footsy under the table, noses nuzzling into necks, coy smiles, you know the drill. It seems that man can't keep his hands out of the cookie jar, or at least off some new conquest every few years. You think he'd be smart and pick a different restaurant. By the way, Bob saw him with this blond in the same one where he used to meet Joanna."

"You're kidding?" said Jane, honestly surprised. "Bob saw Sam with another woman? But, he's such a terrible flirt. Maybe it isn't what it looks like. Though with a shrew like Joanna for a wife I'm not sure I would really blame Sam too much. Leaving Julia was one thing. She was way too good for him anyway, but I don't think that my sympathies lie too far on Joanna's side if it's true. I guess you reap what you sow. Maybe we'll soon be looking at a new mistress of Marsh Cottage if this rumor about Sam Morris is true."

"I do miss having Julia in the neighborhood," Marti replied, wistfully, "but the loss of Joanna won't bother me much or probably anyone else in Herring Run. Bob said they looked pretty serious. Very lovey dovey—my words, mind you, not Bob's. They didn't seem to notice anyone around them; just had eyes for each other, according to my husband. Maybe we can break out some champagne when Joanna leaves Herring Run for good," Marti concluded with a laugh.

This last thought was quite pleasant to Jane. Since Joanna's arrival in the village five years ago, Herring Run had not been the same. It was a small village and everyone knew everyone else's business. The cottage three doors down from Jane's, Marsh Cottage, where Sam and Joanna lived, had once been a place where many of the ladies met after tennis for a glass of iced tea flavored with lively conversations of lobs and volleys. It was a haven where their children had gathered for an evening of games or a movie video. That was when Julia had been mistress of it. Since she had left, it was a house to pass by quickly on one's way to and from the Beach and Tennis Club.

Sam's second wife, Joanna, was a brittle, bleached-blonde woman with a sharp tongue; a woman who thought that everyone in Herring Run was much too provincial for her taste. She rarely had a good word for or about any of them. Well, actually, she rarely spoke to them at all. The heavy gold jewelry that hung from various parts of her slim, toned, overly-tanned body also set her apart from the simplicity of most of these New England summer residents. Her skirts were short, her heels were high and her necklines plunged so far down that she had half the men in Herring Run panting every time she walked by. She looked down her long nose at everyone with an attitude that said she was just tolerating their presence in "her" neighborhood, which she disparaged as beneath her anyway. She often spoke of moving to the gated community in an adjoining town where she thought she would be better suited. Of course, everyone knew she would be tolerated even less there. The wannabe Boston Brahmin sets wouldn't give someone like Joanne the time of day, let alone let her move into their special enclave. And the funny thing about Joanna was that the harder she tried to look and act wealthy, the cheaper she appeared.

Before Sam, Joanna had lived in a small apartment in Boston

with her two young sons and worked as a secretary in Sam's law firm. He had brought her up in the world financially and socially, and she made the most of it by trying much too hard. Jane thought if Joanna would just wipe half of the make-up off her face, get her hair back to a normal color and wear clothes that were appropriate for her age she would be a lovely woman, at least in the looks department. Her personality would take a lot more work. If Jane were to sum up Joanna in one word she supposed it would be shrew;, not the nicest of descriptions, Jane knew.

Most of the village thought Sam had made a very bad choice in his marriage to Joanna, but few would say so to his face, they just quietly faded away from Sam's social circle. It was the hurt that had been heaped upon his ex-wife Julia and daughter, Alex that had been the final nail in Sam and Joanna's coffin socially.

"My opinion is that Joanna won't go quietly out of Herring Run," Jane assured Marti. "Julia was glad to get rid of Sam after all the hurt he put her through. She said that in the end, the only good thing left of that marriage was their daughter, Alex. But Joanna will be out for blood, I can see her long, coral, acrylic nails poised for the attack," laughed Jane as she held up her short, unadorned nails in the air and made vicious scratching motions.

"Blood or money," Marti added with a smile. "If Sam is fooling around, Joanna will be sure to squeeze one or the other out of him, most likely both. Every last drop and every last cent."

Everyone knew that even though Julia had loved Marsh Cottage, she was just as happy to settle for a cute little house across the pond from the village where she and Alex now lived year 'round. This way Alex could easily see Sam on weekends in the summer when he came down from Boston and she could keep up with all her friends in the village. It had also allowed Julia to get a fresh start, not returning to their town in the Boston suburbs as a new divorcee; a town where Sam still lived with Joanna (albeit in a new subdivision in a house with all the bells and whistles that Joanna required, a place that Alex never seemed to want to visit too often). Julia was a quiet woman with the attitude that the glass was more than half full. She was gracious and well liked, not only in Herring Run but also throughout Cape Cod, being an exceptional teacher and a tireless worker in charitable causes. Her settlement with Sam had been fair and her main concern was always for Alex.

On the other hand, thought Jane, *Joanna would never think any settlement was good enough*. Not for her! She would be sure to make Sam squirm if the rumors were true, taking him to the cleaners. She'd probably even try to take Marsh Cottage. She may not like it here but she knew what the family cottage meant to Sam, having been in the family for three generations, and she'd be sure to turn the screws in tightly. Sam could be in for a peck of trouble.

"Well, you might be right, Marti, but let's get going to the Fog Runner so we can catch the boys' first set. After this dinner, we'll definitely need to walk in the morning and if it gets any later I'll never be able to get up early enough," replied Jane as they walked out the door of the restaurant into the balmy, still humid summer evening.

* * *

The Fog Runner was a local after work hangout for the many college students who flocked to the Hyannis area on Cape Cod for summer jobs. Its scarred maple tables had seen quite a few generations of summer youths as they came to unwind and party into the night after putting in a hard day's work. Many of the crowd worked on fishing boats, on ferries, as lifeguards, as waitresses and in shops; all the many places that needed seasonal employees.

Though the air of the Fog Runner never seemed to lose that slight smell of stale, old beer and dirty, spoiled sponges - smells that made Jane's nose wish it were elsewhere - it was just the place for the over twenty-one set of kids to unwind with a beer and some music and maybe find a summer romance.

Jane and Marti walked in, a little miffed that the bouncer had neglected to card them and sat down at one of the few remaining tables. They each ordered something to drink from one of the young waitresses and settled back to watch their sons who were seated on stools by the front windows and had just begun to play. They sounded pretty darn good—that is if you could hear them above the roar of the beer-guzzling crowd that was lined up at the bar.

As she scanned the room, Jane noticed that Julia and Sam's daughter, Alex, who was about a year older than Ian, was one of the Fog Runner's waitresses this summer. Alex was a pretty girl. She had thick, wavy, dark hair that went halfway down her back. She was quick with a smile that lit up her face. Alex was also a very thoughtful, caring girl who worked hard in school and was the apple of her father's eye. His only regret, it seemed, of his wandering ways was not spending as much time with Alex as he would have liked. Despite that, he and Alex had a good relationship. *There's probably a heart in Sam after all*, thought Jane. And even though it might not always be true with his wives, and it surely belonged to Alex. Jane caught Alex's eye and gave her a little wave. Alex beamed back a smile and after she delivered the drinks on her tray, headed over to Jane and Marti's table.

"Hi Mrs. Adams, Mrs. Sanders. Come to see your boys perform, I see. Can I get you something from the bar?"

"Hi, Alex," the ladies answered in unison.

"We're all set here," Jane said. "Hey, how are you this summer? We've hardly seen you at all at the club, or your mom for that matter. Is she still teaching at Hyannis Academy?"

"You bet, and this summer she's teaching summer school. She'll be back lounging on the beach by August. And me, well, I'm working two jobs. Days at the mall and nights here. Got to get through that last year of college, then it's real life for me!"

"This sure looks like real life right here, Alex," Marti observed, remembering her Cape Cod waitressing days back in college, the back-breaking, foot-aching occupation that saw her through four years of summer jobs. One of the best times of her life, she fondly remembered.

"Yeah, but hopefully this time next year I'll have a teaching job lined up while I get my Master's degree part time. Maybe even one at Mom's school. We'll see. Maybe Mom can put in a good word for me and I can take over her class," beamed Alex.

"Oh, is your mom leaving the school? She's been there for a few years now. What's she going to do?" queried Jane.

"You know, I don't know but lately she's seemed restless and says she may not need to work full time next year. So I told her if that's the case it would only seem right if I could take over for her. Well, I'm off, duty calls, great to see you," Alex said with a smile as she turned heel and headed over to a table of boisterous boys who looked like both their alcohol and testosterone levels were on full tilt as they ogled the approaching Alex.

Marti and Jane sat back and listened to Matt and Ian entertain the crowd; always a challenge at the Fog Runner. Though their music wasn't always the taste of Jane's generation she knew they were really good and actually enjoyed hearing them play. She thought of the many summers they had practiced in the Adams' back room with dreams of being rock musicians. Luckily, this was a bit milder with just the two guitars and beautiful harmony.

As the boys finished up their set, their mothers applauded enthusiastically. *That's what moms are for,* thought Jane, hoping they hadn't embarrassed them, as she and Marti got up to leave.

Waving good-bye to Ian and Matt, they stepped out into the cool night air, happy to be breathing in the freshness of the briny Cape Cod air after the stuffy bar. With plans made for the morning walk, both mothers went home with a feeling of contentment. They were having a relaxing summer with good friends, able to share it with their wonderful children and soon their husbands would be joining them. All was right with their world.

Thursday, July 8th

THE NEXT MORNING, promptly at seven-thirty a.m., Marti knocked on Jane's back door. Jane, sleep still in her eyes, blond hair sticking up every which way, stumbled out the door to meet the morning. Soon they were headed out of the village on one of their accustomed routes.

The humidity that had hung around the area for so many days had miraculously vanished, leaving the air fresh with a sense of a great day unfolding. The smell of the new, lighter air with a hint of the ocean coming in with the slight breeze made Jane's spirits soar. They walked through winding, shaded streets filled with quaint weathered gray, shingled cottages that were so popular in this area, many of them covered with the pink roses that seemed to grow like weeds all over Cape Cod. Framed by the clear blue sky the simplicity of the beauty kept the two women quiet for the first part of their walk, enjoying with all their senses the world waking up: birds singing, the smell of bacon frying escaping from various homes, a slight breeze on their faces. Everything seemed so peaceful at this time of day.

As they pumped their arms harder and settled into their familiar brisk pace they began to chat about seeing the boys the night before, the coming day and anything else that came to mind. Walking for Marti and Jane was therapeutic for both body and soul.

Another night out the next time the boys played at the Fog Runner was planned and they hoped that their husbands would also get a chance to hear them play their music sometime this summer. They decided to talk to their boys to see if it could be arranged. Marti said she needed to get to the market after the walk or there would be no dinner at her house that night and Jane said she needed to make a dent in the mountain of laundry that was accumulating before everyone in her family had to start running around the village naked. No matter what, though, they would meet at the tennis courts by ten o'clock for the ladies' round robin, missions accomplished or not!

Winding down toward the end of their walk, they rounded the curve in the road that went past the far end of their great pond and led to the beach. Up ahead they could begin to see the dunes to their left and start to feel the soft, cool sea breeze on their faces. The smell of the salt air and the low tide was a treat to their sense of smell in a way only found on the East Coast. As they increased their speed, they watched the world awaken to a glorious, summer day. Mothers were pushing babies in strollers to catch the day before the sun rose too high, people were walking their dogs, runners passed them by and fellow walkers dotted the sand-dune-edged road.

As the beach club came into view down the road, the serene feeling of mental and physical well-being that was their walk's reward was replaced by constricted hearts when they noticed the flashing lights of police cars and an ambulance, all parked at the front entrance to the beach club. A small crowd had gathered and a siren could be heard in the distance rapidly approaching. Their vigorous strides turned to panicked runs as each mother headed for the club fighting off a thousand thoughts of disaster, each praying that the emergency had nothing to do with their sons or anyone else they knew.

Upon arriving at the beach club, a familiar face came into view as they saw Michael, one of the town's new, young patrolmen. His father, Mike McGuire, was not only a friend of theirs but also the chief of police. Michael was trying to keep everyone out of the club and fending off any questions with noncommittal shrugs. Catching sight of Marti and Jane and seeing their frantic looks, he motioned them toward the beach club office, where they could see Ian and Matt through the sliding glass window. The boys were seated with the other lifeguards talking with Michael's dad, Mike. Relief flooded through every inch of their bodies as they realized that their sons were in one piece, alive and well. Michael told them to stay on the opposite side of the glass where they stood looking in at their boys.

The boys looked much younger than they had at the Fog Runner the previous evening. They sat with their shoulders sagging and their heads hung low. Matt was clasping his hands together while Ian sat holding each side of his head with his hands, elbows resting on his knees. One of the girl guards was quietly weeping while the other was trying to comfort her, an arm wrapped around her shoulder. A policewoman stood beside them.

Jane frantically wondered what could have happened. Could someone have drowned? The guards were in their red regulation guard suits but none of them appeared to be wet. The beach hadn't even opened for the day. Did someone sneak in for a moonlight swim only to have been overcome by a wave, a cramp?

As Jane and Marti tried to get their sons' attention they overheard voices.

"Yeah, they think he was murdered. Found him with his head bashed in."

"No, kidding? Here?"

"Heard one of the guards found him, right in the sand, lying in a mess of blood."

Grabbing Jane, Marti's nails dug deeply into Jane's arm. "Jane, murder? What's happening? Who are they talking about? Why can't we get in to see Matt and Ian?" She asked frantically.

Jane's stomach took a plunge as they stood helplessly, not knowing what was going on or what to do. Jane smelled something unpleasant in the air, but had no idea what it was.

At just that moment, the police chief looked up and motioned them toward the hall around the corner where the door to the office was located. Chief Mike McGuire came out of the office and closed the door behind him before they had a chance to go inside to see their boys. Mike looked like an older version of his son, Michael. He was tall and clean cut. Short, thick sandy brown hair covered his head and a boyishly handsome face surrounded his dark blue eyes that had the requisite weathered wrinkles at the edges befitting a man of his late middle age. He looked as fit as his twenty-five year old son and he always had a kind, yet no nonsense air about him. As a widower since his children were quite young, both year 'round women and the single summer ladies considered him quite a catch. So far, no one had been able to hook him. As a member of the beach club, Jane and Marti had known Mike and his children for many years and at the moment they were relieved to see him.

"Morning Marti, morning Jane," McGuire began. "Need to have a word with you if you don't mind, before you see the boys."

"What's this all about, Mike?" Jane anxiously asked. "They're saying someone was murdered. Who is it? And what's wrong with the kids?"

"Let's go sit down; Jane, Marti," Mike said as he led them over to a picnic table on the center porch.

As they settled themselves onto the benches, Jane's stomach was lurching at the thoughts that rolled through her mind and the smells that assaulted her nose, and she wondered if she looked as pale as Marti. They had no idea what was coming but it couldn't be good if Mike was having them sit before he told them. His grave demeanor told them it was bad but his face gave nothing away as to what or whom this could be about.

"It's Sam Morris," Mike told them bluntly. "He's dead."

Both women gasped. They had just been talking about Sam last night. It couldn't be possible that he could be dead. Not Sam! For all his philandering ways he still had been a good friend (albeit in the past) and Alex's father. They had known him for years. And Alex—they had just seen her last night. They could barely take it in that Sam was no longer with them, among the living. How could a life be ended so quickly? *It just can't be true*, Jane thought.

Mike continued. "The two girl guards, Kelly and Robin, found him this morning a little before eight when they were doing their morning duties. All we know is he suffered a massive blow to the head; good chance that's what killed him. Since the guards all live here at the beach and this is where the body has been found, we need to keep them separated from everyone until we have a chance to question their activities for the last twelve or so hours. The coroner is here now and he'll be able to help us establish a time of death, but at the moment we need to know what all of their movements have been since the beach closed yesterday."

Mike shifted uncomfortably as he explained all this to the

mothers. He'd known the boys since they'd been in diapers and the girl lifeguards, though new to the beach this summer, came highly recommended and reminded him of his own college-aged daughter. Picturing any of them as the one who wielded the blow to Sam Morris' head was unimaginable. But stranger things had happened in his years as a officer of the law and there was no way he would not follow the book to the letter just because these kids seemed to be nice, normal young people. *You never really know someone,* he thought, *or what they could be capable of.* He would bet his badge, even his pension, that Ian and Matt had not been involved.

Looking at Marti and Jane, Mike tried to reassure them by adding, "You know they might hold a valuable piece of information about what went on here last night whether they know it or not."

"Well, what do we do, Mike?" Jane asked.

"Just sit and wait, Jane, just sit and wait." Mike's eyes were sad as he got up to leave, and with that advice, he returned to the beach office and the guards, leaving a stunned couple of ladies. All the morning chores and tennis plans forgotten, Jane and Marti slumped down on the picnic bench on the beach porch and did just that, sat and waited.

Hours later, back at their house, Jane and Ian sat in the kitchen drinking tea, discussing the morning's sequence of events. Actually, it had started the night before when Ian and Matt had returned from the Fog Runner, Ian explained.

As he and Matt returned from their gig at the bar, entering through the guard's private entrance at the beach, they had heard loud voices in what seemed to be an argument coming from the girl lifeguards' room. As they approached the area where their bedrooms where located, Robin, one of the guards, rushed past them in tears. Looking beyond the door to her room they could see an outline of a man. When he emerged fully they realized that they were looking at Sam Morris. He mumbled a hello and something like "got to get going" as he brushed past them. They said hello back, looking over their shoulders as he walked down the boardwalk, between the bathhouses, following Robin. And that was it. Ian said he and Matt each had a beer, put some music on and went to bed.

Jane interrupted Ian at this point. "Why was Robin crying? And what was Mr. Morris doing there with her at that time of night?" she asked Ian.

"I have no idea, Mom," Ian replied and continued with his version of what had gone on at the beach club over the past twelve hours.

Since it was the girls' turn to do the early morning duty of cleaning the bathrooms as well as sweeping the porch and boardwalk, the boys had slept in until eight a.m. Suddenly, they were awakened by the sound of Kelly frantically pounding on their door, screaming something about a dead man. They threw on their red guard trunks and ran out to find Mr. Morris lying on his side on the sand between two bathhouse sections, known as the bays. From what Ian could see, the back and side of his head seemed to be crushed inward. Robin was kneeling beside him sobbing and shooing away curious seagulls. At this point Ian's guard training kicked in and he checked Mr. Morris's vital signs. Finding none and knowing that with a body this cold any attempts at CPR would be useless, Ian ran to dial 911 and to call Craig, the beach manager. Matt stayed with the body and Kelly dragged a hysterical Robin away, back to their room.

After that, everything had been like a dream—or more like a nightmare. The beach was unnaturally still, movement seemed in slow motion and sound muted. Time seemed to have stopped. Waiting for the arrival of the police while guarding over Mr. Morris's body felt like an eternity. Ian thought he would get sick to his stomach, the smell of death was so strong. He and Matt silently hung on until, with relief, they heard sirens in the distance.

First on the scene were the paramedics who moved the boys aside quickly, only to ascertain that they were too late. Next came the police. They ushered Matt and Ian to the beach office at the same time as Craig showed up to unlock it. Now everything seemed to be on fast forward. The police asked them what had happened, sent a patrolman up to get the girls and then left them in the office, requesting that they not speak to one another until they returned, leaving a patrolman to watch over them. The boys sat in numbed shock. Kelly and Robin were red eyed and sniffling with Robin breaking into a mournful sob every few seconds. Ian said he couldn't believe what he had just seen, like it couldn't really be true.

But when Mike McGuire arrived, Mr. Morris's death started to become a reality to Ian. Chief McGuire questioned them each separately, taking each of them, one at a time outside of the office and down to the still not open snack bar. Ian only knew what Chief McGuire had asked him.

"What did he ask you, Ian?" Jane wanted to know.

"Just what had happened, you know, the sequence of events? I told him basically what I've just told you," Ian told his mom woefully. "He told us a formal statement would be required of all us within the next 24 hours and asked that we not leave the general area, which meant not leaving town unless we notified him first."

"Mom, I tried to call you to tell you what was going on but no one answered. I guess you were out on your walk."

"Honey, I'm so sorry you couldn't reach me. But it sounds like you handled everything in such a professional manner. I'm just sorry that you had to go through such an ordeal, but I'm very proud of you," Jane expressed to Ian, not voicing her fear that this would be the start of a very hard time for him, after seeing someone he knew that had been so cruelly murdered. "I wonder why Robin was so upset the night before and why was Mr. Morris there to see her?" Jane asked Ian.

"I have no idea, Mom, but she sure cried a lot. But, that's all I know," concluded Ian with a sigh as he got up to leave.

Jane, brow furrowed, watched her son leave the room. She could see that he was very shaken and trying to cope with the day's tragic events as best he could. She knew that the sight of Sam Morris lying gruesomely dead had been quite a shock to Ian. Death was not pretty, not sweet or floral. She and Marti had caught a glimpse of the scene this morning and she shuddered at the memory of it. Knowing her son had stood guard over what had once been a family friend, the father of a good friend, was heartbreaking to Jane. Ian had known Sam Morris all his life and now this memory would stay with Ian for a long time, if not forever. She longed to just hold him in her lap as when he was little and take all the bad away, not only for him but, also, to comfort herself. She would have to seriously think about getting him to seek some professional help if he showed any signs of not being able to cope with this tragedy; in fact, Jane thought it might be a good idea anyway. She'd talk to Geoff about it.

Since the beach was closed for the day due to the crime scene investigation, Jane thought Ian should stay home to rest and recover. But after an hour or so of Jane's smothering, Ian declared himself fit and went off to find Matt and rescue him from the ministrations of his mother, Marti.

As she watched him walk out the door Jane worried about him and also wondered who could have done this to Sam. A lot of people had disliked Sam when one really thought about it. He was arrogant to start with and as anyone on the tennis courts of Herring Run would quickly confirm, he was a poor loser. He was overly competitive in life, in work and in play. If things didn't go his way he was not always a pleasant man to be around. When he had been married to Julia he had her to smooth things over. Everyone liked Julia and would put up with Sam's bullying ways. But he'd been a good father and always nice to the younger set, that is, until they got a bit older and they began to show him a little competition on the tennis courts, Jane thought wryly. Most of the kids knew not to beat him or better yet, not to play against him. Since Joanna had come on the scene, the village had distanced themselves from Sam. For the most part, people in Herring Run just thought of Sam as an old blowhard and a dislikable one at that. But no one in the village really cared enough about Sam to end his life, Jane thought; at least no one that she knew, or at least she thought she knew.

And Sam did have a few good points. He always donated to the village's yearly charity auction, even if he rarely attended it. Being on the beach committee of the club, he was committed to helping it to run smoothly, albeit often in his favor. But still it did run smoothly. Jane heard he did take some pro bono work in his law practice; that gave him a star in his favor as far as Jane was concerned. He wasn't all bad, just a bit full of himself—oh, and an adulterer—but really, not someone to murder, those couldn't be good enough reasons, Jane thought. Well, then again, the wife cheating part could tip the scales, but in no way could she imagine Joanna getting her hands dirty enough to kill someone. No, she'd rather divorce and go away with the spoils instead if she found out that Sam was cheating on her.

Thinking of his law practice reminded Jane that Sam was a partner in an old, established law firm in Boston and made quite a bit of money. Which was lucky, Jane surmised, since he had two families to support and maybe was looking at another divorce. He was a Harvard graduate and well connected, but she had also heard that there were times he had crossed the wrong people during his years as a lawyer. He had been known for his aggressive, arrogant manner in both the courtroom and the office and it had been said that not all of his partners liked his ways. But would that be enough reason to kill? Jane didn't think so. Weren't a lot of lawyers a bit ruthless; didn't most of them have fairly big egos, especially ones that graduated from Harvard, Jane thought with a laugh. Though a disgruntled client or perhaps someone he sued could have been out for revenge, she mused. But, again, murder is hardly an everyday solution to one's anger.

Her last thought, and not a comforting one, was it could have been just some lunatic roaming the beach at night, not that Herring Run had ever seen a deranged soul on its beach, but you never knew these days with the way the world was going. Attacks on the subways, in schools, churches, and shopping malls, even on military bases, just about anywhere you could think of had seen unthinkable violence. *So, why not our beach?* Jane thought. *It could have been just a random attack by a random person. Why should our little patch of paradise be immune?* Jane wasn't sure she like where these thoughts were going. She got up and rinsed out their tea mugs.

Mike had asked that the boys stay in town. That seemed logical; they would have to give formal statements either today or tomorrow, while all the events were fresh in their minds. With a sudden thud to Jane's heart a thought came racing through her brain. Surely none of the guards was being considered as suspects! Mike couldn't possibly think that Ian or Matt had anything to do with Sam's death. No, she must be having just a panic attack. But what had Sam been doing at the beach last night? Why had Robin run away from him in tears? She was a new lifeguard to the beach this year and it wasn't like Sam spent much time there. He always seemed to be out playing golf or sailing in regattas with his cronies. He preferred the competitive arenas to the sedentary beach lifestyle. Where did Robin fit into this equation, if at all? Ian had not been able to shed any light on those questions.

Jane realized she had two calls to make. One to Geoff back in Arizona to let him know about Sam and what was going on here in Herring Run, and one to Marti. The two needed to do something for Joanna, a casserole and flowers might be nice.

*   *   *

The tennis club was abuzz with somber whisperings when Jane arrived that afternoon. The news of Sam's murder drew many more people than normal to the courts, planning to watch the juniors' tennis team match. Funny how tragedy drew a lot more spectators than the mere regularly scheduled matches; like flies to honey, Jane noticed. When she spotted Trey, he was talking to the pro from the other club. As she drew close she heard the other team's pro saying, "... to reschedule this match if your team doesn't feel up to playing today. We understand it if your players may not feel like playing."

Trey shook his head, glanced at his mom and replied, "No, no; Jay, our pro, says we should go on with the match. He talked to all the kids and they want to go ahead. Most of them are not sure what is going on anyway, and your team is all here. But, thanks anyway. We do appreciate your understanding."

Jane looked around and noticed that all the young kids in their whites did look ready to play, just a little bewildered and excited at all the talk that was swirling around them and all the people that were here to watch them play. She spotted Marti by court number one talking to Nick and decided to head over there until Trey had a free moment to talk to her. As she passed by a group of her fellow tennis pals, other village mothers, she noticed that a hush fell over them and they looked up at her, some with suspicion and pity in their eyes.

Suddenly, one of the more outspoken women, Celia Martin, stepped boldly in front her and asked point blank, "What did Ian and Matt have to do with Sam Morris' murder last night, Jane? We heard from Joanna that they were two of the last people to see him alive and that the police were questioning them this morning. Joanna is devastated, just devastated," Celia pronounced the word emphasizing every syllable, ending especially at the end: *de-va-stay-ted*. "Sam was the love of her life. You know," she prattled on, "there was just no consoling her when I went over to see her. The doctor has had to put her on sedatives so she can sleep through some of this. She's convinced Matt and Ian had something to do with it, if not actually murdering Sam."

As Celia went through her damaging recitation Jane blinked in total astonishment and disbelief. Her heart skipped a beat and her ears began to buzz. Ian and Matt? How could anyone in this village even imagine that two of their finest boys, two well-respected lifeguards, could be even remotely involved in this murder, in any murder? The whole village had known them since they were infants. They were well liked. At least Jane thought they were. What reason would they have to kill Sam? What reason would anyone have to suspect them? The thought of this made Jane sick. It was one thing for Mike to have suspicions until he questioned them and checked out their stories. It was another thing to have this coming from her friends! Well, thinking about it, Celia wasn't a friend, more a meddling gossip, but honestly, where was this coming from?

"For Pete's sake, Celia, the boys live at the beach where this horrible crime happened, that's all," Jane answered as evenly as she could, directing her stare at the catty Celia hoping her voice didn't tremble and betray her fears. She tried to sound casual and not defensive. "They were unfortunate enough just to have come across such a gruesome scene, yet they handled it with the professionalism their jobs as lifeguards require. Why in the world would anyone think they would have something to do with it? Joanna, I am sure, is terribly distraught. But they aren't suspects, they just were questioned this morning because they saw Sam last night at the beach. Then this morning Kelly and Robin found his body and immediately ran to get Matt and Ian. Who in heavens name would ever think that they would be suspects? Totally absurd!" Jane finished, looking as indignant as she could while feeling wobbly inside.

The other women looked away sheepishly, some trying to put a bit of distance between themselves and Celia as she replied, "Maybe you should talk to Marti, Jane." At that, Celia turned to the other women and continued to try to gossip to them in a not-so-low tone.

As Jane walked away and approached Marti, she could see that Marti was in a serious discussion with her younger son, Nick. Not wanting to impose, Jane waited a moment for them to finish. When Marti looked up, Jane saw that her eyes were pooled with tears.

"Jane, you can't believe what people are saying. They think Matt and Ian might be involved with Sam's murder. Joanna said she thinks they did it all because of an argument the boys had with Sam concerning Alex. It's ridiculous; why would anyone think that of our boys?" Marti wondered, trying to keep her emotions in check but having a hard time as a few tears escaped her eyes to slide down her cheeks.

"Oh, Marti, I have no idea why Joanna would say such hateful things. I can understand that she must be mad with grief but we know Ian and Matt wouldn't even think of murder, much less commit it, and deep down she must know it too," replied Jane, seething inside over Joanna's accusations.

Joanna always speaks without thinking of anyone else, tearing anyone down as she goes, thought Jane. What a vicious thing to say about their boys. No wonder everyone was giving them sidelong glances here at the club. With the help of Celia, the whole village was connecting Ian and Matt to Sam's murder. What was wrong with these people, our friends, wondered Jane, and what was this about an argument the boys had with Sam?

"Damn, that Joanna! And I was feeling sorry for her, too. Come on Marti, we have a condolence call to make." Jane declared as she started off in the direction of Marsh Cottage, Marti following close at her heels.

As they approached the cottage they saw several cars parked in front that were unfamiliar to them. They walked up to the front door and knocked softly. The hushed tones inside broke off and a man bearing a strong resemblance to Joanna answered the door.

May I help you?" he inquired.

Jane introduced both herself and Marti and explained that they had come by to pay a call on Joanna in her moment of grief. The tall, slightly thin man had reddish-blonde hair with a bit of a hawkish nose, that was rather attractive in a way, Joanne thought, and he smelled pleasantly of some lemon-lime men's cologne. He introduced himself as Joanna's brother, Stuart McDonald. He told them that Joanna was resting and would not want to see them anyway, seeing as their sons were suspects in the murder of her husband. *Okay, not so handsome*, Jane reassessed!

Marti gasped at that suggestion and Jane was just about to set him straight when a doped-up voice from inside the cottage called out, "Stuart, let them in."

Stuart looked at them with pity as he stepped aside to allow them entry. He warned them as they passed. "Only for a moment; she needs her rest and I will not have anyone upsetting her more than she already is."

"I said, let them in. I have something to say to those two," shrilled Joanna from the couch in the darkened living room of the cottage.

With trepidation, the now not-so-eager Jane stepped into the room with Marti to see Joanna draped across the couch, covered by an afghan, her hair looking wild and her eyes puffy from crying, mascara running down her cheeks. Wadded tissues were scattered around and over her as if she had been involved in a snowball fight. Marti immediately went to Joanna, explaining how sorry they were. What could they do for her? Did she need anything? Jane stood surveying the situation, the room and wondered what they had let themselves in for by coming over to Marsh Cottage. Why did she come up with this dumb idea anyway, she inwardly groaned. She noticed that Joanna's brother stood by the door with it slightly open, an invitation for them to leave as soon as possible.

Joanna turned her red eyes up toward them, her face becoming screwed up in an instant and she screeched, "Haven't you two done enough? Mothers of murderers! I hope your boys hang. You have some nerve coming here to see me. I hate all of you. No one in this village has ever liked me, or my sweet little boys for that matter. It's always been 'poor Julia, poor Alex, Joanna is living in their house'. Well, it's my house and I will see to it that you two will never step foot in it again! In fact, you may never want to spend another summer here in Herring Run." She screamed, spittle spraying the air around them as she ranted on like a deranged woman.

Taken aback at such a vicious attack, Jane and Marti stepped away from Joanna and stood in stunned silence. What could they say to this grief-stricken woman who was so full of hate? Before they had time to even think about a reply, Stuart rushed over and was hurriedly pushing them toward the door and out of the house, telling them he was sorry, Joanna was not herself but it would be better if they did not come back. As they left the porch, the door slammed loudly behind them. The two stunned women slowly walked down the midway path that led to Jane's house in bewildered silence. Each woman was too upset to speak. As they reached Jane's door and walked through it, Marti burst into tears.

"Well, we never really like Joanna, not really, so she was right about that," Jane pointed out. "I mean we tried for Sam's sake in the beginning and we never really excluded her, but on the other hand we never made that big an effort to include her. But then, she never invited us to Marsh Cottage, either. As time went on and we got to know her we really didn't want to socialize with her. She's just so unlikable. Always bragging how much something costs, pointing out that her this or that always costs more, is better, is more popular, no matter what she's talking about, whether it's jewelry or cars, clothes or children. But to accuse our boys of murder is going too far. Marti, I think we need to talk to Mike McGuire as soon as possible. That is, after I call Geoff. Go home, wash your face, give Bob a call and then I'll pick you up in twenty minutes. We're off to police headquarters to see what's going on here. Oh, and by the way, no flowers or casseroles for Joanna from us, she and her brother can just order take out!" Jane angrily proclaimed.

Geoff's reassurances over the phone calmed Jane down quite a bit. He wisely told her that the ravings of someone like Joanna could not be taken seriously. Just hang in there and expect him to arrive at the Barnstable Airport the next evening at seven, as he would be coming to attend Sam's funeral and to calm Jane down. And he added, "Don't get involved in anything, Jane. Let Mike handle it. After all, we know Mike and we know he's good at his job. We can trust him to see Joanna's accusations for what they are, the hysterics of a neurotic woman!"

As Jane hung up, she felt some relief, but not much. Anything threatening her children chilled her to the bone and until the threat was gone she would not rest easy.

Twenty minutes later, Jane picked Marti up in her Tahoe and as they drove over the back roads to the station she told Marti what Geoff had said to her.

"But," Jane said, "I am not going to sit back idly and let anyone accuse my son of murder."

Marti nodded in agreement. Her conversation with Bob had gone about the same as Jane's had with Geoff. Bob also felt that the ladies should just let Mike handle everything and get on with trying to enjoy the summer.

The police headquarters were in a handsome new brick facility. They parked in the front lot, as the back one was reserved for official vehicles. Upon entering the building they saw an enclosed front desk area that went across the whole width of the room. It appeared to have bulletproof glass protecting anyone on the other side. Behind this wall of glass were many other desks and cubicles. People were bustling around, both in and out of uniform. Jane had only been here once before to check on the theft of her nephew's bike. This time it felt so totally different.

As they approached the desk marked information they recognized the young woman manning it. Melissa had hung out at the beach for years with Ian, Matt and Alex. She smiled in recognition as Jane and Marti approached, making Jane feel a bit better.

"Hello, Mrs. Adams. Hello, Mrs. Sanders. How are you?" She asked, then her face suddenly darkened. "Oh, my gosh, I guess you aren't so good. I heard what happened over at the

Beach Club. It's awful. Alex must be so upset. And Matt and Ian being involved."

"Involved? What do you mean 'involved'? Melissa, tell me what you've heard," Jane gasped, her heart beating a million times a minute, not sure she wanted to hear the answer to that question.

"Oh, I don't know really what I mean. I guess because Matt and Ian were two of the last people to see Mr. Morris alive and all of that, you know, such good friends of Alex's and like, you know . . ." Melissa stammered, unable to continue.

At that moment, Mike McGuire walked down the hall and spotted them. He called out, "You two ladies are just the two people I want to see. I was trying to reach you on the phone only moments ago. Could you step down this way to my office where we can have a little privacy?" He motioned as he gave a disapproving look to the flustered girl at the desk.

Melissa buzzed them in. Jane and Marti stepped into the inner sanctum of the police station and quietly followed Chief McGuire down the hall to his office. As they stepped into his office, Jane's thoughts were racing and her heart was pounding. Mike pulled two chairs up for them. As they that sat in front of his cluttered desk he sat himself down into his well-worn seat on the other side. After offering them coffee and having them decline, he began.

"Now, before you say anything," Mike warned, cutting them both off when they began to question him, "I think you should know that we do have to consider Ian and Matt suspects in the murder of Samuel Morris."

As these words were spoken Jane felt her world drop out from under her.

"I know that it just doesn't seem possible that two such fine boys could be involved in such a heinous crime," Mike continued, "but at the moment we're looking at everyone and everything involved. Since the guards were the first on the scene we will have to check each one of them out. Unfortunately, as concerns Matt and Ian, the widow seems to think they have a motive for being involved, something to do with Sam changing his Will in favor of her boys instead of Alex. Some argument that was overheard." Waving his hands at the two ladies as their mouths opened in protest, Mike continued. "I know it seems farfetched, but I have to look at everything that comes my way concerning this crime and I can't discount what Joanna Morris is saying. Believe me, I've known Matt, Ian and Alex since they were babies and I would bet my life that they have nothing to do with this. But I have to do my job and that includes checking your sons, and Alex, out."

"What's this about an argument the boys supposedly had with Sam regarding his will? This is the first I've heard on the subject! What in heavens name would Ian and Matt have to do with Sam's Will?" Jane worriedly asked Mike as he sat looking at them intently.

"Well, now, ladies, it has been alleged that last weekend when Sam was here that the boys overheard Alex talking to her dad down at the beach. As she was crying, Ian and Matt happened along and asked what was wrong. She told them her dad was cutting her out of his Will in favor of his current wife and his stepsons, Jake and Justin. It was said that your boys got angry with Sam and confronted him about it. Supposedly Sam told them it was none of their business and walked off," Mike explained.

"Where did this information come from?" Jane asked.

"Sam's wife, Joanna, said she overheard the original conversation while changing in the Morris' bathhouse down at the beach. She said she heard the boys tell Alex not to worry, that they'd, quote, 'take care of it' for her. She says she didn't come out of the bathhouse until after they'd left but that she'd know their voices anywhere."

Jane mulled this over as Mike continued to talk. "The murder weapon seems to be one of the club's shovels that the guards use every morning for beach clean up. We found it under one of the bathhouses not too far from the body. It had hair and bits of flesh on it that we assume are Sam's but of course we won't know for sure until after the lab reports are back. Not just anyone had access to the beach's equipment and the shovel was supposed to be kept in a locked closet near the office with other beach supplies. But, not only is it left unlocked half the time, that closet has had the same lock for at least twenty years, so I'm sure there are quite a few keys floating around. No prints were found on it, but that's not surprising. So, because your boys were at the scene, had access to the closet and, according to Mrs. Morris, had a grudge against Sam, we have to consider them suspects."

At this news, Jane felt that she could barely contain the contents of her stomach. It felt like her world was crashing in on her; her ability to breathe was compromised and her head felt as if she had just stepped off a carnival ride. As she looked at Marti she knew she was not alone. Marti's face had lost all color and she looked as though she would faint. Pulling herself together as best she could, she asked Mike what they could do, what was next.

"Nothing, ladies. Just tell the boys not to leave the area without consulting me and let me handle the rest. This investigation is just beginning. Meanwhile, try not to worry too much, we know Ian and Matt are good boys. And at this point, what Joanna has said is just hearsay."

Mike stood up, indicating that the meeting was at an end. Jane was grateful that he had been so forthright with them. As upsetting as the news was at least she knew what was going on and felt that Mike was dealing with it fairly.

As he ushered them out of the office he added, "I'll call if anything important comes up."

Both women were quiet as they walked out of police headquarters. Each lost in their separate worries and thoughts, they headed for Jane's car. Jane couldn't believe that their lives could change so drastically in a matter of hours. In her heart she knew that Ian and Matt would never intentionally harm anyone. But her heart was not in charge of this investigation, and she knew that being innocent did not necessarily mean being judged innocent. Her faith in the system was not boundless, though she did trust Mike.

"Why would anyone want to murder Sam?" Jane queried Marti. "Something is missing here. What don't we know? Surely no one would do it over a tennis or golf game, though we all know many murderous thoughts swirled around this village due to Sam's 'winning' attitude. And what is this about a will and the boys championing Alex's cause. That just doesn't sound like them or Alex. In fact that doesn't even sound like Sam; he adored Alex. She was the one right thing in his life, the one place he didn't screw up."

"Maybe we should get an attorney," exclaimed Marti, whose husband, Bob, was one himself. Though a tax attorney, he would surely know someone that they could consult in just such a matter.

Jane thought it might be jumping the gun a bit. But then, maybe she was in denial, she thought. It was decided that both ladies would speak to their sons immediately and see what they find out about this story of the Will. And then they would consult their husbands as to where they should go from there. The rest of the drive back to the village was a quiet one as the two were trying to figure out why anyone would want to murder Sam Morris and why Joanna would try to point the blame at Ian and Matt.

Back in Herring Run, Jane dropped Marti off at her house and set off to find Ian. A note on the refrigerator told her he had already left for his evening job.

Trey returned home from the tennis match and said that whole afternoon had been weird. Everyone kept looking at him and Nick out of the corners of their eyes, which made him feel 'creepy'. The good part of the day was despite all, the tennis team came out victorious, winning by one point, so everyone from Herring Run went home happy. He and Nick would grab dinner down at a friend's house where they were planning to watch a movie. So for the second night in a row, Jane was off the hook for dinner. Too bad she wouldn't enjoy it as she had last night. Though food was the furthest thing from her mind she longed for a distraction such as dinner preparation to help get her through the next hour. What she really needed was to nurture her boys and feel them close and safe at home, like she could protect them from the world by just having them under her wing. *They just don't seem to need that from me*, she thought wistfully.

Jane poured herself a glass of wine and sat down to call Geoff. How she wished he was sitting with her now, with his way of looking at problems in a logical manner to keep her calm. She got his answering machine and decided to page him and wait for his call instead of leaving a message. While Jane sat sipping her wine she tried to figure out who would want to kill Sam Morris. As far as she knew he hadn't done anything so bad to warrant murder. Though, again, she thought, he was a lawyer and had probably stepped on toes during his years of practice, but murder would seem a bit extreme. She clicked on the TV thinking that something mindless could take her thoughts off this puzzle only to see a reporter standing at the entrance to the Herring Run Beach Club sensationalizing the murder of Sam. *That's it!* Jane grabbed the bottle of wine and an extra glass and headed over to Marti's house.

* * *

Watching the same news report at her room at the Tara was Sara. She sat on her bed with tears in her eyes. Sam, her Sam. This is why he never showed up last night, never answered his cell phone, didn't stop by this morning. Because he sometimes got waylaid by that awful wife of his, Sara was not all that surprised when he hadn't appeared shortly after her arrival. But when that happened, Sam could usually get away early the next morning on the pretense of sailing and arrive at Sara's door with croissants and hot coffee, enticing her awake just enough for some wonderful lovemaking. And if not that, he would at least slip out to give her a call.

He hadn't shown up all day and she hadn't heard a word from him as she waited in her room, phone in hand. At first Sara was mad, then perplexed and finally worried. Her thoughts ricocheted back and forth until finally she fell into a worried depression. This was not a good start to their four days together. She began to think that Sam had just had trouble getting away from Joanna due to the fact that he was here on a weekday instead of the weekend. He did have that junior tennis match to go to today. And maybe he had trouble coming up with an excuse, as most of his usual cronies would not be down on the Cape until the weekend. Then Sara had thought that maybe Joanna had gotten wind of their affair. They had been a little less careful lately when they occasionally went out to dinner, usually at their favorite little restaurant in the North End. Sam thought he had seen a friend when they were dining there one night. Could that person have reported back to Joanna, she had wondered. But she still expected him sometime, even if it was just an excuse of an errand and time for a quickie or a cuddle. She had never thought Sam could be dead.

As she sat, her body numb, with the news having moved on to another story her eyes overflowed and her body shook with grief. It couldn't be Sam; she can't have just heard that, her mind screamed. She must have gotten it wrong, she needed to rewind that bit on the television and find she had been mistaken. Maybe at the eleven o'clock news she would find it all a bad dream. But she knew deep down that with his failure to show up, his failure to call, that something wasn't right. She debated whether to try calling his cell phone just in case the report was wrong. He would answer and laugh and say they had gotten it all wrong. Yes, that is what she would do. She would call him even though he had always warned her not to ever call him when he was at home or on the Cape. This was different, he would see that and would rush over to reassure her that everything was a mistake, that he loved her and that he was fine.

Sara picked up her cell phone and hit the automatic dial for Sam's number, something she rarely did. It rang a few times before a male voice answered and Sara's mind flooded with relief. "Sam, you're all right," she exclaimed.

"Who is this?" asked the now-unfamiliar male voice.

Sara quickly hit end. It wasn't Sam. She looked to be sure she had hit the right number and when she saw that she had, her body heaved with grief as she truly realized that Sam was dead, murdered, never to see him again. What would she do with him gone, a big empty hole in her life that she knew she could tell no one about. A hole that she could never fill. Who would understand her grief? She had no right to him, to be the grieving mistress wasn't allowed. So tired, she was so tired. She would have to go to the funeral and act like an acquaintance, another one of his work colleagues who was so sorry, Joanna, to see you have lost your husband. She shuddered at this vision. As she curled herself up into a ball on the bed, rocking her body as she cried herself to sleep she wondered who could have wanted Sam dead. Her sweet, wonderful Sam. Sam, the love of her life.

Friday, July 9th

T HE NEXT MORNING dawned beautifully: a clear sky with the humidity even lower than the day before. Jane was up and out early, walking down to the beach to have breakfast with Ian before he was on guard duty for the day at the beach. As she approached the entrance to the club she saw that the yellow crime tape had been removed and the beach looked the same as it always did. It was hard to believe how different the scene had been only twenty-four hours ago. The guards had moved back into their rooms early that morning and were back to their duties. It was reassuring to see business as usual, though there was something a little unreal about knowing one of their neighbors, one of their friends had been murdered right here on this beach sometime within the last thirty-six hours.

As she walked through the entrance, Jane shivered as she glanced over her shoulder looking for Sam's ghost. She shook that off and followed the boardwalk down toward the snack bar where she hoped to find Ian. Spotting him doing litter patrol on the beach, part of the guards early morning duties, she called out to him.

"Hey, mister, how about some breakfast?"

Ian nodded and held up two fingers. She pointed toward the

snack bar and then headed over there herself. Patti, behind the counter, smiled a good morning and poured a cup of fragrant coffee for Jane. Jane smiled a grateful thank you and picked up the morning paper from the counter. The headline of the Cape Cod Register read: "Beach Slaying of Summer Resident". She read it with trepidation, trying to see what they had to say about suspects. Nothing, no suspects. Well, she thought, at least the local paper hadn't picked up on Joanna's unfounded accusations.

A few minutes later, Ian bounded in and joined his mother. Jane thought he smelled of summer, coconut sunscreen and briny surf. Lovely. They both settled down with BECS, a bacon, egg and cheese sandwich on a fried hamburger bun, one of the snack bar's specialties and their favorites. They began to munch contentedly enjoying a rare moment of breakfast at the beach together. A few moments of bliss. When they were almost down to their last bites, Jane broached the subject of the argument with Alex's father that Joanna had said she had overheard, knowing, unfortunately, it would change the mood of their lovely breakfast together.

"What argument, Mom? I never had an argument with Mr. Morris. What in the world is that crazy woman talking about?" Ian asked, earnestly if not heatedly.

Jane explained that Joanna Morris had said she overheard Alex and her father talking about leaving Alex out of his will in favor of Joanna's boys. She said Alex had become very upset and had begun to cry. "That's when, according to Joanna, you and Matt happened along and decided to champion Alex's cause by threatening Mr. Morris. She's accusing you and Matt of murdering her husband, Ian!" Jane concluded.

"What are you talking about, Mom? We never talked to Mr. Morris about a will. The only time we ever talked about a will was one day joking with Alex as we walked down the boardwalk, saying if she wasn't nicer to her stepbrothers her evil stepmother would make sure she was cut out of any inheritance she might ever get. You know how whiny and spoiled those two little boys are and Alex had just had enough of them that day. She feels sorry for them having Joanna Morris for a mom and even likes them at times but honestly, she really doesn't want to be around them all that much. Her stepmother is always annoyed if Alex won't baby-sit for them at the drop of a hat. She's always pushing the kids onto Alex whenever she's at the beach, which I might add is about the only time Alex has time to relax, with working two jobs. But that's it, Mom. We never even talked to Mr. Morris and we were only joking with Alex, anyway," Ian explained, noticeably angry at the suggestion that such a rumor could be circulating. "Man, I can't believe that Mrs. Morris. What a bitch!"

"Ian, watch your language, kiddo," Jane admonished her son, though truth be told, she agreed with his assessment of Joanna Morris. "Listen, Ian, do me a favor. Don't talk to anyone about the murder. Don't say anything to anyone, including the police. If they want to speak with you let me know first. Something isn't adding up here and I want to get to the bottom of it."

"Sure, Mom, you and Miss Marple find out who really killed Mr. Morris. Hey, thanks for breakfast; gotta get back to work. Sorry I got a bit upset there, but really, Alex's step-mother is a you know what. See you at the beach later, love ya," Ian declared as he got up and went out the door.

Jane looked back down at the headlines and thought, *No, not me and Miss Marple but maybe Marti and I can shed some light on this.* With this thought she headed back up to village.

That afternoon, Jane and Marti sat with their usual group at the beach. They all wore tons of sunscreen and hats on their heads. The old days of baking in the sun were long gone. With today's bright sunlight, even a few brightly striped umbrellas were up to further protect them from the sun's harmful rays, something they should have done many years ago instead of baking like fools on the beach all through their teens. These ladies loved to laugh and they said they earned their wrinkles via their kids, but who were they fooling: they had all tried to get the San Tropez tan as teens and were paying for it in spades now.

As discussion of Sam's murder was the main topic of the day, Marti announced that her husband, Bob, had seemed unconcerned with the predicament the boys might be in but that to be on the safe side had decided to call one of his friends who practiced criminal law to find out what they should or shouldn't do. He would be down on the Cape that evening, as would Jane's husband who was flying across the country as they spoke. Their beach buddies, Sheila, Barbara and Millie, who had shared their spot of sand for the past twenty some-years said their husbands were on their way as well, all from the Boston area.

"I guess we are getting an unexpected long weekend out of our guys this week with Sam's funeral falling on Monday," Sheila wryly observed. "Frank was shocked with the news for Sam's death."

"So was Dick," agreed Barbara. "Not that he was overly fond of Sam, but it's still a shock to hear that part of your weekend tennis foursome has met with such a gruesome end. By the way, I tried to call on Joanna but that brother of hers just about shut the door in my face.

"Well, Jack said he would be here early and stop by Joanna's on his way in to see if he could do anything for them. Fat chance, though," Millie told them. "I tried to talk to Joanne's brother but he refused the casserole I had made, told me to mind my own business and not to bother Joanna, all before I even had time to express my condolences. What's with him? And who is this brother of hers? I don't remember him ever being here before."

"I've never met him before either," Jane replied, "but it's uncanny how much he looked like Joanna, tall, thin, sort of blond with high cheek bones and those startling blue eyes. My brother and I look like we come from different countries, let alone different families. Funny, how some families can look so much alike and others not at all," she said thoughtfully. Hearing how Millie's casserole was turned down, Jane was doubly glad she didn't make one for them as she recalled the bitter treatment she and Marti had received from Joanna and her brother.

Everyone agreed with Jane and a lively discussion ensued over all their siblings and children, family similarities and disparities leaving the topic of Sam's murder temporarily forgotten. Their conversation slipped into the easy enjoyment of years shared on many such beautiful summer days spent on their beach; a relief to them all. Sheila had just recounted the story of a mix up between herself and her younger sister in grade school when their good friend Margaret arrived and plopped herself down in front of them.

Well, ladies," Margaret said as she settled onto the edge of Barbara's blue towel, "have you heard the latest village gossip regarding the murder of you know who?"

Everyone looked at Margaret in morbid anticipation. If anyone knew what was going on and who did what it was Margaret. She always seemed to be on top of every situation. It wasn't that she pried but she was such a warm, sympathetic person and such a good listener that people always seemed to want to confide in her.

"Rumor has it," she continued, "that Sam had a mistress and that Joanna knew about it. Seems that Sam had just about had it with Joanna's selfish way. He was, of course, failing to see that they were two peas in a pod, mind you. It has been reported, reliably, that he was seeking the warm embraces of someone else. Further, that he was thinking about making it a permanent solution to his unhappy situation with Queen Joanna. In fact, I heard that he approached her for a divorce just last month, though none of us has heard boo about that from her," Margaret ruefully remarked, totally disappointed to be out of that loop.

"OOOH, yes, yes," Marti piped in, pleased to be one in the know of the situation, "Bob told me that he saw Sam with a beautiful, young blond at a restaurant in town not long ago when he was out with clients. He said they looked like a lot more than casual or business acquaintances as they nuzzled one another at a dark corner table downstairs at Florentines in the North End."

"Aha, another rumor confirmed!" beamed Margaret triumphantly, sitting up even straighter than before. "Do you think that Joanna would be mad enough, or should I say, crazy enough, to do him in?"

"Well, I wish for Ian and Matt's sakes that were the case and she'd confess to it. And darn quick, too, so police could wrap this up and we could try to get back to a normal summer." Jane said. "I just can't see how Joanna could wield a shovel hard enough to crush Sam's skull. They said the whole back and side of his head was caved in, that you could see his brains and bit of bone sticking up. Maybe she could get off one blow but then she would have had to keep hitting him, over and over and over . . . Ugh, I don't like to even think about that picture," Jane grimaced.

"Oh, I don't know, Jane," countered Marti. "Joanna's pretty deadly on the tennis court with her overheads. I, for one, get out of her way when she attacks a lob."

"But, remember, she's not one to get those pretty, French manicured nails dirty. She's one of the most squeamish women I know. I once saw here almost faint at the sight of a fish Justin caught in the lake one day. She went on and on about the hook being in its mouth and how gross it was," Sheila commented.

With this comment, some of the women defended such squeamish behavior, as they too didn't like when their children caught fish in the lake and brought their prizes home for mom to clean and cook. And once again, thoughts strayed away from the sad subject of Sam Morris' murder and into a regular summer patter.

Later that evening, as Jane waited at the small Barnstable Airport in Hyannis for Geoff's puddle jumper to arrive from Boston, she thought of Marti's remark. Many had been the time that Joanna had wielded her mighty racket smashing an overhead at their feet with the force of a man. One thing you could say about Joanna, she had great arms and really looked great in sleeveless dresses, Jane thought enviously. She must work out with a great trainer or lift weights or something to have arms like that, or quite possibly just be blessed with them, Jane thought. But maybe there was something to what Marti said, Jane fleetingly considered as she caught the welcoming sight of Geoff alighting from the small commuter plane and rushed forward to greet him as he walked into the terminal.

Saturday and Sunday, July 10th and 11th

SATURDAY MORNING DAWNED with a quietness that was unusual for Herring Run. There were few sounds of kids on bikes but not the usual male voices hailing one another after a week away for many of the summer inhabitants and at the tennis courts there were no sounds of balls being hit or line calls being made. It seemed that the entire village was in mourning.

Mothers had kept their children inside and the men who gathered at the tennis courts for their usual Saturday morning challenge matches were subdued, talking quietly, discussing the crime, wondering if they should pack up their families and return home until the killer was caught. Geoff, Jane's husband sought out Marti's husband, Bob, to see what his take on the crime was and what legal advice he had procured regarding his own son, Matt.

"At the moment I don't think we have to do anything," speculated Bob. "Right now the boys aren't charged with anything and anyone that was there at the beach at the time of the murder would be considered a suspect. If they're called in to be questioned again, then we'll consider that a different story. In the meantime, let's just try to keep a positive attitude and try to not worry the boys, or their moms."

"I've talked to Jane about returning to Arizona after the funeral but she's adamant about staying here for the summer. She's so angry about how Joanna treated her and the talk about the boys that's swirling around the village thanks to Celia and that matter, Joanna. She's not about to fly out of here with her tail between her legs!" Geoff stated with a laugh, but his voice rose slightly, indicating that he wasn't happy with the situation either. "How's Marti feeling about all this? Is she ready to pack it in?"

"Well, Marti is tempted to drive home for a few days but I don't think she'll leave Matt here on his own since the boys have been asked not to go out of town. He feels he has his jobs to do and doesn't see what the big deal about all of this is anyway. At least as far as he and Ian are concerned, that is."

Geoff sighed at Bob's comment, "That's Ian's attitude in a nutshell. Anyway, since they can't go anywhere right now, they might as well earn their summer money while they can. I'm glad that they don't seem too worried. Jane is doing enough of that for all of us, I think."

As Geoff said this he noticed a tall blond man join a group of their fellow tennis players by one of the upper courts. After a brief discussion, one of the players pointed toward Geoff and Bob. Eyes blazing, his stride purposeful, the blond man approached the spot where Bob and Geoff were standing just two courts away. Just as Geoff was turning to ask Bob who this stranger was the man bellowed in a voice loud enough for the entire club to hear what he had to say.

"Your boys will pay for this! My sister is inconsolable in her grief. How can you be out here on the tennis courts as if nothing has happened? Her husband lies dead in the morgue and you are acting as if nothing has happened. Well, you'll see, your turn will come," he promised as he turned on his heel and stomped away.

Geoff and Bob looked at one another in utter disbelief. Before they could gather their thoughts or utter a word the man had walked out of the gate to the clubhouse and out of their sight. They agreed that from the description they'd both been given that this must be Joanna's brother, the man that their wives had talked about. He seemed about as sociable as his sister and just as adept in the finer art of etiquette. And they had just gotten a dose of Joanna's brand of medicine courtesy of her brother.

Back at the house after a couple of sets of lousy tennis, Geoff found Jane folding the last of the laundry that she had never gotten to on Thursday. It felt good to her to be getting it out of the way and back to the routine of some of her normal chores. As Geoff walked in dripping with sweat after the game, she knew that her laundry wasn't done and that something wasn't quite right by the look on her handsome husband's red face.

Geoff quickly recounted the incident that had taken place at the courts that morning with what he and Bob assumed was Joanna's brother. "He never even introduced himself or let us utter a word. He just let us have it and left us in the dust with our mouths hanging open. I think he has a screw loose; it must run in the family! I think that it's time that Bob and I go and have a talk with Mike," Geoff finished.

"Now you know what Marti and I have been putting up with. It's really unsettling. But, I don't think you need to talk to Mike," Jane explained. "He called while you were at tennis and said that after speaking with Alex and the boys he doesn't think there's anything to that story of Joanna's, the one about the argument at the beach. He has to keep it in mind and still wants the boys to stick around the area, but Mike, as well as the rest of us, knows that once Joanna decides something to be the truth she can't see anything else. She sort of makes her own truth to fit her life and then believes it. He isn't wasting much time or energy suspecting the boys and says he would be better off looking at more realistic motives. I think we're lucky to have someone that knows this place and its inhabitants handling this case. Mike isn't taking everything at face value."

"Well, that's a relief," Geoff commented with a sigh.

"I agree," said Jane. "But, what I would like to know, is why Joanna started this ugly rumor to begin with. Did someone put this into her mind or is it just another one of her ugly inventions?"

"Who knows with that woman!" declared Geoff. "I'm just glad that Mike isn't taking her seriously. Have you called Marti and told her?"

"Just got off the phone a few minutes ago. Mike had called her, too," replied Jane. "Now, let's forget this for a few hours and go down to the beach for some R and R. You haven't even seen Ian yet and I'm sure he'll be glad to see you're here even though he probably won't let it show."

"Sounds good to me, though how about we make our way to the beach after you show me how glad you are to see me, if you know what I mean," Geoff said with a twinkle in his eye.

With the laundry suddenly forgotten, already making her way to their bedroom, Jane replied, "MMM, sounds good to me! How about I help you off with those stinky clothes and soap up those magnificent muscles and get you sweet smelling first, man of my dreams."

Laughing, Jane turned on the shower, the steam filled up the bathroom and she got to work on what she deemed a much more rewarding activity than laundry.

The rest of Saturday and then Sunday slipped into a numb routine as the Herring Run community dealt with the tragedy and readied itself for Sam Morris' funeral on Monday. Joanna had decided to hold a Memorial Service at a nearby church on the Cape. Most of the people in Herring Run were planning to attend the service, though some were a bit on edge as to the welcome, or lack of it, they would receive from Sam's widow upon their arrival.

Throughout the weekend, the weather continued to be beautiful and people still flocked to the beach and tennis courts despite the tragedy. Many clustered in small groups, whispering theories and details, but no one openly said anything more to the Adams' or the Sanders about the outrageous, in Jane's opinion, accusations that Joanna and her brother had made. Most of the members of the club and community had known Matt and Ian since they were babies and didn't think them capable of murder and since Joanna didn't hold a lot of sway with most of the villagers anyway, Jane tried to ignore most of her feelings on the subject. Joanna's brother was seen coming and going from the cottage and taking her boys to the beach, careful to stay segregated from others, but Joanna remained in her cottage, not venturing out once until Monday for the funeral.

Monday, July 12

THE DAY DAWNED beautifully once again, greeting the mourners who arrived to say their good-byes to Sam on Monday at the Little Chapel by the Sea. The sky was a true sky blue with a trace of wispy, white clouds and the sun shone down benevolently on everyone on Cape Cod. Getting ready for the funeral that morning Jane couldn't shake the feeling of dread at seeing Joanna or her brother once again. Donning a black cotton skirt, a plain white blouse, a short black jacket and tying a black scarf with white polka dots around her neck, Jane hoped that there would be no further outbursts and that Joanna would have come to her senses having realized how ludicrous her words had been. Jane decided to give Joanna the benefit of doubt and allow that it must have been Joanna's overwhelming grief that had caused her to lash out at them that day. At least, Jane hoped that was it and hoped there wouldn't be a repeat performance at the funeral.

Over the weekend, Jane and Marti had gone to visit Sam's ex-wife, Julia and their daughter, Alex, to pay their condolences. Julia was sad but philosophical about Sam's life and death but Alex was devastated and Julia had her hands full with trying to comfort her. Jane knew they would both be at the funeral today, though she also knew that Joanna would see them as an unwanted intrusion, as she always had when Sam was alive.

Traveling together, the Adams' and the Sanders' arrived shortly before the service. They made their way from the parking lot to the front doors of this quaint, white, New England style chapel, walking with many of their neighbors from Herring Run, altogether forming a somber procession. As Jane looked at the weathered wood she thought it a fitting spot for Sam since it had a glimpse of the water and was located a block from the golf course, one could just make out the fourth tee. The Sound and the golf course, his two favorite haunts, she thought and then realizing what that meant hurried into the chapel behind Geoff.

Once the coroner had released the body, Joanna had Sam's remains cremated. Upon entering the nave of the church no casket was to be seen, just a small, square bronze urn on a pedestal and a large photo of a smiling Sam propped on an easel set in front of the altar. To each side of these was a profusion of flower arrangements sent by the many villagers of Herring Run, Sam's business associates and other mourners. There was an enormous wreath in the shape of a sailboat from his sailing buddies at the yacht club and an even larger arrangement, in fact dwarfing all others, sent by his law firm in Boston. His golfing buddies had sent flowers in the shape of a putter and ball, both sitting on a small patch of green grass. *What will they think of next*, Joanna wondered and thought of the donation they had made in Sam's name to the battered woman's shelter in Boston.

Several people were seated in the front on one side. Jane recognized as some of Sam's partners from the firm who she had met years ago when Julia had thrown large summer parties at Marsh Cottage. Across the aisle was Joanna, her sons and her brother who took up the other front pew. Joanna wore a tight, black suit and a hat with a heavy, black, netted veil covering her face. Every few seconds she reached under the veil and dabbed at her eyes with a stark white, lacy handkerchief.

Julia sat directly behind Joanna with Alex, whose eyes were puffy from hours of crying. Julia looked very sad and while Jane was watching Julia put her arm around her daughter and whispered to her in what looked to be a comforting manner, stroking her hair. Jane took all this in as she, Geoff and Trey solemnly walked down the aisle and sat down in an empty pew that was a discreet distance from Joanna and her brother.

Looking around her Jane began to notice that she was not the only one trying not to sit too close to the grieving widow. Though the church was fairly crowded several rows behind and across from Julia and Alex were empty except for Celia Martin and her family. That figures, Jane thought. So like Celia to try to be in the eye of the tempest. Glancing behind her Jane noticed Mike McGuire standing in the rear of the church, dressed in a dark, business suit looking right back at her, giving her a curt nod. Jane quickly smiled then quickly looked away, so embarrassed to be caught snooping that she tugged a bit at her scarf feeling maybe she had knotted it a bit too tight.

So, Mike was here, she thought, checking out who was at the funeral. Didn't they say that the killer always came to the funeral of his victim? Or was that just what happened on TV shows and in mystery novels. It made sense if the murderer was a friend of Sam's. Of course, he, or she for that matter, wouldn't miss the funeral, grieving with the rest of them. It might look suspicious not to show up. *If it was I*, Jane thought, *I'd want to be way far away, like Brazil! But,* she concluded, *I just know the person responsible for Sam's death just has to be here among us.*

As Jane looked around, her eyes wandered up to the front pew on the left and toward the partners of his law firm. Sam had joined his law firm as soon as he finished law school and passed the bar. It was a respected, top firm and he had worked his way up to partner by spending many hours into the night, as all good young lawyers did hoping to make partner. It had been hard on Julia but she had handled it well. Once Alex was born, Julia had quit her own job as a teacher, concentrating her efforts on their new daughter and entertaining whenever Sam needed her to, never begrudging her husband's drive and long hours, always the cheerleader and the wonderful hostess, whenever and wherever the occasion arose, which was often. Julia always seemed to juggle it all with grace and ease.

Did someone want him out of the firm? Maybe Sam had stepped on too many toes in his climb up the ladder to partner. Did he pose a threat in some way to one of these men from his prestigious, old firm? Jane thought this could be a distinct possibility. Sam was ruthless when it came to any competitive sport he played and she wondered if he could have been just as ruthless when it came to moving up in the law firm. Could he have posed a more serious threat to someone there? Did he have some 'dirt' on one of the other partners? She'd recently read a thriller where that had happened, where a partner was not only blackmailing other partners but judges as well, did it happen in real life? Possibly, or maybe she was getting carried away, having read too many mystery novels on the evenings she spent alone when Geoff was on call during Arizona winters.

Looking across the aisle, Jane's eyes fell on Joanna's brother. Stuart was his name, she recalled, from the day she and Marti had called upon Joanna with their condolences. Next to him sat his nephews, Joanna's young sons, Justin and Jake. Not bad kids really, just young and spoiled rotten by their mother. Consequently, it was hard for them to fit in with the other kids in the village when their mother made them out to be better than the rest, having more than the rest and then not allowed to do half of the things the other kids did. Jane felt sorry for them, hoped that one of these days they would be able to break out of the yoke their mother put them in.

Thinking back to the beach conversation of a few days ago Jane noticed that the boys really did look a lot like their uncle. Their resemblance to Joanna had always been there with the boys' blond hair and blue eyes, but their features looked more like their Uncle Stuart's features, close set eyes, narrow face and slim builds, really very good looking boys, but marred by their spoiled attitude. Shame, thought Jane. Of course, that wasn't so unlike Joanna herself, in looks and attitude, must be strong genes on that side of the family. Uncanny how some families can look so alike, act alike, she mused again, as she had at the beach. Jane wondered what their father had looked like. From what Sam said, he was an absentee father who had disappeared years ago. No wonder Joanna spoiled the boys rotten, probably trying to make up for the hurt.

The service had started and Jane stood with the others in the congregation to sing the hymn "Blest Be the Tie That Binds", one of her favorites. She remembered it from the funeral of the young girl in the play "Our Town". Such a sad scene. A life cut short, like Sam's had been. She wondered who had selected that particular song to be sung at Sam's service. Looking at Joanna, Jane thought that she had no idea how Joanna had attributed her time while Sam was being murdered. Joanna had been very busy pointing fingers, but where was she when he took his last breath? Was she the one wielding the shovel? No one had mentioned Joanna's motives or an alibi, so quick was she to blame Ian and Matt. Was she trying to put the focus elsewhere, Jane pondered. Coming out of her reverie Jane noticed the hymn was over and everyone was taking a seat. She quickly sat down.

After a few words about Sam, and his love for Joanna, her

sons and Alex, the pastor introduced one of Sam's partners who got up to speak. He waxed on about Sam's reputation in the law community, his hard working, hard-hitting qualities in and out of court. Could one of the divorce cases he had handled have been more than a little disgruntled, thought Jane, her mind taking off again. Divorces were often messy, emotional and full of rancor, sort of like murder. Having Sam as your opposing lawyer could unhinge anyone, Jane realized. He mostly represented women and went for as much as he could in the alimony department. He couldn't have been very popular with the men his clients were divorcing. Was that reason enough?

As Jane's eyes continued to wander she found herself looking at a group of Sam's sailing buddies and their wives. Could one of them been mad enough at Sam to have bashed his head in? He'd been known to cut one or two off in his rush to win a race. Behind them sat the men that made up his weekly golf foursome and their wives. Jane knew that most of the wives of these men didn't care for Sam and his tactics on or off the course. When he went out to play early on weekend mornings their husbands often came home very late and very potted, leaving the wives with spoiled social plans wondering where their husbands had been and with whom. Though the blame was really on their husbands' they tended to see Sam as the instigator of these forays and spoke not too kindly of him. But Jane didn't think that was reason enough to commit murder. But, one never knew; murder was not a rational act. And how about the men he played with on the tennis court. Like golf, many on the tennis courts didn't like his competitive ways. It was said he would often call balls out that were in and send shots into his opponents' faces. But, again, not a good reason to murder. As Jane mulled all of this over she realized that all in all Sam wasn't a very nice guy much of the time.

Though she had never had a run in with him, nor had anyone in her family, she knew many of the people sitting in this church at once time or another had.

Jane's glance traveled across the aisle to the pew where Julia and Alex sat. Alex was a younger version of her mother with healthy good looks and shiny brown hair. Though older than Joanna, Julia was still beautiful and would still be long after Joanna's brittle, blonde looks faded. What had caused Sam to leave Julia for a shrew like Joanna? Maybe Sam was having a mid-life crisis, Jane reflected, it was not all that unusual. As mother and daughter sat through the eulogies they seemed to be far away from the rest of the congregation, off in worlds of their own.

And what about that rumor Joanna was spreading about a change in the will? That would put both Julia and Alex in positions of being suspects, wouldn't it? Julia probably wouldn't have anything to lose or gain herself but her daughter did. Could a mother's love and the protection of her daughter's inherent rights be a reason for murder? Sam had treated Julia horribly before the divorce with his cheating and verbal abuse until Julia had decided she was better off without him, but did that really mean without him on the face of the earth? Would Alex murder her own father if he cut her out of his will? Absolutely not! Jane was sure of that. Alex was one of the kindest girls Jane knew. There was no way Alex would ever commit a murder. Nor, would Julia, Jane didn't think. And the thought that her son or Marti's son was involved was beyond comprehension. But what was Alex talking about when she said her mother might not teach next year? What was that all about? Was Julia planning to come into some money when Sam died? Had he changed his original will after he divorced her? He was a lawyer so wouldn't he do that right away? But, who knew, maybe he was a typical male who took care of work and details for others while neglecting to get his own house in order. But Julia hadn't even taken alimony from Sam, just child support for Alex. Jane just couldn't think that Alex or Julia could have had anything to do with Sam's murder.

Turning her head slightly to the rear, Jane was surprised to see the new lifeguard, Robin. What was she doing here? It's probably her day off and since the other guards are working and couldn't make it maybe she was representing them, Jane speculated. The more Jane scanned the church the more her head ached and the more she concluded that she was in over her head if she thought she could figure out who killed Sam. Too many people here could have had motives and there were just too many unknowns. There were so many people in the crowd that she didn't know and she wouldn't act like Joanna and accuse anyone wrongly. Anyway, Mike didn't really suspect Ian and Matt anymore so Jane thought she really didn't need to worry, thank goodness. Or thank God she thought, wryly, as she looked up at one of the beautiful stained glass windows of the church.

As the assembly got up for another hymn, this time "Amazing Grace", Jane turned her head all the way to the rear of the church. Sitting in the last pew was a young woman with long, blond hair that sat off to the far side. It looked as though the woman had been crying for days as her nose was red and her eyes were puffy. Even so, it was easy to see she was very attractive, red nose and all. Maybe this could be the mystery lady, Jane thought. The woman Bob had seen Sam having dinner with in Boston. Would she have the nerve to show up at Sam's funeral, Jane wondered?

Suddenly, a movement behind the woman caught Jane's eye. As she looked up she was startled to see Mike McGuire staring right at her with a slightly amused yet irritated expression on his face. Jane half smiled at him and after giving him a little finger wave she quickly turned around, again embarrassed to be caught sleuthing in the middle of a funeral service. Mindful of her manners, she vowed to pay attention to the rest of the service of the dearly departed and joined the congregation in finishing the mournful hymn.

All in all, they did right by Sam and caught his best points with only a few humorous remarks about his bad ones. Not too bad a send off, Jane realized as she exited the chapel with Geoff, Trey and the Sanders. Ian's duty to guard at the beach took precedence over the funeral on such a sunny Cape Cod day. He was probably on tower right now, protecting lives, not taking them, Jane thought defiantly.

In the church's parking lot the Adams and the Sanders families stood, quietly talking. Matt had also missed the service also due to his duties as a lifeguard. Trey and Nick said they needed to get back to the club to help with tennis lessons and hopped in Nick's car and headed out. The adults were trying to decide whether to head for the beach or back to Marsh Cottage with the rest of the mourners. They weren't sure they would be welcome but wondered if it would be rude not to show. Just as Geoff was opting for the beach before he had to catch a late plane back to Arizona that evening, a shrill voice caught their attention.

"Look at them over there. Their boys didn't even show up at the funeral. Too guilty to show their faces. Chief McGuire, I demand you call them in for questioning," screeched Joanna as she pointed her finger at Jane's group. "I demand it!" Joanna screeched as she walked through the parking lot with her family with Mike McGuire standing near the entrance to the church.

Seeing Jane's face turn red with rage, Geoff put his hand on her arm, restraining any impulse she might have to say anything back to Joanna. "Let's go," he said. "Obviously we aren't wanted back at Marsh Cottage. Maybe I should stick around a few days and take a flight out later this week." Jane looked at him miserably with a lump in her throat, thinking that she would like him to stay but knowing that there was nothing he could do at the moment. As they drove away she tried to dispel the sense of doom that had come over her but she knew that she was not the only one with that feeling. Everyone else in the car was feeling the same way as they silently made their way back to the village. Looking back over her shoulder she could see Mike McGuire staring at Joanna as they drove away.

Tuesday and Wednesday, July 13th and 14th

A FTER GEOFF RETURNED to Arizona things began to return to normal. *Or as normal,* Jane thought, *as can be with a murderer on the loose.* She wasn't really afraid for her own safety or for that matter anyone's in the village. The more she thought about it the surer she was that whoever murdered Sam had a reason to murder him. What Jane worried about was that Joanna persisted in her theory that Ian and Matt were involved in this heinous crime and that somehow she thought so was Alex. But Mike continued to let them be, thank goodness. He still wanted them to stay around the area but he wasn't too interested in anything else about them after they had given their initial statements.

Thursday, July 15th,

B Y THURSDAY, MOST of the people in the village and at
the club had turned to other topics of gossip. Except,
that is, for Celia Martin. That little, round, dark-haired
gossip machine (who Jane always thought reeked like the
entire fragrance counter at Macy's) had begun spending more
time than was normal with Joanna in Marsh Cottage. In fact,
it seemed that they had suddenly become much closer than
normal.

Celia continued to give Jane and Marti sidelong glances
of disgust and had gone so far as to pull her children out of
swimming lessons taught by Ian and Matt as well as tennis
lessons taught by Trey and Nick, following, of course, Joanna's
lead. She explained to anyone who would listen that the boys
were a bad influence on her children. Meanwhile, both Celia's
and Joanna's children looked on miserably as all the other kids
continued with their lessons, all of them having a great time.
Celia did her best to get the other mothers to pull their children
out but so far no one had. Yet, it was obvious to Jane that the
Adams and Sanders boys were affected by the campaign Celia
was waging against them even though the boys seemed to
shrug it off as unimportant.

What a summer this was turning out to be! Jane thought as

she took a last swig of her already tepid coffee. The evening of dinner out and listening to the boys play at the Fog Runner seemed ages ago, though it was only a little over a week past. What could Jane do, she pondered as she put the last of the breakfast dishes into the dishwasher. How she hurt for the boys to be living under even the slightest suspicion. Thinking it was time she and Marti had a brainstorming session Jane picked up the phone in her kitchen to call Marti. They could have a nice dinner out on Friday and talk at the same time. Maybe this would lift their spirits a bit. Jane dialed the well-known phone number and waited for Marti to pick up.

Marti and Jane agreed to meet at the tennis courts and get in some fun games of tennis at the ladies' round robin where they would decide where to go for dinner. After the tennis, Jane promised to call for a reservation. With a positive direction to go in Jane felt much better as she ran up to brush her teeth, grab her racquet and head down to the club.

The ladies' round robin had already started when Jane pushed open the gate that led to the courts. Marti was sitting on one of the benches watching a doubles match in progress and talking amiably to Millie, one of their fellow club members. Jane plopped herself down next to them with a cheery hello, all waiting their turn to join in the play. Jane asked how far into the match the foursome was that was playing directly in front of them on Court One. She found they had just started as had Court Three but that the women on Court Two were just about done and then it would be their turn. This was the morning for women only and they rotated in and out playing with many different players. It was always fun, and with the many levels of expertise, the games could prove to be quite challenging.

As Jane looked past the first court to watch the progress on Court Two, her heart sank. There was Joanna pounding the ball at her opponents with her mighty overhead. As the ball left her racquet the two women on the opposite side of the net ducked their heads to avoid injury.

"Set!" yelled Joanna triumphantly, throwing up her arms in victory. "Ha, six-one, six-love! Boy, did we kill you guys." She laughed derisively, a malevolent grin on her face.

Play stopped on all three courts. Time seemed to stand still and the silence was deafening. No one could believe that Joanna had said what she had said and what's more no one could believe she was unaware of it. Joanna stood in the middle of the court hands on hips, looking around her at the other players wondering what had happened. As her eyes wandered toward the bench where Jane and Marti sat her look became downright odious.

Oblivious to the players on Court One, Joanna stalked in front of them heading straight for Jane and Marti, never taking her eyes off them for one moment. Jane braced herself. Whatever would come next did not portend to be pleasant.

"You have some nerve showing your faces here," she spat at the ladies on the bench. "You should be banned from the club, have your memberships revoked. I'm going to speak to the manager immediately!" With that she turned to leave, but not without a parting shot. Turning back around to include all the women that had come to the round robin she glared at them all and yelled, "And the rest of you should be ashamed to be on the same court with these two, mothers of murderers!" At that she turned heel and barreled through the gate toward the office, probably going straight to the manager's office, thought Jane, miserably, embarrassed, but not sure why she was.

"Can you believe that woman?" Millie exclaimed loud enough for the entire club to hear. She had had the misfortune of being stuck between Marti and Jane during this tirade feeling the full force of Joanna's wrath. "She really has a screw loose.

How in the world can she be so vindictive? No one thinks Matt or Ian had anything to do with Sam's death. What's wrong with her?"

Jane, trembling with emotion, gave Millie a quick hug, grateful for such a visible show of support. Being close to tears she could barely squeak out a thank you but Millie understood.

"Listen, guys," she said quietly to Marti and Jane, "no one in the village gives credence to what Joanna and Celia have to say. We all know the boys wouldn't hurt a fly. Try not to let this bother you. She's just a nut case, one who spits when she yells, by the way, yuck!" Standing, she yelled out, "hey, we're here to play tennis, let's go." And with that everyone seemed to let out their breaths at once and resumed their games.

Jane and Marti got up to play but the enjoyment of a morning of ladies' tennis was just not there for them. They couldn't concentrate on the ball and missed some of the easiest shots. Once Jane swung with all her might, missing the ball entirely as it sailed past her.

Marti, known for her awesome serve, double faulted constantly. After two miserable sets they thanked their partners, apologized for their play and decided to pack it in. Sitting on the beach would be a lot easier on the concentration level, they decided.

Walking home, Marti and Jane's moods were seriously deflated but they decided that it was all the more reason to go out to dinner the next evening. As they walked up the midway path toward their houses they began to lay some plans for their night out.

"Let's go to the other side of the Cape," suggested Marti. "It's been awhile since I've been over there. How about eating at the Red Pheasant? It's always been one of my favorites."

"Me, too," agreed Jane. "It's such a beautiful drive and Dennis is such a quaint town. That's a great idea!" Jane's mood was starting to improve already at the thought of driving down leafy 6A to Dennis and maybe having some duck or salmon at the Red Pheasant, good food could always improve Jane's mood. "How about I make reservations for six-thirty tomorrow night?"

"Make it seven," Marti replied. "That will give me a little extra time to get ready after feeding the boys."

"Seven it is. I'll pick you up at around six-thirty. That should give us enough time," said Jane as she veered off toward her kitchen door. "See you later at the beach."

* * *

Time passed relatively calmly with no more run-ins with Joanna. Jane caught up on all the extra chores around the house that materialized after Geoff had been around. Living with three males was a never-ending battle of picking up after them. As much as she reminded them to put the clothes in the hamper, they usually ended up on the bedroom floor or a worse insult, on top or beside the hamper. Wet towels got hung from bedposts, doorknobs and even the vacuum cleaner while the towel bars sat empty. They never seemed to understand the importance of 'if you use it put it back' so that the next time someone (usually Jane) went to use, say, the scissors, it wouldn't take 30 minutes to find them!

Friday, July 16th

J ANE AND MARTI met their friends Els and Breda for tennis on Friday morning and had a close fun match, the murder and Joanna not mentioned once. The beach was back to normal, nothing new on the murder so nothing new to talk about there. All of Jane's friends had their noses into the latest book for their monthly book club meeting. No murder in that book so far, only incest and infidelity, so conversations tended to explore those themes. It was a happy respite despite the despicable subjects. By the time Jane picked up Marti for their dinner out she was wondering if they really did need to have a pow-wow over the plight of their sons and Sam's murder. Everything seemed to have gone back to normal.

Jane had dressed in her tried-and-true black linen slacks that were one of her 'go to dinner' uniforms for each summer! Paired with them was a new sleeveless, white linen blouse and silver and turquoise hoop earrings and a turquoise silk scarf to add some color. She added a black pashmina in case she got cold in the air-conditioned restaurant. Finishing with a dab of her favorite Penhaligon's scent she realized how good it felt to dress up a little and be going out. Marti was ready when Jane picked her up at six-thirty on Friday evening. As she walked to the car wearing a lime green, linen sundress that went so well with her reddish hair, slight tan and cute freckles, Jane noticed how pretty Marti looked.

As they drove up the quiet tree lined route 6A, Jane felt relaxed for the first time in over a week. She hadn't realized how much stress she had been under until just now as it began to leave her body. It was a warm evening on the Cape and she was driving up one of the most beautiful roads in the world. The muscles in her back and neck began to unwind as they drove by old homes and through the small villages on their way to the Red Pheasant. As she drove through Yarmouthport navigating the winding road Jane felt almost optimistic about the whole mess of Sam's murder. Mike would solve it quickly; they could put it all behind them and begin to truly enjoy the summer.

"You know, after this meal we'd better get back to our morning walks on a more regular basis," Marti said. "With all that's been going on this past week I really haven't felt up to it but we really should try to get going again."

Jane agreed. That was one reason she worried that her slacks might not fit tonight, though with all the worry she'd had lately she really hadn't had the greatest appetite. Tonight though, she was starved! She couldn't wait to see the menu and hear about the specials. Definitely a dessert kind of evening!

The Red Pheasant was situated in an old colonial house on 6A just beyond the village of Dennis. With the downstairs rooms serving as several small, intimate dining areas it had a warm, cozy feel. After being seated in what used to be a porch both ladies were quiet as they read over the tantalizing menu. So many wonderful sounding dishes made their decisions difficult. Finally, Jane decided to start with an endive salad then have the duck in cherry sauce for her entrée. Marti chose the Caesar salad and after much debate over the duck or the scrod, as the scrod seemed a more slimming choice she thought, she, too, ordered the duck. They both requested a glass of the house pinot noir to enjoy while waiting for their dinners.

"Well, here's to us, the summer and to Mike solving Sam's murder," Marti proposed once their wine had arrived.

"Here, here," replied Jane. "Things have been so quiet lately that maybe we can get back to a normal summer after all and won't hear another word about Matt and Ian being involved with Sam's murder. I haven't seen hide nor hair of Joanna or her brother since yesterday morning at tennis, have you?"

"No, thank goodness," answered Marti. "I think for the moment we can relax a bit and not worry about running into her. She's either off the Cape or sequestered in Marsh Cottage. Either way, it makes for a better summer."

"I just wish that it was all over. This is sure to be hard on Alex, knowing someone out there hated her father enough to kill him, that it could be someone she knows and sees each day. I know that it is weirding me out a bit, to use Trey's expression."

"It's true. I have been sort of looking at everyone differently lately, wondering if they could be 'the one'. You know, though, it could have been just some fly-by-night guy that no one knows, a transient, a druggie, whatever, which in itself is a horrible thought, though not quite as disquieting as someone we know. But to think it's someone we even socialize with, like, I don't know, Jane, maybe even you, that's awful!" Marti teased and then laughed out loud when she saw the stunned look on Jane's face before Jane realized that she'd been had.

The two ladies got carried away with peals of laughter as if what Marti had said was the funniest thing in the world. It just felt so good to laugh at something silly and at themselves after the stressful week they'd been through that they couldn't stop. They laughed so hard that Jane swore she heard Marti snort a time or two.

Looking around to see if they had drawn attention to themselves for their loud, unladylike behavior they tried to stifle themselves, only to break out once more. As Jane peeked out behind the cloth napkin she had put to her face she saw that they were getting quite a few annoyed looks. As she surreptitiously scanned the room she noticed someone sitting in a far corner that brought an abrupt stop to her giggles.

"Don't look now, Marti," whispered Jane, "but I swear that the woman wearing the pale blue dress, sitting over in the corner to your left, is the pretty young blond that I saw at Sam's funeral."

Marti waited a few seconds and then nonchalantly glanced in the direction that Jane had indicated. Sure enough, it was the same woman. Marti had seen her too and Bob had told them that she was the one he had seen having dinner with Sam in Boston. She appeared to be eating alone and as the waiter cleared her plate it looked like she was just about to order the coffee and dessert stage of her meal. She hadn't appeared to notice the two women, but seemed lost in thoughts of her own. As the young woman laid her dessert menu down and the waiter walked off, she rose and headed for the ladies' room.

Jane immediately stood up. "She's headed for the loo, Marti. I'm going there too," she announced.

"For Pete's sake, Jane what are you going to say to her? Pardon me, were you Sam Morris' lover?" Marti queried skeptically.

"I haven't thought that far ahead, but I'll think of something, I hope," said Jane as she hurriedly laid down her napkin and followed the young woman's path to the ladies room.

Inside the restroom there was only one stall so Jane busied herself by washing her hands, hoping to come up with some bright idea by the time the toilet flushed. When it did and the woman came out Jane still had no clue what to say. But she needn't have worried for the young woman saved her the trouble.

"Excuse me, but didn't I see you at Sam Morris' funeral on Monday?" the pretty girl asked Jane, who had wanted to ask the same question but didn't have the nerve.

"Yes, I was there. Were you a friend of Sam's?" Jane finally got some nerve up and asked.

"As a matter of fact, yes, I was a very good friend," she replied, tears beginning to pool in the young woman's eyes.

"Such a tragedy, Sam's death. I can't imagine who would have wanted to hurt Sam," Jane exclaimed, hoping little white lies didn't count toward heaven, especially when they were of good intention. "Oh, my dear, are you all right?" Jane asked as she noticed the tears beginning to fall down the girl's cheeks.

"I'm not. This is so hard. I loved Sam, and I have no one to talk to it about," she confessed to Jane. "You see, Sam and I were going to get married, but we had kept it a secret so that shrew of a wife of his wouldn't get all of his money when he asked for a divorce. She's an evil woman. Sam always told me that Joanna had married him for his money and they weren't at all happy. He said she had it in for him. He used to kid and say if anything happened to him that was the second place I should look to place blame, right after any unhappy ex-clients he had defended. Of course, he was only joking but underneath it all I think he really felt that way," she told Jane, the tears flowing freely now. "Look, I'm sorry, I've said too much. In fact I can't believe all of that just came out of my mouth! It's probably the two glasses of wine talking. You're probably one of his wife's closest friends. Excuse me," she added as she tried to get by Jane to leave the bathroom.

"Let me introduce myself. I'm Jane Adams, enemy of Joanna Morris, who hates my guts, and you are . . ." Jane extended her hand as she hoped to learn more about this mystery woman.

"Jane Adams! Of course, your son is Alex's good friend. Ian, right? "The young woman seemed to brighten at Jane's name. It's so nice to meet you; Sam has often mentioned you and your boys and what good friends you all are to Alex and to his ex-wife, Julia. I'm Sara. I worked with Sam at his law firm. I'm a paralegal there." Sara explained as Jane silently asked for forgiveness for any bad thoughts she had ever had about Sam. "Sam thought the world of Ian and his friend, Matt, saying that without them, Alex wouldn't have made it through the first year after his divorce."

"Sara, I'm having dinner with Matt's mother at this moment. Why don't you join us? We would love to get to know you. What mother doesn't like to hear a good word about her son? Please, join us," Jane encouraged as they walked out of the ladies room together and chatting, much to Marti's surprise.

Sara sipped her after-dinner coffee at Jane and Marti's table as the other two ladies dug into their duck. They spoke of the Cape, its weather, restaurants in Boston and other safe topics. Sara took her dessert with Jane and Marti, though she only picked at it, mostly just moving the blueberries out of their pie crust and smearing her plate with them while Jane and Marti, appetites only slightly appeased, dug into a luscious chocolate panna cotta with fresh blackberries they were sharing.

As they were finishing the last licks off their forks Jane knew that their time was almost up. Soon they would be saying their good-byes, so she took a deep breath and boldly plunged into the topic she and Marti had been avoiding.

"Sara," Jane quietly said. "I don't want to seem like I'm prying, but since you did say that Sam thought so highly of Matt and Ian I was wondering if you realize that Sam's wife Joanna is accusing the boys of his murder?"

Sara, put down her fork, pretense of eating over. She looked perplexed as she said, "Why, for heaven's sake, would she think that they would have anything to do with it?"

Jane and Marti explained the theory Joanna had been spreading around Herring Run. How the boys had murdered Sam because he planned to change his will in favor of her boys, disinheriting Alex. How she claimed this enraged the boys so much that they crushed in Sam's skull. At this reference to the murder Sara visibly blanched and after a small gasp her lower lip began to tremble.

"Oh, my gosh, Sara. We didn't mean to upset you," exclaimed Marti. "It's just that this has gotten us so upset. Anyone thinking that our boys would do such a horrible crime is beyond comprehension. The police chief has told us not to worry too much. He doesn't hold much in Joanna's theory, but she and her village ambassador, Celia, have spread it all around the village."

"Ladies," began Sara, resolve in her voice, "let me be perfectly honest with you."

At this, Jane and Marti perked up so much that their ears almost bent forward.

Sara explained that she and Sam had been seeing each other for over a year. In that time their love and commitment to each other had grown and they often talked about making it a permanent arrangement. But Sam had yet to approach Joanna for a divorce.

"I secretly think that Sam was a bit afraid of her," remarked Sara. "He knew that she might be aware of something going on but she was toying with him. She told him if he ever had an affair she would take him for everything he had. She would constantly accuse him of having an affair and then she would apologize for mistrusting him. This was even before we began to see one another. It was back and forth, lots of tears on her part, much yelling on both parts. Sam wanted to get his financial house in order to protect Alex's interest before he went through with anything. And quite honestly, I was not sure I wanted to have him leave Joanna for me. I wasn't ready to make a commitment for quite a while. I loved him but I wasn't sure I wanted to put all my trust and life into his keeping. He didn't have the greatest track record. Within the last few months I knew at last that I could make that commitment. Sam had changed and I could trust in him. We were making plans, plans for us, our future.

"You know," she added, "he told me that he realized that he had made one of the biggest mistakes of his life when he took up with Joanna and divorced Julia. He missed Alex, he regretted hurting both of them the way he did, saying he just didn't see it at the time, that he couldn't have it all. Even though he still loved Julia he realized he had gone too far and lost her so he went ahead and married Joanna. He was beginning to mellow in his middle age. He knew it was too late for him and Julia after all he'd done and he knew he had made a big mistake in marrying Joanna. She was just a gold digger. Did you know that Sam came from a family that was quite well off? He had parlayed the inheritance from his parents into a tidy nest egg. Joanna loved to spend his money on herself and her boys, paying little attention to him after she got him to marry her. She took the boys on trips without him, went off for long weekends with friends to the mountains or sometimes even down to the Caribbean."

Marti and Jane were surprised to hear this. They knew Sam wasn't one to spend money foolishly and they would have thought he would have thought a trip to the Caribbean without him would qualify as a foolish expenditure, especially just for a weekend. Maybe, Jane thought, he was just glad to get Joanna out of his hair.

Sara explained to them, "He had tried to make their

marriage work in the beginning but eventually he knew he was very unhappy and he also knew that Joanna would never really love him, just what he could give her. He realized that he'd been had by her. He really wanted to change, turn his life around. I was the one who answered his many demanding and often demeaning phone calls from her at the office. If Joanna couldn't talk to Sam she would give me an earful and this was long before Sam and I had even looked at one another. He sensed I was aware of his problems and he began to confide a bit in me. First, it would just be a look, an arch of the eyebrow, a wry smile after one of her calls. Sometimes a word or two during a slow time at work when he seemed especially down was all he would confide. That led to talks over lunches that later led to dinners when Joanna was on one of her many trips. Somewhere along the line we crossed it and fell in love. We often went to the North End because there's a restaurant there where we could sit down in the basement dining room, knowing it wasn't up to Joanna's standards. She liked to be where she could see and be seen, with all her gold and diamonds. The things she bought with his money. And anyway, we liked the food and the intimate atmosphere."

He paid for that in more ways than one, I bet, Jane thought, unkindly.

"It became our restaurant," Sara remembered with a sob.

Aha, thought Marti, Bob did see them together at Florentines!

"This past week has been so hard. I've taken a week's sick leave from work but I don't know how I can ever go back there now that Sam is gone. Oh, god, I miss him so much!" she exclaimed as tears rolled down her cheeks. "I'm sorry if I'm boring you but I've had no one to talk to about Sam before now. No one, not even at work, I think, knows about our relationship."

"You aren't boring us," replied Jane, thinking it was quite the contrary and feeling genuine pain for this pretty, young woman. "Please, go on. We're so sorry for what you're going through."

"Well, that's basically it. I mean, we've been planning to marry someday. I do think it would have happened. We talked about children, having them. Sam was so sorry to miss a big part of Alex's life. He thought the world started and ended with that girl. From everything he told me about her I looked forward to meeting her when we could finally be together in the open. He had wanted another chance at fatherhood, but Joanna would have nothing to do with that. Didn't want to stretch her stomach anymore she told him, had already had her tummy tuck. Said she wanted to maintain her figure. He wanted to feel close to Justin and Jake but it just didn't happen, they were totally controlled by their mother, though he did try with them, he really did. Took them to Red Sox games, watched their sports competitions, in fact that's why he came down early last week. To see the boys play in a tennis match at the club. But Joanna never let them get too close to Sam, she was afraid of losing their allegiance. We wanted to have at least two children together, so many plans and now . . ." Sara left off, her face now awash with salty tears.

"And that means that there is no way Sam would have written Alex out of his will," declared Jane.

"No, never," confirmed Sara with resolute conviction. "He loved Alex more than life itself, she meant the world to him."

As the ladies walked out of the restaurant that evening they knew that they each had found a new friend. They chatted under the starry sky as they waited for the valet to bring their cars up, exchanging phone numbers with promises to keep in touch. Sara, who had been at the Tara since she drove down to meet Sam over a week ago, said she would stay a few more days. Though she and Sam had been careful about keeping their affair a secret, she felt that a few people at the office might now be aware of it. Her appearance at the funeral may have tipped a few people off. No one from the firm had approached her at the funeral, but she felt that maybe her grief showed more than it should have. She had phoned into work with the excuse of a family emergency but knew she needed to get back to a normal routine. The thought of returning to where they both had worked depressed her, though, and she wasn't sure she would stay there any longer than it would take to find a new position.

Coming to the Red Pheasant was, in a way, her good-bye to Sam as it had been the one restaurant that she and Sam would go to on Cape Cod since it was not near Herring Run, being located on the other side of the Cape and few villagers ventured that far. She had even requested their usual table in the corner. It had been a very sad evening for her until she met Jane and Marti. Spending time with them had been cathartic.

"It was really good to meet you two, thank you for listening," Sara told Jane and Marti, giving them each a quick hug. "Sam's death was such a shock. I haven't had anyone to talk to about him, us. It's been such a secret, which has been hard anyway, but to have him die and have no one whom I could talk to about my feelings has been excruciating. I know that some people weren't that fond of Sam but he had become aware of it and truly was trying to change. I guess you could say he was having a good mid-life crisis. I think I was good for Sam and if we'd only had the chance . . ." her voice trailed off as tears, again, began to spill down her cheeks.

Pulling out some tissues for her, Jane tried to console Sara by saying, "We are really, truly sorry for your loss. I wish I had had the chance to get to know the Sam you knew. If we can do anything for you in the next few days or ever, well, let us know."

"Yes, yes," added Marti. "We're as close as your telephone."

"Sara," Jane added. "You really should try to talk to Mike McGuire, the police chief who is handling the case, about your relationship to Sam. It might help him to get a better perspective on everything."

"I don't know," Sara began. "It's so hard . . ."

At that moment the valet pulled up with Sara's little red Honda. As she got into the car, she lifted up her hand to wave as she said good-bye, tears streaming down her face with a sad, little smile. Jane and Marti stood silently watching the car drive out of the lot. Jane thought she might have misjudged Sam, a little, in the last few years, she knew that she and others had written him off once he had married Joanna. Jane looked up at the star lit sky hoping he would forgive her, wherever he was.

Pulling Jane's Tahoe up to the curb, the valet opened the door for each lady and they followed Sara out of the lot, taking a left onto Route 6A. As they drove home neither woman noticed that a dark gray Mercedes sedan pulled out after them, nor did Sara notice when she took the turn off toward Hyannis that the same car turned with her, keeping a discreet, but sure, distance behind her.

Saturday, July 17th

O N SATURDAY THE nice weather decided to take a break and go elsewhere. After almost two weeks of non-stop, glorious, sun filled days the rain came in with a vengeance. It was going to be a cold, wet day. Mother Nature was again proving that she was the one that planned the weekends, not the golfers, tennis players and beach goers. Jane woke up early, heard the rain pounding on the windows and pulled the covers over her head and slept in until eight. On a day like this, the Hyannis Mall would be swarming with vacationers, the movie theaters would be packed and the main roads to both places, Routes 28 and 132, would be like parking lots. When she finally dragged herself out of bed, Jane decided it would be a good day to catch up on some housework and later settle in with a cup of hot chocolate while delving into the new Mary Higgins Clark mystery that Millie had lent her. They had heard Ms. Clark, a fellow Cape Codder, speak at the Cape Cod Writer's Conference and they had each bought one of her books to swap. Jane thought Ms. Clark was an amazing speaker and had lead a very interesting life, nothing like Jane's boring day-to-day, iron, wash, car pool and so on existence, though honestly, Jane thought *my boring life has taken a turn lately. Hmm*, thought Jane, *maybe we need*

*Ms. Clark here to lead us in the right direction. Don't her books
end well?*

Around one in the afternoon, just as she had nestled into
the couch with her cup of steaming cocoa, the new book open
to chapter one in her lap, she heard the kitchen door slam and
Ian yell up, "Mom, ya home? I need a ride into Hyannis. Greg
called and said the store is jammed with customers. Since the
beach is closed he wants me to come in for the afternoon. Can
you do it? I need to leave right away." He informed her of all
this on the fly as he ran past her and up the stairs for a quick
change out of his guard sweats.

No answer was really needed or expected from Jane but
she managed a feeble yes and rose to get her purse and the
car keys. She put the mug of steaming, heavenly cocoa by the
microwave where she could heat it up when she returned and
pulled on her rain jacket.

As they drove to Hyannis, windshield wipers slashing
madly across her vision, Jane decided to ask her son what, if
anything, he heard at the beach concerning the murder.

"Any new theories on who did it?" she nonchalantly asked
Ian.

His blue eyes looking straight ahead, he answered in a firm
tone, "I really don't want to talk about it, Mom. That's all we
seem to hear from everyone at the beach. The mothers of the
kids in lessons are either thinking we were involved or that
we have an inside track on who did it because we found the
body, so we hear it from them. All the ladies sitting on the
beach can't seem to gossip about anything else, your crew
excepted, of course, and that Mrs. Martin, ugh, she acts like we
have cooties or something. Anytime Matt or I happen to walk
her way she turns around and goes the other way, muttering
remarks under her breath, just loud enough so we can't hear
them but everyone she passes can. I'm sick of the whole thing.

I mean, I feel bad for Alex, and I guess Justin and Jake. I even feel a little sorry for Mrs. Morris and of course Mr. Morris, for getting murdered, but I don't want to talk about it. Mom, I can't always get the horrible way he looked, lying there in the sand, with flies and sea gulls around him, out of my mind. It wakes me up in the night sometimes. And when I close my eyes, there it is. But, like I said, I don't want to talk about it. We just don't at the beach. All of us guards are trying to forget about it and get on with the summer," he stated flatly, turning his face to the passenger side window, making sure she understood that the subject was closed.

Well, thought Jane, for not wanting to talk about it I just learned quite a bit from him. Aloud she said, "All right, Ian, no more talk of Sam Morris' murder out of me. But if you ever want to talk about how you feel about it or anything else that's going on, remember, I'm always there for you. And if you feel the need to talk to a professional . . ."

At this remark, Ian glared at Jane, "The beach committee has already had a 'professional' speak with us all together and one at a time—you know, that pediatrician that sits nears tower three—ugh." At this he rolled his eyes, then decided to glare some at her some more before returning his eyes to his stare out the side window.

Hmm, message understood, she thought. Yet, hearing this made Jane a little misty-eyed but she didn't let on to Ian how she felt, she just kept her eyes on the road in front of her and let him turn the radio on to his favorite rock station. Almost to Hyannis now, they were coming upon the Tara Hotel on the right and the Melody Tent on the left, a place where Jane used to take the boys on Wednesday afternoons, when they were just tots, for the children's matinees. What memories that brought back: she would dress them in their best white shorts, little blue polo shirts and off they'd go to sit under the tent for a couple of hours in the afternoon. They would watch productions of "Little Red Riding Hood", "Cinderella" and other age appropriate plays. Now the little kids at the beach had their own iPods and even some watched movies on little individual players. But, still, the Melody Tent still had their children's matinees and still drew them in, nice thought, Jane realized.

As the kids got older they would go with her to the Melody Tent to hear rock groups or comedians, such as Gallagher and the Beach Boys, but mostly they outgrew her and began going with friends instead. *What pleasant memories it all brings,* she thought. She hoped Ian was having them as well, though she seriously doubted it knowing full well that the male species was wired so very differently than the female. For most males, being sentimental wasn't one of their strongest points.

As they passed the Tara, she noticed looking out through the rain-soaked window the blur of flashing red lights at its front entrance. It made her heart lurch bringing her back to the morning of Sam's murder. But she chided herself, knowing that with a hotel full of guests someone was bound to have some medical emergency requiring an ambulance. It happened everyday in the summer on the Cape. The morning after Sam's murder was still too fresh in her mind to not associate flashing lights and sirens with death, she guessed. Though she hoped it wasn't upsetting her son, how could she expect Ian to feel any differently? As she quickly glanced over at him she saw he was staring at the scene that was unfolding turning his head as they passed. She silently prayed that Ian would be okay and that whatever was going on there would have a better outcome than poor Sam.

As she pulled up to the curb in front of Islands to let Ian out, she told him to call if he needed a ride home and reached over to plant a kiss on his cheek. He bounded out of the car and quickly ran into the store with a shouted thanks and a wave. As she drove off, Jane hoped that they would find out who had murdered Sam soon. She hadn't realized the toll this was taking on Ian and probably all the guards at the beach. His grim face as he got out of the car was all the proof she needed. She needed to talk to Geoff about getting a real grief counselor in to talk to all of the guards if the beach club hadn't already planned on it. She would be sure to ask Craig, the beach manager.

Since she was already in Hyannis, Jane decided to play tourist and do a little browsing in a couple of her favorite stores. She knew Islands was packed, so she headed first for the used bookstore to check out what mysteries and novels they had in that she hadn't read yet. As she wandered up and down aisles and checked out the rows of books her eye lit upon a small plaid book cover that piqued her interest. She picked it up and was pleased to see that it was about Scottish Clans. Scanning through it she looked for the name Henderson, which had been her mother's maiden name. After finding that she looked up Geoff's mother's family name, Kirkby. There it was as well. For two dollars this one was a keeper, she smiled. Pleased with her find of the Scottish clan book, a barely used Anne Tyler hardback that she was anxious to read, as well as two of Ms. Clark's books that she missed when they'd come out, Jane headed for the cash register only too see, much to her dismay, Celia Martin. She was standing in line at the checkout counter with her two children. Just the person I wanted to see, Jane groaned inwardly. Maybe I should just leave my great finds and head out the door, she thought.

But, knowing she had a summer's worth of reading at a steal in her hands she held her head high and approached the desk, standing just behind Celia. One of the Martin children looked up at Jane and said, "Hi Mrs. Adams, how's Ian?"

"Just fine, Jenny, though he misses you in swimming lessons," Jane replied with a smile to the young girl, using her well-known nickname.

"That's enough, Jennifer," huffed Celia as she drew out every syllable of her daughter's first name at the same time putting a protective arm around the youngster. "You shouldn't be talking to Mrs. Adams. And Jane I would appreciate it if you wouldn't mention either of your sons in the presence of my children," Celia quietly snarled at Jane.

"Why, Celia," purred Jane despite an inner desire to scratch the woman's eyes out. "Whatever, do you mean by that? Is there something I don't know about?"

"I don't need to tell you what your son is accused of," Celia blustered. "It's not a secret, you know. Joanna has made it quite clear to me that your son, along with that Sanders boy, is guilty as sin in the murder of Sam Morris. Why they haven't been arrested yet is beyond me but all will come out soon, I'm sure. Joanna says they have more proof now than ever. Just keep your boys away from my family!" With that, Celia turned on her heel, without purchasing her books and dragged a bewildered Jennifer and her brother out of the store leaving Jane with an open mouth in total shock.

The clerk at the cash register looked oddly at Jane as he totaled up her purchases. She was glad when she could leave the store herself. It was one thing to have Celia pull her kids out of lessons but quite another for her to blatantly accuse Matt and Ian in a public place. Jane felt outraged and embarrassed at the spectacle that had just transpired. She knew now that she could not give up her quest to clear Ian and Matt's names. It had gone beyond their little group of friends and their little village of Herring Run.

Feeling down and that her afternoon was ruined, Jane decided to drive home and call Geoff, he might have some insight as to what she should do next, but first she would stop in to see Ian at the store where he worked. She needed to reassure herself that he was all right. Running between the raindrops, she headed down the street to Islands.

Upon entering the store Jane was immediately cheered by the Buffett music playing on the jukebox. Though the store was jammed with people, everyone seemed mellow, taking a cue from the music and the friendly staff. Customers smiled as they riffled through piles of Margaritaville tee shirts and racks of clothing. As she found herself humming along, getting into a better mood, she scanned the store for a sight of Ian. Jane finally spotted him behind the counter helping a couple of cute preteen girls who were trying on sunglasses. Lifting different pairs of sunglasses from the inside of the case to show the girls he caught sight of his mother and sent a smile her way. She smiled and waved back, feeling that despite Celia's vicious outburst, Ian seemed just fine. Reassured she headed back to where she had parked her car.

Driving home Jane again passed the Tara. The ambulance and the police cars were still there, though now their lights were off. Jane felt goose bumps on her arms and the hair on the back of her neck seemed to stand on end. Shaking her head she drove on home, trying to dispel the feeling of doom that was trying to engulf her. Would she ever get over that feeling when she saw that kind of scene in the future? Thoughts of the morning of Sam's death engulfed her. It made her realize how hard it must be for Ian and Matt.

Once back home, Jane reheated her hot chocolate, picked up her book and settled back down to read. But she couldn't get past the first page. She read it over and over until she realized that she had no idea what she had read when she turned to page two. Celia had rattled her more than she thought. What had that woman meant when she mentioned proof? No one from the police had called with anything and she was almost sure that Mike would let her know if something had come up to implicate Ian. But then, maybe Mike didn't know yet. Where had Celia gotten the information? Jane could kick herself for not asking that horrid woman exactly what she meant and who was her source of information. But Jane's pride had not allowed her to give Celia the satisfaction of knowing that Jane was worried and Celia hadn't really given Jane the chance to respond or ask questions anyway. On the other hand, thought Jane, maybe Celia was just full of hot air and there was no proof or evidence. Yet, no matter what, she had rattled Jane.

Jane picked up the phone and dialed their home number in Arizona hoping to talk to Geoff. When no one answered and their machine came on she left a message asking him to call when he could. She tried his cell phone but that just went to his recorded message as well which meant he was probably out enjoying a beautiful, albeit hot Arizona day, probably playing tennis at their club, as he never took his cell phone with him when he wasn't on call and was out to relax. Frustrated at not reaching her husband and not being able to vent to someone, Jane noticed the rain had stopped and decided that maybe she just needed to clear her head by getting out into the fresh air. Maybe a good walk would shake off her dismal mood.

Putting on her old sneakers and grabbing her rain poncho in case it should start up again, she stepped out onto her front porch. Down the midway path she walked, paying little attention to where she was going, just trying to walk free of this mood of doom and gloom. Past the village green and on back down the road that led through the wooded section of Herring Run she went. Before she knew it she had made her way to the end of the road and the last house on the lane that belonged to her friend Margaret.

The gray-shingled Cape-style house was nestled in the

woods with sweet smelling pink roses climbing up a trellis that framed the front door. With an enclosed porch surrounded by blooming hydrangeas and a white picket fence also festooned with roses that surrounded the property the house looked so beautiful and sweet, just like Margaret herself.

As she admired the house she suddenly realized that if anyone knew what Celia was talking about it would most likely be Margaret herself. She always seemed to have the skinny on everything. Knocking on the door, Jane wondered how she would ask Margaret about this new evidence without seeming too worried. When the door opened Margaret's cheery smile and warm hello immediately put Jane at ease. Invited in and offered tea, Jane was trying to decide between Irish Breakfast and Darjeeling when Margaret dropped the bombshell.

"I guess you've heard the latest. Joanna has told Mike McGuire that the new lifeguard, Robin, actually saw Ian holding the shovel that killed Sam while Matt stood by on the night that Sam was murdered."

Jane dropped the Irish Breakfast tea bag and gasped. She felt her stomach going into a spasm. Her ears began to ring. What had Margaret said? Robin had seen what? Jane felt a little dizzy and grabbed hold of the side of the counter to keep her balance, her face rapidly losing color. This is when her low blood pressure was not an advantage as Jane felt she would likely faint.

"Oh, my, god, Jane, I'm sorry. I was sure you would have heard this. It's not as bad as it sounds just that Robin saw them with it late that night as she was walking back from the showers. According to Joanna, Robin told her she saw them throw it under the boardwalk and then go to their room. She didn't think anything of it until the next morning when Sam's body was discovered and was told the shovel was used as the murder weapon. Now, Jane, you know, of course, this is Joanna's story. No one has talked to Robin yet. Joanna said Robin was taking a few personal days off from the beach to get away. She said Robin is afraid of Ian and Matt and couldn't stay at the beach one more minute."

Jane sank down onto one of Margaret's kitchen chairs. This news could really be bad for Ian and Matt, she thought. Why hadn't she heard this from Mike? When had Robin said this to Joanna? Jane felt sick to her stomach.

"God, Margaret, I know this can't be true but why would Robin say such a thing? This could implicate them in the murder if anyone believes it. Where did you hear about this?" Jane asked as she tried with her shaky hand to calmly pick up one of Margaret's delicate teacups.

"The usual source, Celia. So you know that it could just be a wild rumor that Joanna, or for that matter that Celia, started. They've gotten awful chummy lately, have you noticed? Don't put too much credence into it unless you hear it from a reliable source, like Mike McGuire. And now, let me give you chamomile tea instead of the Irish Breakfast you picked out. It will calm your nerves a bit." Margaret said as she guided Jane over to the more comfortable plush wicker chair in the living room and sat her down. Thinking she'd need a bit more than chamomile tea to calm her down, Jane none-the-less gratefully sank into the soft blue and white cushions.

Later, walking back from Margaret's, Jane's sense of doom deepened. She trusted Ian and what he'd told her about the events surrounding Sam's death. She had no reason not to trust him. After talking with Sara, Jane was even more positive that Joanna had manufactured that whole scene between Sam and the boys regarding his will and Alex. But, why was Joanna adding fuel to the fire?

Well, two can play at this game, thought Jane. *And I can play hardball! If Joanna continues to accuse Ian and Matt I will just ask Sara to talk to Mike and tell her side of the story to him. Maybe that will get a few tongues wagging at Joanna for a change!* But, thought Jane, *I don't want Sara ending up hurt. She's such a nice girl and doesn't really deserve Joanna's viscous tongue so I'll have to do this discreetly. First off, I'll go home and call Mike and ask him to go talk to her.* With a concrete form of action to take Jane felt better and picked up her pace toward home.

As she headed through the village green she noticed it was bathed in an eerie light that often comes near the end of a rainy day. As the sky cleared and the sun made its first appearance of the day Jane noticed that several people were out in their yards cleaning up the broken twigs and other debris left by the storm. She waved to them as she walked by, trying to shake off her feelings of apprehension. Starting down the path of the midway Jane saw Marti walking up toward her with her arms waving. As Jane approached Marti's house Marti asked her to come inside for a minute.

"Jane, Matt came home awhile ago and said he and Ian are being asked to take a few days off, with pay of course, because of the rumors circling around them. It seems that Robin told Joanna that she saw them with the shovel the night of Sam's murder and everyone is talking about it. The beach committee has asked that Craig relieve them of their duties until this is investigated," Marti told a stunned Jane. "Matt is crushed and acting mad as hell. He's already moved most of his things from the beach to his room up here. He just left to go tell Ian and he thinks that the two of them should just tell the beach committee 'what they can do with their job'. I'm hoping Ian can calm him down a bit. I think more than anything he's just feeling let down and confused. Bob's on the phone now trying to get his lawyer friend who specializes in criminal defense. Bob says he'll let us know where to go from here." All this rushed out of Marti's mouth in one breath. She was clearly as distraught as Jane was now. Everything seemed to be crashing down on them and their boys.

Stricken by the news repeated made Jane's head reel. "What happened to innocent until proven guilty?" screeched Jane. "What is wrong with Craig? The Beach Committee? They know our boys. What are they doing? Who actually talked to Robin?" she wanted to know.

At that moment Bob walked in and took in the situation at a glance. Looking from one mother to the other he said, "Okay, ladies, yes we have a situation here. But it's not hopeless. For one thing no one has verified that Robin told this story. She doesn't seem to be around. I just talked to Craig at the beach and he said he just wants a few days for things to blow over and for the boys to catch a breath away from the beach and these rumors. He says he has absolute faith in the boys.

"For another thing, my friend in Boston says that until these stories have some veracity and the police take them seriously we should ignore them, as much as we can, I might add. I talked to Mike and he hasn't even been able to talk Robin to question her since the day Sam was found when she gave her formal statement, which by the way, didn't include the latest rumor. He doesn't consider her or any of the guards suspect so it hasn't been that urgent for him to find her, though he did ask her to remain in the area and is surprised that she left. She seems to have disappeared for the time being so, he's looking into it, but not as a high priority, which should tell us something. I know this isn't easy but for now we just go on as usual. Now, Jane, go home and talk to Ian when he returns from work. Then get ready to be picked up at 6:30 for a delightful dinner at the Crab Catcher in Mashpee. My treat! If the skies clear enough, which they look like they're doing, we can eat outside."

Jane looked at him dubiously at the thought of a delightful dinner but was touched by the kindness of his offer. Sometimes Saturday nights were not easy to get through with Geoff in Arizona and all the other women having their husbands down from Boston for the weekend. With the boys off on dates or at work, Saturday evenings could get downright lonely while everyone else paired off and went out. This is when she missed Geoff the most. Certainly tonight would be one of the hardest Saturday nights she had faced yet in all her years at the Cape. So, with gratitude in her heart, she accepted this gracious invitation and started home to do just what Bob had told her to do.

Since Ian wasn't home yet she thought she'd give Geoff another ring to see if he was in yet. She needed, desperately, to share this latest information with him. As the phone rang in Tucson she thought she would start to cry when she heard Geoff's voice. And cry she did. On his first hello she started and couldn't stop. Luckily, Geoff recognized her sobs and listened patiently, speaking soothing words, while he waited for her to get all the tears out of her system.

"What is it, love? What's the matter? Are the boys okay? Are you okay?" he asked with a touch of panic just barely detectable in his voice.

As Jane slowly regained some control she spit out the story that she'd gotten from Margaret and the horrible meeting with Celia. Blowing her nose loudly in Geoff's poor ear, she tried not to leave anything out including the advice of Bob's friend and also the invitation the Sanderses had extended to her for dinner that evening.

"Well, I knew something was up when you called both numbers. I'm sorry I wasn't there for you but it sounds like you are handling it well and Bob has given us some good advice. Until we're given something to worry about I suggest we try not to worry. I promise you that if this thing heats up anymore I'll catch the first flight out there. In the meantime, you just keep your chin up and go on with your life. Nothing wrong with a good cry though, but remember we can't live on what might happen and ugly rumors," Geoff counseled Jane, as he had many times in the past when other crises had arisen. Geoff was always telling her not to project into the future, but for some reason that seemed to be all Jane could do these days. He also reminded Jane to carry her cell phone with her and keep it charged as he had tried to return her calls, but to no avail. Jane was terrible about using her cellphone, she found it more of a nuisance than a normal connection to the world. She was more likely to leave it plugged in at home than to take it anywhere with her. Jane liked to be out of touch where no one could reach her, but Geoff was right. With all that was going on at the moment she would make more of an effort, at least for awhile.

Before they hung up they talked of other matters, the house repairs on their cottage that needed estimates, Geoff's progress on the carousel horse he was carving and what he was cooking on the barbecue that night. Though she had trouble thinking of anything other than her troubles she worked hard to picture him, barbecue fork in hand, standing by the grill over a delicious piece of salmon as he relaxed on their terrace. He was planning to pair his fish with his world famous Caesar salad. That was one of their favorite dinners. He would probably sit under the arbor as his dinner cooked, listen to the stereo play soft jazz, or maybe country western and watch the sun set with the glorious pinks and purples that only seem to happen in the west. She longed for all of them to be sitting there with him this evening instead of being in the middle of a murder investigation on Cape Cod.

After protracted good-byes and Jane promising to tell Ian

to call Geoff within the next two days, Jane sat with her hand still on the receiver, glad she had gotten hold of Geoff. In fact, she was glad that she'd had a good cry. She felt better and clearer than she had all day, though she knew her puffy eyes needed some attending to before she faced the public. As if a cloud had lifted off of her, she felt ready to deal with whatever would come, which did come an instant later with the banging of the kitchen door and an agitated Ian bounding up the stairs.

His face was bright red and Jane could swear she saw steam coming out of both ears. Behind him, looking almost as mad but doing his best to restrain himself in front of her, was Matt. Both boys were carrying Ian's belongings from the beach in their arms.

"Mom, I'm out of the beach. They don't want us back. They think we killed Mr. Morris! I can't believe this. I'm going to give that beach committee a piece of my mind. After all the years there, this is the thanks we get, well, I'll tell them what they can do with their job," Ian exclaimed his voice filled with raw emotion.

Jane could barely stand not pulling him into her arms and soothing him with the voice that every mother reserves for her own. But she knew that would never do in front of Matt, or for that matter would Ian tolerate it at his age. Instead she asked them to sit down, not an easy request in their agitated states, and listen to what she had learned.

As they sat on the edge of their chairs, feet tapping, hands in fists, she explained that Craig was standing behind them with the beach committee. That even the committee was behind them but felt that a few days off might give Matt and Ian some space from the rumors, to let them die down. She didn't add that she thought that if they were really behind them they would just ignore the accusations, but Jane knew Craig was getting all sorts of pressure from all sides and was dealing with the members the way the committee wanted him to. Some of the committee was made up of friends of Sam's and they might just believe the lies Joanna was telling. Successful in calming both boys down a bit, she suggested that they go hang out at the Fog Runner that evening, maybe even see if they could play a few sets and not worry about life guarding.

"Just think, guys, tomorrow is Sunday and you can stay out as late as you want tonight, then sleep until all hours tomorrow because you won't have to get up to guard as usual. This is a first. Take these lemons you've been handed and go make some lemonade with them," she advised. Jane only wished she felt as confident as she hoped she sounded to the boys.

They looked a bit askance at her. She had them with going to the Fog Runner, as well as playing a few sets plus sleeping late on Sunday, a true luxury for them, but she lost them with the lemonade. Maybe she should have tried limoncello instead, she thought, wryly. Taking her advice they took off for an evening out, if not with smiles, at least no longer steaming mad, deciding to try to enjoy a good thing while it lasted. Jane headed up to her room for a quick shower and to make herself a bit more presentable for her evening out with the Sanders. Try as she might, her hair was hopeless even with most of the humidity that had left with the rain, so she just blew it dry as best she could and stopped looking in the mirror!

That evening at The Crab Catcher, Jane, Marti and Bob settled in at the beautiful, curved, mahogany bar while waiting for a table to be free. Reservations only assured you a table at this popular eatery, when you sat down at one was another story. The Crab Catcher was known for it's superb seafood and, summer or winter, it never seemed to lack customers. Jane tried to relax, actually glad for the extra time as people stood three deep at the bar while waiting for tables to open up.

Both women had made an effort this evening. Marti had

dressed in a dark green skirt with a short sleeve, white linen blouse that was trimmed with the same green, which accented her red hair so well. Jane had settled on a slimming, light blue, sleeveless sheath dress that made her blue eyes appear even bluer. Around her neck she wore a long blue and white scarf that she had knotted half way down the front of the dress. As pretty as Jane thought she looked she still felt pretty glum and knew that Marti was feeling the same way, too. But they were trying their best especially since Bob had been so nice to invite them out and try to get their minds off their troubles.

The Crab Catcher was a beautiful restaurant that overlooked one of the many small lakes that dotted the peninsula of Cape Cod. It was situated in a lush grove of trees and the restaurant's views were shown to the fullest by soaring windows and strategically placed spotlights. There was greenery throughout the restaurant as well and the white tablecloths with the dark wood, almost black, of the walls and chairs made for an elegance that belied the restaurant's name. Jane had always wondered why a restaurant located five miles inland from the shore would be called The Crab Catcher. Why not The Grove or Lakeside? Maybe the original owner had gone out to catch crabs to make for the diners. So, Crab Catcher it was and it was good to be out, away from the village, with friends on a Saturday night in such a beautiful setting despite, or maybe because of, all the troubles back in Herring Run.

They each ordered a glass of pinot grigio in anticipation of having some of the restaurant's good fish in a bouillabaisse or maybe some local scrod while trying to pretend that all was well with their lives. That worked for them for the first fifteen minutes or so but soon they had all run out of small talk and were back on the subject of Sam's murder. Bob, diplomat that he was, tried several changes of subject but to no avail and finally realized that when mothers are worried about their children there isn't much one can do to deter them from putting every bit of energy into trying to solve any problem involving their offspring. .

"Do you think that Robin actually told Joanna that she saw the boys with the shovel or do you think it's another one of Joanna's stories," Marti wondered aloud. "She has a habit of exaggerating almost everything, even making things up to suit her purposes. So many times she been caught at making up stories, that are, just that, stories. Or one could say, lies. And then she believes they're the gospel truth and nothing can dissuade her."

"The gospel according to Joanna," laughed Jane, bitterly.

"It's more likely one of Celia's 'stories,'" Bob threw out, wanting to give the ladies as much to calm their nerves as possible. "You know, she's quite a gossip and so many times she's been full of hot air. In fact, I don't understand why she says all the things she does; no one believes her half the time."

Marti looked at both of them sadly and said, "Well, truthfully, I sometimes feel sorry for her. She always seems to be hungry for attention," she reflected as she sipped her glass of white wine. "She sure goes about it in an awful way, though. Not many people care for her or her gossip, but as you said if half the people don't believe it then you have to say that means the other half do," she finished.

"That's the half that don't know her very well," commented Jane. "Joanna is sure using her, though. She feeds something to Celia and soon it's all over the Cape, or at least Herring Run and The Beach and Tennis Club."

"Well, I hope the boys don't hear her latest bit of news. They're feeling bad enough as it is and if they hear one more thing they're libel to blow it all out of proportion and think it's one more nail in their coffin," said Bob. "Look, here comes the

SIB "Liable"

LIBEL IS what everyone is doing in this Book so far!

hostess; bet our table is ready. Let's try to forget this and enjoy a nice dinner."

As they rose to follow the young lady who would take them to their table, Jane said, "Just one more thing and I promise not to say another word about Sam's murder tonight. Tomorrow I'm going to talk to Mike McGuire about Sam's girlfriend, Sara. Maybe she can talk to him and he'll see a different slant on things."

On that hopeful note, they left the bar and were led to their table located by the window, a spot they always hoped to get when they dined at the Crab Catcher. Jane thought this was a good omen. They all ordered the bouillabaisse special of the evening in anticipation of a delicious meal. But somehow the beautiful view and the food they usually enjoyed so much didn't seem to lift their spirits or sate their appetites quite as well that evening. They hardly tasted the wine that Bob chose and it remained mostly in the bottle. Jane knew it wasn't the view or the food or even the well-chosen Italian wine. No, it was the bitter gossip sprinkled by Joanna and Celia that seasoned everyone's meal that night.

The drive home was mostly quiet. Any other time they would have been discussing the wonderful meal, over full stomachs or the next day's plans. Instead, each was lost in their own thoughts, trying to make sense of what was happening, wondering what would happen next. As Jane said her goodnights and thank yous, she was grateful for such good friends as she had in Marti and Bob. Walking up to her door she felt as if the weight of the world was on her shoulders and she was scared by what that meant.

Sunday, July 18th

SUNDAY MORNING BROUGHT the fat Sunday Cape Cod Register to Jane's door. As she stooped to pick it up she noticed that Sam's murder didn't occupy the whole front page. In fact she saw nothing about it until she turned to the local news section where it was mentioned but not much was said, just that the investigation was continuing with no known suspects. The world, even the small one of Cape Cod, has gone on, thought Jane, feeling a bit sad for Sam.

Being Sunday, Jane knew she couldn't call Mike until early afternoon. He would probably be at mass right now at St. Stephen's Church, the local parish that saw many weddings and funerals of prominent Cape Cod residents. Jane had never been in the church, being the lapsed Presbyterian that she was, but she had heard it was beautiful inside. The outside was certainly attractive. It sat on a hill surrounded by pine trees and from the outside looked like it was a stark white New England style church with the tall white steeple so different than most Roman Catholic churches one saw.

Jane decided to try to relax and read the paper while she sipped her coffee. She put water onto boil and took out her favorite coffee from Starbucks, one of their special summer blends. Measuring the grounds into the press and covering them with boiling water always filled Jane with the most aromatic sense of pleasure. She carried it over to the big pine table that had seen so many meals throughout the years and went back to put a slice of bread into the toaster. Grabbing a mug and the cream, some butter, blackberry jam and the toast as it popped up, Jane felt she had all the makings of a nice breakfast as she placed everything onto a tray to take to the table.

Settling down with the coffee, which was ready to press, and the paper, Jane began to scan the pages. As Jane pressed the plunger of the press a small item in the local news section caught her eye. It was only a couple of paragraphs long but it made her stop mid-plunge. As she read the words her heart raced. It couldn't be, could it? No, no way. The article referred to the death of an unidentified woman who had been staying at the Tara. The cause of death was not yet known but appeared to be from an overdose of drugs. No identification was found with the body and the records of her name and address that the hotel had proved to be false. She was a young, attractive woman in the age range of mid-twenties to mid-thirties. She had long, blond hair and blue eyes. The article asked if anyone had any information regarding the identity of the woman that they notify the local authorities.

Jane could barely think. Could this be Sara? That sweet girl that Marti and Jane had just had dinner with two nights ago couldn't be dead. She had so much to look forward to, so much to see and do in life. She was so young. Was she a drug abuser? Was losing Sam too much for her that she took her own life? The thought was too hideous for Jane to contemplate. This was a girl who was not much older than Jane's sons and now she might be gone? Did this have something to do with Sam's murder? *Maybe she should call Mike now*, Jane thought. Maybe this was Sara. Maybe this was not an accidental death.

Maybe the boys could be in danger too! *But, then, maybe I'm over-reacting,* thought Jane, *there must be lots of young woman that meet that description.* But even so . . . it could be Sara. It sounded like Sara!

"Halt!" Jane ordered herself out loud, trying to stop the whirlpool of questions that swirled in her head. "No jumping to conclusions." Don't invent problems where there may not be any, she advised herself, silently this time. It would be just too much if this person were Sara. Her imagination and fears were just taking hold of her again. There were bound to be lots of young women with long blond hair that were staying at the Tara this week. She'd take a deep breath, calmly call Marti, see if she'd seen the paper and ask her what she thought about it.

Trembling, Jane dialed Marti's number. There was no answer. While waiting for the answering machine to click on she concluded that they, too, were probably at church, their church being the Tabernacle in the village. They wouldn't be back for at least a half hour or so. Leaving a message to call her a.s.a.p. Jane hung up. Sitting back down she finished plunging the coffee and began to try to think whom, if anyone, would have done this to Sara, if indeed it was Sara. And for that matter, who had murdered Sam?

Jane needed to do something constructive. A list is what she needed! When clarity was called for looking down at lists in black and white often got Jane's mind in better working order. She ran up the stairs and rummaged through the desk drawer in her bedroom for a legal pad. Finding just what she needed, a nice, new, very blank legal pad she headed back down to the kitchen. Armed with paper and a pen from the kitchen junk drawer she again sat down at the table, not with the newspaper this time but with ideas forming in her head and, at last, a cup of coffee.

Boldly, she headed the top sheet with the name "Sam Morris". Under that she decided she would list any person that might have a grudge with him. First on her list was, of course, Joanna. She probably had lots of reasons to be mad a Sam, not the least of which would be if she knew that Sam was seeing someone else.

After that she was a bit stymied. Jane refused to put Ian or Matt on her list even though she knew some people in the village suspected them. They were certainly not suspects no matter what anyone said. She knew that there were more than a few people that didn't really love Sam or for that matter really like him much. He could be so boorish at times, especially on the tennis court or while playing golf. He always had to be the best and if he didn't win he always found an excuse or blamed someone else for his loss. That's probably why he and Joanna got along so well, Jane surmised. They both had to be the best and have the best or at least what they thought qualified for the best. They probably at one time thought they got the best in each other, sadly that had changed not too far into the marriage. Their relationship had seemed strained the last summer or two, Sam spending less time in the village and at the club, Joanna seen with just her boys most days, at the beach and at village events. Did Joanna know about Sara? Would that be reason enough to kill him?

Trying to think of someone else that would want to kill Sam, Jane realized that her mind kept coming back to Joanna. Too logical, too easy, she thought. Okay, who else? A golf partner, tennis opponent, sailing rival? Coming up with a second name on her list was not an easy task. Murder was such a drastic solution and from Jane's perspective no one else seemed a likely candidate. Even thinking Joanna seemed farfetched. But he had been murdered so . . .

Okay, it could have been a chance encounter with a drifter, someone Sam didn't know but who Sam might have approached at the beach that night. Or it could have been someone who had been doing something illegal at the beach that panicked when they saw Sam, thinking he was a threat and they killed him to keep him quiet. Jane didn't hold much with either of those theories as the most illegal activity that ever took place at the beach were an occasional underage drinker that would most likely get a stern talking to if caught by Sam or whoever caught them. Anyway, with the lifeguards living at the beach not much went on down there at night. But Jane added "Unknown Person/Drifter" to her list as number two.

Thinking back to what she had heard about the night of the murder her mind recalled that the boys had seen Robin, the new lifeguard, leaving her room in tears with Sam behind her. What did Sam and Robin have to do with one another? How were they connected? Maybe Joanna's sons were in Robin's swimming class and Joanna had sent Sam down with some criticism of Robin's teaching skills. Not unheard of at the club. Most parents were pleased with the classes but Jane knew from Ian that every once in awhile a parent felt their child deserved special treatment and Joanna was certainly that kind of mother. This taught the guards to be very diplomatic. But again, not a reason for murder. So, why was Sam in her room and why was she crying when she came out? Could Sam have been having a second affair? Robin really seemed too young for that at seventeen or eighteen but then young girls seemed to mature so much earlier these days, Jane thought with a sigh. Well, because of Robin's involvement, for whatever reason, with Sam the night of the murder Jane would add her to the list.

As she added Robin's name Jane remembered that Celia

had said that Robin had seen Matt and Ian with the shovel on the night of the murder. What if Robin had only said that to implicate them in the murder, to throw suspicion away from her? But also, what if Celia had just made it up to make Matt and Ian look guiltier? Robin seemed like such a nice girl. Feeling very unsure about putting Robin's name on the list, she added a big question mark after her name.

Another name Jane was reluctant to put down was Julia's. Julia had gotten over Sam years ago and had gone on with her life, Jane was sure. But what if something had come up about Sam changing his will, leaving Alex out of it in favor of Joanna's boys? Would a mother do anything to protect what she felt rightfully belonged to her daughter? Jane really couldn't imagine Julia wielding a shovel and bashing her ex-husband's head in, but then there were probably times in their marriage when Julia might have at least pictured something similar. Since the marriage had been over for more than five years Jane thought the divorce was unlikely to be a cause for murder, but when it came to a parent protecting a child one never knew what a person could be capable of doing. Jane sadly added "Julia" to her list.

Tapping the pen to her upper lip, Jane tried hard to think who else might have a motive for killing Sam. His work was a possibility. He was a lawyer. Lawyers always screwed somebody, she thought wryly. And he was a divorce lawyer, even more reason. Divorces got messy, people got mad. He was known for getting huge alimony settlements, almost always for women. That would definitely anger a soon to be ex-husband. Messing with people's lives could bring surprising, sometimes nasty results. Was murder one of them? Jane added "Client's Ex" as her fifth suspect.

What about someone from work? Jane really didn't know much about lawyers but Sam was a partner and maybe he had stepped on someone's toes to get there. Or maybe he had something on someone at work that could be disastrous to him or her if word leaked out. This was an area Jane knew nothing about but it couldn't be discounted just for that reason. She'd ask Bob what he knew about Sam's firm and anyone in it. Jane jotted down "Colleague—talk to Bob".

Thinking of his work brought Sara to Jane's mind and her thoughts clouded over. Could Sara be the unidentified woman in the paper? Jane sincerely hoped not. But what if Sara hadn't told them the truth the other night? It was possible that Sara could have murdered Sam and then couldn't live with herself afterwards. Maybe Sam was breaking it off with her, not planning on leaving Joanna to marry Sara. They were supposed to see one another the night Sam was killed. Maybe they had. Maybe Sam had tried to break things off with Sara and she killed him in a rage. Jane hoped not. In just that short meeting they had had at the restaurant she had grown quite fond of Sara in a motherly sort of way. Jane got the impression that Sara was Sam's last chance to become a caring human being. Regardless, Jane added Sara's name as number seven to her sheet of paper.

Jane looked at her list:

SAM
1. Joanna
2. Unknown Person/Drifter
3. Robin?
4. Julia
5. Client's Ex
6. Colleague—ask Bob
7. Sara

Jane was having trouble coming up with anyone else for her list. None of those she personally knew really seemed like murderers with the exception (well, maybe) of Joanna the shrew, Jane opined. But, truly, Jane just couldn't imagine any one of them killing someone, not even Joanna really, of whom she had never been fond. She didn't want it to be Robin who seemed to be such a sweet girl and so popular this summer with the children and parents, as well. And she certainly didn't want it to be Julia, someone she had long liked and admired. That wouldn't be Julia's style. Julia had never tried to get more than what was needed from Sam, support for Alex. She was independent and had always stressed to Alex the importance of making one's own way in life. Jane put her pen to the paper and put a line through Julia's name.

Feeling better to have Julia off the list, Jane got up and stretched. Looking at the big clock on the kitchen wall, she was surprised to see almost two hours had passed. Her head had begun to throb from her efforts and she thought a cup of tea might be just the ticket as she realized her untouched coffee was stone cold. As she stood at the sink filling the kettle, she saw Joanna's brother walk by along the edge of the pond with his nephews. A light went on in her head. Why hadn't she thought of it! Stuart, Joanna's brother, what did anyone really know about him? He'd never even been to Herring Run before as far as Jane knew. Where had he been the night of the murder? Maybe he had killed Sam for Joanna.

Abandoning her teakettle, she sat back down and penned Stuart's name to the list of suspects. *Well, why not?* she began to think. Maybe he was mad that Joanna's husband was stepping out on her. He could be one of those overprotective brothers with an out of control temper that one hears about. Why not add him to the list? True, Jane had never heard of him before or seen him in Herring Run until after Sam's death but that didn't mean a thing. He certainly hadn't seemed like a very nice fellow when she'd met him.

Jane looked back over her list and felt that somewhere in there was the answer to Sam's murder, if only she could read between the lines.

SAM
1. Joanna
2. Unknown Person/Drifter
3. Robin?
4. Julia
5. Client's Ex
6. Colleague—talk to Bob
7. Sara
8. Stuart

But then again, maybe it was just a list from her imagination. Mentally exhausted, Jane put down her pen and absently took a sip of her long, cold coffee. With disgust she got up and threw the rest of it down the drain and tackled the dishes in the sink, again, waiting for the kettle to boil. Looking out her window toward the lake she reflected on how little she really knew about Sam and his life. For years they had exchanged pleasantries on the tennis court, at the beach and during various functions taking place in the village. For a while there was even the occasional Christmas card after he had left Julia. But she really didn't know what went on in his life, especially since he and Julia divorced. Julia had been a much closer contact to Sam when they were married and as families they often got together. But since the advent of Joanna in Sam's life he had grown to be almost a stranger to everyone in the village. Joanna was not particularly liked and they tended not to be included in as many private social events as he and Julia had. Thinking about this made Jane a bit sad and nostalgic for past summers when they all sat on the beach and watched Ian, Matt and Alex toddle around on the sand.

A knock at her door broke Jane's reverie. Looking up she saw her neighbor, Davis, a retired widower who lived next door. Though he lived in the village year round, he was retired and traveled quite a bit. Jane never knew when he would pop back to home base for a dose of Cape Cod. Having just returned from a three weeks trip to Portugal, he was stopping by to tell her he was home. Jane always kept an eye on his house while he was gone in the summer, watering the garden and making sure that no one arrived in the dead of night with a moving van to empty his house. In return he kept an eye on their cottage throughout the winter, making sure all was well and calling Arizona anytime he thought there was reason for concern. He always teased her that when she was away he was having parties on her deck; it was their standing joke. The whole family loved Davis and he loved them back, such good friends and neighbors they'd been over the years.

"Hey, welcome back, stranger," Jane exclaimed as Davis entered the house. "How was your trip?"

"Great! Think I got some good photos of fishing boats on the coast that I can frame and hang in my cottage. I'll bring them over when I get them back from the developer to show you. I'll save all my tales until then. Meanwhile it feels good to be back. Thanks for watering the garden, it's looking quite spectacular, everything blooming so well this year," Davis commented. "So what's up with you and the village these days?"

"You're welcome regarding the garden, I did get some help

the last few days from Mother Nature," Jane laughed, thinking of all the rain they'd had. "This Sam Morris thing has me so worried. It's really been consuming me morning, noon and night," Jane complained.

"What's he up to now? A fight on the tennis court or another indiscreet affair?" queried Davis.

"Oh, heavens you've been away, you don't know about the murder, do you?" Jane exclaimed, aghast at what she had to tell him.

"Jane, I got in late last night, I've barely had a chance to unpack. What murder? Who did Sam murder? One of his tennis partners, probably," laughed Davis.

"Oh, do I need to catch you up on Herring Run, Davis. Sit down, I'll make you a cup of tea and then let me fill you in," Jane instructed.

A half hour later, Davis was sitting at the kitchen table soberly looking at Jane's suspect list. As a long time friend of Julia's, he just knew she was not capable of such a brutal act and was glad that Jane had crossed her off. The rest of the list he had no clue about as he rarely made it to the beach these days or knew anything about Sam's professional life. Jane had explained that some rumors were circulating that maybe Matt and Ian had had something to do with the murder on Alex's behalf. Davis was surprised that anyone would accuse those two boys of anything worse than playing their music too loud and discounted the gossip as something only Celia would spread around to draw attention to herself.

"Well, I agree with that, Davis, but it still hurts to hear it and to get some of the sidelong glances from people who should know better. Some people are even believing it, or at least aren't sure they don't believe it. Luckily, Mike McGuire doesn't take it too seriously and has really put his energies elsewhere, or so he's telling us. Speaking of which, maybe I can call Mike now. I have something to discuss with him that may have something to do with all of this."

Davis looked at Jane as if she should explain what she needed to talk to Mike about, but instead she said, "I'll let you know if this leads anywhere, but until then I won't speculate like Celia. Try to get down to the beach today, you look like you could use a good nap on the sand to help get rid of your jet lag." With that Jane ushered Davis out the door and then headed for the phone. It rang just as she reached for it.

"Jane, what's up?" asked Marti. "I just got your message. Coffee hour ran more like two this morning and I was in charge of it so I couldn't get out any sooner. Are you headed for the beach?"

"Have you seen today's paper?" Jane wanted to know. When Marti informed her that between getting ready for church having to be there early to set up the coffee and cakes and late to clean up their paper hadn't even been unfolded yet, so Jane launched into a review of the article about the unidentified victim at the Tara.

"It could be Sara, you know, Marti. I mean, I hope not, but, she was staying there, she's got blond hair and she is in that age range."

Marti's voice caught. "Oh, no, not that sweet girl! She didn't seem to be the type to take drugs. It couldn't be her. There's got to be lots of people that fit that description staying at the Tara in the summer, Jane. And why wouldn't she have given her name?"

"Well, I planned to give Mike a call anyway today about talking to Sara so I'll just go ahead and see what he says. Anyway, I'll see you at the beach as soon as I finish talking to him." Jane hung up and pulled out her address book. Finding Mike's home number she began, with a twinge of guilt, to dial it. She hated to bother him with business at home, especially on a Sunday but this couldn't wait as far as she was concerned.

*   *   *

She had been a frequent visitor to the Tara over the last few months, always paying in cash and considered by the staff to be a delightful guest. Known to the hotel employees as Mrs. Brown, she was well liked for her ready smile, sincere attitude and fair tipping, no skimping like so many other guests. The staff felt they had known her and were upset to hear that she had been found dead in her room.

It was one of the maids who had gone in to make up the room in the late morning on Saturday who found the beautiful young woman lying in the bathroom, slightly sideways in the bathtub, with an empty pill bottle near her hand. The maid, a young college student working just for the summer, had made the bed, emptied the wastebasket and had gone into the bathroom with her cleaning supplies when she noticed someone was in the tub. At first the maid thought she had walked in on a guest bathing and was beginning to back out and apologize until she suddenly realized that this person in the bathtub did not look normal. In fact, the woman with the long blond hair had her clothes on and her eyes were wide open and staring at some unknown spot on the wall tile. Stuffing a fist in her mouth, trying to stifle her scream, the maid finally did back out the room. She had the presence of mind to refrain from touching anything else and lock the room back up before she ran screaming down the hall to the front desk, where she was barely able to choke out to the desk clerk what she had seen. Chaos reigned as the police were called, arriving within minutes. Guests quickly heard that someone was dead in one of the rooms and the lobby filled with people talking in hushed tones, wanting to change rooms or just wanting to check out!

The police put a few patrolmen at the exits and explained to everyone that no one would be leaving just yet.

When the police searched the victim's room they could find no identification for her. The woman's purse was on the floor with the wallet gaping open. It contained no license, no credit cards and just a small amount of cash. A few items were hung in the closet and placed in the bureau, cosmetics were scattered on the bathroom counter. She was fully clothed and there was nothing to suggest that there had been a struggle. An empty pharmacy bottle, with label partially torn off lay next to her in the bathtub. It looked to be an apparent suicide.

When Captain McGuire arrived on the scene there was already a beehive of activity going on inside the hotel room. Someone from the lab was dusting for fingerprints, someone from the coroner's office was waiting to examine the body after the photographer finished her work and a contingent from the hotel was waiting outside the door shooing away lookie-Lous while trying to get a peek inside for themselves.

Taking in the situation, Mike conferred with the officer on the scene to see what had transpired so far in the investigation. When he found that as of yet no suicide note had been found he began to think that what he was looking at was not what it appeared to be on the surface. Taking charge, he ordered all hotel employees that were in any way involved in the woman's room to be brought to one of the many conference rooms the hotel had so that they could be questioned. He sent two of his detectives with an officer to interview the staff while he ordered fingerprints of the body to be taken and rushed to see if a match could be found.

While these actions were being taken, the men dusting the room for all fingerprints and other evidence, it was discovered that while most surfaces came up with what one would expect to find in a hotel room, smudged marks on the TV, its remote, the telephone and drawers and other items in the room; the faucets in the bathroom, the bathroom's plastic glasses and all of the door handles were totally devoid of any prints which was especially odd considering that one of the plastic glasses lay fallen from the woman's right hand, having spilled water into the tub beside her, with just a trace of it left. The empty pill bottle also revealed a lack of prints.

Mike's mind began to push suicide out of the realm of possibilities for this woman and began to believe he had a second murder on his hands and though the killer had tried to make it look like a suicide, too many mistakes had been made. Mike hoped that one of them would point a glaring finger at whoever was responsible for the death of this poor girl. He hoped he could get an accurate identification on the girl quickly, that could clear quite a bit up. So many reasons for murder: a drug deal gone sour or a disgruntled lover, a jealous husband, a myriad of ideas began to go through Mike's mind as he headed back to headquarters at about the same time that her body was being zipped up into a bag for its trip to the morgue.

Mike did not go to Mass on Sunday as he usually did and when Jane called his house she only got a recording that said no one could come to the phone and to leave a message. Quickly leaving one for Mike to return her call she hung up and pulled out the phone book to look up the number of the police station, dialed it and asked to speak to Captain McGuire, giving her name and nature of business when requested.

After a few minutes of waiting, Mike picked up the phone. After apologizing profusely for bothering him, Jane warned Mike that what she was going to say was probably way out in left field. She explained that she had read in the paper about an unidentified young girl who had been found dead at the Tara, and, taking a big breath, she told him that she might know something about it, not the death, but the girl. She added that she feared that it might be a woman that she and Marti had met Friday night at the Red Pheasant, as the description in the paper of the victim sounded like the woman they had met, and that this woman had something to do with Sam Morris.

"I know it sounds crazy, but when I read the article I just had a feeling," Jane concluded.

As Jane stopped her ramblings to take a breath, Mike interrupted her and asked, "Was the woman you met named Sara Connor?"

Jane's heart fell, her throat constricted as she realized that it was the Sara she knew who had lost her life. What sadness Jane suddenly felt for such a beautiful, bright, appealing young woman to have her life end so tragically. Why hadn't she told Mike about Sara as soon as she knew about Sara's connection to Sam? If she had, maybe Sara would still be alive.

"How well did you know her, Jane? And what do you know about her connection to Sam?" Mike inquired calmly.

"Marti and I just had dinner with her the other night. We had a chance meeting at the Red Pheasant and she joined us for dessert, actually. But we didn't know her, not really. Was this a suicide, Mike? The paper said a drug overdose but honestly, she didn't seem the type to take her own life even though Sam had just been murdered. Do you think that she murdered Sam?" wondered Jane aloud, thinking that maybe Sara was not quite what she seemed and had pulled the wool over her eyes. Could her feelings regarding the loss of Sam have driven her to take her own life?

"Whoa, back up a bit. Why do you think that she had anything to do with Sam's murder? We know from running the fingerprints that she worked in Sam's law firm as a paralegal and a notary but that's all we have established so far. What did she tell you that night?"

After explaining what she knew from Sara about her affair with Sam, Mike asked her to come down to the station for a formal statement regarding all the information she had just imparted. "And if you think of anything else that might be pertinent please let us know. And Jane, be careful talking about this. This girl did not commit suicide, we have reason to believe she was murdered and now I think it could possibly tie in somehow with Sam's death. You're a little too close to this for my comfort. Don't go poking your nose where it doesn't belong, leave crime solving to the police. Do you hear me, Jane?"

A couple of hours later, Jane finally arrived at the beach. It had been a sad interview with Mike as she told what little she knew of Sara. Feeling that she had not done enough, yet not knowing what she should have done was a disquieting thought as she set her beach chair up among Sheila's and Barbara's families.

Suddenly, Marti came rushing over looking as though she had seen a ghost.

"We just heard on the radio that Sara was murdered! The same Sara we were just talking to at the Red Pheasant, Jane. I can't believe that we just had dinner with her the other night. What's going on here?" cried Marti as Sheila and Barbara looked up from their books, surprised at the outburst.

Jane fell into her chair and motioned Marti to sit down. "I'm afraid it is true. I just came back from making a statement about our evening with her to Mike. He tried to call you while I was there. He left you a message but asked me to tell you to call him if I saw you today. He wants you at the police station a.s.a.p. for your statement in case you remember something I don't. And Marti, he said we should be careful, not to talk about it, someone out here is dangerous."

Looking a bit worried, Marti gathered her towel and headed

home. Barbara and Sheila wanted to be filled in on all the details of what Jane knew of Sara's murder and Sara herself. Jane told them what she could without betraying anything Mike had told Jane was not to be passed on to the public. As they quietly discussed the tragedy, Celia sauntered up and in her haughtiest voices inquired where Ian and Matt were.

"I haven't seen THEM on the guard towers all day. Have THEY been arrested yet for Sam's murder?" The malicious gleam in her eye made Jane want to scream.

"As a matter of fact, Celia, they are taking a few days off; paid, of course. Seems that some truly horrible people are circulating a bunch of unfounded rumors and Craig felt that they shouldn't be subjected to such tripe. He told them to enjoy a few paid days off, away from the wagging tongues of stupid people."

Sheila and Barbara could barely contain their mirth as Celia's mouth dropped open and, finding no words to retaliate, turned and walked off in a huff. "Well, that's telling her!" proclaimed Sheila. "She's probably on her way to Joanna's now to get some help with a retort! Mark my words, we'll hear more from her yet."

Jane hoped not. She was getting tired of gossip, innuendoes and rumors and she was beginning to worry about what would be next. Between nasty tongues and her new fear of the unknown that Mike had instilled in her this morning she was not enjoying her summer, not in the least.

* * *

Sunday was a day that most of the husbands left the beach early to return to Boston. As the beach thinned and people returned to the village to pack up their loved ones, Jane soon found she was one of the few people left on the beach. It was her favorite time of the day there: late afternoon, with the sun having made its way west but still warming to the skin. The quiet of the beach was comforting as she sat back, stretched out her legs and closed her eyes to enjoy her last moments before she too made her way back up to the village. She slowly emptied her mind of all that had cluttered it since Sam's death.

Jane could hear the sea gulls calling out to one another, some of them fighting over the remnants of a forgotten lunch or the pickings of the now filled trashcans. The waves were gently lapping onto the shore sending a soothing hypnotic sound to her ears. The sun wrapped around her like a cocoon as its last bold rays of the day shone down. If only she could capture this feeling of content and bottle it for a rainy day, she thought, or at least take it back to the village for the evening

She was drifting in that world that borders sleep, just barely aware of the beach around her when she realized that a shadow had fallen over her, breaking through her perfect world. Opening her eyes she looked up to see Joanna looming over her, her face contorted with rage.

"How dare you spread nasty rumors about my husband having an affair!" Joanna began in a rage. Jane immediately shot into an upright position, poised in a posture of defiant protection. "You and your son should be shot! If I hear one more thing I will talk to my lawyer about suing you!" With that Joanna turned and marched away. Now Jane was being accused of something she didn't do! Her tranquility rudely stolen away, Jane was left with nothing to do but to pack up her gear and head home. It was time to call it a day.

At home that evening as she finished the dinner dishes and put in one more load of laundry, Jane wondered about Joanna's outburst. Where had she gotten the idea that Jane had known about Sam's affair? It was now obvious that Joanna must have been aware of it. Maybe Mike had told her, though surely that wouldn't seem ethical or at least wise. Marti wouldn't have said anything, she and Joanna weren't on speaking terms at this point and Marti was doing everything in her power to stay away from Joanna. She guessed that somehow Celia could have gotten wind of the news, everyone in the village seemed to have known, it seemed. Joanna's outburst must have been payback time after her conversation with Celia on the beach. But why would Joanna care so much that she took the effort to confront Jane? Why not confront the whole village, why single her out? It was all too confusing.

Feeling dizzy with all these thoughts swirling around in her head, Jane decided on an early evening to bed with a book. Looking around for the mystery she had tried to start the day before she came up empty handed. Looking through her bookshelves her eyes fell upon one of her old Agatha Christie books. Well, that's the ticket, Jane thought. She'd let that super sleuth, Miss Marple, solve a crime, like Ian suggested, instead of Jane trying to untangle the Sam Morris mess. Miss Marple was always able to simply look at all the clues and quite easily figure out that someone quite ordinary, like the maid or the vicar, had some secret that he or she was trying to hide. It always had something to do with a vase of posies, a cigar or something else quite ordinary. Then she'd gather everyone together and solve the murder. Somehow, though, it seemed nothing at all like the complex lives of everyone here in Herring Run in the 21st century, or maybe it was, Jane thought, murder was murder and the reasons didn't seem to vary no matter what century it was.

Monday, July 19th

ONDAY MORNING'S WALK with Marti was consumed with comparisons of each of their interviews with Mike. It didn't seem to them that either had anything extra to add to the other's story. Not really much to tell, except what Sara had told them and what a nice young woman she had seemed. Neither woman could believe Sara had been murdered. Two murders were too much for this little village to cope with, especially in less than two weeks. Everyone wondered if they were in danger. Promising each other to keep their noses out of the whole thing they parted, each to their respective homes, with intentions to wake up their newly idle boys and put them to work around the house. However, when Jane walked into the kitchen she found Ian was already up, looking like he was chewing nails, not Special K, as he ate his breakfast.

"What got you out of bed so early today?" Jane inquired casually.

"Rocks," Ian mumbled, his mouth full of cereal.

"What?" Jane asked

"You know, stones, pebbles, those little hard things," answered Ian.

"What in heavens name are you talking about, Ian?"

"Little rocks, thrown at my window. Well, to be exact I suppose it was gravel. But it's lucky they it didn't break the window. Oh, yeah, and someone yelled 'murderer', too. A bit of a rude awakening, wouldn't you say?" Ian asked wryly.

"My god, of course I would. Who was it?" Jane asked, totally bewildered at who in Herring Run would do such a thing.

"Kids, I guess. I don't know who it was because by the time I really woke up and got to the window they were gone. But I swear that one was that little Johnny from down the street. He's just a troublemaker and his group is a bunch of sheep. Still, I would have liked to have slept in a bit longer so I'm really pissed."

"Hmm, not my favorite word, Ian. Meanwhile, I'm not sure what to say about this. If it was Johnny, Celia's son, then I'd say it's typical but still I don't like the idea of rocks being thrown at the house. Maybe I should go talk to his mother," Jane mused.

"Leave it, mom. I'm not sure if it was Johnny and his little gang of eviler doers, but I'm getting pretty sick of this whole thing. I'm tempted to return to Tucson and get a job out there, but I don't want to leave Matt on his own here and he won't leave. Besides, Craig needs us at the beach and I'm not going to let a bunch of jerks run my life. So, just leave it!"

"Okay, I won't get involved. I've had my fill of this, too. Listen, since you're up I was wondering if you could clean the gutters today. Dad didn't have a chance when he was here and with the rain the other day I could see . . ."

"I'm outa here, mom, sorry. Craig called. He wants us back on tower starting this morning, otherwise I would have gone back to bed. In fact, Matt and I are moving back down to the beach this evening." With a peck on Jane's cheek he was gone.

Jane rinsed out his bowl and began to think about him moving back to the beach, not liking it one bit. But how could she insist that he stay here? She could tell he felt good about getting his life back on track at the beach and return to his normal routine. But she was worried about him. Mike had warned them to be careful and she had passed this on to Ian but he brushed it off as a mother's needless worry. She just wanted him under her wing, to have all of them together during this unsettling time. Maybe she shouldn't give up trying to figure out who killed Sam and now Sara. Jane wondered if it was the same person. Maybe if the killer or killers were caught she could rest easy and her life could go back to normal.

Walking over to the kitchen drawer that held all the family's miscellaneous junk, Jane pulled out the pad with the suspect list on it that she had shoved in there after Davis' visit.

SAM
1. Joanna
2. Unknown Person/Drifter
3. Robin?
4. Julia
5. A Client's Ex
6. Colleague—talk to Bob
7. Sara
8. Stuart

Scanning down the list Jane's eyes went right for Sara's name. Her eyes welled up at the thought of this girl's tragic end. She was so young, sweet and beautiful. Why did she have to die? Jane began to cross out Sara's name when she realized that just because Sara had died did not mean that Sara hadn't killed Sam. In fact, whoever killed Sara may have done it to avenge Sam's death. Farfetched, Jane thought, but still, she shouldn't cross her off her list.

So, where could she put her energies now? Which suspect could she either eliminate or prove did it. Upon reevaluation, Jane thought that now that Sara had been killed, an 'unknown person' seemed unlikely, after all, Sam and Sara were linked. It just seemed too much of a coincidence. What was going on with Robin? Where had she gone? A bit strange that she left after Mike told everyone to stay put. It shouldn't be too hard to find out where she had gone. Jane could start by talking to Craig, the beach manager, when she went down there today.

Joanna; well, maybe Jane wouldn't pursue her as a suspect at the moment. She had had enough of her and her viper ways for a while. One of Sam's client's ex-spouses would be trickier. How could she find out anything about that? Maybe Bob would have an idea, or maybe, if Joanna ever became rational Jane could ask her if Sam had ever had any problems with a client. Bob would also come in handy with the colleague suspect. The law community had a grapevine. She must be sure to corner him this coming weekend. Maybe the Sanders would like to come for a barbecue this weekend and they could all put their heads together. And as for Sara, well, Jane just wasn't sure which way to go with her. At the moment she would leave Sara on the list but deep down Jane knew she would give that lovely young woman the benefit of doubt.

Throwing the list back in the drawer, Jane hurried to get through her morning chores to enable her to get to the beach as soon as possible to talk to Craig. She knew Mike would not be especially happy that she was still nosing around but just talking to Craig about Robin really couldn't be dangerous. After all, as a mother of a lifeguard it would only be normal to inquire about one of the other guards.

A few hours later, feeling extremely virtuous having vacuumed away every grain of sand from her house and dusted every possible surface, as well as finishing a load of the never ending laundry Jane arrived at the beach club looking for Craig. She found him in the office going over the swim meet schedule for the upcoming week.

Knocking on the partially open door she asked, "Craig, got a minute?"

"Sure, come in, I'm about finished here," Craig informed her.

"I just wanted to thank you for putting the boys back to work. It was hard on them to have to sit out but I know you were between a rock and a hard place with the way the committee was leaning on you. Thank goodness, that's all over. The bounce is back in Ian's step today," Jane added with a smile.

"You know, I hated to have to ask them to take a few days off, especially when I really didn't know if it was only going to be for a few days. But Mike seems to have great confidence in them and went to bat for them with the Beach Committee. He convinced them that they weren't seriously being considered as suspects. So I was happy to give them the good news."

"Mike went to bat for them? I had no idea that he was involved with them getting back to work. How nice of him," Jane commented.

"Didn't Ian tell you? He and Matt were so mad and felt they were being treated unjustly. So they asked me to call a meeting of the committee and requested Mike to talk to them. I was quite impressed with how they handled the situation and themselves," beamed Craig.

"Well, I had no idea. Unbelievable! I guess I'm impressed with them too, Craig!" said Jane silently grateful that Craig had never seen the two boys' attitudes when they were letting off steam at home. Some of their comments might not have been taken quite as well by Craig or the Beach Committee.

"Quite honestly, it's good that they're back as we were really short handed. Had to cancel swim lessons, hire some temp guards for the beach, which didn't work out so well, and I would have had to cancel the swim meets if they hadn't come back seeing as Robin hasn't returned."

"Robin's still away?" queried Jane, thinking this is exactly the sort of segue that she could have only dreamed about. "Where is she? And when do you expect her back?"

"Well, she said she was going home for a few personal days but now it's dragged on for over a week and she has yet to return. I called her this morning to see whether she planned to return as a lifeguard. She indicated that she was still nervous about Sam's death and Ian and Matt's possible involvement. I told her that they were not being considered suspects and that she had no reason for that fear. She said she would get back to me in a couple of days. She's been a good addition to our crew here this year and I would hate to lose her, but if she doesn't come back soon I'll be forced to try replace her."

"I'm sorry to hear that she still feels that way about the boys. Maybe, once she knows about how the Chief of Police has confidence in them and how much she's needed she'll reconsider. By the way, does she live close by? " Jane casually asked.

"She lives just north of Boston, in Marblehead. In fact, I was surprised she didn't take a job up that way, as there are many openings for lifeguards this year all over. But I guess like lots of young people, she just wanted to get away from home, have an adventure. Cape Cod is away but not too far. Now, I can't get her to come back. Maybe it was more of an adventure than she bargained for being here.

I know it has been for me. Murder at our beach of one of our members, nasty business," commented Craig as he shook his head.

"I know. This isn't turning out to be one of my favorite summers. Well, thanks for everything Craig," Jane said as she turned to leave. "You've been great to Ian through all of this. Geoff and I really appreciate it."

"Think nothing of it, Jane. Ian and Matt are fine boys. They've worked hard here and are well liked. I hated seeing them being treated poorly. I'm just glad they're back." With that Craig turned back to his work and Jane headed out to her spot on the beach with the information she needed.

Since she'd gotten down to the beach early after rushing through her chores, none of her regular group had arrived yet. She set up her chair and umbrella and gratefully slipped down into her spot. Sitting back in her chair with her eyes closed she tried to relax. With no one around she had time to think and what she wanted to think about was what was the next step she should take.

She knew that Robin had gone home to Marblehead and that she was still there. She said she would return in a few days but she hadn't. Something was keeping her away. She said that it was her fear of Matt and Ian but they weren't suspects anymore and she had gotten to know them well this summer, so could that really be it? *If it were me, Jane thought, I might not be so quick to return to the scene of such a horrible crime if I didn't have to, so maybe Robin just doesn't feel comfortable coming back. I might be afraid that the murderer was still around,* Jane thought, which when she considered it Jane had to concede that's what she thought. She was afraid the murderer might still be around. *Maybe if I were Robin. I'd be afraid he or she might think I knew something about the crime because I lived at the beach. Maybe the murderer thought*

I'd seen or heard something from my room, a room that had windows facing the beach.

Or maybe Robin had seen too many Elm-Street-psycho type of movies and was totally freaked out. Jane thought she might feel that way if she lived in one of the lonely rooms down at the beach. After all there were only a few of the guards that lived down at the beach club and besides them, at night their only company was the seagulls and the sound of the waves crashing onto the shore. It got pretty dark and lonely down there. Ian and Matt loved it, but maybe for the girl guards it was a bit different.

Then, again, maybe Robin had something to hide. She had been seen with Sam the night of the murder. In fact it seemed she might have been the last person to see Sam alive before he was killed so maybe she had set him up to be murdered or had done it herself. Somehow, Jane could not picture Robin doing that at all and she cringed at the thought of a shovel wielding Robin. There were just too many maybes. What Jane needed to do was talk to Robin. She needed to know the reason Robin was not returning to Herring Run.

As Jane thought of the when, where and how she would do this Barbara plopped down beside her. With a start, Jane came out of her reverie and issued a hello.

"Whoa, sorry to startle you. Penny for your thoughts?" Barbara asked.

"Oh, you know, what does anyone think about these days?" Jane replied.

"Well, I see that Matt and Ian are back on tower today, so that looks like a good sign. So what else about this affair has you so lost in thought?" Barbara wanted to know.

"I'm trying to decide whether to drive up to Marblehead tomorrow or not. Think I'd like to talk to the new lifeguard, Robin. You know she hasn't returned since after Sam's funeral.

I heard that she was feeling skittish because of Ian and Matt, so I thought that maybe I could talk to her and allay her fears," Jane explained, not wanting to go into the many other reasons she wanted to talk to Robin. In fact, Jane wasn't sure she wanted anyone to know, as she was feeling quite so insecure about her questions anyway. Maybe she was putting too much significance on Robin. Robin had probably just had it with Herring Run. Mike had told her to drop her inquiries, Geoff had told her to butt out and she knew Ian wouldn't approve. Plus her friends would think she was off her rocker. But Jane needed to get to the bottom of a few things, clear out some clutter in her mind, even if she never solved the big question of who murdered Sam she'd like some answers to a few of the questions.

"Well, I don't think you need to go up to talk to her. What difference does it make whether she returns or not? The club will make do with one less guard and it will save you a trip. It's supposed to be a ten day tomorrow, sunny, in the low 80s, low humidity, absolutely perfect, so why would you want to waste it in the car? Me, I'll be on the beach," Barbara proclaimed.

"You're right," Jane replied. "It would probably just be a waste of time."

With that, both ladies turned around to see Marti and Sheila arrive with their all their beach paraphernalia and the subject was dropped for the much more exciting news of the engagement of their friend Millie's son. Pretty soon they were all off into the discussion of weddings and the bride versus the groom's parental involvement and rights, dresses and flowers, bridesmaids and ushers. Jane put away her worries for a few hours and just enjoyed her day at the beach with her good friends.

That evening Jane walked over to Marti's house as soon as the dishes were done. As she knocked on the door she thought about how she could convince Marti to drive up with her the next morning. If they went they would miss the Ladies Round Robin at tennis, something they both enjoyed. The day was supposed to be gorgeous and Jane knew that Marti hated to miss any good beach day. And one thing Jane knew Marti hated to do was drive anywhere near Boston in the summer. Once Marti got to the Cape she never wanted to cross the bridge again until Labor Day. This was going to be a tough sell. Maybe I should resort to just plain whining and begging, Jane considered.

"Hey, Jane!" Marti opened the door wide so Jane could walk into her well-appointed living room. "What's up with you this evening? I was just thinking that things were beginning to get back to normal in most ways, but still something just doesn't seem right. Can't put my finger on it."

As Jane sank into one of Marti's plush, green and rose-flowered cushioned rattan chairs, she said, "maybe the fact that Sam's murderer isn't caught yet and it's killing us not to know who did it?"

"Well, of course that's a given, but it's more," Marti insisted.

"I know, I feel that way, too. In fact that's why I came by tonight. I don't feel comfortable about Robin not returning to the beach. She was one of the last people to see Sam alive and she ran from him in tears. What was that about? I'm thinking about driving up to her home in Marblehead tomorrow to talk to her. I know that you probably wouldn't want to go, but . . ." Jane trailed off not sure of what else to say.

"Yes, I'll go," replied Marti.

"And you probably would rather play tennis and lay on the beach, but . . ." Jane finally thought to add.

"Stop, you had me at 'drive to Marblehead'. I love the town and I, too feel something isn't right about Robin," laughed

Marti. "I'd like to go. Matt mentioned to me tonight that Robin hadn't returned because she was afraid of them, but something just doesn't seem right about that excuse. Plus, you know, I don't like anyone feeling that way about my son, so yes, I would like to speak to her and I would love to go with you. What time should we leave and do you have her address?"

"Well, Ian said he had her phone number and her address so we're covered there and I figure we should leave around eight-thirty in hopes of missing the commuter traffic on it's way to Boston. Would that work for you?"

"That's great! I'll pick you up, as I'm much better about finding my way around the Boston area than you are. Besides, you're used to the big open spaces of Arizona.

Wouldn't want you to have a hard time on our little highways here in New England," ribbed Marti, knowing that Jane often groused about the traffic patterns and roads of Massachusetts being so overwhelmed by trees one could hardly see the sky.

"You're a true friend, Marti. See you at eight-thirty," Jane said as she got up and made her way to the door. "And let's keep this under our hats. I don't feel like everyone telling us why we shouldn't drive up there. Sometimes you just got to follow your gut. I think we should even just surprise Robin as well, don't you agree?"

"Well, we risk her not being there if we don't call ahead, but if we call ahead she might bolt. Anyway, I know the best place in New England to get a lobster roll is in Marblehead. So even if we come up empty handed on Robin we won't leave with empty stomachs!" Marti enthused.

Later that evening, Jane sat in bed talking on the phone to Geoff in Tucson. She told him the good news of Ian life guarding again. She told him about the beautiful beach day and the news of Millie's son getting engaged. She neglected, however, to tell him about her trip to Marblehead the next morning. Turning out the light about an hour later she only felt a little smidgen of guilt.

Tuesday, July 20th

S KIPPING THEIR WALK the next morning and stopping at a Dunkin' Donuts on their way out of town for a donut (sugared for Jane, plain for Marti) and coffee to go, Marti and Jane were right on schedule as they crossed the Sagamore Bridge at around eight-fifty and headed around the rotary and up Route 3. It was a pretty route, lined with trees on both sides and it made for a pleasant ride. Jane really didn't feel too hemmed in on this pretty highway, she just like to kid Marti, it was when they hit Boston's Route 93 that she felt a bit jammed with no open desert expanses and rising mountains in the distance as they sped, or so often crawled, along this stretch of highway that gave her a longing for the west. While Marti drove, Jane went through the directions she had printed out the night before to find exactly where Robin's house was located in the town of Marblehead. She finally found the street in a section of the town called Marblehead Neck on the final page that she had zoomed in on. Marti thought it would take them a little over two hours to get there.

"I've always wanted to see the town of Marblehead, so I guess if nothing else is accomplished today I'll have done that," Jane commented as they drove up the highway.

"You'll love it, Jane. It's just your sort of place. Right on the water, steeped in history, very New England quaint. It's very picturesque. There are lots of wonderful little shops full of fabulous things. I hope we have time to check out a few. There's even that restaurant on the water where we are going to have the best lobster roll ever. We'll have lunch there," Marti suggested. "We'll try to see Robin first, if no one is home we'll go to the town, do a little shopping, have lunch and then try Robin's place again. Give it two shots."

Up past Plymouth, Duxbury, Hingham, Braintree (what was a brain tree, Jane wondered) and onto Rt. 93 they drove. As they approached the city of Boston the traffic on 93 grew heavier and they lost the picturesque quality of Route 3. Marti took them through the Callahan Tunnel to get to Marblehead by going up 1A and through Swampscott. Jane would never have found her way, she decided, and was glad that Marti was navigating this part of the trip.

Once in Marblehead it was easy to get to the section called Marblehead Neck. As they drove toward Robin's neighborhood she was not at all sorry they had come because true to what she had heard, Marblehead was indeed a beautiful town. Driving out to Marblehead Neck they crossed over a thin strip of land with the harbor on their left and the sea on their right. Looking back, Jane could see a church spire in what she thought from her map reading must be the town.

Finding the right street almost immediately, they drove down it, noticing that it was fronted with beautiful, large houses with sprawling, manicured lawns. As Jane looked for the house number she realized that the ones to her right must be on the water and that by the way the numbers read one of them was going to be Robin's. Very impressive neighborhood, Jane thought, wondering why Robin would have wanted to leave anything as gorgeous a place as this for a summer at the Herring Run Beach Club, living in a little room down at the beach. Robin had everything she could get at the Cape and much more right here in her backyard in Marblehead and Jane was sure it had to be a lot more comfortable.

Finding the house, Marti pulled up a bit past it and the two ladies sat for a moment trying to come up with what they would say to Robin. They didn't know whether she would be in but they had been afraid to call in advance to scare her off. Finally, deciding that they would take the tact of talking over her fears of returning and play the part of Herring Run goodwill ambassadors who wanted Robin to come back to the beach.

"In other words," said Jane, "we'll just wing it."

They got out of the parked car and walked up the long driveway to the front door. Jane pressed the doorbell and they could hear the chimes resonating inside, and then the sound of a dog barking and finally just before the door opened, a voice call out, "Don't worry, Josephina, I'll get it."

Opening the door was a very tall, slim, good-looking woman who looked about their age. She also looked exactly like an older version of Robin with her straight brown hair and long legs. Standing next to her was an old chocolate lab looking up at them with a goofy grin. Jane extended her hand to the woman and said, "You must be Robin's mother."

The woman slowly gave Jane her hand and looking a bit bewildered asked, "And you are?"

"Oh, I'm Jane Adams and this is Marti Sanders. Sorry about that. We're . . ."

"Oh, yes, I know who you are," a smile coming to her face. "You must be Ian and Matt's mothers. Robin has spoken quite warmly of you and your sons. She'll be sorry she missed you. She's out sailing today. And yes, I am Robin's mother, Nikki Thomas. And this furry guy is Turner. Please come in. What brings you to Marblehead?"

"Well," Jane began as Robin's mother graciously led them toward the back of the house to a wonderfully sun filled room that looked out over a rock wall to the ocean. "We came up to see how Robin was. We were concerned about Robin not returning to the beach and we thought if we came up in person maybe we could let her know how much she is missed, maybe convince her to return. The kids really miss her in lessons and..." Jane's mind screeched to a halt. What had Mrs. Thomas said? Robin had spoken warmly of Ian and Matt?

"Jane, are you alright?" asked Marti who was wondering why Jane had stopped talking and walking and was standing in the middle of the room looking dazed with her mouth hanging open.

"Mrs. Thomas, did you say that Robin spoke warmly of our boys?" Jane asked as she awoke from her dazed amazement and followed her hostess into a room furnished with plush, overstuffed furniture that overlooked the ocean.

"Please, call me Nikki. And, yes, very warmly. They have been so kind to her, showing her the ropes, looking out for her, taking her out evenings and just being ever so kind. I have to say, it made me feel much better to know that they were there with her. This is the first time she had taken a summer job away from home and besides living in the dorm at college this year she's never lived on her own," replied Nikki as she motioned for the ladies to take a seat "May I get you something to drink? A glass of water, cup of tea, coffee?" she asked when an older woman in a maid's uniform appeared discreetly at the corner of the room.

Both ladies declined her offer and sat down in what Jane surmised to be the family room which was separated from the kitchen by an island that was made of antiqued white wood and a beautiful shiny, black granite counter top. Jane could see that this was a kitchen she would die for. Double wall ovens, professional gas cook-top, and gleaming restaurant size refrigerator were just a start. The cabinets were also antique white and certainly custom made and the black granite abounded on top of every counter. There was a small under the counter refrigerator with a clear glass door that Jane could see was filled with bottles of wine, above which sat a fancy espresso machine along with a built in microwave oven. Not only could one see the ocean from the kitchen but a flat screen TV was set up to be viewed from any angle of the kitchen as well. A beautiful bouquet of daylilies sat on the edge of the counter closest to the room they were sitting in at the moment and Jane could see that they had come from the garden just outside the room in which they were sitting. This kitchen had it all, Jane marveled. And she was just seeing part of it! Every surface gleamed, every appliance was spotless, but of course there was the maid.

"So, ladies, is there anything I can do for you since you've driven all this way? Robin won't be back for quite a few hours; maybe I can be of some help," Nikki offered.

"Well," Jane hesitated for a second and then decided to plunge right in. "First I'd like to apologize for coming without calling first. We just happened to be visiting a friend up this way and decided to stop in to see Robin. I called Ian to get her address since I knew she lived in Marblehead." Jane thought they did say they'd wing it and a little white lie was okay, she hoped. "Let me get right down to it," said Jane, pretending not to see the look of surprise on Marti's face.

"We were told that Robin didn't want to come back to the beach because she was afraid of Ian and Matt. Now you say that she speaks warmly of them. I'm not sure I understand," Jane said. "You do know why Robin came home don't you?" she asked.

"You must be referring to the murder that happened at the

beach. And yes, I do know about that. Robin was very upset about it and just couldn't stay a moment longer. She is feeling somewhat better these days but maybe I had better explain. This is something that Robin should have done herself but she really didn't have the chance once the horrible death of Sam Morris occurred. She just had to get away, and well, home was the place she needed to be."

"Let me start at the beginning. Robin had a specific reason for taking the job at the beach this summer. In fact, the whole reason was to get to know Sam Morris. You see, Sam was Robin's natural father."

At this piece of news both Marti and Jane's mouths fell open and they were too stunned to utter a word.

"This is all bound to come out so I might as well start with two friendly faces," Nikki continued as she calmly began to explain to Jane and Marti, who sat in mutual silence at the information they had just received.

"I say natural father because she had never met Sam before this summer and he had no part in her upbringing. My husband is the only father she has ever known and she loves him with all her heart, as does he her. But a part of her has always wanted to meet Sam ever since she became aware that she had a father other than the one she had always known. I met Sam my first year out of law school. I got a job at the firm he had joined only a few years before me. When we began dating I knew very little about him. By the time I realized that he was married I had made the mistake of falling in love with him and thinking that Sam was in love with me. He constantly told me how unhappy he was at home. So, I continued the affair with him, even though I knew he was married with a little girl. It was so stupid and naïve, I suppose. You know, I've actually been to Herring Run. Sam would sometimes take me there for a weekend during that winter telling his wife he was away on business. If it wasn't for Robin, I would say that having an affair with Sam was the biggest mistake of my life. I could get through the difficulties of law school but had no experience with getting through life. When I became pregnant with Robin, Sam decided he no longer wanted to see me and insisted I get an abortion. As you can imagine, I was heartbroken. Well, if there was a word that was stronger to describe how I felt I would use it. I wasn't depressed, but I felt used, betrayed and totally, yes, heartbroken. He didn't know it but abortion just wasn't an option for me, so I quit the firm, went home to my parents and had Robin.

"My mother watched Robin so that I could get my career going. I made it a point not run into Sam again, ever. I set up a small practice of my own out here in the suburbs. When Robin was two, I met the man I am married to now and he's been a wonderful husband and father. We have two other children and the five of us have a good life, a wonderful life," Nikki paused, seeming to consider how to go on.

"Robin would never want to hurt her father but she had a deep need to meet Sam. You know, Sam never even knew about her birth. As far as he knew, I had that abortion. I never notified him of Robin's birth. Though his name is on the birth certificate he never knew I even had the baby, let alone whether it was a boy or a girl. After his reaction to the news of my pregnancy I wanted nothing else to do with him. I just walked away and never looked back. It was a good decision. But Robin was curious and since I'd never hidden the facts from her about her beginnings she made the decision to meet him. When she found out he had a summer home in Herring Run she decided to apply for one of the lifeguard jobs at your club. She thought maybe she could just get to know him from afar, as a club member, and then decide whether she wanted to tell him the truth about being his daughter."

Marti and Jane didn't know what to say. Never in a million years would they have ever guessed that Robin and Sam were related, let alone that Sam was Robin's father. As Jane tried to picture any resemblance they had to one another Nikki went on with her story.

"The night that Sam died, Robin had told him the truth. She asked him to meet with her on the pretense of discussing his stepsons' swim lessons. She told him that there was a small problem that she had not been able to settle with his wife and asked that their meeting be kept a secret. She told him she did not want to upset his wife knowing she had gone to Sam about the problem, instead of Joanna. I gather his current wife is not the nicest person, so he seemed to understand completely.

"He said he would have to come down to the beach late as they had plans to be out that evening with friends and the following day he would be out sailing. At first Robin thought he tried to flirt with her, which totally upset her. She says now that she doesn't really think that's what he was doing, that he was just trying to be overly nice to compensate for how he thought Joanna had treated her. But she misinterpreted the signs and at that point, upset beyond caring, Robin blurted out the truth: that he was her father.

"As you can imagine, Sam didn't take the news well. At first he didn't even believe her. He probably saw the implications of the situation and, then, frankly couldn't cope. She said that he tried not to look upset but instead tried to deal with the situation logically by saying that he wanted proof that she was his daughter. He said they should do DNA testing, though Robin said looking back he seemed more flustered by the news than disbelieving. But his reaction upset Robin more than she could control, she wasn't prepared for all the emotions of the evening. The rejection was the final straw, so she ran out of her room crying. I guess as she ran out she passed by Ian and Matt, who were coming home for the evening. Sam ran after her but she said that she couldn't talk to him anymore that night and he left. Now she is sorry that she said that. She wishes she had talked to him, explained things about herself. She has even wondered that if she hadn't run off maybe Sam wouldn't have been killed. That whoever killed him that night might not have had the opportunity. Of course, I tell her that if someone really wanted to kill Sam it would have happened if not that night then some other time. But in some odd way, she feels some responsibility.

"I think all in all, Robin wasn't quite prepared for talking to Sam, for announcing to him that he was her father. I should have been the one to do it with her. I don't know what I was thinking by letting her go down there this summer, but she seemed so determined and I honestly didn't think there was any chance she would reveal who she was to him. Robin was too young to understand how Sam would react and Sam was never good at being emotional, so it wasn't a good scene for either of them. I am sorry that I let her go through this alone," Nikki said sadly.

Jane and Marti looked at each other and then at Nikki. Real raw emotion was showing on Nikki's face and it wasn't a very comfortable feeling to know that they may have come and upset Robin's mother in this way. As Nikki continued her story, Jane realized that they had really not taken the time to get to know Robin at all and felt truly guilty about it.

"She never really knew Sam, so she really couldn't love him yet, not in a concrete way. But he was her father and she had been in love with the idea of this other father for years. She felt special to have one father at home and another secret father she had yet to meet. She also feels a profound loss of the chance of never being able to get to know her other father. So this has been a very hard time for her. She's not sure what to feel. No one at the beach knows, except the police chief, who has been here to talk to both of us. He's been very kind. I know she has loved being at Herring Run, making all her new friends, but she's not sure she wants anyone to know the truth and whether she can go back. It's been hard on all of us, not knowing how to help her through this, but especially hard for Robin. She's not sure how she feels about anything at the moment. She needs time to adjust her feelings, I guess." Nikki looked a bit misty eyed as she wound up her story.

All three ladies sat in silence for several minutes. Jane was just about to ask Robin's mother about what she thought the chances of Robin returning to the beach were when they heard a door bang shut. Turning their heads toward the approaching footsteps, they saw Robin as she came into the kitchen, put her keys on the counter and then suddenly look up. For several seconds Jane and Marti stared at Robin as she stared back at them, then as she looked beseechingly at her mother Jane got up from her seat and walked up to Robin with a warm smile on her face.

"Robin, we've come to see you today in hopes of talking you into returning to Herring Run. Everyone misses you, especially the kids at the beach. Ian and Matt say that without you there to run interference for them they have no respite from the lifeguard adulation that seems to run rampant through the legions of kids at the club. I know they would love to see you return, as would so many of us," concluded Jane, not quite sure what else to say, her "just wing it" theory probably not making the grade.

"Well," Robin began slowly, looking first at her mother and then back at Jane.

"It's okay, sweetheart," Nikki said soothingly as she rose and stood by Robin's side, throwing her arm lovingly over her daughter's shoulder and giving it a squeeze. "Mrs. Adams,

Mrs. Sanders and I have had a long talk. I hope you don't mind but I told them who Sam Morris was to you, and to me, for that matter." As her mother explained this, relief flooded through Robin's face.

"We're so sorry that you've been through so much, Robin. We wish we knew what we could do, but if you come back to Herring Run I'm sure you won't be sorry," Jane said with meaning.

"Oh, I'm so sorry that I used your boys as an excuse for not coming back," Robin blurted out. "I knew that it was wrong. I've never been afraid of Matt or Ian. They've been so great to me. Since they're such good friends of Alex there have been so many times I wanted to tell them that she was my half sister and to tell her, as well. But until I talked to Mr. Morris, my natural dad, I knew I couldn't talk to anyone else. It's just that I could never find the opportunity. He was always with that awful wife of his, or sailing or playing golf or tennis. He was never alone and if he was, I never knew how to approach him. Anyway, I felt like such an impostor this summer. I didn't know if I could face going back to the beach after keeping such secrets. I didn't know how to tell the truth about it after the murder," Robin finished as she broke into hiccupping sobs.

"It's fine, Robin. We understand and the boys will, too. You have to be the one who decides whether to come back to the beach or not and whether to say anything to anyone about Sam Morris. It won't come from us. We would love to see you return but no matter what, just know that we'll support you in whatever you decide," assured Jane as she and Marti picked up their purses and began to take their leave.

At the door Jane paused and turned around to look at Robin's mother. She wasn't sure how Mrs. Thomas really felt about them coming but she had been gracious and open to them, something Jane wasn't sure she could have been if the roles had been reversed. Extending her hand toward their hostess Jane said sincerely, "Thank you for seeing us, Mrs. Thomas. And thank you for being so frank. If there's anything we can do, please let us know and we are so terribly sorry to have upset Robin. I hope you can forgive us for that."

"I should be thanking you. Honestly, it's actually good to get the truth out. Sort of a freeing feeling and I'm sure that Robin will come to that conclusion with a little time," Nikki said as she saw them to the door. "We'll keep in touch and let you know what her decision is. Good-bye, and again, thanks."

Marti and Jane walked back down the driveway to their car in silence, both digesting what they had just learned. Jane could not believe that Sam had a daughter that was only a few years younger than Alex. Did Julia know? Did Alex ever find out? It was obvious that she and Marti had had no idea whom Robin was before today. But then everyone had secrets, maybe this was one of Julia's. Was she aware that Sam had had an affair that had produced this lovely girl? It didn't seem that Sam was even aware of having another daughter until the night he was murdered. The only resemblance Robin and Alex bore to one another was their hair color and their long legs, not enough for anyone to give it a second though or to have guessed the truth this summer. And if Julia knew, would she have told Alex? Would Sam have told Alex eventually? Did someone else know about Sam's other daughter? And the million-dollar question, in Jane's mind, was: did Joanna know that Sam had another daughter besides Alex? Whatever Jane expected to happen when they took this trip to Marblehead, this, surely, wasn't it!

Sitting in the car before Marti started it, they remained silent for a few minutes, until they both looked at one another and exclaimed in unison, "Can you believe it?"

"Well, that's one on me," declared Marti. "I tell you, Jane,

I could not utter one word after I heard that story. I was so dumbfounded I could think of nothing to say."

"I know what you mean. If Robin hadn't walked in at that moment I'm not sure how I would have handled the situation. On one hand I was dying to find out more and on the other I felt that I had invaded this woman's privacy and wouldn't dare ask a thing."

"I can't believe we just heard what we just heard. What a lovely woman Nikki Thomas is. Can you imagine picking up the pieces and going on despite what a schmuck Sam was to her?"

"Chalk another one up for Sam. I think he got his just reward with Joanna. I wonder if he would have really been there for Sara? Do you think that Sara was being duped by Sam?" wondered Jane aloud.

"I don't know. But I'm starving and I do know that there's a lobster roll with my name on it at the Harbor Grill, so let's head over there; we can discuss it over lunch. And then, let's take a walk around the village. You're going to love the shops. Let's see if we can find any goodies to buy while we let this information sink in," Marti said as she started the car up and pulled away from the curb.

Marti was right, the lobster roll was one of the very best Jane had ever had (and she had made it a quest each summer to find the best ones). It was served on a slightly toasted, buttered hot dog roll, which overflowed with big chunks of sweet lobster meat having only a dollop of fresh mayonnaise on top. Heaven on a roll, is what they should call it, she thought. They sat on the outside porch of the restaurant at a little table overlooking the water. The view was truly New England shore picturesque with colorful little boats filling the harbor and a view of a lighthouse at the tip of land across the way.

Browsing through the little shops after lunch proved as

much fun as Marti had promised. They found a shop that was filled with clothes from Europe, one that had every scent of bath soap imaginable, all hand made as well as several little art galleries. A unique florist especially caught Jane's eye as she loved fresh flowers in the house and Marti reveled in the specialty cook shop. Jane ended up buying a black cardigan from Paris and Marti couldn't resist a new vegetarian cookbook to try to lower Bob's meat consumption, which Jane thought futile for such a meat and potato guy, but she wisely kept this opinion to herself and gave Marti an 'A' for effort.

Feeling quite accomplished, they left Marblehead only to find themselves in the middle of the evening rush hour traffic on the way home. Moving in slower than normal traffic they decided to go over all they had learned from Nikki Thomas. They agreed they would not say a thing to anyone about what they had learned, excepting their very discreet husbands (who they could not keep secrets from anyway, but knew they could trust implicitly). They also decided that Robin would not be a very likely candidate for Jane's suspect list and that she should be crossed off immediately. They both felt sorry for Robin, finally meeting her father only to lose him right away, especially since Sam had not been very sympathetic when he learned who Robin was. What a hard time she must be having, they thought.

What they should do next had them at a loss. Where did they go from here with this little investigation of theirs? Maybe Geoff was right when he told Jane, multiple times, to just let the police handle it. But this new information had to mean something, or did it? It was obvious that Mike already knew about it. Maybe this just one more part of Sam's life that had nothing to do with his murder. If so, what was the reason for his murder? Finding that out would be key to finding out who murdered Sam.

As they inched forward in the traffic, Marti seemed to get more and more agitated. This was not the fun part of the trip, for sure. Thinking of a solution, Jane said, "You know, we have to go right by the North End on our way to 93. Why don't we just stop and park in that public lot and have a cozy Italian dinner in one of those delightful restaurants on Hanover Street, my treat? In fact why don't we give Bob a call and see if he wants to join us if he hasn't already left the city?"

"That's a great idea! Let's do it, but we'll go fifty-fifty, or if Bob comes he'll treat us" Marti said with a laugh. "You already bought me lunch."

`"Well, that was payment for introducing me to the best lobster roll in New England, and for doing the driving today. I really appreciate it, especially when you have to deal with this," Jane waved her hand at the surrounding automobiles crawling along with them.

"And that's why I would like you to call Bob. Here's my cell phone. He's programmed into number one, as he's my number one guy," Marti said as she handed Jane her phone. "No way I can talk and drive at the same time. Tell him if he can come that we'll be at Florentine's in an hour. He knows where that is. In fact I think that's the restaurant that he saw Sam and Sara."

Call accomplished, with Bob planning to meet them, the traffic problem didn't seem quite as frantic as before now that they could break up the trip. They relaxed and listened to a demo tape that their boys had made and proudly given them. It was quite good and it helped while away the time it took to reach the old Italian section of Boston, the North End.

Arriving at the restaurant around six-thirty, Jane and Marti found that it was packed with the young after work crowd. Looking around for Bob, they finally spotted him down at the far end of the bar. He waved and motioned for them to join him. They worked their way back through the crowd standing two and three deep at bar that backed so close to the dinner tables that Marti and Jane had to be extra careful not to end up on one of the tables as someone's main course as they squeezed through.

"I've given them our name, they thought it would be about a twenty or thirty minute wait. Can I get you ladies a drink while we wait?" Bob asked as he got off his stool and offered it to Jane, while giving his wife a peck on the cheek.

A champagne cocktail would be just the ticket for me," Marti told her husband as he tried to get the bartender's attention.

"Lovely, thanks Bob, I'd love a vodka gimlet on the rocks, but only if you have fresh lime and wheat-free vodka," answered Jane, gratefully.

The waiter assured them that the bar indeed carried wheat-free vodka, so that made Jane very happy. She turned to her good friends and said, "Did you know that most vodkas are made with wheat, not potatoes? That's a good Trivial Pursuit question, or maybe when one of you gets on Jeopardy!"

"News to me," Bob replied. "I thought vodka was all made with potatoes and made in Russia."

"Not most of the vodkas. I was surprised myself," Joanne told him. "I have a friend who is on a gluten-free diet and she requested gluten free vodka for when she came to one of our dinner parties back in Tucson. I told her I was under the impression that potatoes were gluten-free and that's when I learned that most vodka are made from wheat and many aren't made in Russia. In fact, one is made right here in the good old U.S. A. in Texas! Go figure. Anyway, she's trying to get me to go gluten-free for many reasons and I might just—but since bread and pasta are two of my favorite things to eat I will have to really think about it."

The bar was noisy and they could barely hear what they were saying to each other but it was fun to be in the city, in a popular restaurant that seemed to shout Old Boston. Paul Revere's house was right around the corner and the USS Constitution was just a stone's throw away. The bar was long, made of dark, highly polished wood with a brass rail at their feet and a huge mirror behind the multitude of bottles set up behind the bartender. The floor was made up of wide planks that were well worn and typical of many of the floors found in these old restaurants. Tables crowded the rest of the restaurant with small ones for two and only slightly bigger ones for four. Huge windows opened up to the street with colorful window boxes that overflowed with bright red geraniums and dark blue lobelia. It was a beautiful setting. Everyone seemed to be in a good mood, relaxing after a day of work. A gentle summer breeze wafted in through the open windows as greetings were shouted out. Laughter filled the air. Conversations buzzed around them. Jane wondered which of the tables Sara and Sam had sat at the evening Bob had seen them dining here but then remembered it had been in the downstairs dining room where they wouldn't be seen. How sad not to be able to enjoy the al fresco feel of this evening, she thought.

Thirty minutes later, sitting at a table in the back corner of the restaurant (a little too close to the kitchen door for Jane's taste, but seated, thank goodness), they were scanning the menu, a superfluous task since they had eyed every meal that had been carried by them while waiting at the bar. Dinners having been ordered (pasta with clam sauce for the ladies, lamb shank on top of polenta for Bob, house salads for everyone), both Marti and Jane looked up expectantly at Bob. He knew what that meant. They were busting at the seams with eagerness to tell him something.

"Okay, what's up with you two? Why were you in Boston

today and what do you have to tell me?" Bob asked, knowing these two good friends only too well.

"To start, understand," began Marti, "this is not for anyone's ears but ours. Jane and I drove to Marblehead today, not Boston."

"And that's a state secret?" Bob laughed, as he broke off a piece of crusty Italian bread and soaked it in the olive oil and balsamic vinegar mix on their table.

"Not that," Marti looking a bit annoyed at the interruption of her big news. "But the fact that we visited with Robin and her mother and found out why she hasn't returned to Herring Run is," Marti's scowl turning to a gloat, as she saw Bob's face take on a look of curiosity.

"So, what would make you two go up there? And why, pray tell, did she not return to our illustrious shores of Cape Cod?" asked Bob, looking amused at the look on his wife's face.

"I'm not sure I want to tell you with that attitude," Marti stated, feigning a pout, reaching for the breadbasket.

"Don't look at me, Bob," Jane said, also reaching for a piece of bread, as Bob pointedly looked her way. "I'm not getting in the middle of that one," she added.

"Okay, I give, tell me what did you find out when you went up to Marblehead today," Bob asked, trying to keep his tone serious enough to satisfy his lovely wife.

"Okay, Mr. Know It All. Let me tell you something that will knock your socks off, but you must promise not to tell a soul. Really," Marti emphasized, "this is important."

"I promise. So what's this about anyway?" Bob finally realizing that Marti's serious tone meant business.

"Jane and I drove to Marblehead this morning because we needed to get to the bottom of why Robin hadn't returned. She'd told Craig it was because she was afraid of Matt and Ian.

Frankly, that not only didn't make sense but it bothered us that she would say that about our boys."

"So your mothers' instincts told you to go. Okay. So, what did you find out?" Bob queried.

"Are you ready for this? And this is the part you can't say a word about," Marti warned. "We found out that Robin is Sam Morris' daughter!"

"Whoa, say that again. Robin is what?" Bob asked, his eyes opening wide.

Marti repeated herself and sat with a smug look aimed right at her dear husband. She continued, "It seems that Sam didn't want anything to do with a child from his affair with Robin's mother. A woman, by the way, who just happens to be remarkable. He told her to take care of it and she didn't. She went ahead and had the baby. Mind you he was married to Julia at the time and Alex was just a toddler when this woman, Nikki, got pregnant with Robin. She raised Robin with some help from her parents until she married Robin's stepfather. Though Robin feels her stepfather is really her father, she'd never met Sam, and had this desire to meet and to get to know her natural father. Sam wasn't aware he had another daughter.

"So she came to Herring Run this summer to try to do just that. Her mother knew from years ago that Sam had a summer home on the Cape and it was easy for Robin to just try to find a job close by to it. She'd had a lifeguard job last summer in Marblehead so she just applied at our club and voila. The night Sam was killed was the night she told Sam who she was. Not good timing, I'm afraid," Marti concluded.

"Wow, hard to take that all in but, it makes sense why Robin hasn't returned to the Beach Club," Bob shook is head in dismay.

"And she isn't afraid of Matt and Ian. She just said that as a cover for not coming back to the beach," Jane told Bob.

"I hope that she does return and lay that rumor to rest, though. It would be nice for the boys to have that cleared up and give Celia one less thing to run around broadcasting. But, we can't tell her secret, that's up to Robin, we promised. So you and Geoff must be very careful not to tell anyone."

"Well, that really just blows me away," Bob said as he continued to look amazed. "All these years knowing Sam, playing tennis together, socializing and I never knew he had another daughter. I realize now that I only knew a little layer of his life. He was much more complex than I guess any of us sitting here knew. A daughter so close to Alex's age and none of us knew."

"It doesn't seem that Sam knew he had a second daughter either. He might have wondered about what happened to the girl he got pregnant, but I bet he just thought she'd gone through with his suggestion of an abortion and left his firm because of him. Anyway, he never had contact with Nikki after she left the firm and she never let him know about Robin. It must have come as quite a surprise when Robin told Sam who she was," Jane conjectured.

"Do you think that she had anything to do with the murder?" Bob wondered aloud.

Jane pondered for a moment. She really hadn't after she talked to Robin, but maybe she shouldn't be too quick to discount her as a suspect. After all, Sam hadn't taken kindly to the news that he had this grown up daughter and left Robin in tears that night. Could Robin have seen him later and . . .

"I don't know," Jane answered. "I tend to think that Robin was sincere today but then again she was quite good at not letting anyone know about her relationship to Sam, so maybe . . . well, I just don't know."

Marti looked aghast. "You mean that you suspect Robin still? I thought you said she was off the suspect list."

"I know, I did say that and really my gut instinct is that she had nothing to do with it but she did have an emotional motive and that night her emotions were running really high, so maybe I shouldn't discount her so quickly. But then Mike doesn't suspect her, so maybe he knows something we don't, which he did anyway before we went up today," Jane surmised.

The waiter arrived just then with their salads so talk of the murder ceased. They enjoyed a pleasant dinner and the subject didn't come up again until they were headed for their car in the lot.

"You ladies drive carefully back to the Cape, now. I'll see you this weekend. And maybe it would be a good idea to stop nosing into this and just let Mike handle it. You just might turn something up that won't be quite so harmless as today's find the next time," Bob advised them as he saw them to their car and gave his wife a kiss and a quick hug.

"We'll be careful, don't worry about us," Marti told him as she climbed into the car and put on her seat belt.

"See you this weekend, love," Marti shouted to her husband as they drove out of the lot toward Route 93 and Cape Cod.

As they drove toward the tunnel to get to Rte. 93 they were quiet, each of the women lost in their own thoughts of what had transpired that day. Marti was glad that traffic had lightened up making their evening drive easier. Jane wasn't sure what their new knowledge had to do, if anything, with the murder. She was just glad that Robin didn't really have a fear of Ian or Matt and hoped that she would return to the beach so that everyone else would know it. Neither woman even thought to look behind them where, not too far back, a dark gray Mercedes sedan was coming into the tunnel as well, heading toward Route 93 south.

Wednesday, July 21st.

HURRYING DOWN TO the tennis courts the next morning for her mixed doubles match, Jane ran into Celia as she was dropping her kids off at the courts. Though Celia gave Jane a cold shoulder and turned away as Jane sang out a good morning to all, Jane did notice that Celia was herding her children toward the courts that held the lessons being taught by Trey and Nick. Maybe things were slowly getting back to normal, or at least, Jane hoped.

Once on the court Jane found that she had actually made it with five minutes to spare so she took advantage of the time to stretch a little for once, since her usual M.O. was to arrive just in time to pull her racket out of its bag, jump onto the courts and hit with the ladies as they had already started to warm-up. Today she was feeling pretty good about herself and really looking forward to a few doubles matches. As she pulled the racket over her head with both arms and rotated her body to the left she saw the other three players approaching the court where she stood. Millie was decked out in a stunning light blue tennis dress that fit her body like a glove, Jane noticed as she quickly pulled in her stomach muscles that were sitting under her old black (to look slimmer!) skirt. With Millie was her husband, Jack, who had taken the week off and wanted to get in as much tennis as he could. Walking behind him and obstructed from clear view at the moment was someone Jane didn't think was the fourth player she had arranged to make up their foursome. It appeared to be someone much more slender than her good friend, Ted, who happened to be a bit on the portly side but could play as fast a game of tennis as any of their fitter looking friends. No, it couldn't be Ted. In fact it looked like. . . .

An audible groan escaped Jane as she realized with dismay that the man striding behind Jack was none other than Joanna's brother, Stuart. When he saw Jane was to be his opponent for the morning, as Millie and Jack never, ever played as partners (to maintain a happy marriage they said), Stuart stopped short.

With a look of disdain on his face he grabbed Jack's shoulder, turned him around and from what Jane could see, began to argue with him. Millie stopped for a moment to see what was going on and then progressed toward Jane with a speculative look on her face.

"I wasn't thinking," she said to Jane as she came by her side. "Ted called this morning and said he couldn't make it. He said he called the pro to ask if he could find someone to fill in for him. Jay just probably went down the list of people looking for games and, not knowing who the other three players were, called Joanna's brother. Or maybe he was the only person available. I didn't know what to say when he began following us onto the court, Jane, but, well, I guess he's our fourth. Do you still want to play?"

"Well, I have no reason not to play. He's the one who was so rude to me. I'll leave it up to him but I'm not leaving," Jane said with a conviction she surely didn't feel.

As Jack and Stuart began to approach them Jane busied herself with opening a new can of balls so that she would not have to watch as they walked toward her. As a whoosh emitted from the can of balls a shadow fell over her.

"I'm here to play tennis," a newly composed Stuart said, as Jane looked up at him. "And I also think I owe you an apology. I was quite rude to you last week when you looked in on my sister after she lost her husband. I know some things have been said and I want you to know that it was just grief speaking. I'm sorry if you and your family have been put through any discomfort."

With that, he turned and headed out onto the court. Jane was left speechless, a rare occurrence. Numbly, she picked up her racket and walked onto the court herself. Millie and Jack looked just as puzzled as she felt. What was with the dramatic turnaround? Had a suspect been caught in connection with Sam's murder that she didn't know about? Had something come up the day before while she and Marti were in Marblehead? No, Mike would have called and left a message or the boys would have known. That couldn't be it. Had Joanna and her brother finally come to their senses knowing the boys couldn't have possibly been involved in Sam's death? Had he actually just apologized? And did it really sound sincere?

Jane had no answers, except to be gracious and accept his apology with a nod in Stuart's direction, and with that she hit her first ball across the net. As they warmed up, she partnering with Jack and Millie with Stuart, she tried to figure out how she would get through two or three sets playing against this man who had sent such venom her way not so very long ago. He had apologized. That was something. He didn't seem like the kind of guy who liked apologizing very much so she should just let it go and get on with the game.

Stuart let Millie serve first. Jane received her serve and shot it crosscourt right back to her. Stuart lunged across the court and poached it, neatly putting the ball away.

Whoa, thought Jane, *this guy is good; I'm going to have to get more angle on that ball next time.* Jack took Millie's serve in his stride and he and Jane took that point. The next time Millie served, at fifteen-all, Jane decided to put a bit more angle on it, hoping to keep it out of Stuart's reach. Again, he poached and put the ball away. Luckily, when Millie served to her husband, Jack was again able to win the point for them again. At thirty all with Millie serving to Jane, Jane knew she had to change her return. Watching carefully as the serve came in, she watched Stuart out of the corner of her eye, at the last minute as her racket met the ball she whipped it down his alley while he dove across the court thinking he would again get the poach. Feeling quite proud of herself, Jane smiled and as she glanced across the court she noticed that Stuart glared at her. *Too bad,* Jane thought, *I get one point and he's a sore loser, which makes the winning of that point all the more sweet, to Jane at least.*

Winning the first game due to Jack's superb play, they crossed over to the other side of the court. Jack was their first server and as usual he won his serve without Jane ever having to touch the ball. She could only dream of the aces and spins he could produce. Now it was Stuart's turn to serve. Much like Jack, Stuart had a magnificent serve and they could only get one point off of them before Millie and Stuart had won that game.

Switching sides again, it was now Jane's serve. This was the part of the game she liked least. Too much pressure, Jane thought, especially in mixed doubles. Serving first to Millie the two of them played out the point for quite a few shots until Jack lunged across the court and put the ball away. Sending the fastest serve she had to Stuart just gave him what he wanted and he shot it back so fast that the ball was past Jane before she even knew it was over the net. *What a good player*, Jane conceded, with a nod to Stuart, before she served to Millie at fifteen all. Again, winning the point off Millie Jane served what she hoped would be a wide serve to Stuart as she had noticed he preferred his forehand to his backhand. This time he didn't hit it quite so hard and Jack was able to cut it off at the net for the point. The game stood at forty-five and Jane couldn't decide what to do. Stuart looked prepared for the wide serve so it wouldn't do.

Jane thought, *why not swallow any serving pride I have and give him a dink?* As the ball barely cleared the net and dropped right in front of it a look of surprise was on Stuart's face. He immediately realized that he would have to really hustle up to the net if he had any hope of returning that serve, which he didn't, Jane realized as it took it's second bounce. Game won. Stuart glared at Jane again, this time with a new intensity.

After that, it seemed that war had been declared on the court. Stuart was quite a competitive player and they all had to stay very focused to keep up with him. Jane never won her serve again after that, much to her dismay, but then neither did Millie. The men were really pumped and were not letting much by them. At a set apiece, Jane and Jack winning the first by two games and Millie and Stuart winning the second in a tiebreak, they were now toward the end of the third set. Jane was serving in a tiebreak where the score was Millie and Stuart six and Jane and Jack five. She needed to win both points for them to stay alive. Her first serve was to Stuart and as he returned it she was able to change it's direction and put the ball right past a surprised Millie at the net. One point down, she thought. She took a deep breath and served to Millie. Again, she won the point; what a relief. Now it was Millie's turn to serve. Jane was well aware of Stuart's abilities and knew that he was ready to poach but was also not doing it too soon to leave his alley open. Jane decided to try to lob one over his head if she could, a shot she hadn't tried because he was so tall and the game had been so fast. As Millie's serve came in Jane put her lob into motion but unfortunately it was not deep enough. Stuart took a few steps back, raised his arm for the overhead and smashed it right at Jack. It hit Jack squarely on his face and he quickly went down blood gushing from his nose. Jane was horrified; she had returned a lousy shot and Stuart had spared no mercy and shot it right at Millie's husband. Rushing over to him full of apologies, she grabbed her tennis towel to staunch the flow. Millie said she would run get some ice and quickly left the court. Stuart stood on the other side gloating at his shot.

As Jack stood up, tears streaming from his eyes, blood dripping down his face, yet insisting to Jane he was fine, Stuart said, "Well, you only have your partner to thank for that, Jack. She set you up real well. Think you can finish it out or are you going to want to forfeit?"

Millie, coming back on the court and hearing Stuart's comment, answered for her husband. "I think we'll call it a draw and end it here, Stuart. And a little control would have been in order there, you needn't have sent that ball right at Jack's face!" she added indignantly.

"It was my fault," Jane told them. "I had a weak lob and Stuart took advantage of it. I'm so sorry Jack. What can I do?" she asked though wondering why Stuart had hit that overhead with such a vengeance right at Jack instead of down the middle where they wouldn't have gotten it anyway.

"You see, I told you it was her fault. Call me if you want to play again sometime," Stuart said as he sauntered off the court.

"Not until hell freezes over," muttered Jack under his breath in a newly nasal tone.

After seeing that Jack was taken care of and with a million apologizes to both Millie and Jack, Jane picked up her racket and headed home. She felt terrible. Poor Jack, he would surely be sore tonight and would probably sport two black eyes tomorrow. He didn't think his nose was broken, so that was a relief to Jane, one small blessing. Why hadn't she sent a better lob? Or better yet, why hadn't she just hit a better shot, something low and fast? She resolved to never lob again! Right! And why did Stuart have to smash it so hard right at Jack? They were having a good, competitive, tight match. Good points came from both sides. But Stuart's shot put an ugly end to the match. He could have put that smashing overhead anywhere and won the point. Competitive jealousy at its worst, she guessed.

As she walked through the village Jane remembered the horror she felt at seeing Stuart cock his arm back, come down on that ball with such force and speed, aiming right at Jack. It's a good thing that it wasn't Jack's head that got the initial impact of the racket! Such a forceful smash Stuart took at that ball, like whoever had hit Sam in the head with the shovel. *I wonder . . .* Jane thought as she let her self into her house, threw down her racket and picked up the phone to call Marti.

Marti was sorry she had missed the now famous tennis match, the details of which quickly circulated the tennis club, branching out inevitably to the beach club and the village. When Jane had returned home and dialed Marti's number, Marti was out at the grocery store. She later told Jane that she had heard it first from Breda, who she met while waiting in the deli line for her turn. Breda, still in her tennis whites, had come straight from the courts where she had witnessed most of the match, if not the actual final shot at least most importantly the aftermath of it as she was playing on the court next to Jane's. She described in vivid detail the bloody mess made by Jack's injured nose, and the entailing callous remarks by Stuart. By the time Jane caught up with her at the beach the story had grown way out of proportion due to the village grapevine.

One version Marti had gotten, in the dairy aisle from Breda's partner's neighbor had Jack carted off to the hospital and Jane having a verbal battle with Stuart on the court. The village grapevine at its worst!

Opening her small cooler to retrieve her tuna salad, Jane began to laugh. "You know if I hadn't been there I probably would have thought all that was possible, but Jack's fine. I phoned them just before I came down here and his nose isn't broken, just a little swollen. He plans to keep his tennis date for this afternoon with three of his cronies so I guess he's not hurting that much. I guess a bloody nose can appear to be a lot worse than it is" Jane noted. "But Joanna's brother's attitude after Jack was hit really floored me," Jane added more soberly.

"Well, what did he say? I'm dying to know the real version of this morning's events," Marti stated.

"Basically, he blamed me for the whole thing. And of course, in a way he was right," Jane confessed. "Had I not thrown up such a poor lob, had the shot just gone higher and further back, Stuart wouldn't have been able to hit such a hard overhead. But what I don't understand is why he had to hit the ball right at Jack."

"My guess is that he's as competitive as his sister is, on the court as well as off. And I wouldn't go blaming yourself so much for this. Stuart, like it or not, is as much or more to blame. You just hit a bad shot; he had a choice of where to aim his shot and he aimed it right at Jack's face. Not a nice man," Marti concluded.

"You know, Marti, I almost got the feeling he would rather have shot that ball at me. As he came down on it his eyes left the ball for a second and I swear he looked right at me. I think he did it on purpose. I have no idea what that purpose could be but it was a bit spooky. I never want to play with him again. Wish I hadn't this morning. The funny thing is, he started out with an apology to me for how he acted when we went to see Joanna to give her our condolences."

"What a loser. So, have you digested all we learned from our trip yesterday?" Marti wanted to know.

"Not really. It was quite a bit to take in and understand what the implications, if any, this information would have to do with Sam's death. I'm about ready to give up on all of this. As long as the boys aren't suspects and no one here is accusing them anymore I would just like to forget it all. But you know, this morning after tennis I kept coming back to the moment when Stuart had a certain look in his eye and then the way he came down on that tennis ball. It just made me think of Sam getting his head bashed in by that shovel. And with the remarks he made to me afterward, well . . . it just upset me all the more. I began to picture him standing behind Sam with the shovel, and . . . well, you know. Probably ridiculous, but it's got me thinking again. Something I'm not telling Geoff, by the way. He would like me to just sit at the beach and be a good girl, keeping my nose about of this business," Jane surmised.

"Well, last night as I lay in bed all I could think about was Robin and her relationship to Sam. It's got to have been hard for her being here, meeting Alex, the boys, teaching Joanna's kids, the whole bit, knowing that she was Sam's daughter," Marti commiserated.

"You're right. I wouldn't blame her if she didn't come back to the beach. I wonder if she'll tell Alex or Julia, or even Joanna for that matter," Jane pondered.

"On the one hand, I think it might be really hard for Alex and Julia. On the other, it would stir things up here, that's for sure," Marti stated.

Later that afternoon as Jane folded the last load of laundry for the day she reflected on what the news of a second daughter would mean to all those involved. Julia would probably take it in her stride as she did with all the revelations of Sam's infidelities when they were married that she learned about after the divorce. Julia had moved on with her life, though the thought of a child involved would certainly put a different slant on things. What would concern Julia was how it would affect Alex so that would be her only real consideration. And how would it affect Alex? Hard to know, Jane thought. Alex was an incredibly well adjusted young woman, but, still, that news could be hard to swallow.

Then there was Joanna. Who knew what she would think? Though Jane doubted that she would have wanted Sam to have one more financial responsibility that could take away from the jewelry and trips she liked to spend his money on. Now that he was dead Jane wondered how the Will read. Had he left Joanna well off? What about Alex? Was she provided for in his Will? Time would tell, she guessed. Until then it really wasn't her business, it was just that her curiosity was eating away at her. She'd like to be a fly on the wall when that Will was read! Meanwhile, there was dinner to make. Wonder upon wonder, both boys were eating at home with her tonight, a rare occasion and a cause for celebration.

Sitting at the table that evening, Jane and the boys got into a lively conversation about the members of the Beach and Tennis Club's children and some of their antics on the courts and at the beach when they were at their lessons. Trey taught quite a few of the same kids in tennis that Ian taught at the beach and they found similarities in the conduct and behavior of several of them. Laughing so hard at some of their stories brought tears to Jane's eyes. She remembered her own two boys behaving not so differently during their young years in lessons at the same club. The trick tennis ball had been around for a long time and both Ian, first, and then Trey had been perpetrators of this joke on an unsuspecting new tennis pro. Today, in Herring Run tradition, one of the twelve-year-old boys had secretly put a few holes in one of the balls, filled it with colorful confetti and then during drills handed it to the head pro for him to feed to a player across the net. Surprise, surprise when the ball shot bright paper sprinkles all over the court. Past years had seen water, baby powder and rice fly out of the balls.

Poor Ian had already endured the jellyfish in a plastic pail trick earlier this summer. Hidden in his and Matt's room, left to rot and reek until they finally realized that it wasn't just their dirty clothes smelling up the room they finally found the dead jellyfish behind the dresser in the corner, put there by some prankster. Jane reminded them that they too had been party to some of these ruses when they took their lessons not so many years ago; in fact the hidden jellyfish was one of Ian's favorites between the ages of ten and twelve to any new unsuspecting lifeguards. Ian, with the help of the little boy, was just helping keep the tradition alive by being a recipient of the joke. Some things just never changed at this wonderful little summer community, a fact that Jane was grateful for as the world seemed to speed by them most of the time now with cell phones, DVDs, video games, texting etc.

"Hey, Robin came back today," Ian informed them as they were clearing the dishes "She got in just around quitting time but she'll be back on tower tomorrow. She asked Matt and me to forgive her for implying that she thought we were dangerous. I couldn't believe how sincere she was when she apologized. She actually had tears in her eyes."

"I'm glad to hear she's back," said Jane, feeling much relief. "It will sure help lighten your load down at the beach. Did you and Matt accept her apology? What did you say?"

"Oh, we told her it was fine. No big deal. We're just glad

she's back and we really do like her. Now things will seem a lot more normal down there," Ian stated nonchalantly, as he gave his mom a peck on the cheek, thanked her for dinner and headed back down to the beach and his friends.

"I'm off too," Trey informed her. "Nick is waiting for me at the tennis club. We're going to hit a few balls before it gets too dark. I won't be home too late." With that Trey headed off her concerns as he too walked out the door, swinging his racket in his hand.

As Jane cleared the table she was amazed and heartened by Ian's attitude and his forgiveness toward Robin. She was surprised and glad Robin had come back. Jane wondered if their trip to Marblehead had anything to do with Robin's decision to return. Maybe the summer would finally begin to feel normal again.

Since it was still light when she finished up the dishes, Jane decided that she'd take a walk up to the bluff to watch tonight's sunset. Starting the dishwasher and putting on a light sweater she walked out the door and down the midway toward the bluff. It was a lovely, clear evening and if she hurried she would be able to see the sun sink behind the marsh. Passing Joanna's cottage Jane could hear shouting coming from inside but strain as she might as she slowed her walk she couldn't make out a word. Someone was not happy in that house tonight, she thought. Resuming her speed she made it to the bluff in time to see the sun just as it made its final dip into the west. The sky filled with bright orange colors as the sun sank behind the trees. She sat on the bench totally enjoying the moment and the serenity of her surroundings. Looking over the marsh she could see a loon among the green river grasses. The small river that meandered through the marsh was a steely gray and pink, reflecting the sky. It was a beautiful picture. Wishing she had brought a camera, Jane was lost in thought when suddenly she smelled a whiff of lemon-lime and a voice broke through and asked, "Is this seat taken?"

Jane looked up to see her morning's opponent, Stuart. *Just what I need to ruin a perfect moment: this jerk,* she thought. She nodded no and turned her head back out toward the beautiful scene in front of her hoping he would go away, not daring to open her mouth for fear of what she would say.

"I would like to apologize for my behavior this morning on the court," he began. "I got carried away and just hit the ball too hard. There's been a lot of tension at my sister's and I guess all my frustrations came out on the court this morning. I'm sorry."

"You really should be apologizing to Jack, not me," Jane commented, incredulous at this turn of events, but not sure she trusted him on it.

"I already talked to Jack. He was most kind and seems to have recovered from his injury for the most part. But what I said to you was unkind and I am truly sorry."

"Okay," Jane replied, not sure what else to say, as she got up to leave. "Well then, goodnight."

"Goodnight, and maybe we can try it again on the court sometime," Stuart called to her retreating back.

Jane walked home slowly. This guy is so strange, she thought. First he acts like a homicidal maniac on the court and now he was Mr. Politeness. Which one was the real Stuart? Twice now he had been rude to her and twice he had apologized. He was as weird as his sister, she decided as she followed the path past Marsh Cottage toward her own house. It was quiet now. No lights or raised voices issued forth. Only the front porch light shone. Joanna must have gone out with the boys or made it an early evening, which is what I think I'll do, Jane decided, as she neared her own home and headed in for cozy evening of reading in bed. I'll give Geoff a call and then have an early lights out after last night's adventures and today's stressful tennis match. Despite good intentions it wasn't until three hours later when she had finished her book that she turned off her light. She was just drifting off to sleep when she heard Trey return home as he tried to lock up and walk up the stairs quietly so as not to disturb her.

"Goodnight Trey," she called through her door to him.

"'Night, mom," he called back as he passed by her room. "Thanks for the nice dinner tonight."

"Ah, you're welcome. Love you," she answered.

"Love you, too," he replied.

Now that he was home she could rest easy and finally fall asleep. Having kids meant never getting enough sleep. When they were babies they woke you up all night and now, she thought, *I can't sleep unless I know that they are safe at home. Wouldn't trade that for the world . . .* was her last thought as she drifted off in a state of contentment.

Thursday, July 22nd

THURSDAY MORNING, JANE and Marti met to walk at eight o'clock; something they had been neglecting to do with any regularity for the past couple of weeks and Jane felt it. Today they would not only walk, but also play tennis at the Ladies Round Robin. It felt good to get into a steady, normal routine after all the turmoil since Sam's murder. Today their step was lighter and their pace had quickened. Both women felt full of energy and optimism and it reflected in the walk. Today, they talked of trivial things, groceries, tennis partners, and upcoming village events such as the annual fundraiser. Finally, they could put Sam's murder on the back burner since Robin had returned and it was clear she had not implicated their sons in any way.

Parting company at the end of their walk, they agreed to meet in half an hour to walk to the courts together. Jane ran up the steps to her back door, opening it just as Trey rushed out on his way to work. Wishing him a good day as she went in, she quickly did the breakfast dishes and ran upstairs to change into her tennis clothes. It was so good to get back to a normal summer.

As Marti and Jane walked down the midway past Marsh Cottage on their way to the courts they saw Joanna walk out of her front door, also dressed for tennis. Not sure whether they should politely wait for her to join them or hurry on their way without her they ended up slowing their pace just enough so that she could catch up if she wanted. It was obvious that she didn't when she caught sight of them and quickly walked back into her house without so much as a hello.

"Just as well," Marti told Jane. "I really didn't feel like dealing with her this morning. If we're lucky she won't show up for tennis at all."

"I know how you feel, that's my sentiment as well," Jane agreed. "You know the weirdest thing happened to me last night when I was up at the bluff watching the sunset," Jane said as she began to relate her encounter with Joanna's brother, Stuart, the evening before as she sat on the bluff.

"Wow! That is weird. Maybe he has an anger management problem and is trying to deal with it," she speculated. "It's for sure that Joanna has one and she never deals with it."

"Well, I do know one thing. I don't want to play tennis with him ever again. Next time Ted can't play he should phone me to find a replacement," Jane informed her.

As they entered the club, they were greeted by their usual group. They drew numbers for who they would play with and the pro sent them out for six games on each court before they rotated, winners moving up a court and splitting up, and losers staying where they were to get new partners. It made for lots of fun and at the end of the morning you hoped to be at the top court, which meant that you had been winning.

About ten minutes into the morning of play Joanna arrived on the scene and threw the even numbers off so that soon someone had to sit out at each rotation. Being the strong player that she was it wasn't long before Joanna had moved up and was playing on the same court as Jane. Luckily, Jane thought, she would not have to play with Joanna but had Millie as a partner. As their games progressed it turned very competitive. Joanna smashed the ball down the line, crosscourt and up for magnificent lobs. There was no doubt in Jane's mind who would win this round, Joanna and her partner were killing Jane and Millie, who had only managed to win one of the first four games. Millie was serving in the fifth game and after faulting on the first serve sent in a much weaker second serve. Joanna came into the net and smashed it back at Millie who out of sheer reflex sent the ball back in a high arcing lob. Joanna took one look at that descending ball and with all her might took it as an overhead and smashed it right at Jane who was up at the net. Luckily it missed her face as she turned to avoid it but Jane took all the force of that ball on her upper right arm. Her racket flew out her hand and onto the court as she clutched her right arm with her left hand clearly in pain.

Millie ran over to her to see if she was all right, picking up Jane's racket as she went. As Jane looked up she saw Joanna just standing on the court, hands on hips gloating as she as she waited for play to resume, no apologies. Infuriated, Jane didn't know what to say. Her arm was smarting and had a big red welt, soon to be a big blue bruise. Jane was sure that Joanna had hit her on purpose. In fact, she figured that Joanna was probably disappointed that she'd missed Jane's face. Jane rubbed her arm and told Millie she was fine and they finished out the set. Joanna and her partner shook hands with them after beating them five-one and moved on up to the next court.

As Millie and Jane waited for the next two players to join them on their court Millie said, "I can't believe that woman. Is this genetic? First her brother hits Jack and now she hits you. She didn't even apologize. I don't get it."

"Well, at least she didn't blame someone else like her brother did with me," Jane wryly commented, as two new players came onto the court to join them. Jane didn't really want to talk about it deciding that this was not going to be food for the gossip mill. She gave a warning glance to Millie and they started up the next set without another word about it.

Later at the beach Marti, Millie and Jane sat with Sheila and Barbara discussing what had gone on at the courts that morning. Sheila claimed that she always knew that Joanna had a mean streak and that maybe it was a familial thing, after all her sons could be quite a handful. Barbara agreed. She had worked with Joanna at the beginning of the summer on the fundraiser they were planning to raise money to build a new village playground. Nothing nice had come out of Joanna's mouth. Their job was the pricing of donated items, something Joanna felt only she was capable of doing. At the time the rest of the committee had been quite relieved to have someone volunteer to do the job and Barbara agreed to help. What a mistake that ended up being. Joanna didn't like anything that was donated, saying it was all junk and then pricing it all way too high. When Barbara tried to suggest more realistic pricing Joanna had given her a piece of her mind, more than once. In fact, Barbara had finally just written whatever Joanna said on the tags and attached the tag to the item. Ha! The coward's way out, but also self-preservation, Barbara thought.

Jane wanted to forget about this morning's assault by tennis ball and jumped on the subject of the fund raising auction that was coming up in mid- August. But try as she might her tender arm and the bruise that was appearing there were constant reminders of what felt like a personal attack. When Barbara asked Jane to help price and tag the items the next week in preparation now that Joanna no longer would do it, Jane thought that it would be fun and quickly agreed to do it. Jane had already volunteered to help set up the silent auction and make hors d'oeuvres so that would keep her pretty busy in the weeks to come. Maybe even keep her mind off Sam's murder and her desire to know who was responsible for it. She was determined to butt out of it now that the boys had nothing to worry about.

That evening after dinner Marti stopped by to see if Jane wanted to take an evening stroll around the village. Jane eagerly grabbed her sweater just in case and she and Marti set out to enjoy the cool evening breeze that had begun to waft through the village. The day had been pleasantly hot and now the evening was pleasantly cool, a delightful day all in all on Cape Cod. Jane was glad that she had been able to enjoy so much of it. They walked down the path to the Village Green and stopped to chat with an elderly couple that lived in the village year 'round. The gentleman with the help of his wife had taken the Green on as his special pet project. They had planted many colorful annuals in the spring to brighten up the beds at each end. Jane and Marti marveled at how they seemed to have magic when it came to growing flowers. The beds of impatiens on the Green were twice as big and plentiful as everyone else's in the village.

The couple commented on how sad they were with the passing of Sam Morris. They had known him since he was a toddler and had watched him grow up every summer in Herring Run. They commented that it was nice that he had used the house so much this past winter. It was nice to see more people in the village off-season. In fact, they said, it seemed almost every weekend something was going on at Marsh Cottage. Almost every weekend lights shone from the windows and cars were parked in front. Different cars, too, were there each weekend. Probably lent the house to friends, they thought. Sam could be so generous.

As Marti and Jane said goodnight to them and continued on their walk, they both wondered if someday they too would be living here year 'round, maybe tending to the Green, not that either of them were much good at gardening. But it was nice to see how the generations continued on in Herring Run, each taking care that the next stepped up to the plate and continued the traditions that had been here since the 1880s.

As they approached the other end of the village, they came to the head of the midway path by the Morris cottage. Again, tonight, Jane could hear loud voices arguing. It seemed to be two male voices and at least one female voice, which sounded like Joanna's shrieks. Tonight the windows were open and they could catch a few of the words as voices carried out.

"Sam . . . where were . . . I don't care what she thinks about . . . Absolutely not!" came out the windows.

Marti and Jane looked at one another. With like minds they slowed their walk and moved a bit closer to the cottage. Concentrating on hearing what was being said they actually stopped in their tracks and stood only a few feet from one of the windows to listen. Still they could not make out more than a word here and there, all in angry tones. They were sure they heard the word "murder" and then a few words later the name "Robin". Still straining they stepped a little closer so that they were almost by a window, which, actually, wasn't all that far from the path but too close to look normal if anyone walked by them. Anxiously they looked around. Seeing no one they continued trying to make out what was being said.

It sounded as if the parties arguing were on the other side of the house. At one point they heard a door slam and then they only heard the two male voices. Later when they talked about it they thought one of the voices was that of Joanna's brother Stuart, but they couldn't be sure. As for the other, it was indistinguishable, as they had been too far away to hear. As they went back to the path and began to walk on the front door opened and out rushed Stuart, who glared at them when he saw them on the path. Not breaking stride he abruptly turned and walked down the street, getting into a car they had never seen there before, a dark gray Mercedes.

"Could mean nothing, you know, we really couldn't make out what they said," Jane commented to Marti as they neared her house.

"Wish we could have heard the whole thing. Everyone sounded really mad. Whom did the other male voice belong to?" Marti wondered.

"Could have been someone in the village, I didn't see any other car parked in front of the house other than Joanna's and that Mercedes that Stuart got into. Did he get a new car? I thought that black Acura was his, at least I thought that's what he arrived in originally," Jane noted.

"I have not idea, but that is definitely a weird household as far as I'm concerned. I can't keep track of their comings and goings," Marti replied.

"I wonder what they were saying about Robin. I wish I'd been able to make out that part of it. You don't think that they are going to try to put the blame on her do you? Maybe they know about her connection to Sam?" Jane queried.

"Who knows what Joanna is capable of, or her brother either? Not a nice pair! The less I have to do with them the better. You know, they were so way off base accusing our boys of Sam's murder. Personally, I think Joanna is a few slices short of a loaf," Marti laughed bitterly.

"Well, I can't say that I don't agree with you on that one. Good-night, Marti."

Bidding Jane a goodnight, Marti started on down the path toward her house. Turning, she called back to Jane, "Can't walk in the morning, Nick's got his sports physical for football at nine, but I'll see you at the beach later."

"That's okay, I've got a hair appointment first thing

tomorrow. I'll see you at the beach in the afternoon. Goodnight," Jane called, closing the door behind her.

Later in the darkness of the night, as Jane lay in bed trying to fall asleep, she tried to recall the words and voices she had heard coming from Joanna's house that evening. Why had Robin's name come into their argument? Who else was in the house with Joanna and her brother? As these thoughts tumbled through her mind she had a nagging feeling that she knew something, something just on the tip of her brain. Try as she might to retrieve it, she was unsuccessful. Whatever it was eluded her and at last her mind gave way to sleep.

Friday July 23rd

FRIDAY MORNING BROUGHT a thick layer of cloud cover over Cape Cod. Jane really didn't mind, as her morning would be spent getting her hair color touched up and a badly needed trim. Drinking her coffee and reading the morning paper, The Cape Cod Register, she checked the weather forecast for the next two days. It looked like they were in for lots of clouds and maybe a slight chance of rain until Sunday when things would hopefully clear up so all the weekenders could have at least one day of sun.

Skimming the rest of the paper, Jane noted nothing of great importance had gone on overnight and mostly the paper was filled with good news. That was encouraging. She saw that the County Fair was due to start that weekend, which meant she would avoid running errands in Mashpee until the fair traffic was gone. There had been a few petty crimes to report and more than a few engagements and marriages announced. The school board in the town was holding elections for three spots in the fall and pre-season football tryouts for the high school were being held in two weeks. The ad inserts were full of back to school items. All signs that the summer was half over to Jane. Jane felt that she was on the down side of summer when the fair was held the end of July, all the budding romances had matured into serious affairs, crime was at a lull, and those back to school ads were beginning to appear in the newspaper.

With a sigh, Jane turned to the comic section to get a good chuckle before she was off to Hyannis for her hair appointment. While reading some of her favorite comic strips she remembered that last night there was something that she just couldn't remember about Joanna. What was it? Her mind wandered away from the newsprint in front of her and roamed through the years and conversations she remembered that involved Joanna but still, nothing came to mind.

Realizing that she had better get a move on she folded the paper and dumped the rest of her coffee into the sink before placing the cup into the dishwasher. Still she just couldn't get it out of her head that she was forgetting something. Shaking her head she tried to not think of what she wanted to think of in hopes she would think of it, to no avail, of course. Grabbing her umbrella just in case the slight chance of showers materialized Jane set out for her morning at the hairdressers.

By midafternoon Jane was home and it was raining cats and dogs outside. The slight chance of rain had turned into a torrential downpour. Ian was home because the beach had closed due to lightening. He took advantage of the lousy day to try to catch up on some sleep. Trey had gone to the movies with some of his friends and they wouldn't be home until after dinner, stopping at the pizza place after the movie.

Jane had finished her chores, was postponing her errands and was sitting in their sunroom trying to read. Rain streamed down the windows and every few minutes the thunder, that rolled closer and closer, was followed by lightening flashing high in the sky. Looking out at the downpour Jane's mind wandered to the evening before when she and Marti had stood outside of Marsh Cottage. Still, she thought, there was just something about those voices that nagged at Jane's memory but would not come to the surface. A knock at the midway door interrupted her thoughts. Rising to answer it she could see through the window a wet and wind blown Robin. This was a surprise, albeit a welcome one.

"Come in, come in," Jane beckoned as she opened the door. "It's really nasty out there. Here let me take your jacket and get you a towel to help you dry off." Jane rushed off to the linen closet and pulled out a big, blue towel that she returned with and handed to Robin.

"Thanks, Mrs. Adams. I guess I didn't realize how hard it was coming down."

"So, what brings you out on such a day?" Jane inquired as she ushered Robin into the sunroom and motioned for her to have a seat.

"I was wondering if we could have a talk, you know, about my reasons for coming here," Robin ventured. "And you, uh, know Alex pretty well and, uh, I have been trying to decide, um, you know, well, whether. . . ."

Seeming to be at a loss for words Robin looked pleadingly at Jane.

"Listen, let's make ourselves a cup of tea to drink while we tackle this subject. Come into the kitchen and let's go put the kettle on. Which would you like Darjeeling, English Breakfast or chamomile?" Jane asked as she led the way to the kitchen. Busying themselves with the motions of making tea and putting a few cookies on a plate to take into the sunroom, Jane and the young woman fell into a companionable silence. With Darjeeling steeping in the pot Jane loaded a tray with cups, cream, sugar and spoons and headed back to the sunroom with Robin following carrying the plate of cookies. They sat back into their chairs and Jane played mother and poured the tea, putting cream and sugar in Robin's and just cream in her own.

As they settled into sipping the warmth of the tea while the rain poured and the wind howled outside Jane opened the conversation, "Robin, I was so glad to hear that you'd returned to Herring Run for the rest of the summer. I know that Ian was glad you returned, as were all the other lifeguards. Not just because of the extra workload they had while you were gone, either. Everyone around here has really gotten to like you and we hated to see you go."

"Thanks, Mrs. Adams. I appreciate the vote of confidence, but I'm afraid I might not be so popular if I do what I have been thinking of doing, that is if I come clean and am honest with everyone."

"You mean if you let people know that the reason you came here this summer was to get to know your natural father, Sam Morris."

"Yes, I'm not sure how anyone would take that, especially Alex," Robin replied, looking down into her cup of tea. "The little bit I've known of her makes me think she's so nice. I don't know if this would hurt her, which I would never want to do. Or maybe she would hate me if she couldn't accept me as a half- sister. I've gotten to know her a bit through Ian and Matt and I don't want to spoil the bit friendship we've developed. On the other hand I don't feel I can be her friend if I'm not honest with her. It's got me so confused that I'm thinking that maybe the best thing would be to leave again and just be done with it. Fade away as if I never had been here."

"Have you talked to your mother about this?" Jane asked, gently.

"I did and she says that it has to be my decision. She never looked back once she decided to raise me on her own and then met my dad, you know, my dad who raised me. She never wanted to break up a marriage so she just disappeared out of Sam Morris' life. But she knows that I may have different needs than she did. After all, he was my father whether he was there or not. And Alex is my half sister. I just don't know what to do about it."

"I can't tell you what to do, Robin. I think you have to decide that for yourself. But you know, Alex's mom and dad were divorced some time ago and maybe with so much time having passed it won't seem like such a betrayal to find out that Sam had an affair with your mother. Alex's mom was aware that her husband had been unfaithful a few times, which is why she divorced him. Julia has moved on and has rebuilt her life too and is very happy with where she is now. Alex is a very well balanced and caring person. She had a good relationship with her father but at times it was hard, especially with his new wife Joanna in the picture and Sam didn't run any interference for her as far as Joanna was concerned. That was hard for Alex. Not a lot of love lost between those two, Joanna and Alex, though Alex did try to like her. But Julia and Alex are strong, intelligent women. They just might be able to cope with what you would have to tell them," Jane advised.

"Tell who what?" came Ian's voice from the doorway where he stood looking a little sleepy with one side of his hair flattened by sleep.

Jane looked sideways at Robin, who looked a bit alarmed but also a bit amused at the sight of Ian's hair.

"Just girl talk, Ian," Jane answered. "Want to join us for a cup of tea?"

"Um, that sounds actually quite good. But don't get up. I'll just go grab a cup and join you in this girl talk and maybe I could get some pointers, NOT," Ian laughed. "Can I refresh the pot with some more hot water?"

"No, it's fine. Just get a cup and don't rush," Jane replied.

"Gotcha. I may have to find my special cup and it might

take awhile so don't let me keep you from your conversation. See you in five," he called over his shoulder as he left the room.

"Thanks, Mrs. Adams. You've given me things to think about. Maybe Ian might have some answers for me. Do you think I should see what he thinks?" Robin wondered.

"You might want to consider whether you want anyone else to know before Alex and her mother find out about you being Sam's daughter and if indeed you want them to know. Maybe you need to consider what might happen if they hear it from someone else. This is your secret to keep or tell. Mrs. Sanders and I have not, and will not, let it go beyond us, nor will the police chief. I don't think that Ian would tell a soul if you asked him not to, but you have to come to a decision on whether you want Julia and Alex to know and then maybe whether they want anyone else to know. I think Julia and Alex might feel hurt if others knew before them, of course that's just my gut feeling. I'm sure they will have some feelings on the subject too, that I can't know about. On the other hand, at some point, Chief McGuire may have to let them know. Maybe you should talk to him about it, before he has to let them know, if he needs to, you might want to talk with him. Or maybe not, lots to think about."

"You're right. Maybe it would embarrass them. I'll keep it to myself for the time being. Thanks for your input," Robin smiled for the first time since arriving on Jane's doorstep. "And I will speak with Chief McGuire again."

"I'm glad I could be of some help, Robin. And to be honest it's nice to have a girl in the house occasionally. Between the three males in this house and then their friends I feel a bit out numbered at times. Come by anytime," Jane said with a warm smile. "I think we can let Ian back in now, don't you think?"

"Yes, definitely," Robin enthused.

"Ian, what's taking you so long? Bring some more of those

chocolate chip cookies when you come, will you?" Jane yelled to her son, thinking that it wasn't just herself that Robin had come by to see that afternoon.

* * *

Hours later when Jane finally climbed into bed, pulling an extra cover over her as she was chilled from the damp weather and rain, she thought over the nice afternoon she had spent with Ian and Robin. They had decided to pull out their old Scrabble game and fought a fierce battle of words with the tiles, laughing at some of the ones that Ian had come up with, which to their amazement had turned out to be legitimate. Jane had then left the two to talk as she prepared a simple dinner of pasta with fresh tomatoes, basil and goat cheese, drizzled with olive oil and served with French bread and an arugula salad.

Ian built a fire in the fireplace while Robin set the small table he'd put in the living room so they could enjoy the fire's warmth on the surprisingly cool rainy evening. It was a delightful evening that had happened quite unexpectedly. Thinking about it brought a smile to Jane's face as she settled in for the night. She wondered where the kids had gone afterward, as they both left together in high spirits. Probably to meet up with their beach friends, she thought as she reached up and turned off the light, too sleepy tonight to even read a single page of her book.

Saturday, July 24th

S ATURDAY MORNING WAS bright and sunny, a reprieve
from the weatherman's forecast. The morning was filled
with the noise of all the weekend people down from
Boston and new people arriving to get into their vacation
rentals for the week. Jane was up early and out on a walk by
herself, Marti having slept in with Bob, her usual Saturday
morning routine. She would stop by Marti's on her way back
for a cup of coffee while Bob was at tennis. The air felt clean
and wonderful as her purposeful strides led her down the
road, around the lake and past Julia's house. Looking over she
waved to Julia who was just coming out of her front door to
retrieve the Cape Cod Register from her doorstep.

"Hey, Jane, good morning," yelled Julia. "Come in for a
cup of coffee, why don't you? It's been ages since we've had a
chance to catch up with each other."

"Oh, I shouldn't really, being on my calorie burning, get-
fit-in-one's-middle-age walk and all; but since you twisted my
arm, why not?" Jane replied, laughing.

The two ladies greeted each other warmly with a hug and
kiss on the cheek and Jane followed Julia through her front
door to the rear of the house into her bright white and blue
kitchen. The walls were covered with slate blue cabinets and the

floors with blue and white checked tiles, sort of like a floor of a Vermeer painting. The counter tops were grey soapstone with the backsplash done in white subway tiles with intermittently spaced botanical tiles that Jane loved. She loved the touches Julia had done to the entire house, really making it her own when she moved here after her divorce from Sam.

She'd pulled up old wall-to-wall carpet and sanded the floors herself so that the old wide plank pine floors were once again beautiful. Over the years she'd added some oriental carpets and painted the rooms. A soft yellow graced the living room walls, a Wedgewood blue in the halls and a rich red in the den. The dining room was white bead board on the bottom and a yellow similar to the living room was above the chair rail. The effect was charming in this old Cape Cod style house.

"I've said it before, but I really love what you've done to this house. Especially the kitchen. The tiles are my favorite part of it. Reminds me of some of the Portmerion dishes I have back in Arizona," Jane remarked.

"Yes, I'm quite happy with how it all turned out. I would hate to leave this house. It's been such a great place to live. Alex and I have certainly made this a happy home," Julia acknowledged wistfully.

"Are you thinking of leaving?" an alarmed Jane asked.

"Oh, I don't know. I am thinking of leaving my job and just maybe make some changes in my life," Julia answered cryptically. "But let's not talk of me. Is there any new gossip in the village regarding Sam's death?"

"Not that I know of," Jane answered. "But then I'm not on the inside loop of Celia's crowd," Jane laughed.

"It was really a shame that Joanna made such a fuss about Ian and Matt. Imagine accusing them of such a dreadful crime. I felt so sad when I heard about Sam's death, but you know, I didn't feel more than one would feel when one loses an old friend they haven't seen in a long time. It surprised me, but I realized I really was over my love for him, even more than I knew. I no longer felt any hatred, either, for how he tore my, as well as Alex's, life apart. I guess that shows how close love and hate can be. I mostly mourn for Alex who has lost the father she loved so dearly."

"Sam was a very important part of Alex's life. Thanks to you and how you handled the divorce and how you allowed their contact with each other. They saw a lot of each other. I think as the years went on he was very grateful for that. She was really the light of his life," commented Jane.

"Especially after he realized what a mess he had gotten into with Joanna. He had no idea that he had married such an unstable, self-centered, egotistical maniac of a woman. And those are just the nice adjectives I could use!" Julia laughed unpleasantly. "He just saw a sexy, compliant woman who met all his self-centered egotistical needs, which quickly changed once the marriage vows were spoken," Julia told Jane. "Then the fun began, at least for Joanna! What a fool Sam was, Joanna really played him."

"You know he once called me late at night from his car phone, I think he may have been drinking, mind you, but he confessed to me that he had made a huge mistake leaving me and marrying Joanna. I got the feeling that he wanted sympathy from me, maybe even another chance, but I had nothing to give him. Joanna wasn't the only woman he had cheated on me with during our years of marriage. I wasn't blind. I don't know the other names but there were plenty of signs over the years that he'd stepped out on me on more than one occasion. Late nights, business meeting out of town, perfume smells on his clothes, all the signs. In fact the many different perfume smells are what tipped me off that he had had multiple affairs. I could tell what he'd been up to simply by taking his shirts to the cleaners! Can you beat that! For a few months his shirts would reek of L'Air de Temp or Beautiful and then for a few months I would smell only his aftershave as I carried the bundle of shirts into the dry cleaners. Then inevitably a few months or year later a new fragrance would be on his shirts. I remember Chanel No. 5 distinctly. It used to be one of my favorite perfumes but since I hadn't worn it in awhile I knew it wasn't my perfume that I could smell on his shirts one cold morning. I drove directly home from the cleaners and tossed all of my Chanel down the bathroom drain. Isn't it funny that my nose was what really did him in? I remember Joanna's perfume. I'll never block it out of my mind: Poison! She was the last straw. I just couldn't take one more 'other woman' in Sam's life or mine. My nerves were on edge and quite honestly, it showed with how I got through my days and functioned. I'm sure that had I stayed any longer it would have affected Alex a lot more than it did. Perfume! Can you imagine, Poison! It surely was!"

"Wow, Julia, I had no idea that that is what tipped you off. I'll have to keep that in mind when I take Geoff's shirts to the cleaners," Jane laughed, knowing with her keen sense of smell it would be easy to sniff Geoff's shirts and know, but, ugh maybe not, thinking of what hospital smells she might come up with if she did.

"Oh, I don't think you have anything to worry about, Jane. Geoff is head over heels for you and always has been. You found a winner with that man, don't let him go, ever," Julia advised.

"I've no intention to, believe me. I know a good thing when I have it and I'm mad about him as well so. . . . Hey, how is Alex bearing up these days? This must be so hard for her," Jane commented.

"It has been a very hard summer with her father dying, especially with knowing he was murdered. I think that if they find who did it there will be some closure for her. Not knowing if it's someone that we know or just some stranger out there has made his death so much harder. Having no reason for why he was murdered has made her a bit fearful. I've tried to tell her that I'm sure it had nothing to do with her, but she's still nervous. And honestly I don't blame her. I'm actually a bit nervous at times myself, mostly for Alex. She calls me whenever she leaves work and always lets me know where she is when she goes out, which believe me does make me feel better. But she shouldn't have to go through this. I wish I could just make it all go away. You know, Sam tried to be a good father to her. Despite our differences, he never let that get in the way of his relationship with his only daughter," Julia told Jane.

Jane, thinking of Robin, made no comment, just nodded her head with a doleful smile. It was a sad summer, for the whole village, Robin included, but mostly for Alex. Sam's murder had changed her life in many ways. She would no longer have her father to sail with, play tennis with, laugh with and maybe someday have him walk her down the aisle. Robin had never had those things with Sam but indeed had a very loving father of her own at home, the only father she had ever known. Though she had lost her biological father she still had her "real father" Jane thought. Poor Alex had lost her one and only father to murder. The thought of a murderer in their very midst, that maybe it could be someone that they knew, gave Jane the shivers.

"Are you okay, Jane?" Julia asked.

"Yeah, fine. Just thinking with what you said that we might still have a murderer among us. Not a very comforting thought," stated Jane.

"I know what you mean. I check the doors and windows every night. I make sure the downstairs windows are locked when I go to bed. I've never felt uncomfortable here alone before, but I do now. When Alex comes in at night I let out a sigh of relief."

"Well, I should get on with my walk, but let's plan to go out for lunch or dinner one day next week. We'll get Marti to join us, and maybe even Margaret, she's been asking about you. It's been too long since we've gotten together like in the old days." Jane said to Julia. "And if you need anything give me a call, don't let something spook you and be alone with it," Jane told her, knowing the times she had felt that way.

"Thanks, and getting together sounds great! I've one more week of summer school to teach so dinner would be best for me. When did you think you'd like to go?" Julia inquired.

"You know me, when Geoff is in Arizona I'm pretty free, so any night will be good for me. I'll talk to the others and give you a call on Sunday night or Monday," Jane said as she stepped back out the front door into the splendid day. "Try to get down to the beach this weekend if you can. Everyone would love to see you."

"Well, if not this weekend, maybe next, got some plans of my own on the docket. Talk to you in a couple of days," Julia said with a wink of the eye.

Jane waved good-bye as she started down the driveway, wondering what Julia plans could be that they would be accompanied by a wink. And why was she vague about her plans with the house. Jane remembered that Alex had mentioned her mother might not be teaching next year. Did that have something to do with why Julia might not stay in this house? Was she moving? Maybe some of the answers would be forthcoming at their dinner. And then, maybe not. Julia hadn't seemed ready to share yet and Jane was way too curious, she thought with a laugh.

Forty minutes later as Jane rounded the last curve of the

road leading into their little village, she spotted Marti standing on the side of the road talking to Bob who was dressed for tennis and by the looks of his sweat stained shirt had already played. Waving and yelling a big hello to get their attention she headed their way.

"Hey, Jane, getting your aerobic exercise in for the day so you can have a big fat lobster roll down at the beach? Heard they're on the menu today. I've already got my order in with Nick," declared Bob.

"Lobster rolls, great! It sure sounds a sight better than the leftover, cold pasta I had planned for my lunch," enthused Jane. "And how did you get an order in with Nick? Isn't he working the tennis courts today?"

"That's so, but the snack bar called the tennis shack this morning and asked Nick and Trey to help out on the grill today 'cause they're short handed. With this beautiful day they're expecting a big crowd down there. The boys have to be there by noon, after the men's round robin."

"Guess I better have Trey set a lobster roll aside for me, too, before they're all gone. Wish they had them more often. Patti sure knows how to make the best lobster roll, at least on Cape Cod."

"Actually, I think it's her mom who makes it and only when the price of lobster is down and she has the time to do it," Marti ventured. "I heard her secret is a pinch of horseradish."

"Well, whatever it is, with tennis, a beautiful day at the beach and one of the snack bar's lobster rolls I can't think of where else could be paradise," Bob waxed poetically with a sublime expression on his face.

"Jane, I'm glad you came along just now. I was on my way to your house when I saw Bob coming back from the courts. We wanted to know if you would like to play tennis this evening at five o' clock, with us and a friend from Boston. His wife doesn't play and he would love to get a mixed doubles match in while they're down for an overnight. In fact, they should be here any minute so I should be getting back. What do you say? We could play tennis and then you could join us for a barbecue. Bob's bought some freshly caught blue fish this morning and I have enough for the boys, too."

"Sounds great! What can I bring?" Jane asked.

"Well, how about a salad or wine or something. Don't go to any trouble."

"How about I bring both a salad and a bottle of wine. I've got all the makings in the frig and last time Geoff was here he restocked the wine rack, so I'm golden." Jane offered. "White or red, or both?"

"I guess both, if that's okay, nobody adheres to the white with fish rule anymore, they just drink what they like. So, great! Then we'll see you at the courts at five. Don't forget to tell the boys to join us if they can. Come for dinner about seven," Marti instructed.

"Aren't you coming to the beach?" Jane asked.

"No. Not only does his wife not play tennis, she doesn't sit in the sun either. We're going to go antiquing along 6A, which is her choice. It's fine with me as I won the lunch choice, Capt. Frosty's. Just love their grilled salmon sandwich and it fits right in with her diet of no meat, no fried food and we can sit under those big trees in the back under the shade. You'll see Bob and her husband down there, though. They plan to take the sun fish out for a sail." Marti told Jane as she turned to head back home. "See you at five."

"Okay, have fun antiquing," Jane called back.

Once home, Jane gave a call to the tennis courts and asked Trey to reserve her a lobster roll when he got down to the snack bar. She could tell he was glad to get the call to work at the snack bar today. Though he loved tennis and working at the club, he really didn't make enough money there and liked to supplement his income anytime he could.

Next, she opened the fridge and peered in to see what she could do for a salad for that evening. Pulling out a bunch of greens, she went about washing arugula, endive, radicchio and a bit of romaine, for those who would need the salad not quite as bitter as she liked it. Drying each leaf individually, even after it came out of the spinner, she tore the leaves up and placed them in a plastic bag. She'd cut the cucumbers, tomatoes and avocado later. Next she pulled out the makings for the dressing, extra virgin olive oil, a lemon, Dijon mustard, some garlic, a few seasonings and set about making a dressing that would be light, yet flavorful to compliment the bitter greens. She put the dressing into a small container to easily transport to Marti's and with the greens in the bag placed both in the refrigerator. Now, most of the salad work was done.

Then she perused the wine rack and found both a white and a red that she thought would work for the evening. Though she knew white wine went with fish, lately more and more of her friends were only drinking red. Maybe they all thought it was for the health benefits, maybe they just liked it better, but she was among their number. Picking one of each, a decent chardonnay and a malbec, her favorite, she put the white in the fridge and placed the red on the counter. Now she was ready to dash out to Marti's after the tennis game.

The weekend was shaping up nicely, she thought. First a lovely visit with Julia, then a lobster roll for lunch while enjoying a beautiful day on the beach, then tennis and a barbecue. Marti and Bob were so nice to include her in their plans. The only thing missing was Geoff. She missed him terribly, especially on the weekends when all the other husbands were down. It would be so much nicer to have him here to share this beautiful day with her. With that thought in mind she ran up to her room to give him a call just to tell him she was thinking of him and loved him before she left for the beach.

Jane was glad she had called. Geoff told her that he would very likely be out to the Cape the next weekend as he had business in New Jersey next Wednesday and Thursday, some conference he was to speak at, and thought that he would drive a rental car up on Thursday night or Friday morning and stay a long weekend. With happy thoughts of next weekend filled with Geoff, Jane pulled on her bathing suit, grabbed her beach bag and set off for the beach.

An hour later, standing in line at the snack bar, Jane smiled as she watched Trey and Nick flip burgers and roll hot dogs on the grill. Looking hot and happy, they didn't seem to mind the heat that rose up and surrounded them as they cooked with one of the other employees, joking and laughing as they worked.

Trey caught sight of his mother and he gave her a big smile and said, "What up, Mom?"

"Not much, Trey. Came to claim my lobster roll. It sure looks hot back there," she commented.

"Yeah, well, no problem. I put in your order with Patti. She'll get it for you. I don't know how you can stand those things," Trey grimaced.

Though Trey had grown up spending summers at the Cape, he had never developed a taste for lobster. In fact, he declared that he hated it. Only in the last couple of years had he even tried to eat fish and that was only after a couple years of fishing with his friend Paulie in the Baxter's Fish Tournament, finally venturing to eat what they caught when Paulie's father grilled it for them.

"Hey, Trey, we're invited to the Sander's for dinner tonight. Fresh bluefish on the grill. Seven o'clock. What do you think?"

"Sounds great! I love that chicken of the sea!" Trey shouted back as he flipped a burger a little higher than he had planned based on the surprised look on his face.

"Glad you can make it," Jane told him, feeling relieved that blue fish wasn't a problem anymore. When the blues were running at the Cape every fisherman seemed to have lots to share and it had graced their table many times over the summers without Trey ever trying it. Jane had always had a burger in the freezer just for one of those evenings. "I'm, playing tennis first so I'll see you at the Nick's around seven then if not before."

"Yeah, I know. Mr. S. thought you'd probably jump at the chance to play. When he booked the court today he asked me what you were up to tonight, right, like I'd know. But I'll see you there; I'm on court duty until seven. Just working here for a few hours."

"Okay, see you then," Jane replied, admiring her enterprising young son. He'd be exhausted tonight, but with a bit more spending money for the winter in his pocket.

Jane sat under her umbrella and ate her deliciously, plump lobster roll, enjoying every morsel, the soft New England hot dog bun with just a bit of grilling on the outside, the chunky pieces of lobster with crunchy celery, a dab of mayonnaise and, from what she heard, a hint of horseradish. It was a perfect day, blue skies and few fluffy white clouds reflected in a calm sea with a slight breeze, just enough to keep a person comfortable. She had her best friends, minus Marti, to keep her company and a good book. She didn't see Bob and his friend nor did she see Margaret to ask her about a dinner with Julia. In fact she'd forgotten to ask Marti about it when they had talked earlier. She made a mental note to talk to both ladies about the evening out next time she saw them, hoping she wouldn't forget.

At four Jane reluctantly rose from her beach chair and began to pack up her things. She hated to leave and was a bit sorry she said she would play tennis. She would have been happy to just lie here on the sand as the sun went down. She always felt this way on such a beautiful day. Hurrying home she quickly jumped in the shower to rinse off the sand and then threw on her tennis clothes, rushing back down to the courts arriving just as the big clock on the tennis shack's wall read five.

She spied Bob and Marti on court three. As she walked over to join them, Jane noticed that warming up with Marti was a tall man who looked to be a few years older than they were. On the bench at the sidelines watching them hit was an attractive woman who appeared to be not just a few years younger but almost young enough to be the man's daughter. Her good looks were well-polished. Blonde hair with magnificent highlights, perfect makeup, long, French manicured nails and a perfect (though maybe a mite thin, Jane enviously thought) body to boot. She had on white shorts, a white polo shirt with the collar standing up and lots of gold jewelry on her fingers, neck and wrists. To Jane this screamed 'trophy wife' loud and clear.

"I made it!" declared Jane. "It was hard to drag myself out from under my beach umbrella, but here I am. I don't need much of a warm up so if you want to start in a couple minutes, I'm fine," Jane ran on breathlessly as she threw her racquet cover off and hopped on Bob's side of the court.

Bob offered her a wide smile. "Great," he said. "We've only been on the court a few minutes ourselves so let's give ourselves a few more minutes, then I'll introduce you to our friends.

Everyone amicably hit the balls back and forth. They all got a chance to warm up their volleys and overheads as well as their serves. As they approached the net to spin the racquet for who would serve first Bob introduced Jane to their opponent, one of his law partners, Greg Tanner, and his wife, Jennifer. Jennifer gave a little wave from the bench accompanied by a wide friendly smile. Jane smiled back and began to think more kindly of the Mrs. Tanner.

From the start of their games Jane knew she had to be on her toes playing against Marti and Greg. Marti's backhand was a killer and Greg was the master of the serve, placing it just where he knew his opponent was weakest. Jane spent a good deal of time chasing after the balls he sent her way or watching them whiz by her. Luckily Bob was on to Greg's game as they played once a week during their lunch hours in Boston and was prepared for the unexpected.

By six-thirty they were finishing a third set with a tiebreak. It had been really good tennis with close scores. Jane felt glad that she had decided to play. She was exhausted but she'd had a great time. The third set went to Greg and Marti at a tie break score of eleven to nine giving them the match at two sets to one.

As they stood by the side of the court reliving the final points and laughing at the time where both Jane and Bob had let the ball go right by them, thinking the other would hit it, they heard loud voices arguing coming from court number two. Looking over that way they saw Joanna's brother, Stuart, red faced and angry, berating his bewildered-looking opponent.

"Time to go home and get the barbecue fired up," Bob said. "I don't think I want to stand around and listen to Stuart argue on the courts again tonight. I had enough of that at round robin today."

As they watched, Stuart turned heal and marched off the court. His opponent gave them a sheepish smile of embarrass-

ment and began to slowly put his racquet away, probably hoping to avoid a run in with Stuart in the parking lot.

"Who did you say that was?" asked Jennifer. "He looks
vaguely familiar."

"That's the brother of one of the villagers. You know, Greg,
the brother of the woman I told you about whose husband
was murdered. Stuart McDonald. He's been a real pain in the
ass to have around this summer. Very argumentative and very
competitive, in the worst way. The men's tennis round robin
on the weekends hasn't been as enjoyable this summer due to
his presence."

"You know he looks so much like a man I met in my
singles days. Used to hang out at the bars in the North End
sometimes," Jennifer said. "That guy, too, was an unpleasant
character. Always had to be right and was always hitting
on women in a predatory way. Ugh! What a vile character.
But I thought his name was Scott, Scott Nelson, I think.
We all thought that he might be married and none of my
friends would have much to do with him after awhile," she
added.

"Guess there's a lot of creeps out there," Marti commented.

"Yeah, they probably clone themselves and all look and
act alike. I'm really glad those days are over for me. Meeting
Greg was the best thing that ever happened to me," Jennifer
said with real warmth in her voice as she turned her head and
looked adoringly up at her husband."

"I'm the lucky one. I never thought I'd marry, work being
my passion. Jennifer changed all that. I can't believe it took me
so long to realize how wonderful marriage could be. Better late
than never," Greg countered, putting a loving arm around his
much younger wife.

Jane realized she'd probably been hasty with the thought
of Jennifer being a trophy wife. She seemed like a genuinely

nice girl, young, but not as young as Jane first thought. And Greg was certainly smitten with her. Jane knew she had to stop making such stereotypical, snap judgments, one more fault of hers to work on she thought wearily!

As they packed up their gear and headed out of the club to walk back to the village Stuart sped by them in his car through the parking lot. The anger in his face was being transferred to his accelerator and he almost hit a car when he pulled out into the street with no regard to the traffic already there. Tires squealed as he sped off down the street.

"Whoa, that was scary," remarked Marti.

"What an idiot," Bob pronounced.

As they walked back to the village the conversation reverted back to the tennis game and the men reviewed many points, dissecting each one. Jane and Marti listened with some interest but soon found that talking about the day's antiquing was much more interesting, especially to Jennifer.

Back in the village as the others headed toward the Sander's, Jane veered off to her house to quickly shower, change and to retrieve her salad and wine. A note from Ian told her that he was working that night at Islands and wouldn't be able to make the dinner at the Sander's.

After her shower, Jane quickly blew her hair dry, opting for time over style and threw on her pair of trusty black linen pants this time with a cool, lime green shell and its matching sweater slung over her shoulders. Grabbing her huge salad bowl Jane tossed in her prepared greens and covered them with wrap. She retrieved the dressing, the vegetables and found her wine. Cradling her salad in the crook of her arm with the dressing, tomatoes, cucumbers and avocados precariously balanced on top as well as the wine swinging in a basket from her other side, she headed out the door to Marti's in record time, she thought, at least for her.

Trey was already there when Jane arrived and after a knowing eye from her, jumped up from his perch at the picnic table to help her carry her contributions to the meal into the Sander's kitchen. Marti was buzzing around the kitchen putting seasoning on the fish and throwing a baguette from Pain D'Avignion, Jane's and Marti's favorite French bakery, into the oven. Jane borrowed a knife and began cutting up her vegetables to put the finishing touches on her salad, waiting to dress it until the last minute. Jennifer was cracking ice for the water glasses while the men stood outside around the barbecue with beers in their hands, laughing at each other's jokes as Bob occasionally turned the ears of corn in their husks as they cooked on the grill. The meal preparation was in full swing. Trey settled back down at the picnic table with Nick. They seemed deep in discussion about something or maybe just biding their time until they could eat a quick dinner and bolt for the evening.

"Ladies, shall we eat in or out," Marti queried as she rummaged through the silverware drawer pulling out an assortment of forks and knives.

"I'd love to eat out," replied Jennifer. "Being cooped up in an apartment in Boston all week gets very old in the summer. The only time we eat outside is at the park or al fresco at some restaurant by a street so I vote for outside."

"Me, too," Jane chimed in. "As long as the mosquitoes don't eat us up I would much rather eat outside. The weather is perfect for it tonight. Just give me your placemats and the cutlery and I'll set the picnic table up for us."

"Thanks, Jane," Marti said, handing over the goods. "Tell Nick to come in to grab some stuff for me while you're out there."

"I'll take the water and glasses out," Jennifer added helpfully. With the corn off the grill, Bob came in to get the fish and within a short time everyone was enjoying fresh blue fish, crisp greens with a light dressing, grilled corn on the cob, crusty bread and good wine on a beautiful summer's evening. Hardly a word was spoken as everyone enjoyed every bite. The fish was so fresh and delicious that Jane couldn't resist a second helping, nor could anyone else. For dessert, Marti announced that she'd bought Four Seas ice cream on their way back from their day of antiquing and had all the fixings for ice cream sundaes. A collective groan went up from the table and everyone agreed that maybe a little decaf coffee first while they digested their meals would be a good idea before they challenged their appetites again.

Nick and Trey excused themselves from the table, thanked everyone for the great meal, especially the Sanders and headed down to the beach to spend the rest of the evening with friends. Marti brought out the pot of coffee with Jane following with cups, cream and sugar on a tray and the adults settled down to enjoy each other's company in the aftermath of a wonderful meal. As the light of the day was fading from the sky a bullfrog could be heard croaking down by the pond. Bob lit a few citronella candles to keep the mosquitoes at bay and they all sat on lawn chairs enjoying the evening and each other's company.

Jane learned that Greg had been a workaholic for years, rarely dating until one morning when he was forty-five had begun to wonder why he was working so hard. Professionally he had accomplished what he had wanted and he had begun to feel a real need for something more. He began volunteering at a food bank organized by his church trying to find more meaning in his life. What he found one Saturday was Jennifer, stacking shelves. She had made a career move to Boston the year before and after too many nights trying to meet people by making the single bar circuit with her fellow office mates had decided to find a volunteer job as well. He said it was love at first can for them as they unpacked a donation of can goods.

"To think of all those wasted evenings listening to some moron or other in a bar while I spent money and had a miserable time when my prince charming was waiting for me in soup kitchen," she laughed. "We did have some good times though with the girls going to the bars. Lots of laughs but I was glad to get off that track."

Jane was feeling quite sleepy after a full day and the good food. As she rose to go she said, "Well, I'm going to have to take a rain check on the ice cream, Marti. Greg ran me ragged out there on the court and I'm pooped. The dinner was great. Bob, you cooked that fish to perfection, thank you so much for having me,"

She went inside and retrieved her salad bowl and on the way out addressed the Sanders' guests, "It was so nice to meet you, Jennifer and Greg. And I want to get in a rematch sometime, so keep me in mind next time you need a fourth."

"If you're ever in Boston," Greg replied with a smile.

"Jane, thanks for bringing the salad and wine," Marti replied. "Care to walk in the morning? I'm skipping church tomorrow. Jennifer said she'd like to walk around the village in the morning before they leave, care to join us?"

"Sounds great," answered a weary Jane. "Just not too early."

"We'll be by around ten, see you then, goodnight."

"Goodnight and thanks again for the lovely evening," Jane called back as she headed home.

Walking in the door of her house, Jane was just in time to catch the phone as it rang and quite happy when she picked it up to find Geoff at the other end. She recapped her day for him and he did the same for her. He caught her up on what was going on in Tucson; all good news for them, how nice, she thought. He went over his plans for arriving in Cape Cod the next weekend and she said she'd arrange some tennis matches for him ahead of time. When Jane finally put the phone back on its holder she had a big smile on her face. What a perfect ending to a perfect day. And to think, next weekend Geoff would be here.

Sunday, July 25th

TRUE TO HER word, Marti appeared at Jane's door at ten the next morning. Jane had already had her coffee and read half of the Sunday paper. The day was a bit overcast but still pleasantly warm as the three ladies set out on their walk. Marti and Jane gave Jennifer a running commentary on the village as they walked through it, including its history of starting out as a religious retreat back in the 1800s. They pointed out special spots of interest such as the Tabernacle, the Inn and the old post office as well as many of their friends' houses. They also all admired the beautiful floral displays in many a villagers' garden especially the prolific displays of impatiens that bordered almost every garden and home in a multitude of colors and, of course, the age-old Cape Cod roses that adorned so many of the cottages, framing doorways, windows and hanging from many of the fences that surrounded each property.

From Jennifer they learned what it was like to be married to an older, adoring man (wonderful!), whether they wanted to have children (undecided, things just seemed too perfect at the moment) and where she got her great French manicure! Jane glanced down at her short, miserable-looking nails and quickly hid them behind her back. As they rounded the corner by Marsh Cottage, they caught a glimpse of Joanna and her brother as they got into his car and drove away.

"Probably going to church to confession," laughed Marti. "He's one guy who needs it; or at least a good therapist for anger management."

"I can't wait to see the last of him," Jane added. "I wonder if Joanna will continue to come to Herring Run? I never got the feeling she liked it here all that much; a bit 'beneath' her, is how I think she put it once."

"I wouldn't be surprised if she sold the cottage," replied Marti. "She's never really fit in here and I really don't think she's ever wanted to. That cottage is worth quite a bundle these days. Over the years Sam put in a lot of improvements. It's got a new kitchen, new bathrooms, even a new roof and prices have really gone up in the last few years anyway."

"Well, time will tell," Jane said thoughtfully, wondering if anyone knew what Sam did with Marsh Cottage in his will.

"Ooo, I would love to think about a cottage here," Jennifer gushed. "It's so peaceful. Let me know if it does come on the market. Greg refuses me very little, another added perk of a younger woman marrying an older, successful man who has never married before, ladies," she laughed.

They laughed with her and then cautioned her on the drawbacks of summers spent in a small, gossipy village rather than taking trips to Europe, cruises in the Mediterranean or white water rafting through the Grand Canyon. "And, you do have to spend the summers here to make the mortgage payments worthwhile and give no rise to guilt," concluded Marti.

"Okay, point taken, but do let me know if you hear anything. It's worth looking into."

"Well, we better get back home, Greg wanted to get started before the traffic piles up on the Sagamore Bridge. See you down at the beach, Jane" Marti said as they passed Jane's house and watched her climb her stairs to the door.

"Hope the sun comes out soon. But I'll be there unless it's raining or gets colder. Good trip, Jennifer. It was so nice to meet you and Greg. Hope to see you again," Jane called to their retreating backs. The ladies turned and waved one last time and Jane went in to start on a pile of ironing that had been building for a few days.

A few hours later the sun had still not graced the day, but Jane put on her bathing suit, grabbed a light jacket and walked down to the beach club. Despite the overcast day the beach was spotted with diehards, and she found Marti and Bob in their usual spot and set her beach chair down beside theirs.

Bob was sound asleep. Seems he and Greg stayed up late playing poker with Matt and Ian who had stopped by late. After an evening socializing at the Fog Runner they'd decided to forage for leftovers in the Sander's kitchen. Marti commented on how nice their visit had been with the Tanners and that she'd definitely invite them back. She also commented on how excited Jennifer had been about the possibility of Sam's cottage going on the market and had related the news to Greg when they had returned from their walk.

"You know I was thinking about that, Marti," commented Jane. "What makes us think that Joanna will inherit Marsh Cottage? Maybe Sam left it to Alex. Maybe he wanted to keep it in the family. Of course, maybe he hadn't even thought of dying so young and hadn't done anything about it. But he was a lawyer, so I think he would have done something about where his assets would go if he died. Have you heard anything about a will?"

"I didn't even think about that. And no, I haven't heard anything. I'll ask Bob, maybe he knows something. I wonder what Sam did do about the cottage. I can't imaging that Joanna would let him get away with giving the cottage to anyone but her but then maybe she wouldn't know what he did," Marti answered. Much to Jane's surprise Marti poked Bob in the ribs and said, "Bob, wake up, what do you know about Sam's Will?"

Seeming to be barely aware of where he was, Bob glanced over at Marti and said, "Nothing and it's none of our business anyway, Marti. Let me sleep." And with that he closed his eyes and resumed his sleeping posture.

Marti laughed and whispered to Jane, "I could tell by his breathing that he was half listening to us and only slightly dozing. Anyway, I guess that doesn't answer our question."

"Well, I guess time will tell. He's right, it isn't any of our business but I wish we could get to the bottom of this, his murder I mean," Jane lamented.

Bob half sat up and looked at Jane and then his wife. "Listen, ladies, you did enough snooping around already when the boys were suspected. I can tell by your voice, Jane, that you haven't given up detecting completely yet. No one even connects them with the murder anymore so just let it go. That goes for both of you. Are you listening, Marti? I don't want to find you two with caved in skulls on the beach some morning."

"Well, I certainly hope you wouldn't, Bob Sanders. And I'm not snooping, just discreet inquiries occasionally is all," Jane retorted, half laughing and half annoyed.

"Well, leave the inquiring up to Mike and his department. You two should just enjoy your summer while it's here," and with that Bob resumed his meditative state with eyes closed and soon, mouth gaped open.

Later that evening when Jane spoke with Geoff, she spoke to him about what a nice time she had had over the weekend, wishing that he had been part of it too. She didn't mention Marsh Cottage or the questions she wanted answered. She thought about what Bob had said. Maybe it was time to forget about figuring out who murdered Sam and just relax and enjoy the summer. Mike had everything at his disposal for that task and what did she have? Instead she told Geoff she loved him and to hurry up and get to the Cape. As she said good-bye, she had an overwhelming feeling of loneliness for her husband and best friend. Knowing that he would soon be lying next to her was of small comfort in bed that evening.

Monday, July 26th

WALKING THE NEXT morning with Marti, Jane brought up the subject of having dinner with Julia one evening of the coming week. Marti, ever game for a dinner out, said any night was fine with her.

"How about we shoot for Wednesday, then? Geoff is arriving sometime on Friday so Thursday I'll probably be doing last minute things for his arrival, like taking books off his side of the bed, laying in some of his favorite foods etc. I'll give Margaret a call when I get back to see if she can join us, too."

"Wednesday is fine, then, but don't count on Margaret. I know she's up in Boston for the week. Some family reunion and she made sure it wasn't held here. Last time her family did this she was invaded for a week with all sorts of relatives, sleeping everywhere and not leaving after the reunion was over. This year it's at her sister's on Nahant. She thinks it's her sister's turn to deal with Uncle Dom," Marti laughed.

Jane began to laugh, too. "Uncle Dom, I remember him. Wasn't he the guy who kept drinking out of a flask all day long at the beach, getting merrier and merrier? I seem to recall his solo of *New York, New York* on the beach porch."

"That's the one. And that was on his better day. So, where do you want to go on Wednesday?"

Jane mulled this one over. She wasn't overly fond of the fried food restaurants on Cape Cod. One or two fried fish platters a season was her limit so that left out a lot of the dining choices. She preferred a more discriminating palate when it came to eating out.

"How about the Chatham Fish Market? Their food is great. It's a bit of a drive but they have the best oysters on the half shell there, fresh every day and their grilled lobster is to die for," Jane's mouth was watering with the thought of that dish. "They also have great steamed mussels. Can't get reservations but it will give us time to sit outside and catch up while wait, as long as the weather holds."

"Fine with me. In fact, better than fine. Talk to Julia and let me know later," Marti replied.

"Well, she's in her last week of teaching summer school so I'll give her a call tonight and let you know then. Hey, did you hear anything else about Julia not teaching next year? Remember what Alex said that night at the Fog Runner? I forgot to ask her when I saw her the other day. You heard anything?" Jane asked her friend.

"Not me. I forgot about it altogether. But now that you mention it, it did seem funny how Alex said that. I wonder what Julia has up her sleeve? Maybe she's changing careers, or maybe she's come into a lot of money lately," Marti surmised.

"Well, it must be one of those. Coming into money sounds like a good plan to me," Jane fantasized. "Anyway, I'll let you know about dinner, as soon as I talk to Julia. Well, this is me," Jane said as she started up the stairs toward her door, "so I'll see you at the beach later. Need anything from the grocery store? I'm on my way there next."

"I'm fine, but thanks for asking and thanks for the walk, see you later," Marti said as she headed toward home.

An hour later, Jane was sniffing and tapping cantaloupes in the produce department at the local market when she distinctly heard her name spoken aloud. Looking up to see if someone had called to her she saw that across the way by the vegetables with her back toward Jane was Joanna speaking with her brother as she flung asparagus into her cart. Again, Jane heard her name spoken by Joanna. Stuart looked decidedly bored with his sister and moved on down toward the end of the produce section with his sister trailing behind. Wondering what Joanna could be saying about her, Jane followed at a discreet distance, careful to not call attention to herself, stopping to squeeze lemons and limes on her way.

Try as she might, Jane could not hear anything else, but was disturbed at the fact that when Joanna had said Jane's name she had sounded disgusted by it. As they rounded the corner to go up the cereal aisle Jane closed the gap between them by standing at the end of the aisle studying the multitude of choices of snack chips on display. She found corn chips, potato chips, taro chips, yam chips, even pork rinds. And each of these categories had sub categories, such as salsa flavored, vinegar and sea salt, spicy, barbecue and on and on, none of which would she permit into her cart for fear of an instant two inches to each thigh per chip. Still she was beginning to make out a bit of what Joanna was grousing about making her study of chips pay off.

". . . .can't believe that woman. . . .thinks she can tell me what I should . . . and her daughter. . . ." Come one, Jane silently begged, stop dropping your voice. " . . . as if Julia really knows about. . . ."

"Enough!" shouted Stuart. Startled, Jane looked up to see if Stuart was yelling at her, but, no, they were still just around the corner. A sigh of relief escaped Jane as she grabbed a bag of corn chips, held it to her face and pretended to read the nutritional information while trying to hear their conversation.

"This isn't the place to talk. Get your damn groceries and let's get out of here. We've got to pick up the boys from swim lessons," Stuart informed his sister.

"Fine, get the milk and I'll meet you at the check-out," Joanna retorted.

With that, Jane could hear the cart move away, squeaking as it rolled. Damn, Jane thought. What a waste that was. About all I learned was that they needed milk and the boys were at swim lessons. But what were they saying about Julia and Alex? Could be nothing, Jane knew. With Sam as the common denominator it wouldn't be unusual for Joanna to talk about his daughter. But she had sounded so mad. Of course, reasoned Jane, Joanna usually sounded mad, at least when she wasn't sounding petulant or doing her silky voice act when trying to impress someone, a rare occurrence in Herring Run. Not much learned in that bit of sleuthing, Jane realized. Damn, Jane realized, I'm doing it again. Bob's advice out the window, but it's not like she sought it out, Jane reasoned, so it really couldn't be counted as sleuthing, could it? Man, oh, man, if she could just figure out a way to make her head stop thinking about all of this.

Arriving back home, Jane began to put her groceries away. As she was about to throw a roll of tape into the junk drawer she spied her forgotten, crumpled suspect list and pulled it out. Smoothing it out with one hand against the counter she began to look it over. Sara, poor girl, of course was probably no longer a suspect, in fact, Jane thought, it wasn't just Sam's murder she wanted to solve but maybe Sara's as well. Jane put a line through her name and then, also Robin's. Knowing what Jane did about Robin, it made no sense to have her on the list. Scanning it she realized that some of the suspects were beyond her capabilities. Without special knowledge there would be no way she could know about one of Sam's clients, who had a disgruntled ex unless Julia, Alex, Joanna or one of his partners knew of one.

An 'Unknown Drifter' might be hard unless other parts of the Cape were experiencing similar crimes, which they weren't as far as she knew. And anyway, Sara's murder right after Sam's made that seem like an unlikely solution. How would a drifter have connected the two? Jane didn't really think that Julia was a suspect, did she? She had crossed her out, after all. But what was this about Julia maybe not needing a job next year? Both Alex and Julia had mentioned it, hinted at it, but never explaining it. Jane decided she would ask Julia about it at their dinner. Meanwhile, her name would be on the list with a line through it for the moment. It certainly made Jane feel disloyal to even have it there.

'Colleague' was also one that fell into a category like that of a client's ex. She would have to quiz people who knew about Sam's work life and for her that appeared to be his ex-wife, his daughter and his widow as she now knew Bob wasn't going to help her on this one. She just didn't really know any of his colleagues or who to talk about his current work life, which wouldn't help. Maybe that would have to be put on the back burner.

Joanna was still top on her list, though Joanna as a suspect wasn't panning out lately. She wasn't acting like a homicidal maniac, just her normal crazy self. Seeing Stuart's name made Jane underline it and add exclamation points after it. After all, he was a man with an uncontrollable temper. After seeing him on the tennis courts Jane could imagine him losing his temper and wielding a shovel at Sam, Jane cringed at the thought. Could it be Stuart? With that temper she really felt the answer could be yes, but why and what about Sara? That was a drug overdose, not a fit of temper. He could be a Dr. Jekyll and Mr. Hyde, though. And Sara's death hadn't even been ruled a murder, but a possible suicide. Jane wondered if Mike had found out anything new from the coroner. So many questions and really no motive that Jane could figure out besides petty jealousies or irrational fits of temper. No, she was missing something.

As hard as she tried, no one came to mind. Staring at the list she willed a name to appear or a motive. She let her mind float free, still nothing, except frustration and a knock on her door. Looking up she saw Davis peeking his head into the doorway.

"Are you still sitting here with your list? Didn't I leave you here doing the same thing over a week ago? I've done a thousand things, been here and there, done this and that, and yet, here you still sit, staring at that list!" he said with a grin on his face.

Jane laughed. "Caught me. Come on in, Davis. But, truly, I haven't been here for the past week and a half staring at this list. It's just that nothing has changed. I'm just as stymied about who killed Sam as I was last time you saw me, maybe even more so," Jane complained.

"Leave that up to the police. It's their job. I don't want to come over sometime and see your corpse sitting here staring at the list because you got too nosey. Hey, listen, come over and see the photos of my trip I had framed. I got a great one of a lobster man hauling in his trap."

"That's sounds like a much needed break to what I'm not getting done here," Jane commented wryly, as she threw the list back into the junk drawer and followed Davis over to his house.

A few hours later as Jane sat at the beach with her friends, she began to think that everyone was right. She should give up her quest to find the murderer. Leave it all up to the police, whose job it was anyway. And she should concentrate on relaxing and enjoying her summer on Cape Cod. That sounded like a good plan, all except that Jane just couldn't stop her mind from working on this conundrum.

She sighed and tried to pay attention to the discussion the ladies were having on the latest plans for the fundraiser, something she had sorely neglected. Feeling full of guilt she now gave them her full attention and thus found that Barbara had volunteered her for playing a part in the live auction. Now a groan escaped her.

"What, you don't want to help the auctioneer with the bids?" Barbara innocently asked.

"No, no it's okay. I'll do it. I was thinking about something else," Jane fibbed trying to cover for herself. "That's just fine. I'm doing the pricing, the live auction and bringing three-dozen cookies that night for the dessert. Should be a fun evening. What's everyone wearing?"

In the evening after the dinner dishes were done, Jane dialed Julia's number and got her answering machine. She left a message about dinner at the Chatham Fish Market on Wednesday evening and hoped that would work for her. Jane told her she and Marti would pick Julia up at six forty-five, if that worked otherwise give to give Jane a call.

That done, Jane settled into her favorite living room chair with a book she had been meaning to start all summer, *In the Heart of the Sea*, the true story of a Nantucket whaler, and a book that so many people had recommended to her. A few pages into it Jane was interrupted with the ringing of the telephone. Picking it up, Jane heard Julia's voice say hello.

"Hi, Julia. Did you get my message?" Jane asked her.

"Yes, that's why I'm calling. Wednesday sounds fine and the time is just right. I just thought I'd call you and let you know I'm looking forward to it. It's been awhile since I've been to Chatham Fish Market, should be fun. What happened to Margaret?"

"Family reunion up at her sister's on Nahant," Jane answered.

"Say no more; I remember the one she hosted here a few years ago and that obnoxious uncle of hers. I take it she learned her lesson never to host a reunion again," Julia laughed. "Listen, do you think that we could drop Alex off at the Fog Runner on the way? Her car is being repaired and she's scheduled to work that night."

"No problem," Jane answered. "It's right on the way. Does six forty-five work for her?"

"Well, it gets her there a little early, but she doesn't mind. Gives her a chance to hang out with the kids for a while first. So, okay, we'll see you on Wednesday and thanks," Julia said.

Again, Jane picked up her book and was just getting into it when the front door opened and Trey came in with his sidekick, Nick.

"What's up, guys?" Jane smiled as she looked up at the two boys.

"Not much, Mom, just passing through. Thought we'd go over to Paulie's to watch a movie. They just got a new DVD player and a huge flat screen TV. Plus his dad bought a whole bunch of DVD movies. What are you up to?" her son inquired.

"Trying to finally read that book everyone else has already read," Jane answered as she held up the paperback so that the boys could see its title.

"That's an awesome book, Mrs. Adams, you're going to love it," Nick told her.

"Yeah, Mom, I read it at the beginning of the summer. It's really good," Trey added.

"You read a book this summer? I don't believe it! I just bought this the other day, where did you get it?" Jane asked wondering if she had wasted the price of the paperback if Trey already had one in his room.

"Oh, Alex lent it to me. She told me about it and said I could read her copy and pass it on to Nick. She's really cool. Too bad about her car getting hit last night. Her Jetta's pretty banged up. She was lucky that nothing happened to her, it was a close call," Trey told his mother.

"My goodness, what happened? How come I didn't hear about this before now? I just talked to her mother, too."

"I don't know much except that when she was driving home from work last night another car headed straight for her. She said the headlights blinded her and that she ran off the road and into someone's front yard, hitting their picket fence. She thinks that if she hadn't swerved off the road and hit the fence it would have been a head on collision." Trey told his mom.

"Was it a drunk driver?" Jane worriedly asked.

"Probably, but whoever it was didn't stop. Her car was pretty bashed in on one side."

"Well, luckily she wasn't hurt. How awful for her," Jane commented.

"Yeah, well, I'm just going to grab a sweatshirt and we're out of here. See ya, mom," Trey said as he leaned down and gave Jane a peck on the cheek.

Jane had trouble getting back to her book after that. Poor Alex. She must have really been shaken up. Jane wondered why Julia hadn't mentioned the accident to Jane. But then Julia was not too talkative these days Jane realized thinking about how little she had seen Julia this summer and when she had Julia had seemed to be hiding something. Well, maybe Wednesday night would be enlightening.

Tuesday, July 27th

A FTER TENNIS ON Tuesday, Jane realized that it had been almost three weeks since Sam's murder and still no suspects had been arrested. In fact, the news wasn't even in the paper anymore. Nothing more on Sara had come up either. Jane thought sadly about that beautiful girl who was much too young to die. Had she really taken her life? With these thoughts on her mind, she decided to make an appointment with Mike, the chief of police, to see what new developments, if any, had arisen. If so, Jane wondered if he would divulge them to her. Picking up the phone she called the non-emergency number of the police station and asked for Chief McGuire.

After about five minutes on hold Mike's voice came on with, "Chief McGuire here, what can I do for you, Jane?"

"Mike, do you think that you could spare about ten minutes for me today regarding Sam's murder?" Jane asked.

"What do you need, or should I say want, to know, Jane?" he asked.

"Could I come down to the station and speak with you?" Jane inquired, knowing full well that it would be much easier to tell what he was or wasn't telling if she could talk to him face to face.

"I'll tell you what, Jane, if you can be here in half an hour I can spare about ten minutes. Would that do?"

"Absolutely. Thanks, see you in half an hour." Jane said as she dashed for her car keys and headed out the door.

Once at the station Jane was, again, greeted by Melissa, Ian's friend from the beach. They chatted for a few minutes about different club members and how their summers were going before Mike came out and let Jane into the restricted area of the station. As he led her back through the station he asked her if she would like some coffee. Upon replying no thank you, he ushered Jane into his office and showed her to the seat directly in front of his desk.

"I have some news for you, Jane. We just released it to the paper so it's not a secret, but you won't read about it until tomorrow morning. You were right about that young girl, Sara. She didn't commit suicide. We dusted for prints and found none anywhere, including hers on the pill bottle. What the coroner did find was a very small puncture wound in the back of her neck. We think that someone got into her room when she was asleep and gave her a lethal injection of an animal sedative, something that could be found at any vet's. So, now we have two murders, though I haven't connected them yet."

"I knew she wouldn't have killed herself. She just didn't seem like she going to do something like that. Of course, one can't always tell that about a person. Oh, that poor girl," Jane said with a choked feeling in her throat.

"If it's any concession, we don't think she even woke up so at least she didn't suffer. She had a lot of alcohol in her system as well, maybe she was drinking in grief, who knows, but quite possibly was deeply in asleep when someone gave her the injection. We'll know more eventually. But, she was put in the bathroom with an empty pill bottle by her hand to look like suicide. We found no fingerprints in the bathroom, on the doorknobs, the glass or the bottle. In fact everything was so clean that we knew something was up from the beginning. Finding the injection sight, and getting the toxicology report back today, confirmed any suspicions that we had. I thought you would want to know since it's public knowledge now that it's gone to the papers."

"Thanks, Mike. I really appreciate it. Don't you think, though, that the murders must be connected? If Sara was Sam's girlfriend and they both got killed . . ." she trailed off.

"Well, nothing concrete connects them, but it does give me pause to think, excuse me, Jane I have to take this," Mike said as he picked up the ringing phone and began to get a worried look on his face.

"Jane, gotta cut this short, seems that there's been a robbery at one of the convenience stores near the docks and there's shooting involved. Sorry, but I have to run. We'll talk later; I might need to go over what this woman talked to you and Marti about the night you had dinner together. I'll let you know," Mike said as he hurriedly ushered Jane back to the reception area of the police station and headed out back to his car.

"Things are really happening here this summer, huh, Mrs. Adams," Melissa said to Jane as Jane began to leave.

"They sure are. I hope no one was hurt at that robbery," Jane commented, not liking to hear that any robbery was taking place here in her idyllic summer retreat. Murders, shootings and robberies. It was all too much for this peaceful little part of the world.

"Not to worry. There was shooting but it seems just shots in the air by the owner of the store as the robber jumped into a boat and sped away," Melissa informed her. "I don't think anyone was hurt."

"Well, thank goodness for that. Let's hope that things stop happening now for the rest of the summer. I remember when the worst we could expect was a stolen bicycle or some wicker furniture off a porch, which mind you was bad enough, but nothing compared to murders and robberies," Jane said as she headed for the door. Waving to Melissa as she left had Jane wondering where the safe and peaceful times had gone.

Back in Herring Run everything did seem peaceful and idyllic. Children were biking down the lanes; one could hear the sound of laughter in the air and birds singing. There was a gentle breeze and the sky was bright blue with fluffy white clouds. The scent of honeysuckle filled the air. She spied Davis in his yard, pulling weeds from his flowerbed as she drove up to her house. *Why can't everywhere be like this*, she wondered.

Feeling glad to be back Jane hurried inside her house where she made a sandwich for the beach, packed the book she had started the night before and headed down to the club, not stopping to even think of chores. Doing so might break the mood she had suddenly found herself in and she didn't want that to happen.

She got as far as the bottom of her steps when her conscience took over and she thought guiltily that here she was enjoying the goodness of the day in Herring Run and there Sam and Sara were dead. Their murderer or murderers hadn't been found and now robberies were happening in broad daylight in Hyannis with shots fired, no less. To top it off, she suddenly realized that she had not asked Mike one single question while at the station to satisfy some of what puzzled her.

Retracing her steps, she knew she wouldn't be able to enjoy herself at the beach without having first put the laundry into the washing machine and at least cleaning one bathroom. To anyone else this would probably make no sense at all, but Jane always had a sense of guilt about balancing out life. This meant that for her to be able to relax at the beach she would first have to put her time in at the house getting some laundry in and maybe cleaning a bathroom or two.

Jane opened the door and headed into the laundry room to sort the darks from the lights, the delicates from the hardy items of clothes before starting the washer. With the first load churning away she'd scrub every toilet in the house as well as the entire bathroom that the boys used. By the time that was done she would be able to get the first load of laundry, which were delicates, hang them to dry and get the second load, mostly towels in to wash. Then, with those things accomplished she could head down to the beach with a fairly clear conscience, she thought with a grin.

Later as Jane walked into the beach club, Joanna's brother, Stuart, was coming out. With him were his two nephews, Jake and Justin. Both boys were whining about leaving the beach so soon and their Uncle Stuart had little patience for either of them as he ordered them to shush.

"I don't want to hear anymore out of either of you. Keep walking, mister," he said as he prodded Justin, the younger of the two and the one with the loudest whine." You guys are beginning to look a little too red. Time to go home,"

As Jane tried to slide by them, head down, hopefully unseen she felt herself accidentally bumped into just the person she was trying to avoid. Still looking down and mumbling an apology, she cringed in anticipation of the dressing down she knew she would get from Joanna's unpleasant brother. Steeling herself for an expected unpleasant onslaught she was shocked with what did come out of his mouth.

"Jane, so terribly sorry. I didn't see you there. I'm a bit overwhelmed here. I volunteered to bring the boys to the beach and I think I bit off more than I can chew," he said, laughing pleasantly while he looked first at the boys and then

Jane. "Joanna has been a quite distraught and I thought by getting them out of the house and down to the beach she could regroup and so could the boys."

"How nice of you," was all Jane could think to say, not knowing how to react to the change in this man.

"Well, it didn't turn out quite as well as I thought. Ten minutes ago they were whining to go home acting miserably on the beach. Now they are whining to stay. I can't win."

"I'm sure they don't know what they really want," Jane commented kindly, thinking that this is the way they always seem to act whenever she had seen them. "They've been through quite a bit lately and are probably feeling at odds."

"Well, it doesn't help that Joanna has spoiled them rotten. Personally I think they need to go to obedience school."

Jane laughed politely, knowing that she agreed with him but not daring to say it.

"In all seriousness, things have been tense at Joanna's and all of us have been under a lot of stress. I'm afraid I haven't been myself lately and, well, I know that we got off on the wrong foot when you came by the first day and then with the tennis game the other day. Again, I'm sorry about that. I was wondering if you would give me another chance? On the tennis courts, that is. Would you be interested in playing sometime?" Stuart asked her.

Totally astounded, Jane could think of no way to answer in the negative and still be polite. Instead she nodded and told Stuart to call her sometime if he needed a fourth, hoping that when he did she would have already made other plans. He asked her to do the same if the need for a partner arose with her. Parting amicably and with a smile, Stuart left with his nephews in tow leaving Jane standing with her mouth open feeling that upon entering the beach club she had somehow entered the Twilight Zone!

Plopping herself down on her beach chair among her friends a few minutes later, she was still in a daze over the conversation she had just had with Stuart McDonald. Where had this new attitude come from, she wondered? He was really a Dr. Jekyll and Mr. Hyde kind of guy. Jane didn't know what to make of such a complete turnaround. One day he would be rude and even scary and the next the perfect gentleman. Twice he had apologized for his behavior on the tennis court. Maybe he just couldn't control himself in competitive situations. It was plausible that the stress had made him such a jerk, but what a jerk he'd been. Shaking her head, Jane wondered if he had some kind of disorder that caused him to lose control of his temper so often. Whatever it was, to Jane it was a mystery.

"Jane, are you listening to us? We just asked you where have you been. You're really late getting here today," commented Sheila.

Coming out of her reverie, Jane realized that Marti, Sheila and Barbara didn't know anything about her trip to the police station this morning. More importantly they didn't know anything about Sara's death being looked at as a murder now. Mike hadn't said she couldn't say anything about it; in fact the information had been released to the papers, so Jane, forgetting about Stuart, proceeded to fill them in on the latest information that Mike had given her regarding the murder of Sara.

"I just knew she wouldn't commit suicide," Marti said, sounding just like an echo of Jane's earlier comment to Mike. "She was just too vital, too full of life to kill herself even though she'd lost Sam. That poor girl, she was really so nice. Who would have wanted to kill her?"

"I wonder if this is connected to Sam's murder?" Barbara speculated, voicing everyone's thoughts.

"It's got to be," Sheila piped in. "How could it not be? It's too much of a coincidence for both of them to be murdered within such a short period of time. I wonder what she knew that made someone want to murder her?"

"That's the million dollar question," Marti said. "And one I don't want to know the answer to until they catch whoever did this. It gives me goose bumps just to think about it."

Later that evening, Jane settled into her comfy bed with the Macy and Coffin families of Nantucket, two pillows propped up against her back, as she read *In the Heart of the Sea*. She was so engrossed in the book that she let out a cry when suddenly Trey poked his head in her door to wish her a goodnight.

"I didn't hear you come in. You really gave me a fright," Jane commented to Trey as she tried to regain some composure.

"Sorry, mom," he said. "Usually you complain that I'm too loud. Just was trying to come in quietly for a change."

"Thanks, it's appreciated. I was just so into the book and then to have your head appear, well. . . ." she trailed off.

"Well, good-night, then. Enjoy the book," Trey said as he retired to his room.

Jane tried to settle back into the book on her lap. She still felt a bit unnerved by Trey's sudden appearance. Thank goodness he wasn't someone stealing in to do her harm. She hadn't heard a thing. Maybe it was time to keep the doors locked at night, she thought. Was that what it had been like for Sam? Had someone sneaked up on him and hit him before he knew what was happening? Or had he seen his killer, had a confrontation with him or her? Jane just couldn't get these morbid thoughts out of her mind.

Who was out there with blood on their hands? What had made someone want to kill Sam? And why had Sara been killed? Was it one killer or two? Thinking of her suspect list Jane knew that it could be any or none of them. Would they ever know who had done it?

And what was with the turn around in Stuart's personality? Why was he so suddenly being so nice? Could she trust that he had changed from the wild man on the tennis court? Did he, or his sister, have anything to do with the murders?

So many questions and Jane had no answers for any of them. All she knew was that she wouldn't feel comfortable until she knew whom the murderer was and knew that they were safely behind bars. And now, Jane realized, she had thoroughly spooked herself.

It took Jane ages to finally drift off to sleep. Every creak of the old house brought her back to an alert state of mind and had her listening for another sound, a bump, a footfall, a whispered word, vigilant to every nuance. The last time she glanced at the clock before sleep finally claimed her was around 2:37 a.m. And then her sleep was filled with troubling dreams, monstrous beings stalking her and those she loved. Not the restful night she had hoped for when she had first snuggled down into bed with her book.

Wednesday, July 28th

LOUD KNOCKING WOKE Jane the next morning from her—at last—sound sleep. Sun streamed in through her bedroom windows causing her to squint as she tried to see her clock with her unfocused eyes. From below she could hear Marti calling her name as the knocking continued. Jumping groggily up out of the bed, she stumbled across the room and lifted one of the windows up enough to stick out her head.

"What's the matter, Marti?" Jane managed to croak out to her friend.

"It's 8:30. Don't tell me you just woke up! Aren't we walking today?"

"Oh, god, I can't believe it's so late. I just couldn't sleep last night. I worried about the murderer and then when I finally turned off the light I heard every creak and thump possible to hear in this old house. And I think I had some awful dreams. I guess I overslept."

"You guess you overslept? Good guess," Marti laughed. "Do you still want to walk? It doesn't matter to me, I could use the extra time to get a few other things done."

"Would you mind if I took a pass on it?" Jane asked. "I'm really feeling out of it this morning."

"No problem. I'll see you at the beach later. Don't forget our dinner with Julia tonight," Marti reminded her.

"I haven't. Thanks, see you later," Jane said as she brought her head back inside the bedroom and decided that a shower was her only hope of clearing the sleep from her head.

Gratefully, Jane stood under the streaming water of the shower. It felt so good, so refreshing. Scrubbing her hair vigorously, she began to feel awake. *Thank goodness for showers*, she thought, until the shower scene from "Psycho" suddenly ran though her mind. Turning off the shower she reached for her towel and briskly dried off, thoroughly annoyed with herself for having such eerie thoughts. She was letting her mind run a little too freely in the wrong directions these days. She just wished that when she walked out to pick up the morning paper today there would be a headline proclaiming: "Morris Murder Solved".

Quickly towel drying her hair, she pulled on a pair of shorts and a tee shirt then headed downstairs and out the door to get the paper that was sitting on the second step. Jane could see before she even picked it up that the headline read something about a big drug raid in a town just off the Cape. Sitting down on the step herself, she scanned through the paper's front section and the second section where she finally found a small article on Sara's death. It said the police had ruled it a homicide and that she had been given an overdose of a paralyzing drug commonly found in veterinarians' offices. She scanned the rest of the article but she already knew what was there.

Sad to see so little on such a vibrant life, she slowly got up from the step and went in to brew her morning coffee. While her water boiled so did her temper as she thought of someone ending the precious life of that beautiful young woman. As she waited to push the plunger of the French press down, Jane's hand involuntarily reached into the drawer that held her list of suspects. When she looked down at the names Joanna and Stuart just popped out at her. Jane could go over to Joanna's house when they were both there and ask where they had been on the night of Sam's murder, but she knew that would be fruitless. They were probably each other alibis. No, she thought, divide and conquer would be the only tactic that would work for them. How to go about that was the question. What excuse could she use to get together with Joanna? They certainly didn't have a mutual admiration.

As far as Stuart went, Jane could ask him to play tennis. He himself had suggested that they get together and play. Jane would need to set up a threesome that needed a fourth. Bob and Marti would be the perfect people for that. She'd try to see them at the beach today.

That left Joanna. Jane really loathed the idea of even seeing her, much less talking to her. *No love lost between the two of us*, Jane thought wryly. Maybe the village fund- raiser would be a good vehicle for getting together with that dreadful woman. Jane would have to think of how that might work out. Maybe getting down to the beach early, before the rest of her gang arrived would give her time to think up some strategies.

Feeling better, more organized now that she had a plan of action, Jane suddenly realized she was starving. Rummaging through the cupboard she found exactly what she needed to assuage her hunger: a multi-seeded bagel. Popping that into the toaster she dug out the last of the light cream cheese, poured a cup of fragrant coffee and proceeded to read the paper's comic section in a much better frame of mind than she had woken up with only an hour earlier.

A short time later, Jane lay on the beach with her eyes closed. It was too early for the rest of her friends to show up so Jane had their spot to herself. As she let the noise of other people on the beach recede and concentrated on the sound of the waves pushing into the shore she was able let her mind drift around different ideas on how to corner Joanna. She needed a way to spend some time with her so she could pry information out of that woman without her becoming suspicious. She accepted and rejected a multitude of scenarios before finally alighting on something that just might work. The more Jane thought about it the more plausible it seemed. It just might do the trick. A smile began to slowly form on Jane's face as she plotted.

"What pleases you so this fine day?" Marti asked as she plopped down on the sand next to Jane. "You're looking very content at the moment, not at all like the bleary eyed, wild woman I saw early this morning."

Jane sat up laughing. "Oh, just thinking some wicked thoughts, is all. Hey, what are you doing down here this early?"

"Early? It's already noon. Okay, so it's a bit early, but after I saw you this morning I decided to shorten my walk and take advantage of this marvelous day by sitting on the beach. I see you had similar thoughts."

"Something like that," Jane replied with a smile on her face. She wasn't ready to let Marti in on her plan just yet. "It certainly is a gorgeous day, isn't it? Look, there's Matt just coming off tower."

Marti looked toward center tower and saw her older son headed their way. "He must be coming for his lunch. I told him I'd stop by Lamberts and bring him a turkey sandwich. I don't know what they do that makes him like their sandwiches so much more than the ones I make, but it's a treat for him and he deserves a treat every so often, not to mention it makes me look good," Marti laughed, with Jane nodding in agreement.

"Hi, Mom! Hi Mrs. Adams," Matt politely greeted the two women.

"Got your sandwich, Matt, special delivery," Marti said as she handed him a bag with his lunch inside.

"Great, thanks, mom. Turkey, no mustard, right?" Matt asked as he peered into the bag, checking out its contents.

"Just what you ordered," Marti responded.

"Did you hear that Ian and I are playing at the Fog Runner tonight? Why don't you two come over to hear us? We go on around 9:30 and will play two sets, think you can stay up that late?" Matt said with a twinkle in his eye.

"Hey, that would be great. We're having dinner with Alex's mom and we could stop by for the first set if she's up for it. Maybe Alex is working there tonight, too. It would be fun to see all of you," Jane said, looking forward to the evening. "What do you think, Marti, up for a little bit of the Hyannis night life?"

"Sounds good to me. We can ask Julia when we pick her up."

"Okay, well, later," Matt said as he left to join some friends on the beach for his lunch break.

"This evening looks to be great fun," Marti commented.

"Yeah, I agree. And even if Julia needs an early night we can still go back to hear the boys after we drop her off. Speaking of fun, how about you and Bob playing tennis with me this Saturday?

"Sounds good," Marti replied.

"Great, 'cause I'm going to see if Stuart wants to be the fourth," Jane told her.

"What?" Marti's mouth dropped open as she sat up in surprise. "You've got to be kidding. I didn't think you'd ever get back on the court with that man. And anyway, didn't you say that Geoff would be in this weekend? Where does that leave him?"

"Geoff will be here, but Saturday he's going out fishing with Paulie and his father and Trey. Nick said he couldn't go because he has to work the tennis shack all afternoon on Saturday. So that leaves me at loose ends until they return, so even though I know I said I never wanted to play with that man again, he approached me about playing sometime to make up for his poor behavior. I thought that if I took him up on it, and you were there too, we might glean some valuable information from him or about him. Or maybe just get into his good graces and learn a bit more about Joanna."

"Oh, Jane, do you think that's wise? Now that the boys are in the clear I'm not sure that I want to even think about all of that."

"I hear you, but I can't stop thinking about it. I keep imagining that the killer is someone we know here in the village and every night I get totally spooked. It's like once the sun goes down my imagination flares up. Every creak and groan of the house is a potential mad killer. Like he's roaming around among us and we don't know it."

"I know. I've had the same feelings. In fact, so have Sheila and Barbara and I would guess quite a few of Herring Run's residents. I guess I thought if I could just put my head in the sand it would all go away," Marti told Jane wistfully.

"I wish it would. I wish we could go back to the beginning of the summer and have everything turn out differently. But, I just can't sit around doing nothing. What do you say, in or out?"

"In, I guess. Just don't tell Bob what we're up to; he'll think that we're crazy. But do me a favor, Jane. Don't be too obvious."

"I won't. And thanks, Marti. I'll see if Stuart can join us on Saturday, then I'll reserve a court."

With that settled Jane felt that part of her plan was in place. The other part she would try to put into motion at the same time she talked to Stuart about the tennis. Feeling satisfied that at least she was taking some kind of positive action, Jane could now relax and enjoy the rest of the day chatting with her friends at the beach, taking a dip in the waters of Nantucket Sound, maybe even getting in a cat nap.

On her walk home, Jane stopped at Marsh Cottage and knocked on its door. Joanna's son Justin opened it and looked up at her with an impish grin on his face. He had a face covered with chocolate, probably from a candy bar that had melted as he ate it and his blond hair was sticking up on one side with what looked like the same brown chocolate keeping it in place. Jane noticed that the hand that opened the screen door was also the same gooey, sticky mess.

"Who is it, Justin?" came a call from the back of the house, sounding a whole lot like his Uncle Stuart.

Justin just smiled up at Jane and didn't say a word. Not knowing quite what to do, Jane stepped through the open door into the darkened front room and called out, "It's Jane. Jane Adams? I stopped by to see if we could set up a tennis date."

Coming from the back of the house, wiping his hands on a dishtowel, Stuart hurried toward the front door.

"Justin, get back in the kitchen and help Jake clean up that mess. Now, mister," Stuart said in a harsh voice. "What's this about tennis?"

"I thought you might want to be a fourth and play with me against the Sanders on Saturday around four."

Looking totally annoyed and a bit hostile, Stuart said nothing. This was not quite what Jane expected. Stuart stared at her blankly and Jane began to think that she had imagined the earlier conversation with him and to top it off her idea was really stupid. How could she have thought that he really wanted to play tennis with her, she wondered? Hesitating, she finally blurted out, "I'm taking you up on your invitation to let you know if I ever needed a fourth and I do, on Saturday, but if you're busy . . ."

"Oh, right. I guess I wasn't thinking. When was it again?" Stuart asked, not quite disguising his irritation.

"Saturday, at four. But if you can't I understand, don't feel that you have to . . ." Jane stammered, regretting her decision to ask him.

"Four is fine. I'll see you then," Stuart replied and turned around and headed back from where he had come from.

Standing alone just inside the front door, Jane felt totally ridiculous that she had ever thought this despicable man might have a nice side. Now she was stuck playing with him on Saturday. All I can say, she thought to herself, is this better be worth it because it sure won't be much fun. She opened the screen door and quietly left the house, feeling like an intruder who is trying not to get caught. As she left the yard, she felt someone watching her leave. Turning around her eyes caught an upstairs blind slat snap shut. Feeling shivers go down her back, Jane hurried home to shower and get ready for her evening out, hoping that her good mood of the afternoon would return in time for dinner.

As Jane entered her house she heard the phone ringing. Hitting her shin on the coffee table as she ran to get it before the answering machine picked up, she wondered why she bothered running when she did have an answering machine. It must be a reflex action from the old days before answering machines, she thought ruefully. Catching it just in time to hear the click of the caller, she rubbed her leg briskly as she waited a few seconds for the caller to leave a message. Dialing into her number and putting in her code she found that she had three new messages. The first was from Geoff with his arrival plans for Friday (which made Jane smile). The second was from Ian reminding her that he hoped she could make it to the Fog Runner tonight to hear him perform with Matt (this made her smile wider). And the third was from Joanna telling Jane not to come around Marsh Cottage again and if she had business with Stuart to conduct it elsewhere! Her smile vanished. The venom in Joanna's voice stunned Jane. What was this all about, Jane wondered? Her shin and her feelings bruised, she pondered why Joanna would get so mad.

But shock soon turned to anger. The nerve of the woman, thought Jane as she began to get angry. Where does she get off leaving such a bitter message? She's a maniac, a head case! Business with her brother? What business is it of hers, Jane wondered. Why did that woman ever come to Herring Run? It was true, no one liked her and for good reason. She's a nasty piece of work, a bitch, a mean spirited person and probably a lousy mother. Jane was seething! All of Jane frustrations were coming to a boil.

"How dare that woman call me up and speak to me that way," Jane yelled out loud to her empty house. Jane could feel the steam coming out of her ears as she paced back and forth. "And to top it off my leg is killing me and I'll have an ugly bruise from running to try to get her call". Sitting down to rub her shin, Jane began to laugh at herself. Well, I sure got that out of me, she mused as a few tears rolled down her cheek.

An hour later, refreshed and with a new attitude, Jane left the house to pick up her friends. She had dressed in her favorite green sheath dress with a wheat colored pashmina draped over her shoulders. Jumping into her car she drove down to Marti's who saw her pull up and came right out looking ready for an evening out. Marti had worn her creamy white linen pants with a chocolate brown top that looked great with her red hair. Jane always noticed how Marti knew just how to wear colors that accented her hair so well. Marti had such style! Complimenting each other on how well they cleaned up after a day at the beach, they then headed over to Julia's.

As Jane started to pull into Julia's driveway she saw that

Alex was just backing her mother's car out, and waited for her to exit. Alex waved to the ladies as she turned and headed out toward Hyannis. Julia, wearing a flowered sun dress, was just locking the front door as Jane pulled up the drive and within a few minutes they were all headed the direction that Alex had just taken.

"We just saw Alex drive off as we arrived. Is she on her way to work?" Jane asked.

"Yeah, off to the Fog Runner. Still hasn't gotten her car back so she's using mine. I'm glad you could drive," Julia commented.

"No problem. I thought we were driving her to work tonight."

"She didn't want to bother me at the end of the evening to come get her so she borrowed my car. I must say I'm a bit nervous about her driving home late at night now."

"I know how you feel. I've always been glad when the boys get in. That was scary about the accident she had. I was so glad to hear she was unhurt. Any chance the car will be okay?" Jane wanted to know.

"Looks like it can be saved. Still don't know who ran her off the road. Probably someone who'd had too much to drink. Alex didn't get a good description on the vehicle, just that it was dark in color. Our insurance will pay for it, but that's not the point. Hard to believe someone would run you off the road and then not stop to see if you were okay. Thank goodness Alex didn't run into anything worse than a picket fence."

"We might see her tonight at the Fog Runner, the boys are playing there. First set is around nine, you game to hear them?"

"Well, I'm on my last week in summer school and I should be grading papers, but how can I resist? Count me in," Julia said with a smile. "I haven't seen them play in public, just in our den years ago, so this should be a treat. Alex says they're good."

"Great, then we'll have dinner at the Chatham Fish Market and then head over to the Fog Runner. This should be a great evening," Jane enthused.

Arriving at their destinations about twenty minutes later, they quickly found a parking space in the lot behind the restaurant. Entering the Chatham Fish Market they were seated by the hostess, who had gone to school with Alex and knew Julia from the many sleepovers she had let Alex have through the years. The young lady gave them the primo table by the window and stood and chatted with them for a few minutes once she realized Jane and Marti were the mothers of Ian and Matt. Cape Cod could be a small place, especially when you had outgoing children, Jane thought.

Once their order had been taken and they were sipping their drinks the three ladies began to catch up with each other's lives. Julia was interested in what the boys were doing both on the Cape and back in their respective communities. In turn, Jane and Marti wanted to hear all about Alex's activities and plans. They caught her up on the more mundane news of the village and she gave them the scuttlebutt on some of the year-round residents.

Jane told them that Geoff had called to tell her Arizona license for her staging business had come so once she had her insurance she was in business. They looked at her blankly and both wanted to know what the heck home staging was. She explained that she made houses look their best when they were on the market, by de-cluttering, moving furniture, artwork and other things around in a home to make it stand out and look its best. If the house was empty she would bring furniture into it and "stage" it as though someone lived in it, sometimes all the way down to a fake bagel on a plate!

"I've been working for a very established stager but really wanted to go out on my own. I'll be working with a good friend named Mary. We decided to do the business together. It's been lots of fun working with her to get everything going." Jane told them. "And she doesn't mind that I'm gone for the summer because she likes to take time to go up to Sedona in winter, before I leave for here, and miss some of the worst heat in Tucson. Summer's a slow time with the heat in Tucson anyway so we aren't too worried if we aren't there all the time and I'll cover for her in the winter when she's up in Sedona for all the holidays and school vacations. It's really the perfect set up for both of us. At least we hope so. Time will tell."

Marti and Julia congratulated her and wished her the best of luck. They could tell she was pretty excited about getting back to Tucson to really get into her business in the fall.

It was over appetizers (smoked salmon on endive leaves for Jane, Caesar salads for the other two ladies), when Julia looked from one woman to the other and asked, "Can you two keep a secret? I have some news of my own."

"Of course," they replied in unison, squirming in their seats with anticipation of what Julia was about to divulge. Something about the high school science teacher's messy divorce or the scandal over a town supervisor's false credentials, they wondered?

Putting her fork down and pausing to be sure she had their attention, Julia leaned toward the center of the table and lowered her voice.

"There may be some wedding plans in the future," she stated in almost a whisper with a wide grin on her face.

"Congratulations!" smiled Jane.

"Oh, how grand," Marti exclaimed. "What wonderful news. When is the wedding taking place?"

"Not for a while. Sam's death has put a crimp in our plans

but after we get through this we can set a date and plan the wedding."

Jane thought the idea of the wedding was just what they all needed. The village had been in the doldrums all summer and now would have something to look forward to. She wondered if Alex was marrying the nice young man they had met last summer. Or could it be the boy Alex had been dating the past couple of years at her college? Digging into her salmon and endive with enthusiasm, she felt things were looking up.

"Oh, how grand," Marti exclaimed again. "You and Alex will be so busy picking out a gown, getting a band, finding a caterer. Sounds like fun, to me, mother of two boys that I am."

"Oh, I don't think it will be a big deal. Just a little ceremony at the church with a few of our friends and maybe dinner after," Julia explained. "No fuss."

"Is that because of Sam's death? I remember that Alex always wanted a big church wedding with all the trimmings. Is she a bit disappointed?" Jane inquired as she started to take another bite of her appetizer.

"It's not Alex that's getting married. It's me!" Julia said with a shake of her head and laughter bubbling up out of her throat as she saw the expressions on the two women's faces change dramatically.

Jane swallowed her salmon after almost choking on it and looked up at Julia.

"It's you? You're the one getting married?" Jane exclaimed, stupefied at her denseness and surprised that Julia had kept this under her hat.

"Hush, someone will hear you. What, do you think? I'm too old to remarry? Too old to have sex?" Julia said teasing as she began to laugh so hard at the surprised looks on their faces that tears began to roll down her cheeks.

"Okay, so we have egg on our faces and assumed you were

talking about Alex. Sorry," a contrite Jane said as she started laughing, too.

"Wait a minute, guys," Marti exclaimed as quietly as she could. "You haven't told us who the lucky guy is. And how come we didn't even know you were seeing anyone?"

Julia got a hold of her self and looked around furtively to see if anyone at the other tables was paying attention to them. Satisfied that they would not be overheard she whispered triumphantly, "I'm marrying Mike McGuire."

"WHO?!" Marti asked.

"You know; Mike. Chief of Police Mike McGuire."

"I know who he is, but I didn't even know you two were dating!" Marti exclaimed.

"Oh ... my ... gosh. ... Mike McGuire. That's great, he's such a wonderful guy," Jane said. "But how come we had no idea about this?"

"Well, you know we've all known him for ages. And Mike and I have worked on quite a few projects together involving the school and safety issues in the community. And we both go to St. Stephen's to church and volunteer when needed there. And, well, this past winter it just grew into something more. We thought that once we're married I could quit teaching and get into real estate, something I've always wanted to do but didn't want a chancy income while Alex was growing up. We have such plans! In fact in July we had talked about setting a date and announcing our intentions to all our friends, but then with Sam's death, it just didn't seem appropriate, or wise, me being Sam's ex- wife, Mike being the police chief, working on the case. In fact, he isn't even heading the investigation anymore due to a conflict of interest, though he does pass along anything he hears to those that are, like when you talk to him Jane."

"Well, I'll be a monkey's uncle," Marti exclaimed. "You

could knock me over with a feather. I just don't believe this, but it is absolutely wonderful!"

"It's great," Jane added. "When I think about it, you two are perfect for each other and I wonder why I never thought of it before. Congratulations! You'll have to let us give you a 'girl's night out party' before the big day."

"Thanks, guys. I really appreciate your good wishes. But you can't tell a soul. This is strictly on the QT until the mess of Sam's murder is cleaned up. I wish it could be otherwise but for now we are strictly low key in going out and dating. I feel that even if Mike weren't on the police force that out of respect for Alex and Sam we should wait a bit. I do wish this was over, though. It's been so hard on Alex."

"Even more reasons to find out who did kill Sam," Jane declared. "What do you know about any of this? Do you know anything about Joanna or her brother? They're tops on my list of suspects."

"I know very little. Alex has been around Joanna, of course, so she's the one to ask. She did mention she had never met Joanna's brother before the funeral. Didn't even know Joanna had a brother, but then Alex never did care too much for that woman and I think never tried to find out much about her. Alex mainly was the babysitter for her when Joanna could get her to do it. Free babysitter, I might add. Joanna felt Alex should want to get to know her step-brothers better and imposed whenever she could. Luckily, Sam was fairly understanding about it and didn't let it happen too often, or slipped her a twenty once in awhile when Alex was leaving after an evening with the boys. She liked them, though she thought they were a bit spoiled and ill mannered, especially the younger one, so she tried not to get caught watching them too often. Not easy with a manipulative woman like Joanna trying to pull the strings," Julia pronounced.

"It's too bad about those boys. I think that in some ways they suffer emotional neglect from their mother. I know that Nick thinks that they are a handful at tennis lessons," Marti commented.

"Ian has said that Robin had a really tough time with them in swimming lessons, and an even tougher time with Joanna's interference while the classes were going on," Jane commented.

"Speaking of Robin," Julia piped in. "I think you two ladies have been keeping a secret from me."

Silence fell over the table. The bus boy took away their appetizer plates and the waitress arrived with their entrees. Julia watched her friends, silently, while they looked down at their laps and then took great interest in their newly arrived meals. When the waitress had left Jane began to poke at the lobster on her plate and Marti pushed the lentils around that surrounded her lamb shank. Neither woman spoke.

"It's okay. You can relax. Robin was over this morning. We had a long talk. She told me why she had come to Cape Cod this summer, Herring Run, to be precise. I think it was quite hard for her to come to see me. She was so afraid of hurting my feelings and very afraid of losing Alex's friendship. I had only met her once before when she had come by with the boys to hang out with Alex one evening, but I liked her then and I like her even better now. She was very brave and handled it very well. I have to say I was surprised and then, again, not surprised. Sam had been unfaithful so many times and though I never even thought about him having another child, I can't say that I shouldn't have. After much reflection today, I feel bad for Sam not knowing he had this wonderful daughter. He missed so much, with Alex and Robin. And all this time Alex has had a half sister she didn't know about," Julia mused.

"Does Alex know?" Marti asked gently.

"Yes, after Robin told me and we had talked awhile, I called

Alex to come home for lunch and we all sat around the table and Robin and I told her. I think that she was a bit shocked and I can't say she wasn't a bit disappointed, but she rallied and welcomed Robin to the family. I was very proud of her in that moment. I'm sure it will take awhile for Alex to come to terms with it and the fact that Robin had been here without saying anything, but I think deep down Alex understands and will come out the better for it. And with a sister to boot."

"With you marrying Mike she's also going to be gaining even more siblings," Marti commented.

"Yeah, she thinks that's grand. She's always liked Mike's kids and it seems the feeling is mutual. It's instant family," Julia remarked with a smile. "All these years she yearned for a sibling and now she going getting what she wished for three times over! But you know Alex, eventually she'll be the glue that holds them all together and makes us all one big happy, and unique, family. She even mentioned to Robin that she'd like to meet her mother. Alex never ceases to amaze me."

"She's a great girl. Julia, before you mentioned that Alex wasn't aware that Joanna had a brother. I find that rather odd. You would think that it would have come up at some point, the holidays or birthdays," Jane pondered.

"You would think so, but, as I said, Alex kept her distance from Joanna if she could and anyway, Joanna is an odd duck. But do you think they could have been involved with Sam's murder?" Julia asked.

"Like I said, they're tops on my list. Wouldn't Joanna inherit quite a bit of money from Sam's estate? And maybe she plans to share it with her brother. Not too far fetched an idea, what do you think?" Jane looked from one woman to the other.

"I have no idea what Sam's estate is worth these days, but I do know that he planned to make arrangements in his will leaving most of what he had to Alex. From what little he told me a few years ago he planned to just leave Joanna enough to continue living in their place in Boston, which she would then own, but the rest would go to Alex, including the cottage in Herring Run. That is if Sam didn't change anything recently. Alex isn't aware of this, but she will be as soon as the lawyers settle everything, which shouldn't be too long from now."

"You mean that Joanna will have to move out of Marsh Cottage? I hate to say it but, I can't think of anyone I'd rather see leave Herring Run than Joanna," Marti said.

"Well, keep that under your hat as well, as I don't think Joanna is aware of this either. I'm planning to stay out of it, but I have a feeling the shit will hit the fan when Joanna finds out that Alex can boot her out. I don't think Alex would kick her out, but if Sam did leave her the cottage like he hinted to me that he would, I know that she'll certainly want Joanna out of it after this summer."

"This is going to be interesting. When is the Will to be read?" Asked Marti as she finally began to dig into her lamb shank with relish.

"It's been postponed twice due to scheduling problems, but I think sometime next week is the newest date. We can ask Alex tonight, she'll know, she's the one Sam's firm continues to call. She'll have to go up to Boston for it and she's been too busy with work, plus I think that she keeps putting it off because then Sam's death will be a reality."

"Does she have to sit there with Joanna when they read it?" Marti wanted to know. "That could be very uncomfortable for her. I can't imagine Joanna will be too thrilled."

"I think she said that Joanna had already gone up. But if she has, she hasn't said anything to me or Alex about it."

"If Joanna doesn't like the way the Will reads I'm sure we'll all hear about it, loudly," surmised Jane.

"Enough of sad news, fill me in on the village gossip? How's your tennis?" Julia wanted to know.

Later, at the Fog Runner, all three of the women enjoyed seeing Ian and Matt play. It was a good crowd that evening and Alex barely had time to wave in their direction as she waited on tables on the far side of the room. No more time to talk. Julia was eager to get home to bed after one set, she had her summer school class in the morning, but since it was the last week said she'd catch up with them on the beach next week.

Jane went home feeling happy after such an enjoyable evening. She was amazed that Julia and Mike were getting married and thrilled for them both. They would make a great married couple, both of them being so nice and having so much in common with one another. The news that Sam's will would move Joanna out of the village was met with mixed feelings from Jane. She didn't care much for Joanna but she felt sorry for her in an odd way. Joanna seemed to care so much to fit in and then sabotage that very thing at every turn. But the cottage really should belong to Alex; it was right to keep it in Sam's family.

With a sigh, Jane turned out her light and closed her eyes, vowing to try harder to be nicer to the woman. And she'd start tomorrow by going over for a visit. After all, Joanna was still a top suspect on Jane's list and it was about time Jane explored the possibility.

Thursday, July 29th

AFTER A BRISK walk the next morning with Marti, Jane headed over to Marsh Cottage. As she approached she could see Joanna's two sons, Justin and Jake, on the front porch blowing bubbles and giggling as the bubbles floated into each other and up into the air. They seemed to be having such a great time with such a simple pleasure that Jane smiled from the enjoyment of the moment.

As she walked up the front walk she greeted the boys and asked if their mother was at home. With an answer in the affirmative, Jake bellowed out, "Mom, Mrs. Adams is here to see you," and then he blew a slew of bubbles Jane's way which she proceeded to try and catch and they all laughed as the bubbles broke in her hands.

The door swung open and Joanna stepped out and crossed her arms in front of her.

"Yes?" she inquired, her face stern and forbidding, obviously not inclined to cause a fuss at Jane's disregard for her order to not step foot near Marsh Cottage while standing in front of the boys.

"Good morning," Jane said a little too brightly and immediately tried to tone down her voice. "Joanna," she continued, "I've been given the job of finding a starting price for the silent auction merchandise and I feel totally out of my league. I know you said that you quit the committee but we really need your help. I'm just not good at knowing what things are worth, and no one else has a clue, and I think we, as a committee, really need your expertise in this area," Jane said to Joanna trying not to spread it on too thick or too thin. "You're the one we counted on and now we are at sea as to value. We would hate to lose out on getting a good bid on something just because we aren't smart enough to know how to set a starting price. And well, I've come over to ask you to reconsider and come back and give us a hand in this area," Jane concluded, hoping that she somehow hit the happy medium of flattery.

Taken aback at Jane's almost groveling stature and plea, Joanna seemed not sure what to say. Finally, after checking her nails and clearing her throat she looked at Jane and said, "I'm not sure that I can return. I really didn't feel welcome or needed at the last meeting I went to. Why should I go back for more of the Herring Run cold shoulder?"

Jane felt a bit sorry for Joanna at the moment and said with all sincerity, "I'm sorry if any of us made you feel like that. Sometimes we get a bit old school here but we all like you," fingers crossed behind her back as she knew that she wasn't been entirely truthful. "But it's for a good cause and we really do need your help. Your boys will benefit from the playground, certainly more than mine will at this point. Do it for them, if not for the village," Jane pled her case, ending on a note of sincerity. Not bad, she thought, just a little lie in the middle.

"I doubt that my boys will ever use that playground," Joanna snapped. "But, I'm glad you appreciate the fact that I am the one woman in this village that would have knowledge of pricing all those items," she said with a haughty air. "Well, when is the next meeting? I'm going to Boston tomorrow so that's out. I'm not sure when I can fit it in," she impatiently demanded to know.

"We thought we'd meet for coffee at Millie's on Monday morning." Jane quickly answered. "She's got all the loot stacked around her house and we could all help give you input as to what things are worth. It won't take too long, just a couple of hours. Maybe your brother could watch the boys, that is if he's around on Monday."

"I'll ask and let you know. Come on boys," she said as she ushered her boys into the house turning her back on Jane without so much as a good-bye.

Jane walked away feeling that it had gone well as it could. Joanna was much nicer to her than she had anticipated and maybe had taken the bait. Now she just hoped that Mille wouldn't mind changing the meeting from Friday to Monday so that Jane could wheedle some information out of Joanna without Joanna catching on.

Hanging up from her telephone call to Millie a few minutes later, Jane was grateful that Millie agreed to change the meeting to Monday. She told Jane that she could use all the help they could get as the auction was rapidly approaching with only three more weeks to go and more items coming in each day, so adding Joanna was fine. They agreed to start at 9:30 Monday morning and Jane volunteered to bring something to eat to go with Millie's wonderful Starbuck coffee.

A couple hours later, most of her chores out of the way, Jane headed out for a relaxing few hours at the beach, convinced that all work and no play would definitely make Jane a very dull girl. And Geoff wouldn't want that to happen, she thought as she realized that by this time tomorrow he would be here. A delightful shiver of anticipation ran down her back with the thoughts of three days with Geoff, not nearly enough but they'd certainly make the best use of every minute! Too bad he had promised to go out fishing with Trey but the guys would enjoy it and that gave Jane the opportunity she needed to find out a little bit more about Stuart when she played tennis with him and the Sanders. Big happenings coming up, Jane felt it in her bones.

Friday, July 30th

THE FOLLOWING MORNING, Jane rose early and stripped the sheets to get into the wash before her walk. She could think of nothing else but Geoff's arrival. If traffic wasn't bad he would be in Herring Run in time for an afternoon at the beach. With the washing machine chugging away she ran upstairs, threw on her walking clothes and headed out for a brisk walk with Marti. They kept up a good pace and discussed how they could pry some information out of Stuart the next day as they played tennis. Though they weren't sure exactly how they would start they decided to look for any opening that seemed an opportunity to steer the conversation toward Sam, Joanna or the murder. They also opted not to let Bob in on their plans. If he had any real objections they would already be into it, too late for Bob to stop them.

Returning home, Jane threw the sheets into the dryer and headed up for a shower. She opened a package of her favorite soap, Roger and Gallet Lettuce soap, hoping that Geoff would notice how good she smelled! Humming as she dressed and put on just a touch of makeup, her mind filled with thoughts of her wonderful husband. As each minute crept by Jane grew more excited.

Jane put out fresh towels and made room in the closet for

Geoff's things. Gathering up the dirty towel from her shower and the towels the boys had hung carelessly over a chair here and a door there, she headed back down to the laundry room to start another load. The sheets were dry and smelled springtime fresh thanks to the sheet of softener. She remade the bed with the fresh sheets and looked at her watch. Still a couple hours to go. Good. Just enough time for Jane to go to the store for some fish and the roadside stand for some fresh cut flowers and tomatoes. Heading out for the second time that morning, Jane saw Davis weeding in his yard and called out a hearty hello.

"Off to the fish market. Want anything?" She yelled over the fence that separated their yards.

"I'm fine, but thanks anyway. You look happy this morning," he observed.

"Geoff's arriving today. I can't wait," she replied as she opened the car door and waved a hasty good-bye.

Picking out some great looking pieces of swordfish and some already cooked jumbo shrimp for appetizers, Geoff's and Ian's favorites, at the fish market, Jane paid the fishmonger and headed out the door of the shop and ran smack into Stuart.

"Well, where are you off to in such a hurry?" he asked Jane as he stepped out of her way.

"So, sorry," Jane apologized. "My mind is elsewhere this morning."

"And where is it?" he wanted to know, a smile on his face.

Feeling totally ridiculous, Jane told him that her husband was due to arrive soon and that she was looking forward to seeing him.

"That's nice," Stuart replied. "I've really been missing my wife, but Joanna has been so distraught that I felt I had to stay here until she gets on firm footing again. I hate to leave the boys with her when she is like this, it's hard on all of them, but I should go soon."

"Why don't you have your wife come down for the weekend? It's supposed to be gorgeous and it would take some of the burden off of you." Jane commented, wondering why she was giving this man advice. Interesting though, she hadn't even thought about him being married.

"To tell you the truth, my wife and Joanna really don't get along too well, so it's best that she doesn't come, though I wish she was enjoying it here, it's lovely."

"It is, isn't it? Well, looking forward to our tennis game tomorrow. See you then," Jane said as she backed out the door of the market.

Looking puzzled for a second, Stuart recovered quickly and asked, "What time was that, again?"

"Four. Your memory is worse than mine, must be a senior moment," Jane laughed as she waved good-bye.

Starting her car, Jane reflected on the fact that she couldn't get a handle on Stuart. One minute he was nice and the next he was rude, and he had more senior moments than she did with his memory lapses. Must be a chemical disorder that ran in the family as it was much like Joanna, though thinking about it, Jane couldn't think of many times that Joanna had ever been nice!

Jane drove down Rte. 28 to a roadside stand that sold fresh cut flowers. Today the plastic containers were filled with peonies and dahlias. There were also some plump red ripe tomatoes and corn. Jane got some of each. An elderly Portuguese woman hobbled out of her house to collect the money and to chat with Jane. Jane had heard her story of the family coming over and how they had worked hard to own the land they were now standing on probably fifty times. Jane patiently listened and nodded at appropriate times. She pretended she had never heard the story before and smiled widely.

Jane complimented the old woman on how beautiful her flowers were. She was sure that no one grew any more beautifully than she did. The woman smiled and replied that she knew the secret and it would die with her. She would never let her evil sister-in-law know her secret!

Families, Jane thought. In-laws that were outlaws, she laughed and headed back to get the last minute preparations done before Geoff arrived.

Jane had just finished making the marinade that she would use for the fish that evening when she saw her husband pull up in his rental car. Throwing down her dishtowel, she ran out to greet him, smothering him with kisses and pulling him close to her. He smelled so good, just like Geoff. He was dressed in a suit, having left from a morning meeting to come straight up to the Cape. It always amused Jane to see Geoff in a suit at their beach house; he looked sort of like a fish out of water. She led him inside and told him to throw on his bathing trunks and they could head down to the beach.

It took no urging on her part for Geoff to do just that and soon they were headed down for what Geoff called a few hours of quality beach time. Not having packed a lunch their first stop was at the snack bar where they ran into Ian who had just gotten off tower for his lunch break. Then in walked Trey with a tennis racquet slung over his shoulder, having just finished his morning of lessons. Jane couldn't believe her luck. If she had tried to plan for all of them to have lunch together it never would have happened and now here they all were. Excellent!

As they ate lunch Geoff was able to catch up with what the boys had been up to and what their plans were for the weekend. Trey told him that they would be leaving around five-thirty in the morning to go fishing, causing Geoff to groan, not only at the early hour but how the early hour would feel when he still felt he was on Tucson time. Trey just laughed and said, "don't worry, I'll get you out of bed just like you do for me on school mornings. Anyway, you're so used to doctor's early hours you'll survive. You can nap while the fish don't bite on your line," he laughed.

Later, sitting in their beach chairs, watching the seagulls steal someone's lunch and the young girls hang out under their son's chair on tower, they joined hands and just enjoyed the moment. A beautiful day, in each other's company and the boys close by made for a perfect summer day. Jane felt she was the happiest woman in the world at that moment wanting it to never end.

"Well, look at the honeymooners," Marti said as she set her beach chair up next to Jane's.

"You two sure look blissful. Welcome back, Geoff. When did you pull in?"

Geoff rose from his chair to give Marti a quick peck on the cheek and a hug. He was so glad to be back with family and friends and it showed. Tension was already draining from his body and he was looking quite content, Jane thought.

"Just a couple hours ago. No traffic to speak of, sailed right over the Sagamore, for a change."

"Wish Bob could be that lucky. He won't be able to head down for at least a few more hours and by then the line backing up from the bridge on Rte. 3 will stretch for miles," Marti said ruefully. "I don't expect him until at least nine or ten."

"Marti, why don't you join us for dinner, then. I have enough swordfish and we could rustle up some burgers for the boys," Jane invited.

"Thanks, but no thanks, I have my leftovers waiting and the boys have other plans. But how would you guys like to go out to dinner tomorrow night? I know Matt and Ian are working and Nick and Trey will certainly have plans. I've been dying to go out to try a restaurant in Sandwich so I already made reservations for four at eight in hopes that you would say yes."

"Sounds good to me. You should be home from fishing way before then, right Geoff?"

"I'm up for anything," Geoff said contentedly, "except work, so count me in, we'll just have to freeze all the fish I catch." The ladies laughed, as Geoff was notorious for coming home via the fish market every time he went out fishing.

"So what is this new place we are going to try?" Jane wanted to know.

"It's a restaurant called the Abbey, and it's located in an old, renovated church. It's gotten good reviews and I hear it even has a good wine list, something for you to appreciate, Geoff!"

"Sounds lovely. Shall we pick you up around seven thirty, then?"

"That's great, or we can drive. We'll talk about it after tennis tomorrow when Bob is there."

"Tennis? Will I be back in time for that?" A perplexed Geoff wanted to know.

"You're not playing, love, we have Stuart, Joanna's brother, for a fourth."

"Wait a minute, Jane, you're not meddling into something you shouldn't be, are you? Come clean," Geoff demanded.

"Just a friendly tennis match. You were going fishing and Marti asked me to play. I had to get a fourth," Jane answered, she hoped with an innocent voice.

"You know how Bob likes to get in as much tennis as he can when he's here, Geoff. I asked before I knew you were going fishing. Don't worry about Jane," Marti piped in. "We'll keep her on the straight and narrow."

As they got ready for bed that night Geoff again mentioned

that he hoped that Jane was not sticking her nose where it didn't belong. Jane's answer was to cuddle up to him, and stick her nose into his neck where she began to plant little kisses, soon finding her way to his lips. Nothing else was said about Jane's plans at tennis the next day.

Saturday, July 31st

B Y THE TIME Jane awoke the next morning, Geoff was long gone, off fishing with Trey. She hadn't even heard him get up and for a minute wondered if she had only dreamed that he had arrived the day before. That dream ended quickly with the reality of his damp towel draped on the bathroom doorknob and the realization that the toilet seat was up. He's forgotten he's living with a woman now after his time alone in Tucson, she thought as she lowered the seat so that she could use it without falling in.

She skipped her walk that morning to spend time in the garden weeding while the soil was still a bit moist from the morning dew. As she clipped back some lavender and put it a basket she felt a shadow come over her. Looking up, she saw that Davis was watching her with a grin on his face.

"Finally biting the bullet and getting out here to weed, I see. I was just about to report you to the horticultural society for cruelty to day lilies," he said, trying to hold back a laugh.

"Okay, so I'm not the best gardener, but the lavender sure looks great this year. Here have a little to put in your house," she said as she sniffed and then handed Davis a little bouquet of the fragrant plant.

"Many thanks, my dear. Is that Geoff's rental car I saw

parked here last night? He isn't already gone, is he?" Davis inquired.

"Just up at the crack of dawn with Trey to go fishing."

"Oh, does that mean I'll have fish for dinner tonight?"

Jane laughed. "Only if you go to the fish market to buy it. You know how Geoff's fishing luck is. I'm surprised anyone even asks him to go anymore. No one seems to have any luck when he's out with them."

"Speaking of luck, anything new on Sam's murder? I haven't seen anything in the papers about it and I really haven't kept up on the village gossip lately, been a bit busy these days."

"Well, they still don't know who murdered Sam and I think a lot of people have sort of forgotten about it, or at least they have gone on with their lives. Not a lot anyone can do about it," Jane commented casually.

"Knowing you, I'll bet you haven't given up on it, Jane. You may not like to garden, but a conundrum like this is right up your alley. So, what do you know and what's your next move?"

Jane tried to look deeply offended as she got to her feet and gathered the bag of weeds she had pulled with unwavering determination. "I have nothing planned, Davis. I still have my list of suspects but I haven't made any progress, plus Geoff really doesn't want me involved. So, you see, it's not in my hands."

Davis laughed, thanked Jane for the lavender and said he'd come by later to say hello to Geoff. Jane hurried into the house, threw a load of Geoff's laundry into the washer and decided to get to the beach early this Saturday so she could get there before the weekend people staked out her spot on the beach as their own.

Around three-thirty she and the Sanders dragged themselves back up to the village for their tennis match. It had been a gorgeous day at the beach and hard to think about leaving. Jane still didn't know what she would say to Stuart, how to get information out of him and decided that the best thing to do would see what openings he gave to her. Marti hadn't come up with anything either and they had not dared to discuss it at the beach for fear that the unsuspecting Bob would squash their plans.

Jane arrived at the courts first and proceeded to open a new can of balls. Just as she pulled up on the ring and heard the lovely swoosh sound of fresh tennis balls she heard, "Sorry I didn't get here a bit earlier; I also brought a new can of balls. Everyone has been so kind to supply them each time I play here that I felt it was my turn to bring a can. Let me give you these," he said handing her the can of Dunlop balls he had brought, "so you can use them in your next match."

Turning around to see Stuart standing there handing a can of balls to her, Jane was caught off guard. Accepting the balls from him and mumbling her thanks, she was again amazed at how nice he could be, so unlike the man she had played with last time he was her partner. She also noticed that he was again wearing that lovely lemon-lime cologne. She really should ask him who makes it; she would love to smell it on Geoff.

"That's not necessary, but thank you. I was down to my last can of balls, so this will come in handy. Marti and Bob should be here any minute. Hopefully, I'll be a good enough partner for you, Stuart."

"Oh, not to worry. I'm not the best and anyway, this is just for fun, isn't it?" he asked with a smile. Jane tried to hide her surprise at this change in Stuart and was relieved when just then Marti and Bob appeared on the court issuing greetings and apologies for being slightly late and ready to get their warm up started.

They all played a fun, competitive two sets and were trying to decide if there was time for a third when Stuart said he only had a little time left until he had to leave and why didn't he buy everyone something cold to drink at the snack bar. As it was an agreeable idea he and Bob went in to get the drinks as Marti and Jane sat down at one of the umbrella tables that flanked the courts. As they waited for the men to reappear the two women put their heads close together to try to figure out how to approach Stuart on the subject of Sam's murder. They needn't have bothered because once they were all seated with their ice teas Stuart brought the subject up himself.

"I've really enjoyed being here in Herring Run, with the beach and the tennis. Such a beautiful community to spend the summer in. I wish I'd taken time to come when Sam was still alive. I don't know if you know yet but Joanna found out that Sam didn't leave her the cottage. He left it to his daughter, Alex. Seems the right thing to do, to keep it in the family. This will be the last summer Joanna will be here, so I guess I've missed my opportunities. It has been lovely though and I appreciate the invitations to play tennis."

"Well, this certainly was fun today," Jane commented, not wanting to remember the other match she had had with Stuart as her opponent. He seemed to have turned over a new leaf, thank goodness. Maybe the stress of staying with a distraught Joanna and dealing with Sam's murder had abated somewhat and he felt more comfortable here, she thought. "I'm sure that you've been a godsend for Joanna. It's been a rough summer for her. What do you do that you have so much free time?"

"At the moment I'm unemployed. I start a new job, in the fall, as a professor of history at a small mid western college. Usually I find something to keep me busy over the summer, often traveling to Europe where I visit historical sites that interest me most at the time, but this year because I knew I was moving I only planned to pack up and organize myself. In fact, I'll have to be leaving soon to do just that, as I'm due in my new position the first week of September. Luckily, my wife has been picking up a bit of the slack, but my book, my papers, well, she has no idea what to do with those."

"Joanna will miss you, I'm sure. How is she doing? And have they made any headway to finding out who murdered Sam? Does Joanna think it's anyone she might know," Jane asked trying to get to the subject that brought her to the courts today in the first place.

Stuart face darkened and he rose as he said, "I don't think Joanna has any idea who could have done this and I really must go now. Thanks again for the tennis." And with that he walked off in a decidedly different mood.

"Now you've done it, Jane," Bob said. "You've upset him."

"It's not that I meant to, I just wanted to know what was going on with the murder investigation from his angle. Did you hear what he said about Marsh Cottage? I guess Julia was right when she said that Alex was probably going to inherit it, just sooner than everyone had planned on."

"You two knew that?" Bob asked.

"It was mentioned the other night at our dinner with Julia, Bob," said Marti.

"How come you didn't tell me then?"

"Sorry, love; Julia asked us not to say anything until it was official and the parties concerned knew. Guess Joanna knows now. I wonder if Alex has heard?"

"If she hasn't heard from the lawyers, I bet that she has heard from Joanna. Joanna won't be a happy camper with this turn of events," Jane speculated. "Well, I'm out of here. If I don't hurry and jump into the shower I'll never be ready to leave by seven-thirty."

When Jane walked in the door she could hear the pipes humming with the sound of a shower running somewhere in the house. Entering her room she quickly saw a pile of dirty, stinky clothes on the floor and heard the shower in their bathroom accompanied by the sound of Geoff's singing. Quickly discarding her own clothes, Jane sneaked into the bathroom and stole into the shower with him. Pressing her naked front to his naked back was not only a thrill for Jane but a bit of a shock to Geoff. So absorbed in his aria he failed to notice her until skin touched skin and then he almost jumped out of his. He recovered quickly though and the shower took a little longer than Jane thought it would, with all the soaping up they had to do for each other, not that Jane minded one bit.

*   *   *

A while later, the Adams and the Sanders were peacefully driving down the beautiful, historic Route 6A toward Sandwich. Everyone was eager to catch up on Geoff's life in Tucson. How was the weather? Hot. Had he been playing any tennis? A bit? How was work going? Not too badly. How many fish did he catch today? Ask him no questions, he'd tell no lies, he told them.

"Hey, I heard that the lamb shank at this restaurant is supposed to be wonderful," Jane informed her friend, knowing it was Marti's favorite. "And I was told their wine list is awesome. We should be in for a delightful evening."

"Good, I could eat a horse," Geoff said. "Haven't eaten all day."

"Wait a minute, didn't you guys take that lunch I had packed for you in the 'frig?" Jane asked.

"Yep, and Trey ate his and he ate mine. I was feeling a little green out there, it was a bit rough. But I'm fine now and really ready for a good meal."

"Some seaman you are, Geoff," Jane commented on her desert guy, as she squeezed his arm, so happy to have him here on the east coast, if only for the weekend.

Entering the Abbey Restaurant they were cordially greeted by a hostess and told that their table would be ready soon. They were invited to wait at the bar, which is where they could have a drink before dinner. Walking through the restaurant they marveled at how the old church had so tastefully been turned into a first class restaurant. The atmosphere was elegant, quiet and subdued. They sat at the bar, each ordered a drink and listened as a gentleman played the piano. Chatting amiably it was no time before they were seated at a quiet table for four in one of the front rooms.

After ordering (lamb shank for Bob, baked sea bass for Geoff and the ladies both opting for the irresistible sounding duck confit on lentils and a good Chilean wine for all), the four of them sat back and relaxed. They commented on how lucky they were to be able to be doing exactly what they were doing with whom they were doing it with. Despite some bad weather and often overcrowded roads, they wouldn't trade being here for anywhere in the world each summer. It was a great place to raise their kids and they only wished they could spend a lot more time on this little arm that jutted out into the Atlantic Ocean.

The wine arrived and after tasting it Geoff pronounced it worthy. Glasses were filled all around and a toast made to each other and to many more summers. They ate the freshest looking salads Jane had ever seen. Hers, of arugula, radicchio and endive was to die for with its light touch of lemon dressing and topped with goat cheese and pine nuts. The others had opted for sliced tomatoes with fresh mozzarella cheese and basil that looked wonderful, too, with its touch of olive oil and an aged balsamic vinegar. Talk ceased as they savored their food and only an occasional satisfied sigh was heard for a few minutes.

Their entrees did not disappoint either. The duck sitting on a bed of lentils was tender and flavorful. Geoff said his fish was so fresh that he wondered if the boat fishing next theirs had caught it for that boat seemed to just reel in the fish all day. Bob's lamb shank was finished clear to the bone with all the juices sopped up by the crusty French bread that was on the table. Not a complaint to be heard at the table.

Sitting over their various coffees, after dinner discussion was already under way about when they would have a chance to return to the restaurant for a repeat performance. Geoff wasn't sure if he would be out again until he took two weeks toward the end of August but that they should try to eat there again when he returned.

"You'll be back in time for the fund raiser, won't you, Geoff?" Jane asked. "I told you the date and bought you a ticket. Please, don't tell me you forgot."

"No, I'm on top of it. I return the day before if all goes according to plan. Got any good auction items we should bid on?"

"I haven't seen them yet. Millie has them at her house and Marti and I are going over, with Joanna, on Monday morning to price them so I'll get a good look then."

Bob looked up surprised. "You two are going to be working with Joanna on the pricing? Please say it isn't so. What madness drove you to do such a foolhardy thing?"

"It's just the committee that was formed at the beginning of the summer, Bob," Marti informed him. "Don't get into a fit about it."

"Look, she wasn't easy to get along with before, but now that she knows she's losing Marsh Cottage, she'll be impossible. Don't you think you should gracefully bow out?"

"We can't bow out, where would that leave Millie? Besides it will give us a chance to see what Joanna knows," Marti told him.

"Wait a minute," Geoff implored. "What do you mean, Joanna's losing Marsh Cottage? Why is she losing it and to whom?"

"Oh, that's right, you don't know. I guess with the shower and getting dressed I forgot to say anything," Jane said coyly, looking lovingly into Geoff's blue eyes. "Anyway, Stuart told us that Sam's Will stipulated that Alex inherit the cottage. Guess Sam wanted to keep it in the bloodline part of the family. So, I guess, Joanna is out after this summer, though that's up to Alex, of course. Weird that after all the trouble she's caused the village that I feel sort of sorry for her that things turned out the way they did," Jane mused. "Of course, not that sorry. She's still conceited, delusional and maybe even evil. The most unwelcome person we've ever had in the village by a long shot."

"Wow, I never even thought about that," Geoff disregarding his wife's commentary on Joanna behavioral quirks, knowing too well how true they were. "I guess it makes sense that Sam leave the cottage to his daughter, it's been in his family for a few generations. It seems to me I heard his great-grandfather built it."

"Too much time spent where the javelinas roam, my love," Jane chuckled. "Around these parts Sam's murder and everything related to it are about all we speculate on and talk about. You need to get with the program here."

"Jane, try to stay out of it, please. I know that you can't always help yourself when it comes to a problem to solve, but this is murder, not just some minor hitch, and you shouldn't get mixed up in it," Geoff warned his wife, with Bob echoing the warning to Marti.

Giving Jane a quick smile, Marti turned to Geoff and said, "Don't worry about Jane, I'll keep a leash on her." At that moment the waiter returned with their credit cards and they rose to leave. Geoff helped Jane out of her chair and then put his hand on her elbow steering her close to him and he saying quietly in her ear, "I mean it, Jane, don't get mixed up in murder. It's not a game. Somewhere out there is the person who killed Sam and whoever it is doesn't want to be caught. Keep your nose out of it." Releasing her elbow, he took her arm and followed Bob and Marti out of the restaurant into the soft night air.

Monday, August 2nd

TOO SOON, GEOFF was on his way back to Arizona, with Bob back to Boston. It was Monday morning and fresh from her walk, Jane walked down the path to Millie's house carrying the cinnamon nut coffee cake she had made the night before, something to keep their energy up throughout the ordeal of volunteer work. Knocking on Millie's door, Jane could smell the rich aroma of the coffee wafting through the screen as she waited.

"Come on in," Jane heard Millie yell from the back porch. Jane let herself in and followed the scent right to its source, where Millie's coffee maker sat amid a jumble of castoffs, lots of junk and some interesting pieces of people's lives that they had been willing to part with in the name of charity.

"Good morning, Jane. Look at this mess! Can you believe what some people think we should be able to get a good price for?" Millie moaned as she held up a platter with a chunk missing from one end. "And look at this," she ordered, holding up an old, stained sundress. "We said 'no clothes, items in good condition only' and this is an example of about half of what was left in boxes at my door. I think people just didn't want to pay to have some of this junk hauled away! What am I going to do with that table over there, missing one leg?

A note was left saying 'just needs a leg, I'm sure you can find someone to make one and attach it'. Too bad I can't recognize the writing or I could have sent it back with a note saying 'send it back once it's fixed'. I'm going to have to get a dump run together and that will definitely eat into our profits. Geez, what cheapskates."

Jane stood holding her cake on its paper plate and trying to hold in her laughter. Every auction they did was like this and every time they had one Millie had the same valid complaint. Maybe it was time they thought of a new way to raise money!

"Here let me take that, Jane. Ooo, that looks great. I'll just get a knife and some plates. Help yourself to some coffee, the mugs, and spoons, napkins, cream and sugar are over there on that table, on the other side of that pile of books. I can't wait to get this junk out of here," she commented as she walked into the kitchen and came back with a knife and small plates.

"It doesn't all look bad, Mill," Jane said as she sorted through some odd pieces of china and mismatched wine glasses.

"No, actually, there's some really good stuff, too. Mrs. Weatherby called me to come over to get a whole set of china. Place settings for twelve. She said she no longer entertained and none of her kids wanted it. It's very sweet, white with blue flowers around the edges. She said that it wasn't her good china, just an extra set she picked up over the years."

"Lucky her," commented Jane. "I'm still waiting to complete a first set. Always seems to be something else to buy, like braces, hot water heaters, you know. Maybe I'll bid on that myself."

Just then Marti walked in, paper and pen in hand, stickers also. "Private Sanders, reporting for pricing duty," she said with a salute and a laugh. "Boy, what a mess. How can you stand to live with this all over your porch?"

"EEEE, don't start me on that. It's driving me crazy. I need us to not only price, but to sort and bag up what we don't want in the auction. Some stuff will be donated to Goodwill and the rest to find its way to the dump. We'll put throw out stuff by the door and donation things next to the wall. The rest we'll just price. Here are some heavy-duty trash bags. Why don't we get started with the sorting? We can price as we go."

"Oh, I see I've made it just in time," Joanna said as she stood at the entrance to the porch.

The ladies looked up from the pile of items they had been examining to Joanna, who was dressed as if she was going to price items in Neiman Marcus for a gala charity ball. In one hand she dangled her sunglasses from her perfectly manicured finger and in the other, lo and behold, she carried a cut glass plate of assorted croissants that looked delicious.

"Oh, lovely," Millie cooed, eyeing the goodies as she took the plate from Joanna "Where did you get such gorgeous looking croissants?"

"Stuart went up to Boston yesterday and brought them back early this morning with expressed instructions for me to bring over to you. I told them probably no one would want all those calories but he insisted. . . ." She trailed off, looking disdainfully at the offending, fat-filled but beautiful pastries.

"How nice of your brother. Is that an almond one?" Jane asked eyeing the plate. "Anyone want to split one with me, or will I have to eat the whole thing myself?"

"All yours, I'm for the chocolate one," Marti answered, getting a napkin and helping herself to one even before Millie had a chance to get the plate to the table.

Contentedly munching on the unexpected treat and sipping their coffee, any work was temporarily postponed until every last crumb on each one's plate was devoured. Jane figured her coffee cake would freeze well anyway, and fresh from this morning croissants didn't get delivered every day in Herring

Run, calories be dammed. Meanwhile, Joanna was poking around the different piles that Millie had set up by category, as best she could.

"Are you ladies ready to work? I don't have all day and Jane said you needed my help, so could we get going?" She held up a piece of unidentifiable clothing with the tips of two fingers and scrunched up her nose. "You can't be serious? I hope this isn't representative of what you want me to price. This is ghastly!"

"Actually, Joanna," Millie said, quickly taking the offending item and placing it in one of the throw out bags. "We have yet to sort the good from the bad. Thought we'd do it all at once. Maybe Marti and I could sort and since you and Jane know a bit about pricing you two can put opening prices on each item. Remember to mark them either for the live or the silent auction."

"Okay by me," Jane said as Joanna shrugged.

Work went pretty fast. The sorting wasn't too hard and most of the items were for the silent auction with very low starting bids. Joanna and Jane worked quite well together. They priced an old chess set, a cute teapot, several serving platters of no great value but pretty anyway and other small items that people felt they could part with. Joanna would give Jane a price and Jane would write it on a sticker and then put the sticker on the item. Millie checked all the electrical donations with the help of Marti and were surprised that over half of them worked. She commented that she thought she'd try to bid on the waffle iron as both of her kids loved waffles and they didn't have one in their summerhouse.

Jane came across a beautiful little blue and white dish that she didn't have a clue how to price. Passing it over to Joanna she said, "This might be something you would know. I think it's Wedgewood so it should be worth something."

Joanna taking the dish from her turned it over in her hand to look at the underside to assure of its authenticity.

"It's not an antique. I really can't guess its value. I'll see what I can find on the Internet and get back to you about it. It's so pretty though that I think if we start the opening bid at about two thirds of whatever I find it might go for on-line then it might go for value or a bit more. Probably not terribly valuable but it really is a pretty little piece. If I was staying I might even bid on it myself," Joanna said wistfully.

"I heard about the Marsh Cottage, Joanna," Jane said softy so the others wouldn't hear. "I am sorry."

Joanna looked up in surprise, then her face began to contort in rage, "You aren't sorry, I'm sure that you of all people are glad that I didn't get the cottage. All three of you are probably planning to celebrate. Did you pop open the champagne yet? You know I never fit in here so it's just as well; this is a stupid little village anyway. I would much rather be at a luxury resort than have to hang out in damp, old Cape Cod in an old decrepit, moldy cottage!" And with this Joanna burst into tears, hiding her face in her hands.

Millie and Marti looked up in shock. Jane gave them a warning look and shook her head.

"Joanna, I am sorry and I'm sorry you feel that way. We didn't mean to make you feel like you didn't belong. It's just partly because we felt you didn't like us. We're glad you're here today helping us," Jane finished lamely, not really knowing what to say.

Joanna looked up, her face red, her eyes swollen with black mascara streaming down her cheeks. "I know that all of you thought that I ruined Julia's marriage. I know that you took her side. But I want you to know that Sam and Julia's marriage was over before I came in the picture. They just hadn't done anything about it yet. I loved Sam. He really cared for me when we first met. I was so excited to marry him but he stopped loving me just as he had with Julia. I didn't have him anymore and I never fit in here so I didn't have any of you either. And now Sam is dead and I have nothing left." And with that Joanna ran the house in tears, the screen door banging shut behind her.

"Oh, boy, I didn't handle that well at all, did I?" Jane commented as she watched the retreating back of Joanna running down the midway path toward Marsh Cottage. "And actually, we were all doing quite well this morning, getting along, working together. I have to admit, Joanna really does seem to know her stuff when it came to pricing a lot of these items. Anyway, I feel really horrible. I shouldn't have said anything. Maybe I better go apologize for making her feel so bad." Jane said as she turned to go. "She probably won't listen to me but I should at least make the effort. I'll try to be back before you guys are finished here."

And with that Jane left Millie's and strode off toward Marsh Cottage wondering what she could say to make amends that wouldn't sound contrived. Knocking on the door with trepidation Jane steeled herself for another one of Joanna's onslaughts. The door opened and Jane looked down to see Justin holding the door with one hand and the thumb of the other hand in his mouth. Stepping in she said, "Hello, Justin. Remember me, Mrs. Adams? I'm Ian and Trey's mother. Is your mother home?"

Justin let her in and then let the screen door slam and Jane walked in the direction that he was now pointing. She could hear sniffling coming from the den at the rear of the house and headed back toward the sound. Joanna lay face down on the sofa and was sobbing. Jane sat on the coffee table by her and put her hand on Joanna's back, giving it a slight rub.

"I'm sorry, Joanna. Maybe we haven't been fair. I'm not sure

why or when it all came about. But I want you to know that I
take no pleasure in you losing the cottage or your husband. It's
got to have been a very hard summer for you."

Sitting up and blowing her nose in a crumpled tissue that
she had been clutching in her hand Joanna's sobbing subsided
and she took a long look at Jane.

"I owe you an apology, too. I don't know what I was thinking
when I accused Ian and Matt of Sam's murder. I just needed
to lash out at someone and they were the ones that were there
that night and the next morning, standing with Sam's body. I
just got crazy and thought that they had done it. I'm sorry that
I put you through that," she said, beginning to well up again,
in tears. "I've just never felt I belonged here and I guess part of
me wanted to lash out at anyone I could."

"Well, it's water under the bridge for both of us then, isn't
it?" Jane said with a sad smile. "Look, I hope you're planning
to come to the fund raiser and if you're up to it we really could
use your help with the pricing, so if you want to return, well,
we'll be there for at least a couple more hours."

Jane rose to leave. "You know, Joanna, it's too bad that we
can't all start over again. But at least let's make the best of what
we have now. Call me if you need an ear, or a shoulder for that
matter."

Walking back to Millie's, Jane was surprised that she no
longer felt the tremendous loathing for Joanna anymore.
What she felt now was pity for the woman who tried so hard
to look like she had so much, for whom objects and status had
been her prime objectives. Joanna looked broken. But, Jane
had a feeling that this glimpse of Joanna was just a small crack
in the usual brittle façade that Joanna generally put on for the
world. By tomorrow, no most likely by later this afternoon,
she would be back to her old tricks. Most people can't change
just as tigers can't change their stripes, she thought.

Millie and Marti looked up expectantly at Jane as she returned to the scene of the crime. They were bagging up the items to go to Goodwill and had yet to bag up the junk for the dump. Still knee deep in other people's treasures, Jane thought to herself, with a laugh.

"You're back in one piece, I see," commented Marti. "I thought we'd have to call out the Mounties to rescue you."

"No, here in one piece, feeling kind of rotten, though. Maybe Joanna isn't as bad as we thought."

Millie looked at Jane incredulously. "She just let her mask slip for a moment. She is human, but basically she's a bitch and we all know it, so get over it and let's finish this job off. Oh, yech," Millie said as she threw a dog-chewed Frisbee into a trash bag, using the tips of her fingers. "Who donated that?"

"Don't start feeling sorry for that woman, Jane," admonished Marti. "She really did a number on us with no holds barred. She made us miserable and what's worse she made our children miserable. No one attacks my son and then gets my pity!" she declared.

"You're right, I'm sure. In fact, my thoughts were headed in that direction as I walked back here but I still can't help feeling sorry for her because there must be a reason that she is the way she is. But, I guess, there's not much I can do about it. She did apologize for accusing Matt and Ian, so that's something. Oh, well, let's get on with the work so we can get down to the beach before the sun sets," and with that Jane got back to work.

Two hours later most of the sorting, pricing and bagging were done and Millie's porch had some degree of order restored to it. While Marti filled out auction forms, Jane helped Millie clean up the leftovers from their snack. Picking up the plates she realized that Joanna had left her glass platter behind when she fled so abruptly. On it sat three, now not so fresh, croissants from the original half dozen. Jane thought it an extremely nice gesture of Joanna's brother Stuart to bother to pick up fresh croissants this morning on his way out of town. Just remembering that they were working on the auction was amazing enough, but to buy them such a treat was above and beyond. Shaking her head she felt she just couldn't figure that family out. Most of the time Joanna was a conniving, nasty bitch, but Jane had seen another side of her today and a few times before with her children. Her brother, Stuart, on the other hand flip-flopped from being very nice to being very rude. One never knew what one would get with those two so she guessed it paid to be on one's guard when dealing with them, she thought with a sigh.

"So, what do we do with the rest of these and the plate?" Jane asked as she held the croissant platter aloft for Millie and Marti to see.

"I'd love to take the croissants, if no one else wants them," Marti commented. "They'll perk right up if I nuke them for ten seconds tomorrow morning and I'm having the our minister over on parish business."

"Fine by me," Jane replied. "I'm not sure I'm still going to fit in the dress I thought I'd wear to the Fund Raiser so I don't need them, of course, want is a different thing, they were delicious. By the way, Millie, keep the coffee cake. You can throw it in the freezer if you want to save for later. It freezes well and, again, I don't need it on my hips and Trey won't eat anything with nuts in it so . . ."

"Thanks, it'll come in handy when I have the relatives over for brunch in two weeks. And I'll volunteer to return Joanna's platter. I have less history with her than you two and she hasn't picked on me for a while, so I can take it. In fact she's probably been waiting for the opportunity. I know I'll hear plenty about the auction items even though I'm not responsible for what people dropped off," Millie said with a roll of her eyes.

"Okay, then if we're done for the day I'm going to head for the beach," Marti said as she rose to go.

"I'm right behind you. How about we skip packing our lunches and meet at the snack bar in half an hour. I could go for one of their hot dogs," Millie salivated.

"I'm on. Make sure I order nothing but a salad sans dressing, though. See you in half an hour, then," Jane said as she followed Marti out the door. "And, Millie, thanks for having this at your house. You've been great. I don't think I could handle this mess on a daily basis, but you've kept it incredibly organized. I can't even do that with my own stuff, let alone half the village's," Jane said as she went out the door.

Thursday, August 5th

A FEW DAYS LATER, Jane was at the grocery store filling up her basket when she ran into Julia, who was dressed in a pair of khaki shorts and a tee shirt, looking the picture of a woman on vacation. Both ladies chatted as they waited for their turn to be served at the deli.

"So, are you done with the summer school?" Jane asked her friend.

"Yes, thank goodness! And I'm caught up on laundry, bill paying and general housework, so I just may make an appearance at the beach today," Julia commented happily.

"About time!" Jane pronounced cheerfully.

"Hey, Alex finally made it up to Boston regarding the will. It's as we thought, Sam left the house to her. She's overjoyed on one hand to get it back, she felt so displaced when Sam brought Joanna and her boys to stay there each summer. In fact, she hasn't spent a night there since Sam remarried. You know, she actually avoided driving by it whenever possible. On the other hand, she feels a bit strange about kicking Joanna out. But as the legal documents will take some time, she probably won't take possession of it until at least the fall and by that time Joanna will be gone which will make it easier for everyone. I just hope that Joanna doesn't abscond with any of the family pieces in there, the will states 'and all contents', but I don't think there's much we can do about it if Joanna gets light-fingered about it," Julia rationalized.

"I had a bit of a set to with Joanna the other day while working on the auction items for the fund raiser. She took something I said the wrong way and flew off the handle in a rage and then ran out of Millie's house in tears. I went after her to apologize and do you know she was actually acting like a normal human being. No posturing, no airs, no 'richer than thou' stuff that she usually pulls. I think the stress of everything that's happened this summer is getting to her. And a lot has happened to her, " Jane observed.

"She can't be all bad. Honestly, Sam could really be a jerk sometimes, a womanizer and a macho prick. But he wouldn't have married her had she not had some redeeming qualities about her. Lord knows what they are but there must be some," Julia said. "Listen, they're calling my number. I'm going to get my cold cuts, run home to make some sandwiches and then get down to the beach. Alex is coming, too. I'll see you there," Julia said as she moved off to show the deli man the black forest ham she wanted a quarter of a pound of as well as some slices of cheddar cheese.

Jane finished her shopping and stood in one of the many long lines. She should know better than to shop just before lunch, she thought. Idly scanning a *Bon Appetit* magazine from the rack as she waited, she had just found an interesting article about fish marinades for grilling when she felt a cart bump her heels from behind. Ignoring it as just a slight misjudgment of someone in the overcrowded store, Jane continued to read the section on the Cal/Asian influence on grilling. Again, she felt the carriage hit her from behind, this time with some force, enough to hurt. Turning around to see what the problem could be, Jane came face to face with Celia and her two children.

Loudly Celia berated her children for causing the shopping cart to run into "MRS. ADAMS," and to "BE MORE CAREFUL NEXT TIME! NOW SAY YOU'RE SORRY." Both kids colored a deep shade of red mumbled incoherently and looked quickly away while their mother stared brazenly at Jane.

"Oh, hello, Celia," Jane said in a calm voice, knowing fully well that the kids had nothing to do with her contact with Celia's carriage. Willing herself not to turn her cart around and bash it into Celia's (*Be good, be good*, she told herself), Jane smiled; she could just see the Cape Cod Register headlines now: "Summer Residents in Shopping Cart Battle."

"How are you today, Celia?" Jane asked, in a cloying voice.

Celia, not sure if Jane was truly being nice, straightened her back and said huffily, "I'm just fine, a lot better than my poor friend Joanna. You must be quite pleased that she won't be with us in the village much longer. Happy that you won?"

Jane couldn't believe it. Not this again. First Joanna and now Celia. Would they never leave her alone? She never really cared that much where Joanna spent her summers before she and Celia had accused her son of murder, now she was the guilty of heavens knew what. Unbelievable!

"It's none of my business," she replied to the little toady woman, and turned her attention once more to the magazine.

"Well, you seem to have made it your business, though, haven't you?" Celia sneered.

Jane turned to stare at Celia and said quietly, yet firmly, "No, actually, you've tried to make it my business and frankly, I'm sick of it. Enough has been said." Jane could feel heat rise into her face as she turned around and attempted to ignore this awful woman. Jane really hated confrontation.

"Well, I see you sure were getting chummy with her brother at the tennis courts last weekend. What was that all about?" Celia goaded her on with emphasis on the word brother.

"Tennis," came Jane's two-syllable reply as she scanned the other check out lines in thoughts of moving over to one.

"I don't think her husband was very fond of you, though, especially your tennis game" Celia sneered.

Jane did not know where this conversation was coming from or where it was trying to go but she did know that she was headed into the adjoining checkout lane that had just opened up. Swinging her carriage rapidly back, she turned her carriage into the next lane, whacking Celia's in the process, and began unloading her groceries.

"Hey, watch it," Celia thundered. "And how dare you butt in front of that line," she said with righteous indignation.

"Yes, how dare me and frankly, how dare you, Celia," Jane said, her face burning, as she quickly moved ahead and dealt with the process of checking out her groceries. Leaving an odious Celia behind with Celia's face turning as pink as the shocking pink, too-tight Lily Pulitzer dress Celia had somehow managed to squeeze her tubby, little toady body into.

Driving home, Jane realized that she was more upset than she had thought. Her hands were shaking as she clenched the steering wheel and gritted her teeth. Rationally, she knew that she shouldn't let Celia upset her. Celia most likely realized that she'd backed a losing team and just couldn't let it go. But what was all of that about Joanna's brother? And tennis with Joanna's husband? Jane hadn't played with Sam in many years. His desire to win at all costs took all the fun out of tennis whether playing with him or against him, so she steered clear of him on the court. So why would Celia mention him? Shaking her head to clear it and she took a deep breath. She couldn't let that vile little woman rattle her this way. Deep breaths, deep breaths. Inhale, exhale. A few minutes later Jane was only two ratchets above calm when she pulled up to her house.

Climbing out of her car she looked up to see Trey coming out the door of the house.

"Need some help?" he called down toward the car.

"I'd love it," she smiled. "You're just what the doctor ordered, the sunshine in my day, a sight for sore eyes, a blessed relief."

"Don't get all worked up, Mom," Trey said, cocking his head warily. "I'm just helping you carrying some groceries in, I'm not the second coming."

Jane laughed. "It's not 'just' and it's very appreciated. Sometimes, Trey, the littlest thing can make the biggest difference, and besides, in this house you were the second coming, my own little miracle," she said, smiling up at him, as they walked companionably, side by side with groceries in their arms, toward the house.

Later that night as Jane sat in bed getting ready to put the light out after reading a few more chapters of her book, she thought again, how Celia had been so vindictive at the grocery store that day. Why had Celia even started in on her? Having no answers Jane tried to clear her mind. She wanted no nightmares tonight. She turned off the light and tried to get to sleep, trying to turn off Celia's strange comments. Jane just wanted a good night's sleep.

Sometime in the middle of the night Jane was slightly roused from her slumber by the sound of people arguing and car doors slamming. Pulling the pillow over her head she barely registered where it was coming from and quickly went back to sleep, so she was only slightly bothered that someone was so noisy and rude in the middle of the night.

Friday, August 6th

GREETING THE NEXT morning with renewed vigor, Jane hopped out of bed and quickly threw on her walking shorts, tee shirt and walking shoes. By seven-thirty she was out the door and on her way to Marti's to see if she would join her for the morning walk. As she proceeded up the road she saw Marti walking her way and they both gave a wave.

"Glad you had the same idea as I did," Marti commented. "We forgot to hook up yesterday about our walk and I was a bit afraid to knock on your door this early but, here you are!"

"I slept pretty well last night and woke up raring to go this morning. I did hear some commotion in the middle of the night though, but went right back to sleep. Did you hear anything?" Jane asked.

"Not me," Marti said, "I slept like a log."

"Well, what a gorgeous day. Where would you like to walk this morning?" Jane inquired.

"If you don't mind, I would love to walk up that lane with all the hydrangea bushes. You know the one, way back near the end of the road close to Margaret's house, just a little past the old cranberry bog. I bet they're all blooming now and I would love to drink it all in."

"Sounds good to me, lead on," Jane said as they began to

pick up their pace and head along the pond, back to where the road would eventually end abruptly a bit past the old cranberry bog that was only used by mosquitoes and varmints these days. "So, what do you and Bob have on your docket this weekend?"

"Let's see, so many exciting things we have planned. Digging up the front bushes that died over the winter to be replaced by new bushes that hopefully will last through the next winter. Bob is hoping to finally set up a bicycle rack on the side of the house, something he's talked about for ten years but for some reason thinks this is the year for it. Mind you, the boys hardly ever ride bikes anymore and mine has had a flat tire for at least a decade. There is talk that his mother may show up on Sunday but she threatens each year and each year I prepare and then she doesn't come."

"So, why don't you skip the preparing part and just expect her not to show up?" Jane asked.

"Because I fear that my preparations are all that's keeping her away. If one year I don't clean and cook in anticipation of her arrival, she's sure to show up, probably when I'm in my old clothes without my hair washed!" Marti chuckled.

"See what you mean," Jane said, joining Marti in her mirth.

"Anyway, it gets me into action. So, how about you? Got any wonderful things happening this weekend?"

"I'm afraid not quite as stimulating as your plans. Mine include mending a hem, ironing a pile of clothes and talking to Geoff as much as possible to dispel the weekend blues. Wish he could come as often as Bob does. As much as I love to live in Arizona, I sure wish it was closer to Cape Cod," Jane moaned.

"Ouch," Marti said, slapping her leg. "I think I just got attacked by a mosquito. Wish we didn't have to pass this old bog to get to the end of the road. You would think that someone would fill this in or at least spray some kind of bug killer over this area."

"It's really a mess around here. More of a swamp than a cranberry bog. And it really smells bad. I wonder if an animal died in here recently, there's been lots of raccoons roaming around this summer. I can't believe it, " Jane said pointing to trash lying off the side of the road, just into the bog. "People are even dumping their trash out here now. That's disgusting. I'm not sure this is worth seeing the hydrangeas for," Jane commented as she too began to slap at her legs. "Mosquitoes, trash, yuck, look there's even an old, dirty wig."

Glancing over at the pile, Marti spied the wig and stopped dead in her tracks.

"Come on, Marti, what are you doing? This is no time to check out the trash. I can't take the smell. Let's get by this as fast as we can," Jane suggested as she continued to walk and slap her legs, trying to leave the mosquitoes and smell that had grown stronger with each step behind her. With no response from her friend, Jane stopped and turned around to see what the hold up was. What she saw was Marti looking stricken, color draining from her face.

"What is it?" Jane wanted to know. "Are you all right? Did you pull something?"

"Jane, what is that in the bog there?" Marti muttered as she pointed to the pile they had seen.

"Just a bunch of junk. You thinking we can hose it off and use it in the auction?" Jane asked laughingly. "Come on, it really stinks, let's go."

"I'm serious, Jane. Something doesn't look right. Look at that wig. It doesn't really look like a wig, if you know what I mean. It looks like it has something attached to it."

Forgetting the mosquitoes and holding her breath, Jane moved slowly closer to the pile. It looked like someone had dumped a trash bag containing some clothes and a wig. As she got closer she grew leery as to what it was that she really saw. Could it be someone's pet, she thought, knowing that even as that thought popped into her head that it couldn't be true. This was no one's pet.

"Marti, I think that we need to call the police. There's a house just up the road a bit. Do you think that you can go up to it and give them a call? Or better yet, Margaret is just down the road a little further, maybe you could go use her phone. Or would you rather I went to make the call while you stay here?" Jane asked, using her fingers to hold her nose.

"NO," Marti said loudly, almost shouting at her friend. "I'm fine, I'll go make the call. I don't think that I want to stay here alone. Are you going to be all right?"

"I will be if you hurry," Jane said, her stomach starting to get queasy not only from the smell but from what she thought had been dumped in the bog, or maybe she should say whom. No matter what, she didn't want to hang around for long. "But, please come back once you've called and please hurry," she begged her friend.

"Okay, okay, I'm on my way," Marti said, not moving an inch. "I just have to get my legs to work. Give me a second."

Jane turned to face her friend. Walking toward her she put her hands on Marti's shoulders and said, "It's okay. This is just something we have to do. We're okay." And with that she gave Marti a quick hug, turned her around, and gave her a shove giving her the impetus to get moving toward Margaret's house. Watching her retreating figure, Jane was trying not to look back at the bog and what it contained. Finally when Marti turned the corner and was out of sight, Jane, with trepidation, took a quick peek to confirm that what had at first appeared to be a wig seemed to be attached to something that was the color of shocking pink. Sure enough, just below the hairy mass was something that stuck out from the end of the bag, a piece of material, and it was the color of shocking pink.

It seemed ages until Marti returned, driven by Margaret in her little green VW bug. Margaret pulled off to the opposite side of the road and both ladies hurried over to where Jane was standing. Margaret had brought her cell phone and nervously redialed the 911 emergency two times before the operator just told her to stay on the line this time and not keep repeating the call. Then as the three of them stood there it seemed centuries before the police finally showed up. When the police did show up they immediately called for more help after examining what Jane and Marti had seen lying just off the road in the bog. There was a flurry of activity as one officer taped off the area, another two went over to the body, and one officer who they didn't know questioned them. After initial questions and then giving of all their vital statistics they were told they could go and that someone would call them within twenty-four hours.

Moving away from the four cars and the officers who had arrived in them, the three ladies got into Margaret's car at her urging as she insisted that nothing but a cup of tea was called for at this moment. She drove them to her house and soon Marti and Jane did what they were told and were sitting in wicker chairs on her porch sipping the soothing hot liquid as she fussed over them offering them cookies and kind words.

"Who do you think that was?" Margaret wondered aloud.

"I've no idea. Hard to say with only brown hair and a bit of shirt to go from," Marti shakily said.

Jane sat mute, her face drawn. She kept sipping her tea as if nothing in the world mattered but that she gets that hot liquid down her throat. Realizing that her friends were waiting for her to make a guess about the identity of the body they had just found in the bog she looked up. At first her voice just wouldn't cooperate. She tried to form the words but they just wouldn't come. Her mind reeled with what she was thinking, and as it made no sense she just couldn't get it out. Finally she managed to squeak out, "Celia," very quietly.

"What's that you say?" Margaret inquired. "Speak up, we can't hear you."

"Celia, Celia Martin," Jane repeated loudly this time. "I think," her throat catching, "it's Celia Martin."

"What?" shouted Marti. "Celia? What makes you think it's Celia? Jane, we couldn't even see a face, a body, nothing but a blob and hair. Why in the world would you think that that was Celia?"

"I don't know, but yesterday at the grocery store I had a run-in with Celia and she was wearing a dress that same color of pink. I even had the wicked thought that she must have poured herself into it and wondered why anyone would wear something that tight in that color in public, especially someone as chunky as Celia. It was the same color of pink. I have a very bad feeling about this," Jane said in a quiet voice.

"Well, let's not jump to conclusions, ladies. Time will tell and then we'll know. How horrible, two dead bodies found in little Herring Run this summer. Let's hope that this isn't one of those things that happens in threes," remarked Margaret.

"But this is the third," Jane said. "First Sam, then Sara and now Celia. Oh my god; what is happening here? Are they all connected?"

"Now Jane, maybe it's Celia and maybe it's not. Lots of people wear pink, so let's keep an optimistic attitude," Margaret instructed, always the one to keep a level head.

"I'll try, but I really think I'm right. Oh, god, I hope not, think of her poor kids. Their mother murdered right in the place where they come each summer to be happy." At this Jane put her face in her hands and began to sob. Within seconds Marti had joined her. And as optimistic as Margaret was trying to be for the two women in tears on her porch, the thought of two possibly motherless children was just too much for her and she soon joined them in their tears. And that is how Chief of Police Mike McGuire found them a few minutes later as he knocked on Margaret's door.

"Thought I might find you ladies here," he said through the screen door. "The young officer who questioned you saw you head down this way. Mind if I come in?"

Margaret quickly stood up and opened the door for Chief McGuire. Grabbing a box of tissues she wiped her eyes and handed some on to the other ladies who were looking up at Mike with red, swollen eyes.

"Mike, is it Celia?" Jane asked.

"Jane, what makes you think it is Celia? From what I gather it was hard to even tell it was a body there, let alone who it was," the chief commented.

"The hair, the color of the clothes, I don't know. When I remembered where I had seen that color of pink before I realized it was on Celia at the grocery store yesterday."

"It looks like you might be right. Pending a positive identification I can't officially say, but it sure looks like Celia to me, and like she's been there maybe eight to ten hours," Mike added.

"Then since last night," Marti figured in her bewildered state.

"Yep, I'm guessing that's about right. Is anyone aware of Celia having any problems? Do any of you have any idea why someone would want to see Celia dead?" Mike asked seriously as he stared down at them.

From each woman came a low-toned "No". Each was into her own thoughts trying to put some reasoning to what seemed unreasonable. Why would anyone want Celia dead, Jane wondered? Sure, everyone had times when they would have loved her to shut up or leave them alone, but no one really cared that much to want her dead. Not even close. At least, Jane hadn't thought anyone would.

"Jane, you saw Celia at what time yesterday and where?" Mike asked, pulling out a small notebook.

"It was at the grocery store, The Market on the corner of Main Street and Herring Run Road. It was sometime in the morning. I ran into Julia there. We talked at bit and then I ran into Celia. She was behind me in the check out line. We spoke a little and that was it. I will tell you we didn't really have pleasant words, at least hers weren't. I noticed that she was wearing a shocking pink dress, probably because it was a bit too tight for her and she looked awful in it," Jane said sheepishly.

"Was anyone else with you or Celia?" Mike wanted to know.

"Well, I was alone, just doing the weekly shopping and Celia was with. . . ." Jane broke off. Standing with a look of horror on her face she began to head for the door.

"The kids, she was with her kids. Where are her kids? If she died last night that must mean the kids are alone. Oh, my, god, we've got to get to them," Jane said in a panicked tone as she stood by the door.

"Hang on there, Jane. I've already sent one of one of the officers on the scene to go straight over to her house to check on the kids. Don't worry, he's probably there already," Mike assured her. "It's one of the older guys that has six kids and ten grandkids, he'll be great with them. "I'll go out and check on the situation," Mike said as he left to go out to his cruiser to use his radio.

Silence hung over the porch. Everyone's ears were pricked up to hear Mike talking softly into his police radio. They all looked lost and stunned as they waited for his return. The orderly and idyllic village of Herring Run didn't seem to exist anymore. How would they ever recover the sense of well being they all came to expect each summer in this little patch of paradise?

Stepping up to the porch, Mike leaned toward the screen door and said to them, "seems I'm needed back at the scene. We'll be in touch with each of you sometime soon, probably tomorrow. Meanwhile, try not to jump to too many conclusions and I'd appreciate it if this didn't spread like wildfire until we know some of the facts. Oh, and Jane, if you still have the receipt from the grocery store yesterday, would you save it for me?"

The three ladies agreed that they would keep their lips sealed and with that Mike was off. Marti and Jane thought they should be going too but neither lady wanted to have to pass the bog where the body had been found to get to their homes. As it was the only way out from Margaret's house she suggested they stay for another cup of tea, by which time maybe the body would have been removed and she would drive them home herself. It was agreed upon and Margaret busied herself with the task of brewing another pot while Jane and Marti sat sullenly on the porch. Finally, Jane got up and gathered their cups to refill them, just do something. The idleness was driving her nuts. Marti watched them both through the doorway of the enclosed porch.

"If that is Celia and she was murdered, then what is going on here?" Marti asked plaintively.

Returning to the porch with Margaret behind her, Jane just looked at Marti and said, "What is going on here is murder. This is getting spooky. First Sam, then Sara and now Celia. It just can't be a coincidence but what does Celia have in common with Sam and Sara?"

"Frankly ladies, there is one thing they all had in common," Margaret said in her self-assured manner. "All three had a connection to Joanna. Sam was her husband of course. And it looks like Sara was Sam's mistress, so she would be Joanna's rival. And then there's Celia, who is, or was, just about Joanna's only friend. So to me, Joanna appears to be the common denominator."

Jane looked thoughtfully at Margaret. She was, of course, right. But was that the only common denominator, she wondered.

"How well did you know Celia?" Jane asked Margaret.

"Not well at all, really. I talked to her occasionally on the beach, but only in passing. With her children so much younger than mine and with that attitude, I can't say that I really tried," was Margaret's answer.

"And how about you, Marti? How well did you know Celia?"

"Not more than from around the village and beach. Like Margaret, our kids were in different age brackets so I have to admit that since I didn't have to run into her for any reason I certainly never sought her out. Now I feel badly that I wasn't nicer to her," Marti said mournfully.

"I really didn't know her at all either," commented Jane. "And like the two of you I had the same reasons. She wasn't a very likable person. In fact at times she was quite unlikable, especially with all that went on this summer. She was quite hard on Ian and Matt, and us for that matter, after Sam's murder. She spread vicious rumors, verbally attacked me in a store and even assaulted me with a shopping cart at the grocery store yesterday. I think of all that, the rumors bothered me the worst. Once she started about Matt and Ian being suspects it spread through the village and the club like wildfire and made their lives hell. She was a mean, petty woman but I still feel sorry for her. No one should end up face down dead in an old cranberry bog."

"And her poor motherless children," Margaret added. "This will be so hard on them."

"And her hen-pecked husband," Marti chimed in.

"Maybe he wanted her dead," Margaret said remembering the wimpy husband who Celia had led around by the nose all summer.

"It's just too much of a coincidence, three murders in one summer. I don't think there's ever been a murder in Herring Run's history and all three of the victims can be connected to Joanna. This has got me thinking," Jane murmured.

"Well, I for one would like to head home," Marti said. "Think the coast is clear yet?"

"We'll see," Jane answered. "Let's walk, we could use the air."

"Oh, no you don't," admonished Margaret. "You are not going to rob me of a legitimate reason to drive back down the road to see what's going on without seeming like a lookie-Lou."

"If you're sure you don't mind then, thanks," Jane said looking gratefully at her friend. After this morning's adversity she really didn't feel she had the strength to make it home under her own power.

Driving slowly by the scene of the crime they took in the yellow tape and many officers behind it picking through the debris of the bog as quite a few spectators looked on. But the body was gone, a relief to each of them, punctuated by three huge sighs as they drove on by.

"I'm glad that's over with," Margaret commented. "I know I'll never feel the same driving by the spot ever again, but I got through the first time with you two with me, so thanks."

"I don't think Herring Run is ever going to seem the same again," Marti shivered. "It feels real spooky these days. I'm not sure I want to stick out the rest of the summer here, anymore."

"I know what you mean," Jane commented. "Paradise lost. If the dinner and auction weren't only two weeks away, I think I might even want to pack it in, and that's a biggie for me! I hate to leave every year, knowing it will be nine months before I can return."

"Jane, do you think anyone will even want to come to the auction now?" Marti asked.

"I hope so, despite all that's happened, we still need to raise funds and everything is in the works, the caterer has our down payment, auction items piled up, volunteers committed. We'll just have to make it solemnly festive, if that's possible, which somehow doesn't sound like it," Jane sighed, thinking that maybe it would be better to call the whole thing off.

"Given a week of mourning and a week of getting back to normal, we should be okay," Margaret surmised. "Not everyone coming was friends with or even knew Celia, that is if it was Celia, which we all know deep in our hearts it was. God Bless her poor kids."

Margaret came to a halt in front of Jane's house. Wearily, Jane climbed out of the car. Turning to Margaret she said, "Thanks for the ride, for the tea and sympathy, too, Margaret. I'll probably see you down at the beach later. I'm thinking, maybe we should just keep quiet about our suspicions as to whose body we think that was until it's made official. If we're wrong we could really cause some panic and needless misery here."

"I agree," Margaret said. "Don't think I'll make it to the beach today though. Feeling much too restless. Think I'll head over to 6A for a little antiquing. Spending money just might help me feel better, or at least I'll get a perspective on life and time as I look at all those old items that once belonged to someone else way back when."

"Alright, then, thanks again," Jane replied.

"Wait up, Jane," Marti called. "I'll get out here too and walk to my house. Thanks for everything, Margaret. See you tomorrow."

As the ladies watched Margaret drive away Marti asked Jane, "Are you really going down to the beach after all this? God, I don't think I could just go down there and relax after what we found this morning. I'm so keyed up, yet so tired. I don't know what to do."

"I know how you feel, Marti, that's how I feel. Like I just want to crawl into bed and cry, yet my body feels like it's going to jump out of its skin," Jane said with a shudder. "But I want to get down to the beach to see what's being said and what anyone knows. If there is one place in this village to find out what's going on, it's at the beach. Anyway, I feel a bit too spooked to stay in the house alone even in broad daylight. I'm thinking I'm going to beg my boys to spend the night at home tonight."

"Not a bad idea. Listen, give me ten minutes to change into my suit and I'll meet you back here and we'll walk down together," Marti said as she hurried off in the direction of her house.

Jane slowly climbed the stairs to her door. Each step was thoughtful, Sam, Sara and Celia. All came back to Joanna in her mind. Sam was Joanna's husband. Sara was Joanna's rival, her husband's lover. Celia was Joanna's friend. As she reached the top step she stopped, deep in thought. Jane could almost understand why Joanna would want Sara dead, but why Sam and why Celia, supposedly someone Joanna loved and someone she liked. That didn't make any sense. What would be gained by killing either of them? In fact, losing Sam had meant she had lost the summerhouse as well as his steady paycheck, but then there was always life insurance which someone like Sam would have had. It wouldn't make sense to kill Sam, unless it had been in a fit of anger about Sara and his affair. And why kill Celia? Celia was the one person in the village that seemed to like Joanna, in fact not just liked but was a true ally to Joanna, against anyone else. What would be the reason for killing Celia?

Putting her key into the lock of the door, Jane felt there must be more to all of this. Something was missing. That the murders must eventually lead to Joanna in some way, or at least be tied into her seemed a given, but how? Shaking her head, Jane entered her home, ran up the stairs to shower off the icky feeling she had and hopefully to get the smell out of her nose by using some lavender soap. After a long shower she quickly changed into her bathing suit, the modest black one out of respect for the dead of Herring Run. Marti was waiting for her on her steps when she emerged from her house, so they headed for the beach.

*   *   *

The beach was abuzz with news of another murder in their midst. Rumors were flying around about the identity of the victim and who had found the body. As they walked in, Marti and Jane were told by one young mother that the tennis pro had found the body behind the tennis shack early in the morning when he had taken out the garbage for the daily pick-up. They listened politely, nodding, making appropriate murmurs and excused themselves as soon as they were able. Walking down the boardwalk, they overheard another version that had the crime take place at the beach and a third version was had when one of the lifeguards said he heard that a body had been found hanging from a tree on the beach path. One had to wonder where had these stories come from.

In the snack bar as Jane got a salad and ice tea for lunch, she encountered a bunch of teenagers who claimed to have heard screams around midnight as they went on their nightly foray around the village. Thinking this might be valuable information, she told them to let the police chief know about it. Quickly the kids said, well, maybe it had just been some of the feral cats that roamed the village at night. She smiled with acceptance, but made a mental note of what they had said.

The village did have a bit of a problem with cats; there were many nights when their cries startled Jane awake as the cats had a run-in with a skunk or a raccoon. They could sound quite human. So if they could sound human, so could a human sound be mistaken for that of the cats? She also knew that a few of those kids had eleven o'clock curfews, which meant that some of them had sneaked out after coming home, a not-uncommon occurrence with the youth of the village. Most the parents knew and most of the parents let it go on as long as they stayed out of trouble. But the kids didn't know that the parents knew and they would not want it found out that they had sneaked out after curfew. Noting who had told her she thought she should pass the information on to the police when she talked to them.

Returning to her beach chair with her lunch, Jane found that Sheila, Barbara and Marti were deep into discussion of the morning's tragedy. Discussion came around to Celia's children and where they had been. No one had seen hide nor hair of them all day and everyone wondered if they were all right.

"They can't have disappeared off the face of the earth," Sheila, always the practical one, commented.

"Who can't have disappeared?" a voice asked.

As a group, the ladies all looked, shielding their eyes from the sun, to see Trey and Nick standing over them, dressed in tennis whites and holding tennis rackets in their hands.

"Hi, guys," Jane said. "We were just wondering where Celia Martin's kids were."

"I can't imagine why, but we had them for tennis lessons this morning. Mrs. Morris brought them over with her kids," Trey informed the group. "Since when do you ladies keep tabs on the younger set? Especially, those two."

"Sit down, boys. You might as well hear this from us," Jane said and related the morning's finding, stressing that even though they weren't sure it was Mrs. Martin in the bog, it sure looked a lot like it was. "Try not to play post office with this story, but if you do, at least get it right. We've heard some really far out versions of what happened. But you say that the kids are safe? They were with Mrs. Morris?"

"Yeah, think they had a sleepover at Marsh Cottage last night, from the way they were talking. Mrs. Morris sat and watched the whole lesson and then took them all away afterward. They seemed fine to me. It's really too bad about their mother, though. I don't think they knew anything while they were at the courts," Trey said shaking his head, wondering why his mother worried so much, especially about someone else's kids, for Pete's sake.

"Well, good. Then that's one less thing for me to worry about," Jane said at almost the same time that Trey had his thought, which made him laugh.

"Don't worry so much, Mom, you'll get gray hairs. Listen, we're out of here. Just wanted to let you know that we're going wake boarding with Paulie. I'll be home in time for dinner, though. Any chance steak could be on the menu?" Trey asked.

"No way; tonight's chicken. But I'll make you garlic mashed to go with it. How's that?" Jane replied, glad to know that her son would be with her for dinner.

"Sounds good, Ma, see ya. Bye, ladies," Trey said with his winsome smile as he took off down the beach with Nick.

"So, at least we know that Celia's kids weren't marooned by themselves at home all night with no adult," Barbara said. "That's a relief. I wonder if they've been told what happened to their mother by now."

Another discussion ensued about who would tell the kids, what they would be told and how they would take it, that is, of course, if it was Celia's body that had been found that morning, which no one doubted was the case. Jane's head began to ache from all the thoughts that were trying to crowd in and swirl around her brain, while she tried to make sense of them. She sat back in her chair, closed her eyes and listened to the opinions without saying a word. Before she knew it, she had dozed off waking only when Marti shook her shoulder, saying everyone was leaving, did she want to go too?

Drowsily, Jane said yes, time to go, she'd meet Marti at the front entrance and they'd walk home together. She just wanted to find Ian and have a quick word with him. Marti lumbered off under the weight of her beach accouterments as Jane went in search of her son.

Finding Ian putting the rescue equipment away for the night, she asked him if she might have a quick word. Putting down the red rescue buoy he quickly came out of the storage closet and looked a bit worried at her.

"What's it now, Mom? Someone saying that I killed someone else?" he asked, sounding irked, but there was a tinge of fear in his tone.

"Oh, no, Ian, nothing like that, but I gather you've heard the rumors?" Jane surmised, feeling that her son had reason to feel annoyed.

"The only thing I really know is that a body was found in the cranberry bog by you and Mrs. Sanders. She told Matt and me while you were snoozing away on the beach. I thought she'd saved the bad news for you to tell me. Sorry if I sound a bit jumpy, but this summer has done that to me," Ian exclaimed, ruefully.

"Ian, I'm sorry that you've been through all this, but this time no one is pointing a finger at you, thank goodness. I just wanted to know if you'll be home for dinner and to ask you if you'll spend the night under our roof instead of at the beach. I'm a little spooked and would feel a whole lot better if all of us were under one roof for the evening and the night," Jane added, hoping he heard the plea in her voice, without the desperation. Not only was Jane a bit spooked about staying alone or just with Trey in the house, she also worried about any of them out and about where they could be in harm's way.

Ian looked at her with a soft smile, and put his arm around her shoulder. "Sure, Mom, I'll stay at the house tonight. In fact, we can have a family evening, play trivial pursuit or something, but just one night. I don't want you to get in the habit of having me around," he said with a grin.

"Thanks, Ian. I'll feel much better. And we'll see about how many nights, maybe one will be enough, or maybe two?" she asked hopefully.

"One, Mom, don't get greedy," he laughed. "I'll see you around six-thirty for dinner. Love ya." And with that he was off down the beach to finish his duties for the day.

Jane hurriedly stowed her beach gear in their bathhouse and headed for the front entrance to catch up with Marti, who she found deep in conversation with Craig, the beach manager.

"There you are, Jane," Marti said as she caught sight of her friend approaching. "Craig just told me that it is confirmed that the body we found was Celia. It's so distressing. He said it's been on the local news radio station as well as the cable channel."

"Not only that, but quite a few members have been talking about it as they came and went today. A few are talking about leaving the Cape until a killer is caught. Can't blame them, but then there's a lot of us here that call the Cape home and don't have that option. I've heard a few people saying that they are considering arming themselves, a scary thought in its own," Craig commented.

"Oh, dear, poor Celia," Jane said with tears in her eyes. "I knew it would be her when I saw the shocking pink but now that it's verified it's hard all over again. Her poor kids and husband. What a horrible summer this is turning out to be for Herring Run."

Craig looked uncomfortable at the sight of a woman crying and excused himself to get back to his duties. Turning to go, Jane and Marti started their walk back up toward the village in silence. After a few minutes Jane turned to Marti and said, "I have to admit, I'm feeling a bit eerie about this whole thing. Who could be doing this? It's got to be someone we know, and that just makes my skin crawl. Anyway, I'm spooked enough to have asked Ian to spend the night at home instead of the beach tonight. Maybe you should get Matt to do the same, so he's not alone," Jane added.

"Already done. And I told him to tell the girl guards that they're welcome to stay too, if they like. Without the guys down there, they're more vulnerable than ever," Marti told her.

"Oh my god, you're right. I should have thought about those poor girls. You're so nice, Marti. If you want to send one our way let me know," Jane said, feeling badly that she hadn't even thought about Robin and Kelly.

"Thanks, we're set for tonight, but if this drags on maybe they can rotate houses. I just hated the thought of them down at the beach all alone tonight," Marti replied.

Walking on through the village toward home both women noticed a flurry of activity outside of Marsh Cottage. Two police cars were just pulling away and standing on the front porch with Joanna and her brother was Celia's husband, Spencer. He looked exhausted and bewildered. Sitting on the grass in the front yard were the two Martin children looking lost and adrift. No one noticed as Jane and Marti quietly walked by.

As Jane walked up to her house she reminded Marti of her offer to take the girl lifeguards off her hands if things dragged on. "And Marti, tell Bob that I'm going to try to get Geoff to come out a week early, in case Bob wants to try to get some tennis in. I'd be more comfortable with Geoff here, I think."

"Sounds good, I'll talk to you later," Marti said as she headed on down to her house.

Hair still wet from her shower, Jane sat down on the side of the bed in her chenille bathrobe and with a heavy heart dialed Geoff's office number. She knew that he wouldn't feel good about their being apart at this time. He picked up immediately and Jane proceeded to tell him the day's event, downplaying her involvement in it. Shocked when he heard the news of Celia's death, he immediately tried to talk Jane into closing the house early to return to Tucson with the boys.

"You know I can't do that, Geoff," Jane whined. "Both boys have jobs and the fundraiser is coming up in two weeks. We have commitments. Besides, Ian is staying at the house, so all three of us will be under one roof," Jane informed him hoping to ease his worried mind, and hoping that he wouldn't ask how long tonight's arrangement with her sons would last. "Why don't you think about coming back a week earlier than you had planned? That way we can ride out this storm together."

"I wish that I could, love, but that doesn't look like an option. Jane, these murders are real. This is not some mystery novel that you can put down whenever and then go about your business. This is serious stuff and I wish you would consider what I said about coming home. But if you won't do that, at least keep you nose out of it and pay attention to what is going on around you. Keep your doors locked at all times. No unnecessary risks. Make me a promise," Geoff insisted.

"Don't worry about me, Geoff Adams," Jane assured him without promising a thing. "We'll be just fine here. You just get here as soon as you can so we can enjoy Cape Cod together."

"Well, I'll see you in two weeks, but in the meantime have Ian call me this evening. Tell him if I'm not at the office to call my cell phone. I plan to go to the gym after work, but I'll be sure to take my cell. And, listen, I'll try to come out at least a few days earlier if I can," Geoff told her and then rang off after Jane told him she loved him, sentiments returned with a 'ditto' which meant that someone must have entered Geoff's office while they were saying their good-byes.

Staring at the now mute phone, Jane pondered Geoff's fears. Should she pack up and leave the Cape with the boys in tow? As eerie as she had felt, deep down she didn't really feel in danger, not the kind of danger that truly threatened them. She would never knowingly put her boys in danger. But was she doing that now without realizing it?

First Sam was murdered. Ian and Matt were on the suspect list of his murder for a short time, so in a way they were connected. Then Sara was found dead, right after she and Marti met her at the restaurant, and later it was concluded that Sara had been murdered, also. Now Celia was laying in the morgue, the third victim of murder within a month in their seaside paradise. This was after Jane had seen Celia at the grocery store. But as far as Jane knew, the murders of the two women didn't even remotely connect with the any or them. Maybe, just maybe, Jane was not seeing things as they were and she should heed Geoff's advice and get her children far away from here. On the other hand, that seemed like panicking to

Jane and no one else in the village was beating a hasty retreat off the Cape or out of Herring Run.

Rising from the bed with a sigh, Jane threw on some shorts and went to fix dinner for her lovely sons. She decided to take it hour by hour with the dilemma of what to do. She'd be vigilant over their safety, take her cues from what everyone else was doing and most importantly, use her motherly instinct. Hopefully, that instinct wouldn't fail her. In the meantime, she had chicken to marinate, potatoes to peel and a grill to heat up. She wanted to be sure the boys were glad to be home having dinner with their dear old mom!

Later in the evening, as Trey was slaughtering his mother and brother in a game of Trivial Pursuit, Jane remembered that Geoff had asked her to tell Ian to call him. Glad to have the excuse to get out of an overwhelming defeat at the hands of his younger brother, Ian excused himself and called his dad. Jane tried to overhear the conversation but Ian's end was full of uh huhs and yeahs and noes which nothing could be garnered from that would help her know what the gist of the conversation was. When she heard Ian finally ask his father if he wanted to speak to Mom, Jane started up from her seat only to see Ian turn the phone off.

"Didn't dad want to talk to me?" she asked.

"Said he already had and was in the middle of his workout so he'd talk to you tomorrow," Ian told her. "He sounds really worried, Mom. Wants me to keep an eye on you. Truth be told, what he really wants is for all of us to get on a flight tonight and return to Tucson. I can't believe he's that worried. Beginning to sound a lot like you, the worry wart."

"He just wants us safe, Ian," Jane told him.

"Well, he can forget that. I'm not missing one day of this summer," Ian said as he returned to the couch, pulling out a deck of cards from a side table. Starting a game of solitaire Ian ignored the fact that his brother was sitting by the game board waiting to clinch his victory by acquiring one final wedge in the game of Trivial Pursuit.

"Hey, we're not finished here," Trey complained to his brother.

"I'm finished, bro. You wiped me out and I think I've had enough humiliation for one evening. Your brainpower is beyond me tonight. I declare you the winner," he said with a genuine smile for his younger brother.

Trey beamed at the unaccustomed praise and was happy to wrap up the game, especially since he had not acquired that final wedge and Ian had been known to come from behind in a sweep of good luck and right answers. What a Hallmark moment, Jane thought wryly. Too bad Geoff wasn't here to share this. Jane just had to think of a way to get him out to them sooner.

Saturday and Sunday, August 7th and 8th

THE WEEKEND WAS filled with good weather and somber villagers who felt too guilty being alive to enjoy it much. Celia's death and funeral plans were all that anyone seemed to have on their minds. Spencer, her husband, had decided that she would be laid to rest back in Ohio, where she was originally from and where her parents still resided. Since that would keep most of the villagers from attending her funeral a memorial service was hastily put together in the village tabernacle, their open-air church, for Sunday evening.

Jane and the boys, in their Sunday best, walked solemnly together up to the church that evening. They stopped at the Sanders' house to pick them up and they, with Kelly and Robin made a quiet procession toward the village green where the church was located. Most of the village was on their way as well and people greeted one another in hushed tones.

Approaching the church Jane noticed that Joanna was standing at the door with her two young sons. Jane felt a stab of pity for this woman whom shortly after losing her husband to murder had now lost her best friend as well. But these thoughts reminded Jane that Joanna could be the connection to both murders, she could even be the murderer herself! If that was so, then Joanna was quite the accomplished actress as she stood looking totally distraught and grief stricken, tears wetting her cheeks, Jane saw as they came abreast of her.

"Joanna, I'm so sorry you've lost your good friend," Jane said with real feeling. "This must be just too much for you."

"It *is* too much. And it's gone too far, I don't know what I'm going to do about it," Joanna snapped as tears ran down her face. Just then her brother, Stuart, came out of the church and quickly took Joanna's elbow and steered her inside, giving Jane a startled, unpleasant look.

Startled herself at this abrupt removal of Joanna, Jane was speechless and watched as Stuart led his sister into the darkened church to sit right behind Spencer and his children in the second row. As at Sam's funeral, Jane opted to sit near the back to get the best vantage point. Jane sat with her boys beside her, Robin by Ian, and Kelly next to Trey, the Sanders seated themselves in the row directly in front of her. Jane settled into the quiet of the church. Glancing around she noticed that Julia and Alex were seated halfway up the aisle next to Mike McGuire and his son, Michael. While Julia and Alex seemed to have their heads bowed in prayer, Mike was casually glancing around the assembled congregation. Their eyes met and Mike gave Jane a look that was worth a thousand words—or maybe just four, like: "Stay out of it". Feeling caught with her hand in the cookie jar Jane primly lowered her eyes in meditation, meditating on who she had seen at the church and what they might have to do with the murder.

Besides the bereaved and Mike and his crew, the church seemed to be filled mostly with villagers, which made perfect sense, as this was a service for the village. Jane hadn't noticed anyone that would be a stranger to her. A few people from the beach had come, that was about it from what she could tell, but they all looked familiar even though she might not know them by name.

As the service commenced, Jane's mind wandered over reasons that anyone would have wanted to kill Celia. Besides being a pest, a gossip and reeking of horrible perfume, which were hardly reasons to resort to murder, Jane could not come up with a single reason that would warrant Celia's murder. Maybe it was just one of those random acts of violence. Woman attacked as she took an evening stroll. Jane wondered if there had been a rape involved. She hadn't heard a word about that or what had actually caused Celia's death. Jane hoped that she could corner Mike after the service and ask him a few questions.

As the minister droned on, Jane knew that there were just a few pieces that could bring the whole puzzle together. What were they? What did Celia's death have to do with Sam and Sara's, if anything, Jane wondered with a sigh. Maybe she was just trying too hard to link them. Maybe it was nothing.

Rising to sing one of Celia's favorite hymns, *All Things Bright and Beautiful*, Jane took the opportunity to glance behind her. A few beach goers sat in the last remaining pews and Jane nodded a greeting. Beyond them in the darkened doorway of the church Jane noticed a man standing by himself in the shadows. She could not make out who he was as he could only seen in silhouette. She noticed that he was tall and lean, casually dressed in dark clothing with a baseball cap pulled forward and down to obstruct any chance of her seeing his face. Turning back to join in the singing Jane wondered who it could be.

After several eulogies Jane had the chance to sneak a look behind her again when the congregation rose to sing. The stranger was gone from the doorway. Jane surmised that he must have been a passerby curious to see what was going on at the church that evening. The doors to the tabernacle were open as were the sides to let in a breeze so there were bound to be a few curiosity-seekers. She turned her attention back to her hymnal and tried to put thoughts of mysterious strangers out of her mind. As the service continued she worked at connecting the dots of Sam, Sara and Celia, but could come up with nothing except the obvious. *Maybe they were in a menage a trois, or* quatre, *if Joanna was involved,* Jane thought with a chuckle, hardly bearing to picture that in her mind, but irreverently seeing Sam between a pudgy Celia and a svelte Joanna anyway. Could they have been involved in something illegal? Didn't seem likely after her talk with Sara or knowing Sam the way she did. Or maybe, just Joanna and Celia were doing something that wasn't on the up and up. Even that seemed farfetched. Something was very wrong here in Herring Run. But what was it?

Suddenly Jane realized that the benediction was being said and everyone was rising from his or her seats. The organist was playing a dirge like tune that did nothing for anyone's spirits, appropriate though it was. As Jane and party began to exit she noticed that Spencer had not left his seat and as quite a few of the villagers were heading up to express their sympathy, Marti and Jane decided to join Bob, who was headed that way, to express theirs.

After waiting a few minutes for her turn, Jane reached out to take Spencer's hand in hers and tell him how sorry she was. Spencer looked up at her from his seat and his eyes took on a wild look. He took the hand that Jane offered and pulled her down close to him and whispered frantically, "She never should have been involved with that family, she never should have," and with that he let go and began to cry. Jane straightened up and, mildly embarrassed with this outburst, looked around to see if anyone had noticed what had just occurred. Her eyes met the steely stare of Stuart, who was seated behind Spencer and had taken it all in. Unreadable as his stare looked, Jane knew for some reason that it was not friendly. Jane walked away, feeling stung and a bit on edge.

Retreating to the back of the church where coffee, tea and cookies had been set up Jane found Ian and Trey waiting for her. They were helping themselves to some food and talking with Matt and Nick.

"Ready to go, Mom?" Trey asked.

"Give me a minute, Trey. Let's wait for the Sanders and we'll all go back together," she replied, feeling a bit spooked by Stuart's malevolent gaze. "We came with them and we should at least see if they want to leave with us," she explained, really thinking that safety in numbers was a more comfortable thought in walking home now that it was beginning to get dark.

"Here come my parents now," Nick commented. "I'll go get the girls and we can get out of here," he said as he left to get Robin and Kelly who were talking with Alex and Michael. Jane noticed that it looked like Robin and Alex had hit it off, both girls had big smiles on their faces. Alex seemed adjusted to the reality of suddenly discovering that she had a half sister.

"Well, Jane, this is turning into a depressing summer," Julia said as she and Mike approached the refreshment table. "I'm thinking that there must be something in the water and that I should stop drinking it."

"Anything new officially, Mike?" Jane asked.

"Not a thing," Mike said in an unconvincing tone of voice. You glean anything during the service?" Mike said alluding to having caught Jane in the act of spying while others' heads were bowed.

"Not me," Jane said truthfully, "unless you count pathetic, licentious imaginings."

"Say what?" Julia asked, looking surprised.

"Nothing, just frustration at what is going one here and not being able to figure it out," Jane complained.

"Just don't try to," Mike admonished. "That's our job. I mean it, Jane, this is getting pretty serious, if it wasn't so already. I think you'd be wise to be extra careful. Lock your doors, don't walk alone, keep your car doors locked, you know the drill. Until we figure this out and have an arrest made everyone must be extra cautious."

After Stuarts's stare Jane didn't have to be reminded to take extra precautions.

"I've got the boys staying with me tonight and Marti has her sons and the girl lifeguards with her, so we're battening down our hatches, so to speak," Jane informed him.

"That's good. We'll be canvassing the village this week to see if anyone noticed anything unusual leading up to Celia's murder and at the same time handing out safety fliers and answering anyone's questions. So expect someone in the next few days, but be sure to ask for an I.D. before opening the door to anyone you don't know."

"You got it," Jane replied.

"I'll call you later," Julia told her as she and Mike walked toward to door on their way out. Jane nodded and decided after that stern warning to gather her troops and get home.

Later that night, talking to Geoff on the phone, Jane described the memorial service, the people that attended, the eulogies and then Spencer's odd comment about how Celia "shouldn't have gotten involved with that family". Jane assumed that the she was Celia, but wondered whom "that family" could be when he spoke to her at the memorial service. She could only think Spencer meant Joanna's family, yet there he was, sitting with them. Or were they sitting with him, she wondered? Geoff told her that he had nothing to offer on the subject and that she should stay out of it. All of this was better left to the police.

Jane agreed and, again, asked if there was any way Geoff thought he could come out a bit earlier. He told her that it was very unlikely, but that he would if he could. Meanwhile, he told her to be sure to lock up tight every night and to heed Mike's warning not walk alone, which he told her included her early morning walks.

"Stick with Marti on your walks and stay in at night. It will help me rest easier," he told her.

Agreeing, she told him she'd talk to him tomorrow and that she loved him. He loved her too, he said, and was looking forward to seeing her soon. It was only after she hung up that she realized that she had forgotten to tell him about the man standing at the back of the church in the shadows. But she reminded herself it was probably nobody other than a passerby, someone curious to see what was happening in the church on a Sunday evening. With that thought, she turned off her light, rolled over, and promptly fell asleep, a miracle with all that was going on in her mind.

A couple of hours later she was awakened by some shouting and a car door banging. Annoyed to be robbed of such a sound sleep she got up out of bed and walked over to the window, and then carefully peered out through the slats of her blinds. Briskly walking up the road was a tall, slim man dressed in dark clothing with a baseball cap pulled down over his face, the man from the back of the church! It must be! How similar the build, the same silhouette. Jane still didn't know who this was but she thought the stride looked familiar. As she studied the retreating figure she was startled when he stopped and looked back over his shoulder, straight at the bedroom window where she now stood. Letting go of the blind, Jane stepped back, unsure if she'd been seen, feeling as if she had been totally exposed, yet knowing, rationally, that there was no way he could have seen her peering out her window through slats an inch wide, if that, in her dark bedroom.

Shaken, Jane stood still, taking deep breaths, finally getting the nerve to slightly lift up a slat again and look out. Looking up and down a now-empty road, Jane could not find the mysterious figure that had stared up at her only a few moments ago; he had disappeared into the night.

Making her way quietly back to her bed, Jane searched her brain for whom that could have been. Something familiar, she thought, something familiar, but what? Climbing into her bed she shivered as she pulled the covers up to her chin. A man walking down the street at night, not so unusual in this vacation spot. She was making a mountain out of a molehill; but she just knew it was the same man she had seen outside the church. A visitor, a houseguest, someone she knew slightly from the village, who could it be? Just because she didn't recognize him didn't make him sinister, but why did he look up at her window just then? Could he feel her eyes on him? Did he see the movement of the blinds out of the corner of his eye? She felt a prickly feeling on her skin, an eerie sensation all over. Don't be silly, she told herself. You're just imagining all sorts of strange things with all that's going on this summer. Trying to calm herself she eased under the covers, ever so quietly. And why? She wondered was she so worried about being quiet anyway! Damn! She was spooked!

Sleep wouldn't come now and Jane lay in her bed listening to every rustle, squeak and knock in the night. Finally, after an hour or so, falling into a troubled sleep around four a.m. Jane began to dream of the *ménage a trois* scene with a shrewish Joanna, a selfish Sam and a chunky Celia, all entwined on a big bed with a tall, dark man standing in a shadowed doorway staring at them as they cavorted on the bed. The scene soon became macabre with the figures in the bed melting away as they laughed hysterically, while the man in the doorway just stood there and watched. Joanna was the horrified observer from afar, trying to stop something from going wrong but not quite knowing what she was trying to stop. As the figures melted away and their laughs turned to cries of terror, the man standing in the doorway began to turn toward Joanna, but before he could turn all the way around the lights went out in the room and Joanna's nightmare became like so many dreams, lost in the circus of one's nightly wanderings.

Monday, August 9th

JANE WOKE UP late the next morning with a throbbing headache. She recalled bits and pieces of her nightmare and got shivers down her back. Heading straight for the shower, she let warm water run over her head, trying to soothe the pain. Raising her face to the spray she let the warmth beat on her forehead as her mind tried to push the feeling of dread that the night had left with her. Was there any meaning to her dream? Why had Joanna melted along with Sam and Celia? Was this a premonition that someone was going to kill Joanna? Why wasn't Sara in this dream and who was the dark figure in the doorway? Could it have been the mystery man at the doorway of the church?

Finding no answers and conceding that her headache needed more than just warm water, Jane finished her shower and got out to towel off. Taking a couple of aspirin and throwing on a pair of shorts and a tee shirt, Jane headed downstairs to make herself some strong coffee. She would not subject herself to a blow dry this morning, not with this headache. Walking into the kitchen she saw that both boys were already up and were sitting at the kitchen table having bowls of cereal. Coffee was made. This rare occurrence brought a smile to Jane's face as she poured herself a cup. She couldn't remember the last time she had seen them both up this early having breakfast and with coffee made!

Bless them, she thought.

"You're up late, Mom," Ian commented. "Mrs. Sanders came by earlier to see if you wanted to walk but when I knocked on your bedroom door I got no reply so she said she'd catch you later."

"Thanks, Ian. I had a night filled with weird dreams and woke up with a dreadful headache. That last thing I feel like doing is a power walk. In fact I'd love to crawl back into bed, truth be known."

"Know how you feel, but I've got to get to work. Lessons start in twenty minutes. Think you'll make it down to the beach today? It's supposed to be gorgeous."

"I'll see how I feel. There's nothing worse than sitting at the beach with a headache. Maybe I'll catch up on my ironing," Jane said wincing from both the pain of her head and the thought of the mound of ironing that was growing at an outlandish rate in her bedroom.

"That should be good for your headache, a real cure," Trey commented wryly as he rose from the table to deposit his bowl in the sink.

"Hey, buster, into the dishwasher, you know, that appliance right next to the sink," Jane informed him, while she rubbed her temples.

"Yeah, yeah, Mom," Trey laughed. "I gotta go, too. Hey, Ian, I'll walk down with you, hang on a sec."

"That's a good idea, boys. I would be very grateful if you two would stick together as much as possible. Safety in numbers, you know."

"Oh my god, Mom, I can't believe that you think we can't take care of ourselves," Trey said with a roll of his eyes.

"Just humor me. There's been too many deaths this summer

not to take precautions; just do it for your old mom, please," Jane said, trying to find the right balance in her tone of a lightness and seriousness without sounding too much either way, an impossible task but one she continued to try whenever she had advice for her boys.

"Sure, Mom. We'll see you tonight for dinner, if not before at the beach. Hope you feel better," Ian said as they ran out the door.

"Thanks, have a good day," Jane called after the two as they let the door slam after them, causing her head to almost explode.

Settling down with her cup of coffee, Jane tried to empty her mind and let the aspirin do its trick. She closed her eyes and let her mind float free, hoping to rid it of any unpleasant thoughts. But the scene of Celia's body in the bog kept parking itself in the way. Giving up she pulled the morning paper toward her and looked at the headlines. No more murders, that was good. In fact nothing traumatic was on the front page, just news of the shenanigans of various politicians in Washington, D.C., some malicious mischief in a nearby town and a bake sale at a local church. It made things seem almost back to normal, she thought with a sigh.

Thumbing through the different sections of the *Cape Cod Register*, she came upon the obit column where she saw a flattering photo of Celia and a short bio of her life. No mention of the murder was mentioned in the piece and funeral arrangements were also omitted except to say she would be interred in Mansfield, Ohio, where her parents lived. To her surprise, Jane saw that though Celia had been born in Ohio she had left as a baby and grown up in the Boston area until she was sixteen. Her parents were originally from Ohio but she had only lived there when her parents had moved their family back during her last of high school. She had returned to

Boston for college where she had met Spencer and had lived in the Boston area ever since. The piece went on to say that Celia was survived by her husband, two children, her parents, a sister, a brother and various nieces and nephews.

So sad, Jane concluded as she thought of Celia's kids and parents. No child should have to lose a parent when they were young and no parent should outlive a child. It gave Jane a moment's pause as she thought of her own parents and children. Oddly enough, the fact that Celia had lived most of her life in Boston was new to Jane. She thought Celia had been from Ohio, since Celia and her kids made a yearly trek out to visit her parents there for a week each summer.

I wonder where in Boston she grew up, Jane thought idly, sipping her coffee, which with the aspirin was beginning to work a minor miracle on her head. Was she feeling well enough to iron, she wondered, or maybe just go to the beach and rest?

A few hours later, Jane was relaxing on the beach, half the ironing done, half waiting for a rainy day. Her head was almost back to normal and she had lost that disconcerting feeling of dread that had assailed her when she woke up in the morning. In fact, she was feeling positively great when Marti arrived with her beach paraphernalia in tow.

"So, you're up and about," Marti said as she set up her beach chair and sat down with a sigh of relief. "You were sure a lay about this morning. You missed our walk."

"Woke up with the most dreadful headache," Jane replied. "You didn't walk alone, did you?"

"Of course, why wouldn't I?" Marti asked.

"I think that with all that's been happening here it just doesn't seem safe. Geoff has asked me not to walk unless I have a walking partner. It makes sense to me. In fact, I've asked the boys to go in twos," Jane informed her.

"That'll last long," Marti said with a laugh. "You'll never get them to keep that up, or us for that matter. We've got to live our lives. Besides, I don't think the murders have anything to do with any of us. And I don't think they are random acts of violence. I think Sam, Joanna and Celia had a *ménage a trois*," Marti said with a guilty grin.

"Oh my god, you too? That's why I woke up with a headache. I was having this horrible dream about the three of them, in bed, mind you. There was a shadowy figure in the door watching them in a menacing way and then they melted. It really was hideous."

"Gee, I'm sorry about your headache. But I didn't really mean it about a threesome with them, but you know, it could be possible. If I thought of it, even in jesting, and you dreamt about it, there might be something to it. But then, who would want to kill them, Spencer? And is Joanna next?"

"I don't know but this talk is bringing back my headache. Maybe Mike and Geoff are right and we should leave it up to the police. But I just can't get these thoughts out of my mind. Did you hear shouting out on the street last night around one a.m.?"

"Not me, I was out like a light the minute my head hit the pillow. Anyone we know?"

"I don't know. The shouting woke me up and by the time I got up to look all I saw was a dark figure walking down the street, looked like a man, vaguely familiar."

"Probably a lover's quarrel; sometimes this village can seem too small."

"I know what you mean. How about we put the murders to rest and enjoy our good weather. Can I talk you into swimming out to the raft?" Jane asked her skeptical friend.

Coming back in from the raft about thirty minutes later, Jane saw that Sheila and Barbara had joined them. Both ladies were in deep discussion on the topic of last night's memorial service. Inwardly groaning, Jane sat down to join them. It was inevitable that Celia would be foremost on everyone's mind but Jane felt it had been the only thing on her mind all night and she was ready to drop the subject and be engaged in a frivolous conversation.

"Did you know Celia knew Joanna and her brother back in high school?" Barbara asked Marti and Jane.

"I didn't," replied Marti.

"Nor I," said Jane, suddenly interested. "How do you know that?"

"She told me. One day at one of the tennis tournaments I sat with Celia, or should I say, she sat down next to me," Barbara went on. "Stuart happened to walk in on the other side of the court and Celia boasted that she had actually dated him in high school. He is quite good looking, you know, in a Nordic sort of way. Anyway, she really didn't say too much, but then I wasn't really too interested. Personally, I couldn't imagine the two of them together, but who knows."

This gets more and more curious, Jane thought, recalling last night's dream and her conversation with Marti. Looking up she caught Marti's eye, which seemed to be telling her, *See, I told you so.*

"That must have been in the Boston area, then," Jane surmised. "Until I read this morning's paper I always thought that Celia was originally from Ohio and just went to college in Boston."

"I think she was from the Quincy area, you know where Joanna and her brother grew up," Barbara told them. "At least that's what I assumed when she said something about dating Joanna's brother. I actually don't know much about her at all, when I think about it."

"Well, her kids are quite a bit younger than ours so we've never hung around her that much," Sheila reasoned.

Everyone, feeling less guilty now about how little attention they'd paid to Celia over the years, agreed with Sheila. Soon Jane's wish came true and their conversations went to more frivolous topics. Seating arrangements were discussed for the night of the fund- raiser and Jane told them about some of the better auction items in hoping to pique their interest to bring higher bids.

At the end of the day as Marti and Jane walked back home, they fell into a deep conversation about all they never knew or would know about other people's relationships. They both had advised Barbara to relay the information about Celia dating Stuart to the police even though she felt it wasn't an important detail. Jane knew that only time would tell what details were important and what ones weren't. Marti suggested that maybe she could tell Julia, Julia could tell Mike and then if Barbara hadn't called him then he could call Barbara. Feeling a sense of accomplishment at that idea, Marti volunteered to get in touch with Julia as soon as she returned home.

"Want to come over for some burgers tonight? Robin and Kelly are still staying with me and I'm firing up the grill with something easy. I've got plenty and you don't need to bring a thing except the boys, around seven. Rest that pretty head of yours," she laughed.

"You're on, thanks, but I'll at least bring a bottle of wine," Jane replied unlocking her front door and waving a cheery good-bye to her thoughtful friend as she stepped inside.

Throwing her beach things down on the kitchen floor, Jane began to walk over to the phone to check her messages. Turning back around, she grabbed the dead bolt on the door and turned it, feeling a bit foolish but a lot safer. She never thought she'd see the day when locking the door in broad daylight in this sleepy little village would even occur to her. Shaking her head, she dialed into her message service, put in her code and found she had two messages.

The first one was from Ian telling her he would have to have a quick dinner that evening because the Fog Runner had called and asked him and Matt to play that evening as the planned talent for the evening had canceled at the last minute. He sounded exceedingly pleased and Jane thought with a laugh it was just like one of the boys to throw a monkey wrench into her and Marti's plans. The boys would just have to do with a sandwich if dinner at seven was too late for them.

The second message was from Millie. She wanted Jane to come over the next day to work on pricing and sorting for the auction. More things had been dropped off and she was drowning in junk, most of it "unusable let alone sellable". Then she added, "And forget Joanna; she packed up and left this afternoon. I saw her loading her Suburban with half of the house on my way back from the beach today. She told me she's not sure she'll be back for the auction, let alone the rest of the summer. See if you can get Marti to help, will you? I'm desperate." And with that Millie had hung up.

That was a new development, Jane thought: Joanna leaving before the end of the summer. She couldn't really blame her, losing her husband and her friend and soon to lose the house. It was probably all too much for her, thought Jane. Or was she running away from something? "I wonder if she told the police that she was leaving town," Jane wondered aloud. Skeptical at that thought, Jane headed up for the shower.

Later at Marti's after burgers, chips and watermelon for all, including Matt and Ian who didn't have to report to the Fog Runner until at least eight thirty, Jane and Marti sat and talked about Joanna's abrupt departure. Why had she left in such a hurry? Was she trying to hide something? When Joanna had first arrived in Herring Run she had rubbed everyone the wrong way even though most of them had tried to bring her into the community and accept her as Sam's new wife. But in typical Joanna fashion, she proceeded to make everyone sorry they had ever bothered. They grew tired of her attitude and soon all they could do was barely tolerate her for Sam's sake and then, only when they had to.

Now as Marti and Jane sat quietly talking under the darkening skies, watching the briquettes of the grill lose their glow, they realized that they now felt pity for this woman who just didn't fit in here. She had lost the one friend she had in the village on top of losing her husband and now she was losing the house. It didn't really make them like her any better but it did put some perspective on her as a woman who was in pain. They questioned if they could have been more approachable toward her but thought they'd both done the best they could seeing the circumstances of the situation over the years.

No, they couldn't feel guilty over what couldn't have been. But both felt badly for Joanna with where she now found herself. Hopefully, Sam had left her adequately cared for with his life insurance and in his Will. Jane wondered if Joanna's first husband paid child support for their two sons. She'd never heard anything about Joanna's first husband except for some malicious gossip about him being a deadbeat dad.

Out under the open sky an increase of insect activity, the biting kind, soon drove the two friends into Marti's house where they put on a pot of decaf coffee. The older boys had departed for their gig and the girl lifeguards along with Trey and Nick were playing a wicked game of Balderdash in the living room. They listened to peals of laughter ring out as the kids tried to define the most obscure words Jane had ever heard. Sitting at Marti's kitchen table she held the warm mug in her hand, sipping it slowly, savoring the moment brought by a good cup of coffee and the sound of joy in the air.

"Are you going to Millie's tomorrow to price?" Marti asked as she joined Jane at the table. "She wants me to go over to her house for last minute pricing, said she'd like you there also. Seems she got a flurry of donations over the past few days."

"Yeah, I'm going. Though I can't imagine anyone is in the mood for a gala auction night after all that's gone on here lately," Jane opined.

"Probably not, but the catering is set, the hall is paid for and the show must go on. Won't be too upbeat, I dare say. But maybe it will be a healthy shot in the arm for the village. There's nothing we can do to change what's happened but at least we can try to do something good for the village. A new playground isn't a controversial subject, which is good. Just about everyone seems to agree the equipment isn't safe and the grounds could use some beautifying so. . . ." Marti's voice trailed off, remembering how run down the current playground looked.

"You're right, of course. So what time are you planning to show up at Millie's?"

Marti got up and looked at her crowded kitchen calendar. Each date seemed to be crammed with some activity or appointment that one or the other of the Sanders had going.

"I've got a hair cut at eleven-thirty, so as early as we can make it would work for me," said Marti. "How about eighty-thirty or nine?"

"Sounds about right. I'll give Millie a call as soon as I get home. Marti, thanks so much for the lovely dinner," Jane said as she got up and rinsed her coffee cup out and put it in the dishwasher. "I'm going to head home for a good night's sleep, hopefully with no more weird dreams." Calling into the living room she said, "Trey, I'm off. Do you have a key to the house? I'm locking up as soon as I get in."

"Got it, Mom. See ya later."

"Well, then, goodnight, Marti, and thanks again for the lovely evening. I'll stop by tomorrow morning to pick you up on the way to Millie's."

And with that Jane walked out in the dark night, switched on her flashlight and walked swiftly home, feeling a bit spooked the whole way. Once inside her house she relocked the door and headed straight for her bedroom and was quickly in a deep, dreamless sleep.

Tuesday, August 10th

P
RICING THE NEXT morning went smoothly once they
had waded through the junk that just couldn't be sold.
All three ladies had quite a few good laughs over some
of the more outrageous donations. A moose head that was
quite moth-eaten, donated by one of the more eccentric family
of the village whose great uncle had been an avid hunter. No
one could think of a polite way to phrase a 'thanks but no
thanks' note to them as the family had waxed poetically about
what the moose had meant to all of them. They'd put a note
about what it was worth with references to tax deductions in
the moose's mouth, of all places.

Then there was the bag of size 42 triple E used bras, with no
note. No note needed, as everyone in the village knew who had
worn those, though probably no one realized what beautiful,
lacy bras this particular matronly lady wore. After howling
with laughter and a few good-natured lusty remarks, the three
women vowed to keep their find a secret. Also in the reject
pile was a small box filled with some very lifelike erotic toys.
When Millie opened that box she almost strangled with mirth.
She plugged one in, held it up and they all crumpled with
laughter. No note had been left with this unusual donation
and they didn't have the slightest idea who the toys could

have belonged to, thinking they might have been donated by mistake. Whomever the previous owner was, Millie declared them unfit to auction off at this year's fundraiser and threw the toy back into the box, taped it shut and announced she felt a great need to go wash her hands. With that Jane dissolved once more into hysterics, with Marti right behind her.

At about a quarter after eleven Marti announced she had to run for her hair appointment but that she thoroughly enjoyed their morning. Millie and Jane said they'd catch her at the beach later and expected to be done pricing within the hour. Working diligently it took them another two hours to finish but they ended with a great sense of accomplishment. The items were cleaned, priced and ready for the event that was less than two weeks away.

Jane left Millie's and hurried up the Midway heading for the post office, which was located on the village green. The post office was a tiny building with two small rooms. One room was where the post office boxes were located with their funny little locks. The other room was for the postmistress to do whatever a postmistress does. Jane saw through the clear glass of her box that she had several deliveries. Pulling the box open, she reached in to get the envelopes out one at a time causing a small piece of paper that had been stuck between them to flutter to the floor. Jane pulled out the rest of her mail and then bent to retrieve the errant piece of paper. It was folded in thirds, with no envelope, no stamp, and no address. Just the words written in tiny, cramped handwriting in black ink stating: *Stay Out of It*. There was also a dagger drawn on it, dripping red ink from its tip; Jane assumed this was to represent blood.

Stay out of it? What was that about? Jane wondered. Going up to the window, Jane tried to get the attention of the grandmotherly postmistress who looked like she was deeply involved in some project with a laptop computer on the high desk behind the counter.

"Morning, Mrs. Ambrose," Jane called out. "I hate to interrupt you, but I was wondering if you had put a note in my mailbox."

Looking up from her computer, Mrs. Ambrose at first looked a bit distracted, then with a smile said, "I'm sorry dear, what did you say? I was working on beating this computer at a game of solitaire. Wasn't having much luck, as I can't cheat a little like I do at home with a deck of cards. What was it that you wanted?"

Jane laughed. "I know what you mean about the solitaire. I was just asking if you had left a note in my post box."

"Note? What kind of note? Nothing from me in those boxes, just what gets delivered from the main post office in Hyannis. Does it have a postmark?" Mrs. Ambrose inquired sweetly.

"Never mind, it's not important. Hey, how are those grandchildren of yours?" Jane inquired.

"They're great. Had a few over a couple of days ago. Stayed for three nights. Those are Gina's kids. They'll be coming back soon to stay again. I'm just taking a few days to rest up for the next round. They certainly keep me jumping. I forgot what three kids under ten can get into and how hard it is to keep up with them. Todd's children are older, teenagers, and they're easy all day. Just go to the beach. It's the evenings when they wear me out the most, wanting to be out for all hours and such and me wondering what they're up to."

"I hear you on that one," Jane said with a smile. "See you later. Good luck on beating the computer," Jane added as she walked out the door.

Heading back down the midway, Jane pondered who could

have put a note in her box without sending it through the mail. Putting it there wouldn't have been too hard. With Mrs. Ambrose engrossed in her game it would have been easy for anyone to reach around and stick something into her box, in fact lots of people walked on back just to chat to the sociable lady so anyone could have access to all the boxes as they were open in the back. Herring Run's little post office was a throw back to the 1800s and a very casual affair these days, it closed at two and was run by Mrs. Ambrose who lived in the village. And what did "stay out of it" mean? No answer came to her except just kids fooling around. It really did look childish. Sticking the note in her pocket she started glancing through what had arrived. Being in Herring Run only in the summer Jane never had to wade through bills here. They still went to her Arizona home. In fact, not much mail came to her in the village so she only checked her box two of three times a week. Today was a windfall. A thank-you note from a friend's daughter who had recently had a baby, a Pennysaver newspaper, an ad for a cleaning service addressed to Occupant and last, but most importantly, a 'miss you' card from Geoff. Jane loved it when Geoff did these sentimental things. And mostly, she missed him, too.

Unlocking her door she walked in and threw the mail onto the kitchen counter. She put Geoff's card on the refrigerator with a magnet and sighed. Only a week and a half to go and he'd be here. Pulling herself back to earth she relocked the door, something she just couldn't get in the habit of doing and walked up the stairs to her bedroom to get ready to go to the beach. Throwing her shorts in the clothes hamper she forgot about the note as she got out her blue bathing suit, white beach cover and straw hat. She suddenly realized that it was getting late and her stomach was growling. She'd buy lunch at the snack bar, a good old tuna melt. Pulling on her suit she took a sideways look in the mirror, sucked in her stomach, stood a little straighter and with a sigh of acceptance threw the beach cover over her head, down past her hips, plopped the hat on her head and without a further thought she headed down to the beach.

Friday, August 13th

THREE DAYS LATER as Jane was pulling weeds and errant grass out of her bed of lavender,

Marti came by waving a small piece of paper. She had a grim look on her face and worry lines creased her forehead.

"Jane," she called as she approached the garden. "Jane, look at this. The oddest thing appeared in my mailbox."

Working to stand up straight after remaining in such a cramped position, Jane realized how stiff she had become. Shielding her eyes from the sun she reached out and took the small piece of white paper that Marti had thrust out in her direction. Letting her eyes adjust for a second to make out the tiny writing Jane saw that the only words that were written on the paper were: *Hands Off or Else*. Drawn under the words was a skull and crossbones.

"How weird," Jane said slowly.

"What do you make of that? It was mixed in with my mail. I wonder if the letter sorter let something get into my stack of mail by mistake. It's sort of creepy-looking, though."

Jane turned the paper over but the reverse side was blank.

"Did this come out of an envelope or with anything else?" she asked Marti.

"No, it was just stuck between a couple of the letters in our post office box." Marti explained.

Remembering her note from a few days ago, Jane hurried into her house, telling Marti to follow. She started going through her papers on the counter and then began to look through her junk drawer. Impatiently, she threw things out willy-nilly, making a mess all over the granite counter top.

"I got a strange note the other day, too," Jane informed her friend, as she continued to search. "It wasn't quite the same, but similar. If I could just find it." Stumped that she couldn't find the note she began to rifle through the counter top accumulation again. "I can't remember quite what it said, something like 'stay out', but I do remember it had what looked like a dagger dripping blood under the message. I'd forgotten about it until just now. Where did I put that thing?"

Jane stood stock-still and tried to remember what she had done when she had gotten home from the post office three days ago. She'd unlocked the door, walked in, put all the mail down on the counter except for Geoff's card, which she hung on the refrigerator. So, it had to be right on the counter. She was terrible about throwing things away and even the occupant-addressed card was still there even though she knew she'd never spend the money on a cleaning service. So the note had to be there, didn't it? But it wasn't.

Taking her memory further back, she thought about when she was at the post office and then walking down the midway toward home. *That's it*, she thought. "Stay right here," Jane told Marti as she bounded up the stairs to her bedroom and lifted the top of the hamper. There on the bottom of the pile of dirty clothes were the shorts she had worn that day. She stuck her hand in the pocket and pulled out the note. Taking it back downstairs, she handed it over to Marti.

"*Stay Out of It,*" Marti read. "You know, the handwriting looks similar. Let's compare them side by side."

Both notes were written in small letters and both had drawings. The handwriting looked similar and the type of paper did too. Other than that and the idea that it was a bit of a veiled warning Jane and Marti could draw no conclusions.

"Do you think this has to do with the murders?" Marti wondered aloud.

"I have no idea," Jane responded. "It's not like we've been too involved in them lately, in fact I thought that on the whole we had backed off the entire thing. Maybe we should show these to Mike."

"Do you think?"

"Well, I originally thought it was the work of some kids, and granted that may just be what it is but I don't know about you but I find it a little scary, both of us finding these notes. I think we should hand them over to the police," Jane said firmly.

"Okay; should we do it today?" Marti asked.

"If it's okay with you I'd feel better if we got it over with. Can you run over there with me now? I'll just wash my hands and run a comb through my hair and be ready. We can take my car," Jane said as she ran her hands under the kitchen sink.

Twenty minutes later Melissa, the young woman behind the desk, ushered them back to Mike's office. She was not as chatty today, clearly trying to keep everything official. She'd probably gotten a reprimand from the desk sergeant who had observed her conversation with Jane the last time Jane was stopped by her desk.

Mike rose from his desk as the ladies entered and told them to take a seat in one of the chairs that sat right in front of it.

"For what do I have the pleasure of your company today ladies? I heard from Julia that you are aware of our news."

"We are and congratulations, Mike. You two are perfect together," Marti gushed.

"We couldn't be happier for either of you," Jane said. "Just you treat that friend of ours right or . . ." she made a fist and gave Mike a big smile.

Mike laughed and then took a more serious tone of voice. "Really, now, what brings you to over to my official sanctum? You aren't meddling into these murders are you?"

"Absolutely not!" Marti said indignantly. "We've backed off just like you told us to."

"But maybe someone doesn't know that we have," Jane added and pulled the note she had received and laid it on his desk. "I got this in my post office box a few days ago and Marti," she indicated to her friend as Marti pulled out her note and placed it next to Jane's, "got this one today."

Mike looked the notes over then looked up at both women. "I don't suppose you handled these with rubber gloves on, did you?" he asked with a grimace, knowing the answer as he stared at notes.

"Well, I never thought of it," Jane replied honestly. "In fact I forgot about it and shoved it into one of my shorts' pockets. I honestly didn't think much about it until Marti showed up with hers this morning."

"When did you get yours, Jane?" the police chief asked.

"I think it was three days ago. Let's see last time I did laundry was on Monday so it must have been on Tuesday because the shorts were on the bottom of the pile," she replied triumphantly.

"Run that by me again," Mike said, looking a bit confused.

"My shorts, where I put the note. They were in the laundry

hamper still, at the bottom of the pile. So that means if the last time I did the wash was Monday than it had to be Tuesday that I picked up the mail."

"I see," Mike said, not really sure he did but taking her word for it.

"But then it might have been in my mailbox for days because I only check my post office box a few times a week at the most."

"And how about you, Marti?" Mike asked. "When did you last do your laundry or pick up your mail?"

Marti looked at Mike a bit askance and then realizing he was trying to make light of it told him, "I'm a bit like Jane. I only get my mail once or twice a week since most of my mail goes to our Boston address. I rarely get things down here unless it's an invite or a thank you from someone down here on the Cape," she explained. "So I don't know how long that note may have been there."

"Well, that certainly clears things up and makes things easy," Mike said as he picked up his phone and requested the person at the other end to bring two evidence bags to his office immediately.

"So you think this had something to do with Celia or Sam's murder?" Marti wanted to know.

"I don't know what it has to do with but if you don't mind, or even if you do, I think I'll keep these notes just in case. I appreciate your coming down with them. You know, we'll have to get a copy of your fingerprints so we can try to identify any others on the notes," Mike added.

"Oh, I never thought of that," Marti said, "but it's fine with me."

"Me, too," Jane added "Anything new on the case, Mike?" Jane wanted to know.

"If there was I couldn't tell you," Mike told her earnestly, as he got up and began ushering Marti and Jane out of his office to escort them down to the lab to get their prints taken. "We are looking into a few possible leads but I really can't go into that now. One thing I will ask of you two is that you don't talk about your notes to anyone else. The less people know, the better for us in helping us solve the cases. And ladies, we don't even know if these two, or I should say three cases are at all related. Now, go on back to the village and enjoy some tennis or something. Summer is almost over. Let us worry about solving the murders."

"Hey, did you know that Celia once told Barbara that she had dated Joanna's brother?" Jane asked Mike.

"Barbara did call me about that. It's something I'm looking into," he replied, without adding any information.

Jane and Marti hesitated, but with nothing more forthcoming from Mike began to leave with the lab attendant to have their fingerprints taken.

"One more thing, Mike," Jane said as she stood in the hallway. "You haven't said how Celia died."

"No, I haven't, have I?" Mike replied, rubbing his chin and giving Jane a meaningful look. "Jane, this is serious business. We have had three corpses turn up this summer, all seeming to have to do with something or someone in Herring Run. I will tell you that there was head trauma, but I don't think that's what killed her. Now, keep your head safe by keeping your nose out of police business."

"Did you know that Joanna left the village to go back to Boston," Jane persisted.

"Yes, as a matter of fact I do have that bit of information. She phoned me to be sure it was all right. So get this done and then off with the two of you. Go relax at the beach. I'll look into this note business and you two keep your noses clean." And with that Mike turned and headed back to his office.

"I guess he's made his position clear," Marti noted, as she held out her hand to the young man taking their prints.

"Guess, so," Jane replied as her mind whirled with questions that she desperately wanted answers to.

*   *   *

Back in Herring Run, life looked the same as it did any other day of the summer. People were laden with beach chairs on their way to the beach, a mother and her kids were rowing across the pond, a man was walking his dog and three young boys rode by on their bikes with tennis rackets slung across their backs.

Jane's weeding tools were right where she'd left them, among the lavender, and the sun was now too hot to even think of finishing the job. Picking them up, she trudged to the shed where they kept their tools and put them away. Lost in thought, she wondered who could have left the notes. What kind of a warning was "hands off"? Marti hadn't really had her hands on! This was just meant to scare them, Jane was sure. And it had worked; Jane was scared. But she was more scared to do nothing than she was to "stay out of it". This village needed to be free of this onus of a killer roaming free hanging over its head. She especially needed to be free of it.

Jane entered her kitchen and went straight to her junk drawer and pulled out her list of suspects. Scanning it she realized that none of it made sense to her and she crumpled it up, depressed the trash lever of her compactor with her foot and threw it in to be pressed into oblivion with all her other trash. Maybe Mike was right and the best thing to do would be to do nothing.

Standing at the counter deep in thought, she was startled to hear the kitchen door open. She gave a small yelp as she looked up, realizing she had forgotten to lock the door when she returned home

"Didn't mean to startle you, Jane. I knocked as I opened the door. I thought you heard me," Davis said as he stood in the doorframe looking quite embarrassed. "Are you okay?"

"Yeah, yeah, I'm okay. Just a little jumpy, that's all," Jane replied, looking quite pale to Davis despite her reassurances.

"I'm sorry if I scared you. I heard about Celia from Mrs. Ambrose at the post office when I picked up my mail today. I just came to tell you I'm back from my visit to my daughter's but I'm leaving in a few days, this time to Montreal. It seems like every time I leave on one of my trips someone gets murdered. You're not still nosing into this one are you? Who's left on your suspect list?"

"I threw is away, thank you very much. I'm done with all of that."

"That look in your eye doesn't agree with what's coming out of your mouth, Jane Adams. You better watch yourself and keep you doors locked."

"I plan to, I just keep forgetting. Guess I'm not in the habit," Jane told him, pushing her blond hair out of her face, ignoring the part about the nosing around.

"Listen, I'm off to the store, need anything? I could at least make amends for giving you such a start."

"I'm fine, really and I don't need anything from the store, thanks anyway. Did you have a good trip?"

"I did. My new granddaughter is adorable and I'm very glad that I only had to spend three days listening to the music of a newborn's cry," Davis laughed. "Catch you later."

Jane watched Davis go down the walk toward his house and then put the dead bolt in place. She wondered if she should retrieve her list from the compactor or just start a new one. Nothing wrong with speculation, she told herself. No one would know she thought as she pulled a new piece of paper from the pad, grabbed a pen and began a new list. She made three columns. One headed with the name "Sam", one with "Sara" and one with "Celia", all three names underlined.

Under Sam and Sara's names she put "Joanna". Joanna had been married to Sam and Sara was having an affair with Joanna's husband. Under both Sam and Sara's names Jane put colleague and then client. Both worked in the same firm and could have had some dealings that angered someone. What about Celia? Who would want to kill her? Celia had seemed to have been one of Joanna's good friends, a friend, Jane now realized, since high school. Did Joanna hate her for some reason they weren't aware of, some old grudge? Jane added her name under Celia's. There was always Stuart who it was rumored Celia had dated in high school. Jane scribbled his name under his sister's in Celia's column. And Stuart could be thought of as a suspect in Sam and Sara's murders, doing it for his sister. Celia's husband could have wanted her dead and though it might not have anything to do with Sam or Sara, maybe Spencer got caught up in the frenzy of the summer's murders and decided for reasons of his own to murder his wife, hoping no one would suspect him. Adding Spencer's name below that of Stuart's, Jane recalled that most murderers knew their victims well, and who better to know you than your spouse, so he was a good bet, though Jane really couldn't imagine Spencer even kicking anyone. But then it's often those mild, meek types in Agatha Christie books that are the murderers. Spencer didn't go under Sam or Sara's names as Jane couldn't think of any involvement he would have had with them. She'd never even seen them socialize together.

SAM	SARA	CELIA
Joanna	Joanna	Joanna
Colleague	Colleague	Stuart
Client	Client	Spencer
Stuart	Stuart	

Jane looked at the list and realized that only two of the names were listed under all three of the victims. Could Joanna and/or Stuart be the murder? Murderers? Could they have done this together or were they not even connected. Was there another person that Jane had no idea existed that belonged on the list? Jane's head began to throb. She decided to take a few aspirins and lie down for a bit. These murders were causing so many headaches that Jane was tempted to give the whole thing up like Geoff and Mike wanted her to. Taking the list up to her room she tucked it away in her underwear drawer, the one place she didn't think anyone in her family would ever run across it, unless of course, she thought with a chuckle, one of them had a deep, dark secret. Sitting down on her bed, Jane thought she'd take a short nap and try to get rid of her headache.

Jane awoke to the ringing of the telephone. Groggily, she pulled herself up in the bed and answered the phone.

"Mom, you okay?" came Ian's voice over the wires.

Looking at the clock, Jane realized that she had slept a good three hours. Jumping out of bed she replied to Ian, "Wow, I really slept. Sorry, Ian, I had a bad headache and the phone woke me," Jane told him.

"Gee, mom, sorry to wake you but I wanted to let you know that a bunch of us are off to go wake boarding this afternoon after work. Trey and the Sanders boys are going with us and we're all stopping to eat at Hyannis Pizza and Sub. Hope that's okay," he ended.

"Sounds fine to me, just be careful," Jane told him.

"Thanks, Mom, see you later," Ian said as he rang off.

Bye, thought Jane to the dial tone. Now what? Again, no one for dinner, that was par for the course. Maybe this night would be a Lean Cuisine night. It certainly wouldn't hurt. Running a comb through her flattened hair and making a face in the mirror she decided that she would be good and eat a low cal dinner and clean out a few drawers. No more eating out and no more trying to solve murders. Mike was right, she should just try to enjoy the rest of what was left of the summer.

Jane was good. After eating two Lean Cuisines (one was never enough) she began to work on the mess of the junk drawer in the kitchen. What wasn't in here she wondered as she pulled out twist ties, rubber bands, a three-year-old pocket calendar and other items that gave the drawer its name.

She was just lining the drawer with some new paper when there was a knock on the kitchen door. She looked up to see Marti's face peering in looking down at Jane as she sat on the floor cutting the paper. Jane motioned her in and as Marti tried to open the door Jane remembered that it was locked and struggled to get up quickly to let her friend enter.

"This is what I hate," she told Marti. "We can't even trust our neighbors. I never locked the door except when we went to bed, and now, well, it's always locked, day and night. This is so annoying."

"What are you doing?" Marti asked with a chuckle, knowing full well that Jane was not the most domestic housewife of her friends. Neat drawers and paper-lined cupboards were not in Jane's character.

"I'm doing my drawers," Jane replied. "Can't you see?"

"Yes, but why?"

"Well, because—well okay, because I'm trying very hard not to think about the murders and to heed Mike's advise."

"Good for you, Jane, but how long do you think this new you will last?"

"One drawer. I've had it. This is not my thing," answered Jane as she threw the misshapen cut paper away, tossed the remaining items back in the drawer and shoved it back into place. 'But I'm trying."

"Okay, that's good. Now, let's go to a movie. The boys are out, I'm bored and we need to occupy our minds."

"Give me two seconds to get my purse," Jane replied.

Saturday and Sunday, August 14th and 15th

OVER THE WEEKEND Herring Run seemed to get back to normal. Jane and Marti were able to fall back into their summer routine. Julia even talked them into looking for a dress for her to wear for her upcoming nuptials. They drove over to the Mashpee Commons where Alex met them and they had a great time watching the two women try on dresses. Everything looked great on both Julia and Alex but nothing was decided on that day. Afterwards the four went to have lunch at one of the restaurants on the Common. No one spoke of the murders, just happy thoughts of dresses and weddings, flowers and champagne. They all had a great afternoon.

With the auction night a week away Marti talked Julia into coming insisting that she buy two tickets even though Mike's schedule might not allow him to attend and they hadn't really made a public announcement of their engagement. Jane thought Alex could always pinch hit for Mike in case he was busy and she would have fun seeing lots of the old Herring Run neighbors. Alex's reply to that was a cross-eyed look at the two ladies!

The next day as Jane and Marti finished three set of tennis with the ladies in the round-robin they noticed that Joanne's brother was talking to the tennis pro. When the two ladies passed by them the men stopped talking as Stuart turned to say hello.

"How was your game this morning ladies?" he asked with a wide smile on his face.

"Luckily, we squeaked by in a tie breaker in the third set, so I guess it was good," Jane told him.

"Glad to hear it. Listen, Joanna is going to come back to stay for the rest of the summer. She's talked to Julia and Alex and they encouraged her to bring the boys to finish out the season with their swim and tennis lessons. I hope that everyone's okay with that," he asked them with a knowing look on his face.

"That's great," Jane replied quickly. "We still need her help with the auction so we'd love to see her return."

"Well, good, that's settled. Guess I'll see you around," Stuart said, dismissing them as he turned his attention back to the tennis pro.

Walking home, Marti said the Jane, "That's great? Boy, how did you come up with that? You know we really don't need Joanna for the auction anymore unless it's to cart the stuff up to the dining room and put it in place and you know she'd never risk her nails."

"Give me a break. I didn't know what to say to him. Anyway, maybe she will want to help out with the decorations or something. I was on the spot and you know that I really don't think that quick on my feet, Marti!"

"Okay, well, you be the welcoming committee 'cause there she is getting out of her car now. I'm going home to change for the beach, I'll see you later," Marti said as she veered off in the direction of her own house.

Waving good-bye to Marti, Jane took a deep breath and

slowly headed toward Joanna. She had not yet caught sight of Jane, as Joanna was busy unpacking the back seat of her car so that when Jane approached and said hello Joanna seemed a bit rattled at the intrusion.

"Oh, I didn't mean to startle you, Joanna. I just wanted to say hello and welcome back."

Joanna mutely stared at Jane as if she were an alien from Mars. Jane stood in great discomfort as the silence lengthened. Finally Jane said, "We were hoping you would still want to help with the auction. It's only a few days away and there still the decorating to do the day of it. I know that you really have a talent for that sort of thing."

Joanna blinked a couple of times, her mouth opened and closed and in a very atypical manner said, "I would love to help with the decorating. Just let me know when you need me. And thanks for the compliment."

Jane feeling a bit floored, said she'd give her a call in the next day or two when she knew what the schedule was and bid her good-bye. On her way back home Jane wondered if Joanna had been captured by aliens or had been possessed. This was not the Joanna that Jane knew and didn't love; she'd actually been a bit civil.

When she arrived home she immediately called Mille to let her know that a new meek and polite Joanna was back and that she would love to help them with the decorating for the auction. Jane added that when Millie got the schedule Jane would be happy to call Joanna with it. Millie, not one to let a good opportunity pass her by, told Jane that she would be happy to make the call to Joanna herself. Millie was dying to talk to the new Joanna herself. Jane, also, not one to miss a beat, told Millie to be sure that she was included in the decorating team.

The auction looked like it was going to be a fun evening

after all. Most of the people coming had signed on in advance of Celia's death or even before Sam's murder and weren't going to let their money go to waste. Anyone who was thinking of not coming was taken to task by the chairwoman, Lanie, a woman who could charm a cat out of a tree. Plus everyone knew it was for a good cause, new playground equipment for the kids. A charity function like that always tugged at the heartstrings of the villagers. Now, if it was for a new flagpole for the Green, or a new organ for the community church, well, that might be a different story. But, just about everyone in the little village of Herring Run had a soft spot for the kids.

The rest of the week Jane let all thoughts of the murders go and enjoyed getting ready for the auction and the good weather by going to the beach. Everything seemed to have returned to normal in Herring Run, including Jane and Marti. No more threats and finally Jane began to relax. Mike hadn't called regarding their notes, Joanna didn't bother anyone and for the most part the front of Jane's brain had forgotten about most of it. Herring Run was in its countdown days until Labor Day and everyone was determined to enjoy the days of summer that were left.

Thursday, August 19th

THURSDAY MORNING, JANE went to her closet and began rummaging through it trying to find something to wear for the evening of the auction. It had to be something she wouldn't roast in because at the old Inn, where it was being held, there was no air conditioning, just open windows and a few floor fans. She loved to dress up, especially with a slight tan enhancing her looks. And she wanted to look spiffy because Geoff would be there and she wanted him to be reminded of just one of the reasons he married her!

After rejecting about everything in the closet and not even bothering with some of it, Jane concluded that she needed to do some shopping herself. She didn't really want to go back to Mashpee Commons since it was a bit of a hike. Grabbing her keys, Jane decided to skip the beach this afternoon and head to Hyannis and one of her favorite stores, Puritan.

Parking behind Puritan and entering through the back door, Jane headed straight for the section she thought would have something that would work for the night of the auction. If she was in luck it might even be on sale as it was late in the season for summer clothes and the fall arrivals were already appearing on the racks.

One of her favorite saleswomen, Linda, spotted her and

with a smile joined Jane and asked her if she could help her find something. With the two of them busy going through the racks they found four dresses and two skirts with some tops that just might work and Linda led Jane to one of the wonderful, roomy Puritan dressing rooms.

The first two dresses Jane refused to come out of the dressing room, even to show Linda, due to how bad they looked on her. They added five pounds, on each hip! They would never do. And on top of that, whoa—what a matronly look! Sometimes having boobs at middle age wasn't the best! Now, put this same dress on Alex or Robin and they would look very svelte. The third dress was a real possibility and Jane came out to look at herself in the three-way mirror. Not bad, in fact pretty darn great! The dress was a cotton sheath dress, black with tiny white polka dots. It wasn't revealing but mid-knee length with a slight sexy slit up one side. Making it a bit "in" and fun was the back zipper that was wide and visible. It gave the dress a young, stylish look without looking too young for someone Jane's age.

It would look great with the cute little black sandals that she already had. Since it worked when she looked in the three-way mirror Jane knew she had found exactly what she wanted. In fact she loved it. She headed out of the dressing room to find Linda to show her the final choice and ran smack dab into Joanna!

"Oh, my gosh. I am so sorry," Jane apologized to Joanna as she steadied Joanna to keep her from tipping over. "I didn't mean to run into you. I really should look where I'm going and not go so fast. Are you okay?"

"Jane, wow, you look great! And yes, I'm fine," Joanna told an astonished Jane. "What's the occasion?"

"Well, gee, thanks, Joanna. I'm getting something for the night of the auction."

"Me, too! What fun, maybe we can look together."

Now Jane was really mystified. This really was not the Joanna that she had known for the last few years. What was going on here? Though as Jane looked closely at Joanna, she did think she was noticing a bit of a tic to the side of her left eye and an overall strain in her face.

"Thanks to your confirmation, I think this is what I plan to buy," Jane said as she stood at the three way mirror and eyed her rear end, feeling relieved that it didn't look bigger than normal and maybe even a mite smaller.

"It's lovely. You really look nice in it."

Now Jane was really perplexed at the changed woman before her. Turning to her she said, "Joanna, we're about the same size, you might want to check out what I had in my dressing room. You've got the long legs for the two dresses that just wouldn't work for me.

Ten minutes later the two women, each with a Puritan purchase in their hands, left the store and headed for a nearby coffee shop to have a latte together with Jane still mystified by the change in Joanna. When they had settled into one of the tables with their drinks Joanna told Jane that she thought she made the right choice in the polka dot dress and would knock the socks off all the men there that evening. Jane returned the compliment in spades as Joanna had chosen a dress that hugged her body beautifully in all the right spots. As soon as the words were out of her mouth Jane knew something was wrong.

"I'm sorry, Joanna. I didn't mean anything. I know you must wish that Sam would be here to go with you. It must be so hard. Is your brother going to accompany you to the auction?" Jane wanted to know as she tried to steer the conversation away from the subject of Sam's death.

"Scott said he'd come, so I guess so. I have two tickets," Joanna answered.

"Scott? Do I know him?" Jane asked.

"Did I say Scott? No, I meant Stuart. Scott is a friend of Stuart's and I was thinking about him today. Sorry, just a slip of the tongue. Yeah, Stuart's going to the auction with me. He really likes Herring Run and will be sorry to not be coming after this summer. Me, too. I know I never really fit in here. I found it so difficult with all of the friendships that were so entrenched in the village and, of course, with me stepping into Julia's shoes as Sam's wife, living in Marsh Cottage."

Jane shifted uneasily in her seat. Having no idea what to say, she kept quiet for once. Joanna let out a big sigh and they both sipped their lattes in silence. Finally, Jane reached across the table and put her hand on the back of Joanna's as it rested on the table.

"You know, Joanna, you can make a fresh start. In fact I think you have. Let's just say that today is a new beginning for you. We had a good time today. Now, I best be off and I'll see you tomorrow at the decorating party. We're doing it a day in advance I'm going to order pizza in and make it a fun evening. Only two nights until the big night."

"I know. Millie called me and gave me the details. It sounds like fun. Jake, Justin and I are going to bake cupcakes tonight to bring for dessert. That is if I can keep those boys of mine from eating all of them," Joanna concluded with a sad smile as they walked out the door and headed for their cars.

On the way home, Jane kept rerunning the last hour and a half through her mind. She really had never seen this side of Joanna. Where had this woman been every summer she had been in Herring Run since Sam had brought her as his new wife? Maybe, Jane thought, her marriage to Sam wasn't a very good marriage. Maybe that's what had made her the shrew that they had all known. Did that make Joanna a prime suspect? A shiver went down Jane's spine. Could she just have had coffee with a killer? No way, Jane thought. Joanna just didn't seem like the type. Yet, sometimes the least likely people turned out to be killers, like scout leaders, ministers and nurses. Even priests were in the news as pedophiles. Nor were our elected officials immune. All these people who should be trustworthy, weren't. What was the world coming to? Maybe Joanna was a psychopath or whatever those people were that could be charming one day and a killer the next.

Stopping at Cape Fish and Lobster on the way home Jane bought a nice piece of halibut that they could put on the grill after seasoning it up a bit. She had the makings of a spinach salad, one of Ian' favorites, and could roast some potatoes with garlic for the boys, another favorite. She just hoped that they were staying home for dinner for a change now that she had the fish.

Arriving home, she found Trey and Ian already lounging on the deck. Ian was playing his guitar and Trey was just sitting with his feet up enjoying the music.

"Hi guys!" Jane greeted her offspring. "Please, tell me you'll be home for dinner."

"Not only are we home for dinner tonight, Mom, but you have us for the next three nights. Low on funds and pay day isn't until next week," Ian explained.

"That's not my problem," Trey chirped in. "I've saved plenty of money this summer. I just want to be home and relax and get a good home cooked meal."

"Great," Jane smiled. "If you guys get the grill going I've got a nice piece of halibut we can marinate right before it goes on and I have the makings for a spinach salad. But to tell the truth, the next two nights I won't be around to cook for you. Tomorrow night I'll be decorating at the inn and having a pizza party. The next night is the dinner and auction for the fund raiser so you two will have to be on your own."

Groans were heard from both boys and Jane laughed. For once they would be staying home and she wouldn't be here to feed them. Murphy's Law!

"Hey, Dad comes in to the Barnstable airport tomorrow night. Why don't you guys pick him up and grill something special for him? He'll be tired and he would love that. Ian, your lamb chops are great. What do you say? I'll pick them up tomorrow if you want and I'll make enough potatoes so you can reheat some for tomorrow night and then you can just make the salad. It's Dad's recipe and anyway, it's easy and so delicious."

Groans were replaced with smiles and assents. Jane put the halibut in its wrapper on the kitchen counter and ran upstairs to put her new outfit away. She wouldn't show it to Geoff until the evening of the auction, not until she was dressed and ready. Hopefully, it would be just the ticket.

Friday, August 20th

THE NEXT MORNING, the sun did not greet the day. Instead, a steady drizzle rained down on the village and it was gloomy and cold. No walk this morning for Jane, instead she pulled the covers over her head and decided to sleep in another hour.

Around nine when she finally went down the stairs to the kitchen, she turned on the TV to see if she could get a weather forecast. Though the television stations generally only gave the Boston weather report with any accuracy, which was often quite different than that of Cape Cod, she still wanted to see if a weather pattern of rain had descended on the east coast. Crummy weather would really put a damper on the auction fundraiser plus her new outfit was really meant for warm weather not this cold, wet stuff.

She had missed all the local reports so decided to take an optimistic attitude and count on this just being a passing storm. Brewing up some coffee and popping a piece of whole wheat bread into the toaster, she got set to have a leisurely breakfast with time to read the paper for a change, which she just realized she'd have to run out into the rain to retrieve.

Throwing her yellow rain slicker over her robe Jane ran out, grabbed the paper and quickly shut the door against the howling wind. Her toast popped up as she came back into the kitchen so she threw the wet plastic covered paper into the sink and buttered her toast, got some beach plum jam to top it off and poured herself a cup of coffee. Retrieving the paper she pulled it out of the bag and sat down at the table opened it up and took a bite of her toast at the same time that she read the headline "New Allegations in the Sam Morris Murder".

Jane gulped. What was that all about, Jane wondered as she set down her toast and used both hands to hold the paper. As she read Jane grew quite skeptical, "an anonymous tip sent by letter into the newspapers office has charged that Sam Morris was involved in illegal drug trafficking . . ."

Oh, right, thought Jane. That was as far from Sam's personality as one could get. He was such a straight arrow about those things. He wasn't even a big drinker and he was always on the kids' cases about drug and alcohol abuse. This didn't sound at all like Sam. But then she wondered if she had really known Sam as well as she thought she had? His affair with Sara had come as a surprise. I wonder who would have sent in such a letter, Jane mused. The article mentioned that the letter had been left in an overnight drop off box at the newspaper's offices. No addresses, no signatures, no stamps or other identifying features were found. Too many people at the newspaper had handled it for it to be a good piece of evidence though the police were still looking into fingerprints, not much hope was held out for that. At least the newspaper was good enough to say there was nothing to prove that the story was true but the headline was damaging enough, Jane thought.

Well, this is really a new twist to things, Jane thought wryly. And on a gloomy day like today she really didn't feel like thinking about it at all. Leave it all to the proper authorities was her motto this morning as she had all week and she turned to Dear Abby for a chuckle. This was way beyond her.

Later that day Marti called Jane and wanted to know if she wanted to go to a movie matinee.

"Horrors," Jane replied. "Can you imagine how many people will be at the mall and at the movie theater on a day like today? Count me out. In fact, I don't think I'm doing much more than getting ready for Geoff to arrive tonight, you know, changing the sheets, getting some groceries in, that kind of stuff. Thanks for asking, though."

"Okay, see you at five for the decorating party, then. Don't forget to order at least six pizzas, Kelly, Robin and Alex are coming to help so we'll need extra and make them all large," Marti reminded her.

"You got it. Have fun with the crowds," Jane laughed, truly glad she wouldn't be a part of them. On rainy days the Cape Cod Mall was filled to the rafters with people and just finding a parking spot was usually an adventure, one that Jane avoided whenever possible.

Later as she smoothed the bedspread on her newly changed bed, Jane thought back to the morning paper's headlines. Such an odd idea to think of Sam involved with drugs. She supposed anything was possible. Maybe Sara was involved with them as well, thought Jane. She had died of an overdose of something, Mike had said.

Smacking the last wrinkle out on the bed, Jane turned her attention and frustration to cleaning the bathroom. She would have it sparkling for Geoff's return, for at least the first few minutes of it. Five minutes of him in the house usually set all things topsy-turvy, turning a house into a home, as Jane thought of it, with a grin.

By the time Jane finished her all her chores, around four, the sun had finally shown its face and her house almost sparkled with it. With a sense of accomplishment Jane turned her attention to gathering up what she would need for the decorating that evening. She rounded up her scissors, masking tape, scotch tape and some thumbtacks and threw them into one of her many huge tote bags along with a few personal items she thought she might need, like a flashlight for the walk home in case they finished late.

At a quarter to five, Jane put in a call to the pizza shop for three plain pizzas, two veggie pizzas, one Greek pizza with feta and to be on the safe side two more pizzas, this time with pepperoni, yuck, as far as she was concerned. Eight large pizzas should be plenty for the crowd; at least she hoped so. She asked for them to be delivered to the Inn around sis-thirty, figuring even if they weren't finished decorating, they'd be ready for a break.

Jane propped up a welcome home note for Geoff, an arrival time note for the boys so they'd remember when to pick him up and tonight's menu so they wouldn't forget what they were making for dinner. Picking her brain she tried to think if she had forgotten anything. Ah, a stepladder, she realized and went to grab one from the closet. Feeling ready Jane grabbed her bag, the small stepladder and her keys. She locked the door behind her and set out for the Inn to meet up with the other ladies.

It was a festive atmosphere at the Inn's main function room where the dinner and live auction where to be held. Millie had brought her CD player and had Jimmy Buffett music playing. Alex, Robin and Kelly had joined in with the ladies singing along with the CD. Barbara, Sheila and several of the other tennis ladies had started hanging the fairy lights when Jane arrived and some were twinkling already. The theme was a magical garden so Mille had procured small topiaries for centerpieces for each table and there were small unicorns scattered up and down the long serving tables. Jane recognized them as one of her friend's daughter's toy collection. When decorating on a shoestring, creativity came in all forms! Fake ivy from the craft store was to be hung from the rafters, the lights and around the doorways. The auctioneer's podium would be wreathed in green leaves. Jane hoped that the arty Richard wouldn't decide to appear dressed as Puck while being the auctioneer! She wouldn't put it past him. He was a real kick and quite the actor. Though, on second thought, that might be a good idea, she pictured with a chuckle.

Everyone turned around when the door opened and Marti's husband, Bob, appeared with Matt and Nick, each carrying a three-foot tall garden gnome. After a stunned silence all the women burst out laughing.

"Where did you get those?" Millie wanted to know, trying to contain herself.

"These slightly naughty gnomes, I'll have you ladies know, are the contribution of the Garden Center. I told them we were having an auction and that we were looking for contributions. Then I happened to mention the theme, well . . . here we are. They can be decorations and then auctioned off, we hope," Bob added, with a slight grimace. "I'm not sure to whom, but there must be someone who would love to have them in their yard, hopefully someone outside this village."

"Well, we can certainly try. If anyone can sell them, it will be Richard. In the meantime, they'll make great decorations. We'll find someplace for them, maybe one on each side of the podium and one as everyone walks into the room," Millie said.

"Sounds good to me, "Bob said, as he and the boys placed the gnomes in the spots that Millie indicated.

They actually looked very cute and livened the place up with their colorful hats and clothes. Jane thought she'd be surprised if anyone bought them but then stranger things had happened at their auctions, especially after a few glasses of wine. In fact, maybe they would really be the hit of the evening!

As Bob and the boys left, Joanna walked in apologizing to Millie for being late. Her brother had arrived down at the Cape later than usual due to heavy traffic with the rain so she couldn't leave until he could watch her boys. She handed over her box of yummy looking cupcakes and immediately started to pitch in with the decorating. Marti caught Jane's eye and gave her a meaningful look. Jane wasn't quite sure what the meaning was but she smiled back.

By six-thirty, most of the heavy duty decorating was finished and shortly thereafter the pizzas arrived. Sheila had brought some sodas and Barbara had brought some bottles of wine and with those open and the paper plates handed around everyone began to devour the food. Jane was beginning to worry that the eight pizzas were not going to be enough. With only one piece of pizza left in one box the women had finally had enough to turn their attention to the cupcakes and Jane was able to relax, and grab the last piece, her first.

The cupcakes were delicious. Chocolate cupcakes filled with a coconut cream that was divine, and they were all topped with a fudge icing. The decorating crew was swooning with pleasure.

"Did you bake these yourself, Joanna?" Barbara asked. "They're out of this world."

Everyone was nodding with agreement, their mouths too full to say much of anything besides Mmmmm. Joanna was smiling with pure pleasure.

"I love to bake. It's one thing I'm really good at and really enjoy doing." Jane swore Joanna actually blushed as she said this.

"We could auction off a dozen of these tomorrow night if you'd be willing to bake them." Nikki said.

"I'd be honored, make it two dozen," Joanna smiled.

"Well, these are really fabulous, I will be bidding on them

for sure," Millie added. "Thanks for bringing them, and thanks everyone for all the help you gave in getting all these decorations up. I think we're just about ready. Just some finishing touches to do here and there. The caterer will arrive tomorrow around four-thirty. Cocktails will start on the lawn around five-thirty unless it's raining and then I guess we'll have to move them in here which means we'll have to move the silent auction items in here also. Do I have any volunteers?"

Just about everyone agreed to help out at the last minute to get the silent auction indoors if it was needed. The moods were high and everyone was looking forward to tomorrow night. Dresses and hairdos were discussed. Even the three young girls, Kelly, Alex and Robin, who were acting as servers during the cocktail hour and runners during the auction, were excited. For Herring Run this was the event of the season! After another hour of decorating they left with high hopes of a successful auction.

Millie, Marti and Jane stayed behind to pick up the last of the remnants of the pizza feast and do the general clean up. As they worked Millie turned to the two other ladies and asked them if they'd seen today's Cape Cod Register headline. Jane said she had and had been surprised that no one had mentioned it during the decorating party.

"I think everyone was too afraid that Joanna would walk in at any moment and no one wanted to be the one to be the recipient of her wrath," Millie commented.

"Which reminds me," Jane told them, "I think that a new Joanna has emerged." Jane then proceeded to tell them about her experience at Puritan clothing store and the coffee shop the day before. "I've never seen a nicer Joanna, in fact she was just a regular person. I really don't think she's ever been very happy here. Maybe we're guilty for her feelings of rejection.

We didn't really greet her with open arms when she married Sam and showed up with him the first summer."

"We hardly greeted her at all," Marti remembered. "When I think back, we were pretty awful to them both. But then, it was a real feeling of betrayal for me. I really felt that Sam had landed a low blow to Julia and I really don't like a woman who gets involved with a married man."

"I know what you mean," Jane agreed. "But you know, we both liked Sara when we met her at the restaurant even though she was having an affair with Sam behind Joanna's back."

"Well, maybe that was because we so disliked Joanna," Marti theorized.

"Who's Sara?" Millie queried. "Wait a minute, you don't mean that girl that was found dead of a suicide at the Tara."

"Cripes, we weren't supposed to let anyone know we knew about that," Jane cried smacking her head. "You can't let anyone know a thing, Millie, please. Mike would have our heads!"

"Lips sealed," Millie said as she demonstrated zipping them shut. "But can't you just spill a little more now that the cat's out of the bag?"

Thank God, thought, Jane, it was only to Millie she had let that slip, she knew Millie always kept her word but she added, "Let's just let it drop for now. We promised we wouldn't say a thing and a slip of the tongue is one thing but actually elaborating on it is another, please, forget what you just heard."

"Forgotten," Millie promised. "At least until you're allowed to say something and then I want to be the one you call!" Millie couldn't resist wanting to be the first to know now that Jane let the news of Sara slip.

With a sigh of relief, knowing that they could trust Millie, Jane and Marti said their good-byes and started their walk home.

"Thank goodness Millie is good at secrets," Jane commented as they hurried along the dimly lit streets of the village. "Can you imagine if my loose lips screwed up the case for Mike. Who knows where one little innocent comment can end up?"

"You don't know how many times I've almost said something to Barbara and Sheila at the beach catching myself just in time. It's really hard to know something and remember it's not something everyone else just knows. And you were right back there, I can't always judge someone just because they are having an affair but mostly I don't like it at all if they're married."

Jane looked at Marti and said "Me, too. In fact I really didn't like it about Sara but I did like Sara so I really shouldn't have said what I did, sorry. There was just something real about her and she seemed to have seen the better side of Sam that had somehow gotten lost for awhile."

"I agree. And, no apology necessary. I liked her too. I was sorry we didn't get to know her a bit better. And you know, now that we know that Julia is so happy with Mike and things are working out so well for her, I think that she would have been glad to see Sara coming into Sam's life."

"Yeah, maybe you're right. And maybe if we'd only given Joanna half a chance," said Jane who looked at Marti and in unison they both said, "Not!"

They were just about to Marti's house when they saw the dark outline of a man approaching them on the street. Stopping and trying to make out who it was both women were ready to bolt toward Marti's just in case. But as he neared them, Jane realized his silhouette was very familiar and she called out, "Geoff, is that you?"

"You bet!" was the reply. And with a sigh of relief they both moved forward, Jane picking up her speed and embracing her too long gone husband with a huge bear hug and a kiss. It felt extra good to be in his embrace, she hadn't realized how much she had missed him until she was sheltered in his arms.

"I am so glad to see you!" she gushed as she held her head against his chest.

"Me too, honey. Hi Marti!" Geoff said as he gently held his exuberant wife.

"Hey, Geoff, welcome back. Well, here's my house. I'll see you guys tomorrow at the beach. Geoff, give Bob a call, he was hoping to get some tennis in around nine if you're up for it. Goodnight, you two love birds," Marti laughed as she headed up her walk to her door.

Arm in arm, Jane and Geoff walked to their house. "Did you guys eat yet?" Jane asked.

"No, we've been hanging out, waiting for the grill to heat up, listening to Ian play his guitar and I decided to head up toward the Inn to see if you were ready to come home. Did you eat?"

"Yeah, the dregs of the pizza, but I could go for some of your Caesar salad if you've got a little extra, the boys were going to make it."

"Well, we do and they didn't. They left that chore for me with all the compliments of nobody does it better etc., etc.," he laughed. "So, the dressing's sitting on the counter with all the ingredients mingling together to perfection. All we need is the romaine to be washed and torn."

"Tell, you what, I'll do that while you guys barbecue and talk and then we'll sit down together, what do you say?"

"I say great!" Geoff smiled as they walked up to the deck where the boys were waiting for them.

Saturday, August 21st

THE MORNING OF the auction came bright and sunny with a promise of low humidity and a perfect day. Jane rolled over to give her sleepy husband a hug and found that he was already up and in the shower. Recalling their amorous night before, Jane thought to continue the fun by joining him in the shower. But, alas, she was too late. Just as she rolled out of bed the water stopped and he hopped out of the shower with a towel around his torso.

"Damn, man, I was just going to join you," Jane told him as she sidled up to him and tried to remove the towel from his waist.

"Sorry, love, no time this morning. Ian, Trey and I are going over to the courts for a quick set before they have to be at work. The pro is going to be our fourth. And then Bob and I are going to play at ten. I e-mailed him before I left yesterday and told him I'd play. Why don't you and Marti come and join us, we'll play some doubles."

"Well, maybe we could. I'll give her a call. But honestly, don't you have a few minutes to spare before. . . ."

"Dad, let's go, I don't have all day, I have to be at the beach in less than an hour," came Ian's voice from outside their bedroom door.

Deflated, Jane gave up and went to make the bed and then some coffee. She'd give Marti a call and see if she wanted to play doubles and then hop into the shower herself.

A shower and two cups of coffee later found Jane at the tennis court ready to play doubles. She was just in time to see the end of the match the boys were playing against Jay, the tennis pro, and their dad. It looked pretty even, youth versus wisdom and age. But in the end the pro and wisdom won the day.

As Ian ran off the court to get to the beach and his job as life guard, he stopped long enough to give his mom a quick peck on the cheek and tell her he'd see her later. With no chance to reply except with a smile, Jane turned her attention to Trey who was looking a bit sulky as he walked off the court. Jane knew that being an assistant to the tennis pro, Trey had expected to do a bit better against his dear old dad on the court. She knew that his plan was to keep the ball away from the pro and hammer it at his father to win more points. What he didn't count on was that his father had a few tricks up his sleeve with the finesse of his slice and the placement of his overheads that more than made up for Trey's brute strength.

"Good game, honey?" Jane asked her younger son.

"Yeah, sure, but we didn't get to finish because Ian had to get to work. They were a bit ahead of us but we were coming on strong and would have had them in a third set if we'd had time to play it," Trey, the boy who hated to lose, told her.

"Well, there's always next time," Jane told him. "Speaking of work, that's where you should be headed as well. I'm sure that Jay has something he needs you to do around the courts."

"Yeah, well, see you later," Trey said as he walked away with his racquet slung over his shoulder.

"Bye, Trey, love you," Jane called after him wondering where his kiss was. Oh, well, he never could take losing quite as well as Ian, but he always bounced back fast ready for the next challenge, she thought.

"Hey, Jane, Geoff, ready to get on the court and play some tennis?" Bob asked as he and Marti approached the courts. "How you doing, old man?" Bob asked Geoff. "Did you fall to your sons or did you hold on this morning?"

"Well, we won but I have to say, I am wiped out so go easy on me. Don't tell Trey this but it was all I could do to hang on against him. That kid is some savvy player and boy can he hit that ball hard." Jane smiled when she heard this, she'd have to remember to tell Trey what his dad had said.

"How about we play the men against the women, then? That should make it a bit easier since you're a bit tuckered out," Bob suggested.

"Good idea, we'll go soft on you ladies, play a nice easy game," Geoff agreed.

A little over an hour later, after the women had soundly beaten the men 6-4, 6-3 with their finesse, placement and style, much to the men's surprise. Marti and Jane suggested they all get their suits on and head to the beach because they would need to leave early due to the evening's auction. The men were good to go and a short time later everyone was relaxing under their umbrellas.

As Geoff snoozed away on the sand and Bob read his book, Jane and Marti discussed last minute details that had to be seen to for the auction. Nikki and Millie had most of it in hand but Jane and Marti had told them they would be there early to help with the cocktail hour's silent auction. That meant setting everything up, looking its best so lots of bids would come in, as well as placing the correct tally sheets with the correct items. No putting antique porcelain bowl description with a pair of cheesy hoop earrings as had happened one year!

Both women discussed how they wanted to bid on a few

items themselves and hoped that working wouldn't interfere with their bidding. Jane had her eye on some antique flatware that she had seen come in and was going to put a bid in on a few interesting stray pieces like the pickle fork she'd seen with the bone handle and the olive spoon that had stars for it's holes. She had also seen a twisted handle butter knife that would make a nice gift for her friend, Mary, back in Tucson.

Marti, on the other hand, liked some of the bigger objects. A couple of paintings that had come from a local artist of Herring Run village scenes had caught her interest and there was an old porch rocker that she really was yearning for that would be in the live auction. She knew she would have Millie bidding against her for a couple of those items so she'd have to stay on top of things. They promised to keep an eye out on each other's bids as they made their rounds to see that one of them wasn't getting outbid by someone else, unless, of course, it went over their limit. It got very confusing, though, with so many people milling around, lots of conversation with folks they'd seen little of during the summer and wine and cheese being served. One hardly had time to put a bid in let alone keep an eye on it. And that didn't even account for the women, or on the rare occasion men, that stood right next to an item that they really wanted and each time someone upped the bid they just upped it again. At times it got a bit hairy when two people were determined to "win" that item so both bidders stood by it. When the bell that ended the auction sounded, well, just stay out of their way, Jane thought.

"I'm listening to you spend my money," Geoff said with a groggy voice, having just woken up from his catnap. "You guys do all this work to get items for an auction, get a caterer, decorate the place and then you are the ones to spend the money. Why don't you just donate the money in the first place and make it easier?"

"What fun would that be, Geoff?" Marti asked, with a smile on her face. "This way we periodically clean out our houses of our stuff and then fill them back up with someone else's stuff. Year to year we pass it around, maybe eventually we'll get our original stuff back again, but meanwhile we'll be having fun and making money for the village."

"What's it going to this year? New bushes or something?" Geoff wanted to know.

Jane looked askance at Geoff. "It's for the new playground equipment. Last time we had new stuff for the kids was when our boys were little. It's worn out and needs to be replaced. Gee, I told you this at the beginning of the summer."

"Oh, yeah, now I remember," sure he did, thought Geoff wryly. "Hey, I'm hungry; what did you bring for lunch, anything good?"

"Yes, I did," Jane replied, "your wallet. We're going to the snack bar today. I've got too much to do to worry about lunch. So, what do you want? A burger? Tuna Melt? Hot dog? How about a veggie burger, they're good for you and they have really good ones here."

"How about a tuna melt with fries and an ice tea," Geoff contently ordered as he lay back down on his towel and closed his eyes again, the change in time zones was catching up to him.

As Marti and Jane walked up to the snack bar, Jane told Marti, "Today I get him lunch; tomorrow, he gets mine!" Marti laughed. First day back with husbands was always a bit trying when husbands thought the wives were on "vacation". What they'd really done was just switch houses. They were in houses that needed to be cleaned, with groceries that needed to be bought, with lunches and dinners that needed to be made, and to top it off, these were houses that usually had more houseguests and enough sand to start their own beaches!

As they waited in the long line that was inevitable at the Snack Bar on a sunny Saturday, they saw that they were just a bit behind Joanna and her brother Stuart. Upon seeing them Stuart turned around, tapped Joanna on the shoulder and the two siblings waved hello. Letting the couple separating them from Jane and Marti go ahead, Stuart and Joanna stepped back to stand next to the two friends.

"I hear you guys did quite a job on the decorating," Stuart said to Marti and Jane as he sidled up to the ladies. "Joanna told me that it looks quite magical and that she had a wonderful time with everyone last evening. It's a pity that this will be her last summer here. She was finally feeling that she was making some headway with all of you women and now with Sam gone and the house going to Alex, well, anyway, at least she's enjoying herself now. "Pity no one has stood up for her or cared more for her", he said under his breath with a hint of malevolence in his voice, his eyes staring steadily at Jane.

Feeling a bit creeped out and full of guilt, Jane didn't know what to say and neither did Marti. She didn't think that Joanna had heard her brother's comments as Joanna had been talking to someone else and now when she did join them she had a big smile on her face and began to talk enthusiastically about the evening's event.

"I'm so excited about this evening! Stuart said he'd accompany me and I bought the cutest little sundress with the most darling little red, spiked heeled sandals, you remember, Jane, the one at Puritan." Joanna enthused. "Millie wanted to know if I could make some more of those cupcakes for the dessert table tonight so I did that this morning. That way it would really spike the bids on the ones being auctioned. I was so thrilled that you all liked them so much."

Glad to be on safer ground, both Jane and Marti began to exclaim over the delicious cupcakes that they'd had the evening before. Stuart said he'd never had them and they told him he was in for a treat. Soon they were ordering and then Jane and Marti were off the hook as far as Stuart was concerned.

As they returned to their husbands on the beach, Marti and Jane wondered about Stuart.

"He is such a Jekyll and Hyde. At times he is so nice and concerned about his sister and nice to all of us. Other times he is out and out mean. Just then I thought he was going to be nice but then he sort of started to dig at us. I mean what was that all about anyway?" Marti wondered aloud.

"I don't know," Jane replied. "Maybe it's just some kind of protective, brotherly thing he's into. I can't figure him out either. You're right, it's like he's two people, not just the professor, sometimes, he's like the mad professor. Maybe it's all that intellect," Jane mused.

"Anyway, let's try not to let it bother us and ruin tonight's fun. But, let's be sure we really compliment Joanna on her outfit," Jane said with a laugh, "whether we like it or not. And I for one like it. I helped her pick it out!"

Marti laughed in agreement and for the rest of the afternoon at the beach they put Joanna and her brother out of their minds.

Like Joanna, Jane was excited as she got ready for the auction. She just knew it was going to be a fun, and profitable evening. Most of all, she couldn't wait for Geoff to see her in her new outfit. She had just finished blow-drying her hair, happy that the humidity was low for a change so it just might last through the evening, when he walked into the bathroom ready to take his shower.

"Oh, no you don't; not until I get my make-up on and can get out of here. The steam of your shower is not going to ruin my hair!" Jane declared.

Geoff backed out of the bathroom with a chuckle. He never

could see what all the fuss was about but since Jane always made him wait to take his shower until after her hair was done and she was finished in the bathroom there must be something to it. He was just glad that he didn't have to worry too much about what little hair was left on his head. No bad hair days for him!

Later when he emerged from his shower and walked into the bedroom, there stood his lovely, smiling wife looking stunning and quite sexy in her new black, dotted sheath dress with the slit up the side that made Geoff want to see more of Jane. As Geoff looked at her he decided that the auction could wait as he had a much better idea of what they could do with their time at the moment. Seeing the wide zipper in the back was surely an invitation, he thought. Dropping his towel he headed right for his wife, whose smile was replaced by a look of horror as if a monster was approaching.

"Geoff Adams, don't you dare touch me. You are still wet and I am totally ready to go," Jane informed in a shrill voice, as she tied a little sexy black scarf around her neck to finish her outfit off with a bit of sophistication. Very Audrey Hepburn, Jane thought.

"But, babe, you look much too good in that outfit to leave it on for long. We have a few extra minutes," Geoff informed her.

"Not for that we don't. My hair is done, my make-up looks great. Now how do you like my new outfit and how do I look?" Jane asked her husband as she twirled around for him to see it from all directions.

"Didn't I just let you know?"

"No, come on, Geoff, how do I look, really," Jane implored.

"You look great, honey, and we'll save this for later; rain check, okay?" Geoff asked.

"You got it. Anyway, I did want to knock your socks off, I

just didn't realize it would be your towel that would go," she said with a laugh, realizing she got the reaction she had hoped for.

Ten minutes later as they left for the auction, they ran into their boys returning from work. The boys promised to be up to the Inn in time for the live auction to help out and Jane reminded them that if they came earlier there would be dinner for them as well. That perked them up a bit and they said they'd be up by six-thirty.

"Don't forget to wear a collared shirt," Jane yelled after them as she and Geoff walked out the door.

* * *

The evening was going splendidly. White and red wine were offered and there were trays of cheese and crackers as well as an assortment of hors d'oeuvres. People milled around the silent auction items and they were bid on heavily. Though Jane didn't get the pickle fork she wanted she was able to get the butter knife and the olive spoon which delighted her and kept Geoff happy to only pay for two out of three. Millie and Marti had battled over a painting of the village post office but in the end Millie won out. Marti decided that she would save the extra money to go toward the rocker in the live auction after the dinner.

As the silent auction wrapped up and the party slowly made its way into the Inn Jane noticed that Joanna and Stuart were on their way down the walk, arriving just in time for the dinner. Joanna didn't look very happy and Jane noticed that Stuart had a tight grip on Joanna's arm, almost as if he were forcing her to join in the evening. Not wanting to confront Stuart after the incident at the snack bar Jane quickly slipped into the Inn and found her way to the table that she and Geoff had been assigned to sit at for the evening.

Looking around, Jane saw that she and Geoff were seated with Millie and her husband Jack, some ladies she barely knew from tennis with their husbands and Julia, who was on her own tonight. She waved across the room to where Marti and Bob were seated at a round table with the tennis pro and his wife and Sheila and Barbara with their husbands. Jane noticed as Joanna entered the inn that she seemed to be confused about the assigned seating and after searching for a table realized that they were seated at the same table as Jane and Geoff. Taking the empty seats across from the Adams, Joanna and her brother sat down, not without giving off an unpleasant vibe to the table.

What's this about, wondered Jane. She so wanted this to be a lovely evening and instead it seemed that she would be dealing with the Mr. Hyde part of Stuart this evening. *Drat,* Jane thought.

"You look lovely tonight, Mrs. Adams," Stuart said with a bit of a sneer on his face.

Not knowing quite how to take this and thinking that maybe she was the only one to notice the look he gave her Jane decided to answer as politely as possible, "Why thank you, Stuart. As do you and Joanna. We do clean up well here in Herring Run," she exclaimed. "I hope you will enjoy our little auction this evening. We have some wonderful things to bid on. Joanna was a great help to us in organizing this evening."

"Yes, I know. Too bad Justin and Jake won't get the benefit of the new playground equipment that will be built with the money from the auction," he replied.

"Well, neither will my sons, Stuart," Jane replied tartly, and with that she passed the rolls that were sitting on the table to Geoff so forcefully that Geoff felt compelled to take the two that fell out of the basket before passing them on.

Jane busied herself with talking to the woman next to her

about tennis and refused another look at Stuart. As dinner was served she noticed that Joanna was looking miserable. She picked at her meal and whenever her brother said anything to her she looked like she might cry. Jane was so annoyed with the whole thing that it was hard to feel sorry for Joanna. Damn it, they were ruining an event that she had looked forward to all summer. Try as she might, it was hard to put them out of her mind and pretend they weren't there.

As the tables were being cleared, the desserts were being served and coffee poured, Jane was at last able to turn her chair around and face the auctioneer as the live auction was about to start. Though she didn't plan to bid on anything that was being sold at this part of the fundraiser, she also didn't plan to have to sit facing Joanna and her brother for one more minute than she had to this evening.

The auction was well under way when Jane heard Stuart whisper to Joanna that it was time to go. Joanna was reluctant to leave and made it known to him in a low whisper that Jane could barely make out. To her chagrin, she had tuned out Richard's voice as he auctioned off the wares and was now tuned in to Joanna and Stuart. As they argued, she heard Stuart tell Joanna that he was waiting for them outside. Instinctively, Jane looked up and thought she caught a glimpse of Stuart through the window outside of the inn.

Wait a minute, Jane thought, *Stuart is sitting behind me, how could he be outside*? She looked at the window again but saw nothing. Sitting in her chair she tried to figure out what she had seen. A reflection? Someone that bore a resemblance to Stuart? A brother? As Jane pondered these questions she remembered the time that Joanna had called Stuart Scott, and then corrected herself. She thought of the Jekyll and Hyde personalities. Pieces wanted to fall into place but she still couldn't make sense of it all.

When she heard the sound of their chairs scraping back and saw the two walk quietly out toward the exit, Jane made a rash decision. She would follow them outside and find out what was going on.

Telling Geoff that she was going to the ladies' room she excused herself and left the table, slipping out the door of the Inn that was on the side of the building closest to the front. As she came around to the front, she could see three retreating figures walking quickly down the street in the direction of Marsh Cottage. Keeping her distance, Jane followed them, wishing she had worn her low sandals instead of her spiky black sling back heels. They were hard to keep on and made too much noise as they clicked on the pavement.

As she neared Marsh Cottage, she noticed that the gray Mercedes and another car were parked outside of it. Standing just inside the open front door were the three people that Jane had seen walking away from the Inn. The light in the hallway of the cottage gave Jane a perfect view of all three of them as Jane hid in the shadows of the trees. There was Joanna holding her high heels, smart girl has taken hers off, thought Jane as she slipped hers off, too. The men had their backs to her and seemed to be arguing. They suddenly turned around and Jane gasped; it was Stuart and Stuart!

Jane blinked her eyes and looked again. Two Stuarts stood flanking Joanna, arguing. Then Jane noticed that one of the Stuarts was holding a gun. He had it pointed at the other Stuart and Joanna. Joanna seemed to be pleading with the Stuart with the gun while the other Stuart seemed to try to reason with him to no avail. *My God,* thought Jane, *a good twin and an evil twin, it really does happen.*

The Stuart with the gun motioned the other two toward the outside and they both led the way out toward the cars, close to where Jane was hiding. She would be seen if she didn't move, so she cautiously tried to get behind a tree so she would be unnoticed as they went by and then she could somehow call for help, cursing herself for leaving her cell phone in her purse at the auction. Unfortunately, as Jane quietly moved toward the tree she stepped on one of the Joanna's boy's squeaky toys, which alerted the Stuart with the gun to Jane's presence immediately as he looked right at the spot where she stood.

"Okay, Miss Nosey Parker, you can come with us, too. You've just about worn out my patience this summer. I'm so sick of all you goody-goodies here in Herring Run and it's time we got rid of another one."

Joanna stepped in front of him and said, "No, there's been too much killing, Scott. I won't play your game any longer. I sent the boys to my mother and she knows that if anything happens to me that you are to blame. I put the whole story down for her just in case. You can't use threats against them anymore to make me do what you want. Leave Jane alone. She hasn't done anything."

Jane wasn't sure, but she thought pieces were beginning to fall into place and make sense. There were two of them. A good Stuart and a bad Scott. Identical twins. Somehow they were wrapped up in this and this was why she could never figure Stuart out. Scott must be the bad twin. Scott must have been the one that committed the murders. But why? As these thoughts flashed through her head Scott grabbed Jane's arm and pulled her over to stand with Stuart and Joanna. Jane began to think the why could wait; she needed to concentrate on how to get out of this mess.

Scott began leading them to the Mercedes. Jane knew that if you got in a car with a killer your chances of surviving were greatly diminished. She did not want to get in that car. She did not want to end up like Celia or Sam or Sara. Scott was holding a gun, she had nothing, they had nothing. But, she thought, there were three of them, there must be something they could do.

As he nudged them forward, Jane looked down at her spikey heels, and then over at Joanna's. Strictly speaking, they weren't weapons, but they could do some nasty work if applied hard enough. She looked at Joanna, pleading with Joanna to look back. When she finally did Jane motioned her head toward her shoes and then Joanna's shoes, hoping that Joanna would get the message. It took a few seconds but it seemed that she understood.

By the car Jane thought would be their opportunity to attack, so she cocked one finger up by her side and then pointed it toward the car, hoping Scott wouldn't notice. Joanna made a slight nod of her head. As they drew close to the Mercedes and had to turn to get into the back seat, Jane raised her hand quickly and came down hard on Scott's hand with the gun. A second later Joanna's spike heel drove into the side of Scott's head, making him reel backwards. As the gun hung limply in Scott's hand, Stuart grabbed the gun and threw it in the bushes and tackled his screaming brother to the ground.

It all happened so fast that Jane couldn't believe it was over and was shaking so badly that she had to sit down. Only then did she notice that beside her was Joanna, crying uncontrollably.

Within a few minutes, Geoff and Mike came running down the street. Mike had come to the fundraiser after he had learned about Stuart and Scott's background and his relationship with Joanna. When they realized that Joanna had left with Stuart/Scott and that Jane was missing, the two men had hurried down to Marsh Cottage just in time for Mike to take over for Stuart. He quickly cuffed him behind his back and began to read him his rights.

Mike called for a backup and when the police cars arrived

he ushered Scott, Stuart and Joanna into them and rode off to the police station. One of the patrolmen took a brief statement from Jane and asked her to come down to the station the next day for a more complete one. With that, Geoff put his arms around his beautiful wife and decided not to scold her until tomorrow for sticking her nose where it didn't belong and took her home and put her to bed with a warm cup of Sleepy Time tea. All the while, Jane wanted to know if Geoff remembered to get her butter knife and olive spoon.

Sunday, August 22nd

THE NEXT MORNING around eleven, Mike and Julia arrived at the Adams' bearing bagels, cream cheese, coffee, and for Geoff, Bavarian cream donuts from Dunkin Donuts. A short time later, they were followed by the Sanders who came bearing the antique olive spoon and the butter knife that Jane had bought at the auction the night before. News of the auction was that it had raised more than enough for the new playground equipment and there was enough left over to buy a few benches for the parents to sit at while the children played.

Mike told them that Stuart and Scott were indeed twins. And just like Jane had thought the night before, one was a good twin and one was an evil twin. Joanna had once been married to Scott, and he was the father of her two boys. Stuart was their uncle. Scott had been a very poor husband. He had been involved in drugs and would beat Joanna on occasion whenever he was high or strung out, which more and more seemed to be the case as their marriage progressed. When Sam had met her, she had already left Scott and was hiding from him, supporting her boys by herself. She had kept in touch with Stuart because he was a good influence on their lives and was such a nice man. She was glad to have a steady, strong presence in her sons' lives.

"It's the old story of the good twin and the evil twin," Mike said.

"Eventually, Joanna landed Sam as a prize husband, a man with money and influence. She was sure she would have it all, but she really didn't fit into his world and it began to wear on her. Just being in Herring Run showed her what a duck out of water she was. She had grown up in a lower-middle-class neighborhood that skirted the better ones in Boston and had always aspired to grander things. To her that meant lots of jewelry, cars and anything else money could buy. What she didn't understand is what it took was just to be relaxed and at ease with oneself, to accept and just be yourself. She always was trying to be someone she wasn't and it just never worked. Her striving for something she wasn't began to wear on Sam and their marriage began to erode.

"Somehow, Scott had found out where Joanna was living and that she was remarried to Sam. He was enraged; he felt he was the only man that should have Joanna. He began stalking her and then even Sam. Sam was aware of Scott's stalking as Joanna had told him all about her past once Scott came back into her life, but he was so involved with Sara that he really didn't see it as a threat. Finally it came to a breaking point, after over a year of stalking them, Scott became mentally unhinged. Scott was stalking Sam the night when Sam went down to talk to Robin that evening at the beach. When Sam was leaving the beach club a shovel happened to be lying there in the sand. Scott saw the perfect opportunity to get rid of Sam as a rival. Scott just picked it up, swung as hard as he could. Sam probably didn't even know what hit him."

"With his stalking Sam, Scott knew about Sara and didn't

want to chance that she knew and had told anyone about him, that's all we could get out of him on her death so far. Funny, he seems quite proud of himself in all of this, like everyone he killed deserved it, wanted to tell us a lot about it," Mike said sadly with a shake of his head.

"Where does Stuart fit into this?" Jane wanted to know.

Mike explained, "Stuart wasn't sure that Scott had really done the killings and then when he began to think it was true, well, it was too late. Scott had threatened to harm Justin and Jake if they went to the authorities. Scott had begun to come to the Cape and call himself Stuart, saying he was Joanna's brother. It really was a mess for the real Stuart. The real Stuart should have come to us from the beginning but I guess being a twin makes some bonds much stronger than we can understand. Plus, Scott's threats were real; Joanna and Stuart were afraid he would harm the boys, despite the fact that they were his children. He had always seen them as an impediment to his marriage with Joanna, blamed her for having them, yet also saw them as his property. At times the real Stuart was here trying to see what he could do to protect Joanna and the boys, but when Scott came down he had to disappear, per Scott's orders."

"Well, now I understand why I could never figure out why one time Stuart was nice and the next time he wasn't. I just thought he had a screw loose. I guess he did, Scott, I mean, but being two of them made it very confusing. Also, a friend of the Sanders thought she recognized Scott but knew him as Scott Nelson but Stuart's last name was McDonald, how come there were two different last names?" Jane asked, thoroughly confused and shaking her head.

"Yeah," Marti said. "She used to see him in bars when she was single. Said he wasn't a very nice fellow back then, when she saw him here she thought it looked like someone she knew named Scott Nelson, but then she wasn't sure and we forgot about it."

"From what we have gathered in the last 24 hours, we found that Scott had a few aliases. He rarely went by his real last name that is, by the way: McDonald. He more often used Nelson, Neilson and also Johnson. Something to do with looking Nordic, he told us proudly," Mike told them in wonderment. "She probably met him when he went by the name of Nelson. I don't think this is the only trouble he's been in. He has some arrests for possession and there may be other crimes he's committed that the authorities are unaware of at this time. Right now he seems to want to sing, so we'll just let him."

"I don't understand why Sara didn't tell us about this Scott thing. Why would she keep it a secret? She would still be alive if she had gone to you." Marti lamented.

"I can only guess that she didn't know," Mike surmised. "Probably Sam didn't want to bring that ugly part of his life into the new part. Or maybe he really didn't think it was a real threat. Sam always thought he had a handle on things and was immune to most of the ugly side of life."

Mike continued on, "Stuart continued coming to the Cape to try to get Scott to leave Joanna alone. When he found out about the two murders he tried to get Scott to give himself up with a plea of insanity. You see right after high school Scott had spent quite a bit of time in a mental hospital. Stuart has always been so protective of him it seems. But Scott wasn't having any of that. Said he'd never go back to one of those places again."

"Okay, but did Scott also kill Celia, and how does she fit into this?" Jane asked.

"In high school, Celia dated Scott, right before she moved away to Ohio. She knew that Scott had a twin. She knew them both. We haven't gotten everything out of him, yet, but I'm guessing that Celia realized that Stuart was really Scott at times and was going to spill the beans. Though I don't think she knew about Scott's time in the mental hospital. But, you know, she never could keep a secret and Scott knew that. He couldn't chance her 'blabbing' as he put it."

"What about all the other little things that happened?" Marti wanted to know. "You know, crazy rumors, running people off the road, rocks thrown, whatever."

"From what we can tell, that was just to throw people off the track or just part of his insanity," Mike said. "Time will tell us more as we interview him and have professionals work with him."

"But why kill Sam?" Jane wanted to know. "Sam was divorcing Joanna. So, why would he bother to kill Sam?"

At this Mike looked over at Julia and could see that she was looking a bit sad and dabbing her eyes. Even though Sam had not treated her well, Mike knew that they shared a daughter and a history together and she would always be sad that his life ended so tragically.

"We think that Scott couldn't take the fact that anyone else had his 'property' is how he put it. Joanna belonged to him, the boys belonged to him, even though he had no love for Justin or Jake. He couldn't stand that Sam married Joanna and was acting as a father to his boys. And then when Sam treated her badly by having an affair that was just another mark against him. For all of that, and more, he felt Sam should die. It really didn't matter. This guy isn't all there," Mike added.

"What will happen to Joanna and Stuart? Did you arrest them, too?" Geoff wanted to know as he munched on his Bavarian cream donut.

"Yeah, but I think they'll become witnesses and will plea out of getting any time. They were victims, too. What a mess one person can make of people's lives."

"Here's another thing I don't understand," Jane wondered aloud. "Joanna was such a shrew for so long and then all of a sudden around the time we were setting up for the auction and also when I ran into her at Puritan she was like a whole other person. She was actually really nice. What caused her to have such a changed attitude?"

"Stuart shed a bit of light on that last night. Seems he had talked his brother into going back up to Boston and Scott had promised that he wouldn't return to Herring Run under any circumstance. In the meantime, Stuart tried to figure out what to do about the whole mess Scott had gotten them into. Stuart had told Joanna a few days ago that she needed to change her attitude toward everyone. I guess she'd never been one to win personality contests; very self-centered and mean spirited unless there was something she wanted, then she was like honey for a fly."

Marti and Jane nodded as they remembered some of her antics.

"So, Stuart had asked Joanna to lighten up on everyone here in the village, thinking that maybe it would help calm Scott down. If her hysterics about Sam and her feelings about everyone in Herring Run were more amenable then maybe Scott would cool off and stay in Boston without another—what Stuart calls it—incident. Stuart said Joanna was always a very unhappy woman, but her marriage to Scott had made things even worse. And after her marriage to Sam, Joanna never felt very adequate socially, especially here in Herring Run, such a tight knit little village where everyone seemed to dislike her from the start; I guess we all had a bit to do with that. But that doesn't make anything that happened right. Just maybe helps us understand how Joanna felt," Mike concluded as he motioned to Julia that it was time to go.

The group silently nodded as they all thought how the

community had sided with Julia when Sam had brought his new wife, Joanna, to Herring Run. They knew they hadn't given her a fair shake. Dealing with a crazy ex-husband on top of that must have been hard to bear whenever Joanna spent time at the Cape in their happy, little village.

"You know," Jane said to Mike, "this will sound strange, but I always wondered why the nice Stuart always smelled sorta lemony and the mean Stuart didn't, that was always in the back of my mind, but I didn't really connect the dots that there were two of them", Jane said. "Not until last night. I guess I should have trusted my nose a bit more."

"Well, you should have kept your nose out of it, Jane," Mike admonished her. "What if you hadn't been wearing spiked heels?" he asked with a knowing look in his eyes. "We'll need to get your side of the story, Jane, so come down to the station later today and we'll do that. And Jane, next time, let the police handle the case."

Jane looked abashed as she nodded, she knew he meant it about leaving it to the police and she fully intended to, if—God help her—there ever was a next time. But she also knew that all's well that ends well! And with that thought and thoughts of sitting on the beach later on this glorious day, she popped the last bite of her everything bagel into her mouth and gave it a good chew.

Geoff's Caesar Salad

In a small bowl:

Pour ¼ cup good extra virgin olive oil,

Squeeze lemon juice until you get a slight tangy flavor

Press 3 cloves of garlic

Mix above ingredients and let stand for 30 minutes

To Serve:

Pour dressing through strainer over 2 heads of romaine lettuce (washed, dried and torn into bite size pieces, according to Jane)

Add shaved, aged Parmesan cheese in great quantity

Add a can of flat Anchovies (chopped)

Toss and serve and enjoy!